HELIOGRAPH

THE **SKYLIGHT SERIES**

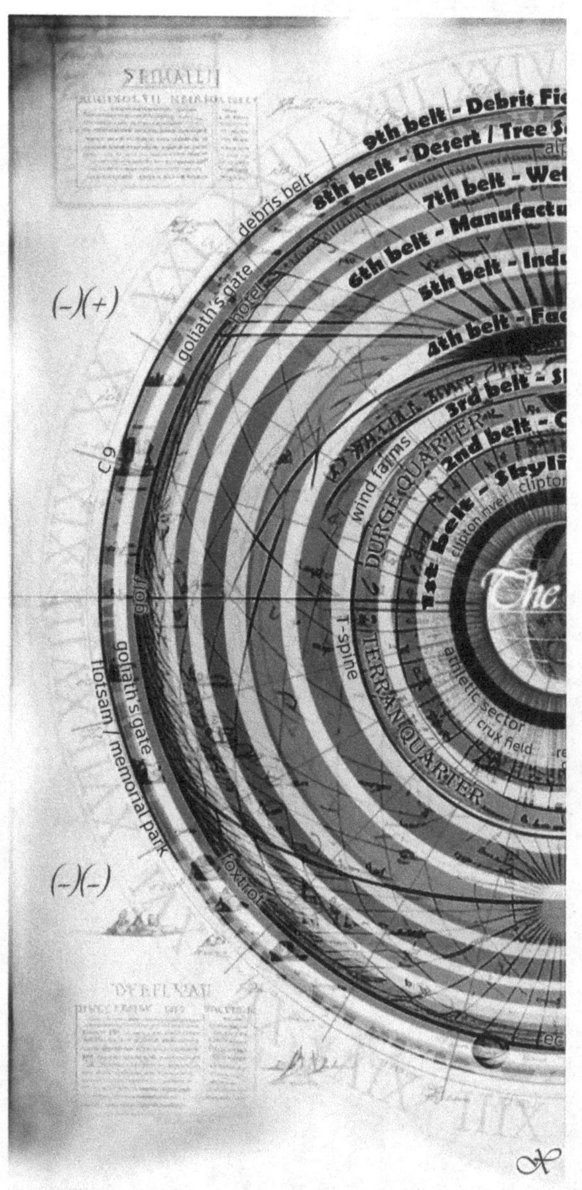

9th belt - Debris Fie
8th belt - Desert / Tree S
7th belt - Wet
6th belt - Manufactu
5th belt - Indu
4th belt - Fac
3rd belt - S
2nd belt - C
1st belt - Skyli
debris belt
goliath's gate
hotel
wind farms
DURGE QUARTER
TERRA QUARTER
T-spine
athletic sector
crux field
clipton river
clipton
The
(-)(+)
(-)(-)
c 9
golf
goliath's gate
flotsam / memorial park
foxtrot

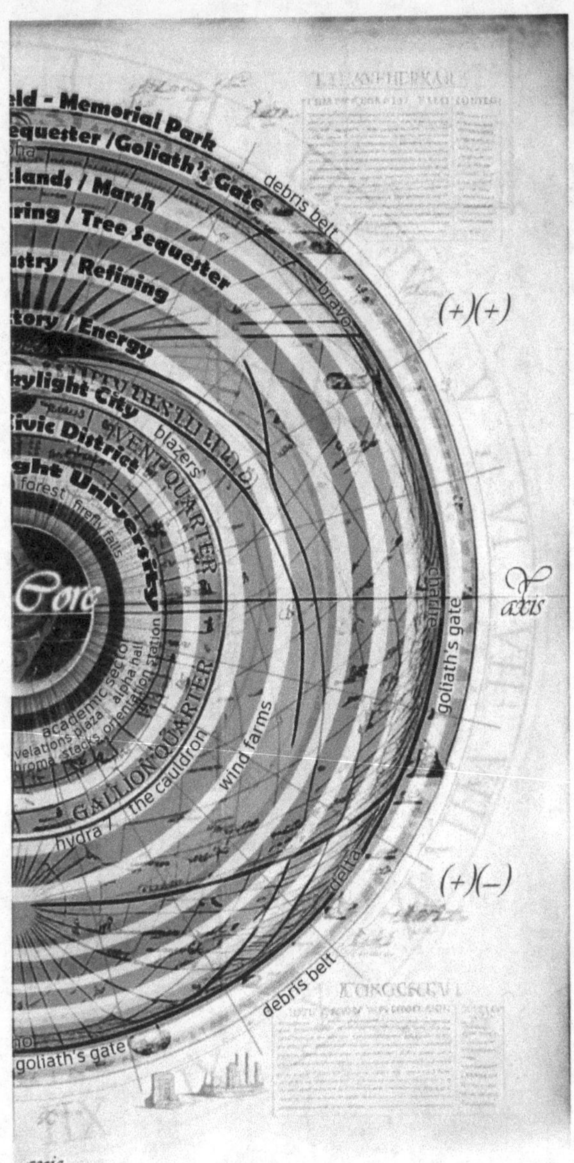
eld - Memorial Park
equester / Goliath's Gate
dlands / Marsh
ring / Tree Sequester
dustry / Refining
tory / Energy
kylight City
Civic District
ght University
forest
firefly falls
Core
academic sector
revelations plaza
alpha hall
orientation station
chroma stacks
GALLION QUARTER
hydra
the cauldron
wind farms
VENT QUARTER
blazers
debris belt
bravo
chaine
goliath's gate
delta
debris belt
goliath's gate
(+)(+)
(+)(−)
axis
axis

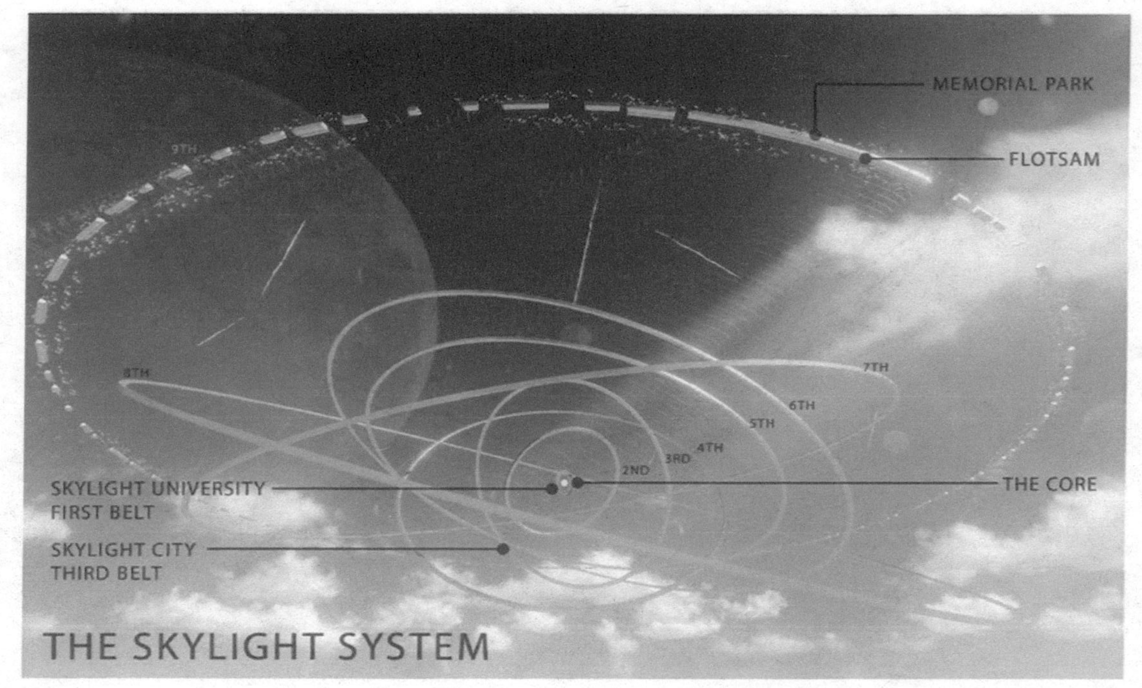
MEMORIAL PARK
FLOTSAM
THE CORE
SKYLIGHT UNIVERSITY
FIRST BELT
SKYLIGHT CITY
THIRD BELT
2ND
3RD
4TH
5TH
6TH
7TH
8TH
9TH
THE SKYLIGHT SYSTEM

SKYLIGHT UNIVERSITY

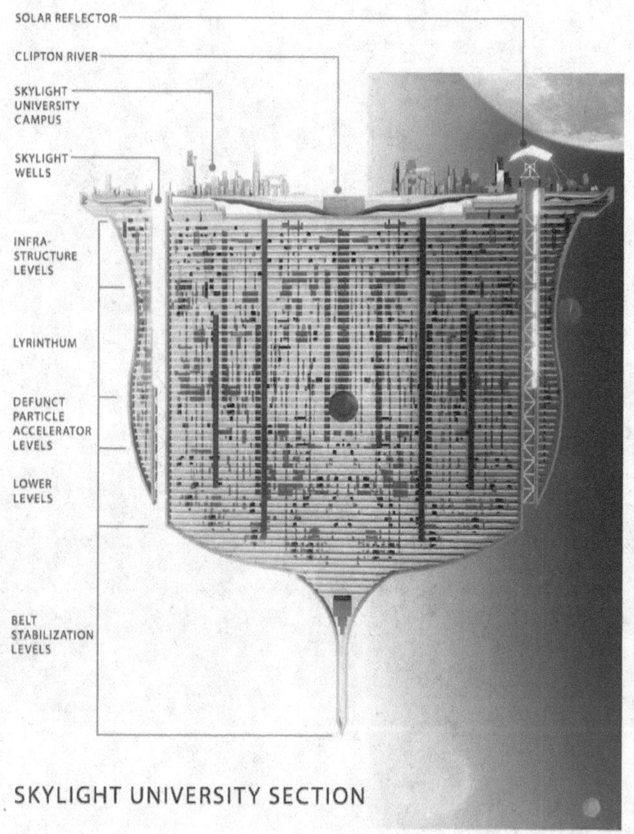

SKYLIGHT UNIVERSITY SECTION

ALBRIGHT
SHILOE
ANNAKA
TYBERIUS
BOOKER
HARRIET
DIJINN
TI-LEER
CORD
SOLAN
KAMBER
JET
VAIL
BRIT
BOFISTO
JOSHIA
SOJAHN
BO
HURSE
TETRA
MYRANDA
RENZIE
MOSSTROM
SYBOLD

THE SERPENT EFFECT

BOOK FOUR

OF

THE SKYLIGHT SERIES

www.theskylightseries.com

ISBN: 978-1-7363029-7-2
Edited by Caroline Barnhill
Artwork by Ghilmanul Faton

On the cover: Vail Hart

A CHARADE OF IMMORTALITY:

BOOK ONE: *A STORM of IMMORTALITY*

BOOK TWO: *A SHROUD of IMMORTALITY*
(forthcoming)

BOOK THREE: *A RAGE of IMMORTALITY*
(forthcoming)

THE SKYLIGHT SERIES:

BOOK ONE: *THE PRISM EFFECT*

BOOK TWO: *THE SKYLIGHT FALLOUT*

BOOK THREE: *THE HELIOGRAPHI MEMOIRS*

BOOK FOUR: *THE SERPENT EFFECT*

BOOK FIVE: *(forthcoming)*

THE SERPENT EFFECT

J WINT

*"If your hate could be turned into electricity, it would
be enough to light up the whole world."*

–Nikola Tesla

For Elaine

CONTENTS

PART THREE: A LOOPHOLE IN TIME

PART ONE

A SICKNESS IN THE AIR

CHAPTER 1
A Court of Titans

ΑΒΓΔΕΖΗΘΙΚΛΜ
ΝΞΟΠΡΣΤΥΦΧΨΩ

THE **TITANS MOVED** past the stars and galaxies and beyond the edge of known existence. Port-Shear disliked these gatherings. Mostly, it disliked the other celestial bodies, save Mal-Freer. Simply put, most Titans disagreed on the way of things, when it came to those who dwelled in the lower regions or lower dimensions. It had been 'time out of existence' since they had gathered to appoint laws for such beings. Most of the celestial bodies—or Titans—fancied their free time and cared not for rules and other such matters. Thus, the creation of the Heliographi Order. That lower subset of Titans roamed somewhere between their two planes. The idea had been to 'free' the Titans from the burden of setting rules.

…Shepherds… Port-Shear and the other Titans had commanded of them.

But the Heliographi Order continued with their warring nature, which in turn had derailed the Titans' intent. There was little hope of bringing the Heliographi back together. Another failed Titan initiative, it seemed. It took away from Port-Shear's favorite pastime: creating matter. Forming planets from dust, shining light on those that deserved it…and punishing those that didn't.

At the dawn of another universe, they gathered in a realm with no matter, space or time. This was where they held court, where they decided rules for the dimensions and those within them. Of the higher dimensions, the Titans had little to say and were, in fact, never allowed in for visits. That dimension remained beyond even them.

But in this realm, the two prime Titans always had final say, at least over the lower dimensions. Of course, Rend-Shear eternally disrupted flow. That celestial body's dark light was made of murky intent, like so many galaxy clusters it had created. *What use was it to hide matter from view?* Why not display such creations? It was beautiful to behold. Only the two primes held the power of creation. But the balance of matter was also crucial, and Port-Shear understood that as well.

In all the infinite universes, the topic of their current gathering was a troubling matter—one they must decide before the creation of the next universe. Once again, the Heliographi Order had caused disruption. The two Heliographi who had caused the disruption were bending the rules the Titans had set forth. It was forcing their decision now, and they had no choice but to intervene. The Titans had slowed the flow of time to decide the matter.

The court assembled as the dawn set on another universe. Eons later, they had decided. Each of the Titans, all twenty-four, would parlay an atom's worth of their own essence. That essence of starlight would be given over to the Heliographi Order in the form of a vessel. The vessel would create the headpiece of a powerful artifact, which would guide them. Of course, the Heliographi would continue to fight, and the lower dimension beings beneath them would pay the price of their war.

Port-Shear held to the hope that they might find a way, though. There was one Heliographi who might save them, if he could find the courage.

If not, there were infinite other Heliographi across the multiverse of creation.

Star-light could shine through.

Dark-light might cloud all.

A preordained destiny could still be reversed.

The essence of their likeness was all the Titans could give, lest the higher dimension being grow upset at their interference. It was up to the Heliographi to settle their own matters now.

Port-Shear left the court, left behind the white space. It disliked being in places where matter didn't exist, and it would be eons before they returned.

CHAPTER 1
The Double-Cross

ΑΒ Δ Ζ ΗΘΙΚΛΜ
Ν ΞΟΠΡΣ ΥΦ ΨΩ

VAIL HART STOOD in the corridor outside the Lucem control room. Her mind raced in circles, and her hands twitched nervously. She could barely stand still as she thought about what had just happened.

The Heliographi Memoirs had been unlocked!

She'd had only a split second to steal them, as Joshia had commanded her to do.

And…she had blinked.

A moment of goodwill, or mercy, or weakness perhaps? Either way, she'd missed her opportunity. And all because of her feelings for Stroud.

Joshia was going to kill her. What excuse could she give now?

Vail was half tempted to flee and never return. Maybe she could find some small port town on the ninth belt and fade away from existence—hope that the Atrum might never find her. But a split second later, fear crept into her soul at that thought.

If she fled, she'd be alone forever. Life within the Atrum's sphere of existence was the only thing she had left now that they'd betrayed the Lucem. Besides, Joshia would track her down and kill her no matter the cost. Once you were inducted into the Atrum, there was no walking away. Vail would die as an Atrum. Not that she minded it, if she were being honest. She got along with most of them: Sojahn, Bofisto, even Joshia, most of the time, though Mosstrom frightened her. She'd kept her distance from that man ever since becoming a part of the Atrum four years ago. Of course, she'd never actually met their leader, Sybold. But if she was anything like Mosstrom, she would probably avoid her as well.

Vail cloaked and raced from the control suite. She heard the whispers of the tortured spirits as she sprinted along the old rusty corridors of Lyrinthum. The defunct particle accelerator had been the Atrum's headquarters for the last several months now, after teaming with the

Lucem—an agreement between the two clans, which was now at an end. Like fire and ice, they detested each other. But it had gained them the memoirs, at least.

Obviously, the Atrum had always planned to break the truce. They had no need for the Lucem, now that the memoirs had been unlocked. Even still, she was returning empty handed and needed to think of an excuse, and quick. But if she was good at anything, it was hiding her thoughts and being deceptive. Joshia was powerful and would try to probe her mind. Vail was about to be tested—she'd know soon enough if she would live or die.

She popped up through the Clipton Forest portal, moving the vegetation to the side. Then she closed the portal and raced along the dirt paths beneath dark skies. Stray moonlight lit her way through the skeletal shadows of tall pines, its luminance a deep red in the summer air. Her blurry figure was barely perceptible amongst the fog and shadows, thanks to the way her cloak bent light.

Just a few minutes later, Vail slowed and stopped. She hid in the underbrush and listened. The soft sound of crickets chirped as the breeze ruffled her cloak. Her glowing eyes lit the surrounding area in a turquoise light, causing the shadows to melt away. Five meters to her left was a cave, and it seemed to beckon to her—some darkened maw looming from the forest's edge.

She moved inside, stepping gingerly and trying not to disturb the silence. Gravel crunched beneath her tactical boots and sent echoes around the moss-covered walls as she moved deeper.

Some twenty meters in, two pairs of glowing eyes stared back at her and blinked. Two Atrum stepped forward and met her, cloaks drawn.

"You can relax now, Vail." Joshia stopped just a meter in front of Vail, her tall frame imposing in the dark. Joshia's silver hair seemed to glow from the light of their eyes, the red streak down the middle ever prominent. She squared her broad shoulders to Vail, tense, as if ready to strike. Vail felt an instant of fear but quickly brushed it aside.

The other Atrum moved around behind Vail, though. She noticed the color of his eyes: an impossibly dark indigo. Mosstrom's presence made her twitch, a barely perceptible blink as she rotated her head and watched as he settled behind her.

"That'll do, Mosstrom," Joshia said and crossed her arms as she faced Vail. "I'm sure Miss Vail has a good excuse."

Vail tensed, her muscles quivering and at the ready.

Mosstrom paused behind Vail. "Why, of course. Hopefully, I haven't frightened the young lady."

Vail's anxiety shot through the roof at hearing his melodic voice. Mosstrom was an ancient Atrum, an entity who'd been around for eons. He was the eldest of the current Atrum—powerful and cunning…and evil. If they were here to kill her, she didn't stand a chance.

"Well?" Joshia asked. "I can see that you're empty handed. What do you have to say?"

The tone of her voice held an undercurrent that made Vail's skin crawl. It sounded dark, accusing almost. There was a clear threat in that tone.

"Stroud was there," Vail said, which was a lie, she knew. She was placing all her hope in her ability to deceive, and her voice didn't waver. "He's been there ever since the memoirs were unlocked. It was just as you said, Joshia."

Mosstrom stepped around to face her. Vail looked into his glowing eyes. Her turquoise gaze seemed to clash with his. But his darkness began to overwhelm her light, and she took a step back. Her palms grew sweaty, her heartbeat ticked up a notch. But her expression didn't falter, and Vail calmed herself.

"My dear, if I didn't know any better, I'd say you weren't being honest with me." Mosstrom remained close to her, unmoving, his hands folded calmly behind his back.

Vail knew if she spent too long staring into those bottomless dark eyes, she would fall under his spell. She looked past him at Joshia and addressed her instead. "It's true, what I say. Stroud hasn't left the control suite. Solan also arrived just after the memoirs were opened. The timing wasn't right."

Joshia lifted one corner of her lip in a malicious sneer and pushed her way past Mosstrom. "You're a clever girl, Vail. Maybe too clever, though I see that 'gift' in you. Yes, I know." Joshia leveled a finger at Vail and lowered her voice. "Your task isn't over. I'm giving you another chance. Bring me the vessels, the memoirs, and our staffs."

Vail took a deep breath, then exhaled and straightened her shoulders. She wanted to ask why the hell Joshia wanted her specifically to do this. There were eight other Atrum who could easily accomplish the task. In fact, there were enough Atrum to simply storm the control suite and take whatever they wanted.

No. Joshia was simply testing her. Vail could see that now. Still, her inner defiance wanted to lash out at Joshia, tell her to figure it out herself. But that would be the last thing Vail said. She needed to 'play the game,' and bide her time till she could think things through.

"Will you at least tell me why we're leavin'? Seems like things were going smoothly with the Lucem."

Joshia tilted her head and gave Mosstrom a sidelong glance. "In time, yes. I will share all of it with you. Just know that plans are in place, and a time is approaching. We must have everything ready soon. Play your part, and you *will* be rewarded."

…a time is approaching? Vail mused, trying to interpret what Joshia was saying—and what she heard was, 'follow orders this time.'

"How long do I have?" Vail asked.

"A few hours," Joshia replied. "The Atrum are leaving at daybreak. We must be away from the first belt before the Lucem organize." Joshia stepped up to Vail and placed a hand on her shoulder, then cupped it around Vail's neck as if she might choke her. "Return with the vessels, memoirs, and staffs this time."

Vail didn't have to read between those lines. If she came back empty-handed, she knew Joshia would kill her.

CHAPTER 2
The Memoirs Revealed

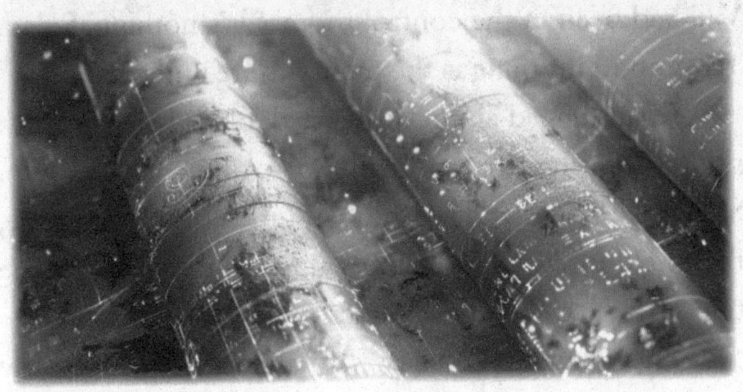

ΑΒΓΔΕΖΗΘΙΚΛΜ
ΝΞΟΠΡΣΤΥΦΧΨΩ

JET BARGED INTO the control room with Solan right behind him. "It's done, see," Jet said, trying to control his voice from the excitement. He walked over to the table, expecting the staffs to still be glowing. But their light was gone, the table was back to normal, and all had gone silent. However, the remaining memoirs lay on the table along with five colored jewels. They glowed and pulsed, similar to the one in his staff.

Jet froze for a moment in confusion. *How had the memoirs ended up on the table? And the jewels as well?* He

narrowed his eyes as he looked on. Solan noticed his confused expression.

"Something else wrong?" she asked.

Jet walked around the table, shaking his head. "I'm…not sure." But he had a sneaking suspicion that Vail had been in the control room. "It's nothing, Solan. The important thing is the memoirs are unlocked now."

Solan tugged at her disheveled, black hair, her dark skin still flushed from the sprint to the control room. She walked over and set the ninth memoir on the table, then held a few of the others up to the dim light. She traced the text with her fingertips.

The memoirs' yellowed parchment was nearly transparent. The text was written in a mix of mathematical language, charts and three-dimensional holograms. There were even microchips embedded into the paper.

"This portion of the map…right here." Solan pointed at a section in particular.

Jet walked over, set his staff down, and took the memoir. "Yeah, I noticed that too. But there're no coordinates. I'm guessing it's where this so called 'fulcrum' is located. Look." Jet pointed at the three directives.

I ~ LOCATE FULCRUM DEVICE FROM MAP ABOVE.

II ~ PLACE MEMOIR TO GAIN CONTROL
OF BELT'S ARMAMENT.

III ~ FOLLOW CODE PROVIDED TO
INITIATE SEQUENCE.

Jet sat back and rubbed his chin. "It seems these memoirs are a key to unlocking each belts' weapons or defenses or something. I hope I haven't unintentionally opened some pandora's box that could lead to war."

Solan sat back and considered. "We're already at war."

"But this might make things worse."

She shook her head. "Let's not jump to conclusions just yet. I want to understand these more before we make assumptions." She reached over and held up some of the jewels and examined them. "What do you make of them?" she asked.

Jet moved around the table, sorting through all the staffs. "I think these jewels are some sort of accessory for our staffs." Jet sifted through the pile until he found his own. As soon as he gripped it, the white jewel lit up, and a barely perceptible moan floated around the chamber.

Solan lifted her head and squinted her eyes suspiciously. "Did that just come from your staff?"

Jet slowly nodded as he held the war staff, looking into the clear jewel. Inside was the skull, and it started to shift in the light. Its eye sockets gleamed as it looked at him. Jet felt his skin begin to crawl. Like before, it made him uncomfortable and somewhat nauseous. He only assumed that this 'thing,' or entity, perhaps, came from another place—another dimension maybe.

Jet pulled his gaze from it and held the staff away from his body, as if trying to distance himself. "Yeah…well, I think this thing is alive. Does that make sense? Sounds crazy, I know, but can't you see it?" He walked over to Solan with the staff held out. But as soon as he neared her, she pushed him away. It was an involuntary motion and one he'd never seen from her before. Solan's skin turned pale, and she had to look away.

"Take it," she said through clenched teeth and looked at the jewel through the corner of her eye. "Explain this. How did it happen?"

Jet set his staff down, happy to be away from it, and found the yellow jewel. Then he grabbed Solan's war staff and handed it to her. She gripped it, placing the spike through the hole in her right hand. It lit up when she did. Jet brought the yellow jewel closer, and the staff's endcap opened. As the jewel glowed brighter, he felt the magnetic pull and let it fall into place. The room lit up in a yellow glow. Inside the jewel, a tiny heart began to pulse and come to life, an avatar perhaps.

Power surged from Solan's body. It was similar to what had happened to him, and he sensed a greater power descending upon them, emanating from her bejeweled staff.

Jet waited for the moment to pass. "I'd say our staffs, at least some of them, just got a major upgrade."

Solan continued to look at her staff in wonder. Then she set it on the table and looked at the other jewels. "What is Albright up to?" she whispered.

Jet shook his head. "I don't know, but I get the sense things are about to get interesting around here."

Solan arched her eyebrows and leaned forward. "Back to these memoirs. If there was any doubt before, it should be clear now. Albright must have designed some sort of weapon into each belt, and these are the key to unlocking them. It's a race to find these so-called 'fulcrums' now."

"I'm sure Cord will be thrilled," Jet muttered. "Another riddle."

Solan gave him a serious look. "Once these memoirs are placed, Skylight will be in a civil war."

Jet returned her look and grimaced. "First, it's a race to collect these memoirs. Now it's a race to place them. I wonder what's next?"

"Everything is being revealed sequentially, it would seem," Solan said. "Just as Albright planned it a century ago. It's obvious that finding the fulcrums and placing the memoirs will be crucial. You can bet Lybra will do the same; she craves the power. If these memoirs really do arm the belts, then we need to figure it out before she does."

"There's more to this, I think," Jet said and pointed at the symbols on the parchment. "I see a lot of ancient text in these. I wonder if there's more information about these jewels?"

Solan bent back to the table, leaning on the edge and giving each memoir a good look. She shook her head. "I don't understand this language. Let's get Cord involved. I sense that some of this wasn't meant for mortal eyes."

"I'll check on him. He's probably still practicing anyway."

Solan clenched her jaw but continued to stare at the six memoirs on the table. "We have to protect the memoirs. After you find Cord, let's call a meeting. Wake the other Lucem and meet me back here within the hour. I'll talk to Joshia."

Jet nodded as Solan left the control room. He didn't disagree with Solan—the memoirs were more important now than they had realized. Whoever controlled the memoirs would rule the Skylight System. But he was still curious about the jewels and what they really meant. Could they be equally important? If Albright had included them along with the memoirs, then there was indeed some significance to them. However, Albright spoke through riddles, and nothing was as it seemed.

But Jet lingered, staring at his war staff and the skull inside the white jewel. It continued to morph and elongate, grinning at him with its toothy smile. Just a few minutes earlier, he'd felt nauseous being near it. But now, not so much. Was he already getting accustomed to its presence? Did his 'gift' have something to do with it? He sensed one thing—these jewels were not of this world.

Jet stood to leave, then felt a strange impulse. Something whispered his name, and he looked down at the staff and into the skull's eyes.

Had it just spoken his name?

As if in a trance, he reached out and grabbed the remaining jewels and placed them in his pocket along with the eighth memoir. Then he hurried off to find Cord.

CHAPTER 3
There and Back Again

VAIL STOOD NEAR the control room, cloaked, and hidden in the shadows. She waited until Stroud and Solan had left, then tiptoed into the control suite for the second time that night.

Laying on Albright's table were all the Atrum's staffs *and* the memoirs.

Missing were the colored jewels, or *vessels*, as Joshia had called them.

Stroud! Of course he'd take the jewels!

Joshia was going to be furious.

But she couldn't worry about that at the moment. She didn't have long before the Lucem discovered that all the Atrum were missing.

Vail compressed all the Atrum's staffs, placed them in a small bag and carefully stashed the memoirs on top. She hesitated for a split second as she looked at all the Lucem's staffs. *Why not take them as well?* But that would place them—place Stroud—in a dangerous position.

Vail cloaked and moved quickly out of the control suite and into Lyrinthum.

Just as she reached the lower level, someone behind her cleared their throat.

"Where you goin', lass?"

Vail turned to see Ti-Leer standing behind her with his arms crossed. He was wearing a torn pair of boxer briefs and a stained T-shirt that read, *Luck o' the Irish*. Ti-Leer's stubby frame and reddish-brown beard bristled in the dim light of the corridor.

Vail sneered at him. *She didn't have time for this!* But she knew there'd be no reasoning with Ti-Leer. He was as stubborn as she was.

Vail immediately dropped the bag and decompressed her war staff. The corridor lit up in a turquoise light, the sound of the energy crackling in the air. "You sure you want to do this, Ti? You have no staff."

"Oi, I have a staff, missy," he replied, then nodded to the bag. "It seems we're being a wee bit sneaky. Why don't we empty that sack?"

Vail gave him a wicked smile. "Come and get it."

Ti-Leer returned her smile. "Fine. I'm always up for a bit of fun first thing in the morning." He crouched, then barreled at her.

Ti-Leer's short stature and large belly gave him a comical look. But she knew not to judge him by his appearance. He was an older Lucem and if he managed to get her on the ground and into a wrestling position, he could choke her unconscious.

Vail sidestepped his charge, and he crashed headfirst into the rusty bulkhead. She spun and brought the blunt end of her staff down on his head. Ti-Leer rolled to one side, then wobbled a few steps. He shook his head, then dropped to the ground and swept his foot at her. She hopped and brought the blunt end up and under his chin this time. Though her staff had a spear on the other end, she had no desire to kill Ti-Leer. As much as she hated to admit it, she kind of liked him. In another time and place, she thought they might even be good friends.

Ti-Leer stood and teetered for a second, then collapsed to the floor, unconscious.

Vail walked over and checked to make sure he was just knocked out. *He'll have a hell of a headache*, she thought. Then she slung the bag of goods over her shoulder and sprinted out of the control area.

Before long, she was pushing her way through the Clipton Wood's portal and into the early morning light. A fifteen-minute jog brought her to the same hidden cave, where she paused and breathed a sigh of relief. She walked into the dark recesses and set the bag down. Vail took a seat on a large boulder and waited for Joshia, Mosstrom and the rest of the Atrum to arrive.

CHAPTER 4
A Bit of Fortune

ΑΒΓΔΕΖΗΘΙΚΛΜ
ΝΞΟΠΡΣΤΥΦΧΨΩ

JET WOKE ALL the Lucem. Then, he and Cord walked into the control room to find Solan hurrying about the space in a frenzy. Kamber searched the equipment while DiJinn rifled through some holopads. The chairs about Albright's table had been shifted out of the way and sat randomly around the room. As soon as Solan saw Jet, she rushed over to him.

"Do you have them? The memoirs?" She grabbed him by the shoulders and practically lifted him off his feet. Her eyes were wide, and her voice trembled. Her dark skin was flushed, and her hair was tangled as if she'd been pulling at it.

"Hold on, Solan." Jet tried to push back from her, but she held on, her fingers digging into his cloak.

"All of the Atrum are missing and so are the memoirs," Solan said, a hint of rage in her voice. Her nostrils flared and her brows furrowed as she slowly released Jet and turned to pace the room. Everyone stopped searching and waited.

The silence was broken by Ti-Leer when he stepped through the doorway. He leaned against a wall to steady himself, a large welt on his forehead. DiJinn rushed over and propped him up. Ti-Leer's stubby frame teetered, then he shook his head, trying to get his bearings.

"Ti," Solan said. "What happened?"

"Ah…that pretty lass. She…"

DiJinn waited impatiently. "Come on, Ti, let's have it!"

"She took 'em, the memoirs. I tried to stop her…but she…" Ti-Leer paused, and his face turned red with embarrassment.

"You let that girl beat you?" DiJinn said.

"Oi, she had her staff. She's tricky, that one. Thought I had her but—"

Solan held up her hand, and he stopped midsentence. "That's enough." She moved over and sat down heavily in her seat and slouched.

"Knew we couldn't trust 'em," DiJinn said but didn't say more, realizing it was a moot point now.

Jet moved over to the table. All of the Lucem staffs were still there. *She could have taken our staffs too*, he thought. Vail could've put the Lucem in a very dangerous position…yet she hadn't. There was still some inner conflict in her, it would seem.

"Blast it," DiJinn said and hammered the table. "What now, Sol?"

Solan continued to sit and stare at the ceiling. The dimly lit control room remained silent; only the soft beep or purr of defunct equipment could be heard. She finally stood, as if resolved. "There's no sense in dwelling on it. What's done is done. We have to regroup and consider our options."

"She left our staffs," Cord said. "That's not like the Vail I know."

"I noticed that too, Cord," Jet said. "She's different lately. I might even say she's not fully committed to the Atrum. There's still a chance I can talk to her and see about—"

"No, Jet," Solan said. "We are no longer tied to the Atrum. They've made their decision. Do not go near her. She's cunning, like Hurse was. She will find a way to manipulate you."

"Agreed," DiJinn said. "We're down to six Lucem now. I don't think Albright, Tyberius, or Shiloe will aid us in the war ahead."

Jet listened but was still thinking about Vail. He felt hesitant about abandoning her. She was vulnerable now, no matter what anyone else thought. In his heart, he knew she was struggling. But he didn't have to tell the others about it. If the opportunity presented itself, he would track her down and find out. He felt confident he could help her. The fact that she'd left their staffs had been a sign of peace. A sign that she still cared for the Lucem, perhaps.

No, that wasn't it.

It was because of him. *Vail cared about him.*

Taking their staffs would have placed him in harm's way, especially with all the chaos in the system right now. Without their staffs, the Lucem were doomed.

"So, what now?" DiJinn asked again. She finally stopped pacing and leaned against Albright's table.

Jet stuck his hand in his pocket, felt for the colored prisms and the eighth memoir, then pulled them out and spread them across the table. "We're not completely out of business."

Solan stood and immediately raced over and gripped him by the shoulders. Jet witnessed the smile on her face, which was something rare. "How…how did you guess?" she asked.

Jet shrugged as he pushed his way out of her grip. "I dunno, really. Just a hunch, I suppose."

"This is our ticket," DiJinn said. "Joshia'll have to come to us now! She needs these jewels for the Atrum staffs."

"What exactly are those?" Kamber said. She walked over to stand next to Jet and nudged him.

"Honestly, I don't know yet," Jet replied. "I was hoping Cord might give some insight. I've already placed one in my staff and Solan's too."

Jet walked over and picked up his staff. When he did, the white light from the jewel lit up. Then a whisper emanated from it, making everyone turn and look around the room.

In Jet's mind, a thought formed.

…Leave me…in peace…

Jet looked down at the staff, at the skull inside the jewel. It was moving again, staring at him with vacant eye sockets. The voice in his head hadn't been the ghost Lucem named Brindall this time. It had been the skull in the jewel.

Cord walked over and looked at the staff but didn't touch it. Jet watched Cord's reaction, and his olive-toned skin turned a shade paler. Like Solan, Cord seemed to have a similar reaction. *What was it about this thing that made everyone so uncomfortable?* When Jet looked around the room, he could see that everyone had the same expression of fear on their faces too.

Jet moved the staff to his side and out of view. "Cord, hand me your war staff." Cord did, and Jet took the jewel that matched it. He placed it in the end piece and watched Cord grin as he handed it back.

"Intriguing," Cord said. He stood, letting the power flow through him.

"Looks like there's one for Albright and Tyberius's staff too," Jet said. "Any idea what this is about, Cord?"

Cord pursed his lips but shook his head. "Negative. I imagine the answer is within the memoirs, unfortunately. Perhaps we might find something in the Book of Vishmu. Let me do some research."

Solan stood. "While Cord's figuring that out, let me say that our first goal is getting the memoirs back. Thanks to Jet's quick thinking, we have the eighth memoir *and* the jewels. That's our bargaining piece. Our second goal is to evacuate citizens. We need to get as many people to the inner belts as possible, I feel. If there is a civil war coming, I want the citizens closer to us."

"I thought Stell was handling that?" Kamber said.

"She is, but we need to do our part too," Solan said. "Lybra's already regrouping, and there are dozens of mercenary factions around the ninth belt. That's her territory, and the prized ally will be the Dreadnaughts. It's dangerous for citizens to be near those areas now."

"Aye, Solan," Ti-Leer said. "The Dreadnaughts are formidable, and they're as likely to turn on us as help us. If you've got your eye on 'em, be aware of that."

"I have to agree, Sol," DiJinn said. "Those are dodgy outfits. I've spent plenty of time in the debris field. There's nothin' good to find out there."

"And yet, we can't stand by and let Lybra snatch them up," Solan said. "We need to make an effort, at least. Kamber and I will also handle evacuations with Dane—"

Cord drew everyone's attention. "I think I have something." He took the eighth memoir and laid it on Albright's table, smoothing it out.

Jet watched Cord's expression and could tell he was excited. The smile on his face was like a kid on Christmas morning. Cord traced the rough parchment with his fingers, reading some of the mathematical language under his breath. "This is something we've already seen from Albright in the paintings by Shiloe Van Saint. See here?" Cord indicated an area near the middle of the memoir as the other Lucem gathered around. Jet felt Kamber lean against him as he looked on.

The memoir had a jumble of scribbles on it, all written in the rust-brown color, which Jet knew to be Albright's own blood. Some of the text was in holographic format and floated over the parchment. There were hand sketches, maps, and portions with integrated technology.

Cord continued. "Says here that the fulcrum device is located below each belt, in the lowest levels called the 'stabilization levels.' No one ventures into those areas willingly."

"Makes sense," Solan said. "They'd be well hidden that far down. What else can you make out?"

Cord leaned in closer and scanned the document. "I can't speak for the other memoirs, but it looks like this one is called a 'prime' fulcrum. It lists the first memoir as a prime as well, see?" Cord pointed at the top right corner of the map. There was a hand sketch that Jet had noticed before. Nine loops circling an orb, with a serpent indicated on the eighth loop and a prism on the first loop. "It notes these two memoirs as primes, the first and the eighth, that is."

"Meaning?" DiJinn asked.

Cord shook his head. "Jinn, there's a lot of information here. I need time to research it."

"What about these 'armaments' it mentions?" Jet asked.

"Unknown at the moment," Cord said.

"We don't have much time, Cord," DiJinn huffed impatiently.

"I agree," Cord replied. "It might help if I could see the site first, though."

Solan leaned back and rubbed her chin. "You want to go find this fulcrum device?"

"I think that might shed some light on some of these questions."

"How long would you need?" Solan asked.

"I think I can locate it fairly quickly," Cord said. "A day or two perhaps, once I get started."

Solan considered as she sat on the edge of the table, arms crossed. "It's a good idea. See what you can find."

"By the way," Cord said as he stood. "It states that only a 'prime Heliographi' can initiate the final fulcrums. Just thought you might want to know."

"What does that mean?" Kamber asked.

"I'm guessing that means only Sybold or Albright can initiate these 'so called' armaments," DiJinn said.

"Sybold was assassinated by Albright and Tyberius several years ago," Solan said. "Albright is in hiding and likely will not return."

"Actually, I'm not so sure that Sybold's missing," Jet said. "It's a feeling I get. If she does return, then maybe Albright will be forced to return as well."

Everyone looked at Solan. She was quiet for a moment. "I believe that Jet is right—Sybold is out there, waiting. Our enemy is on the move, and I have no idea what the next few months will bring. For now, Cord will locate the eighth fulcrum and study it. See what you can figure out and report back as quickly as possible. In the meantime, the rest of us need to discuss our recruiting and evacuation plans."

CHAPTER 5
A Sequence of Events

ΑΒΓΔΕΖΗΘΙΚΛΜ
ΝΞΟΠΡΣΤΥΦΧΨΩ

"RECRUITING?" KAMBER SAID. "The Lucem are recruiting now?"

They all stood around Albright's old table and stared at Solan in surprise.

"Yes, and very soon," Solan said. "Otherwise, the Atrum or Lybra will draft all the factions."

"How will we sway them?" Jet asked. "Seems like we don't have much to offer. I mean, the Atrum have the memoirs. Lybra has the troops."

"Oh, I think we have plenty to offer," Solan said. She stood and held up her staff. The yellow jewel sparked as she tapped it to the metal floor. "Yes, the Atrum may have the memoirs, but I feel we have the advantage since we hold a majority of these jewels. In particular, I feel that Jet's staff holds a greater power. I think a show of force might sway some of these factions."

Solan walked over to the main console and kicked the wall. A three-dimensional map of the Skylight System sputtered to life over Albright's table. "Most of the powerful factions are located around the ninth belt. For now, we'll focus on that area."

"Solan," DiJinn said. "I'm not sure just walking into the Dreadnaught's territory is a great idea. During my days as an undercover agent, I spent a lot of time in those ports along the fringe. Some of the run-ins I had weren't pleasant."

"That's why we're sending Jet," Solan said and leveled her gaze at him.

Jet had been sitting, staring at the holographic map. His head snapped up and his eyes narrowed. "What in Skylight are you talking about?"

"You heard me," Solan persisted.

"Wouldn't Jinn be better suited? I mean—"

"Trust me, Jet. They'll listen to you. Besides, it's time you got out on your own."

DiJinn raised her eyebrows. "I dunno, Sol. It's dodgy territory, even for a Heliographi. They will only respond to a show of force."

"And that's exactly what we're going to do," Solan replied. "We have these new staffs. Let's use them to our advantage. Eventually, we may have to give up the Atrum's jewels in return for some of the memoirs. But before we give the Atrum these artifacts, let's use what we have. It may be just the ticket to convince the Dreadnaughts to join us."

"Sounds dangerous," Ti-Leer said and rubbed his hands together. "I like it."

"What about General Dane?" Kamber asked. "Maybe he has some connections out there?"

"I'm sure he does, and he'll go with Jinn," Solan said.

"And Stell?" Kamber asked.

Solan nodded at the map and the third belt. "She's primarily recruiting in the Galleon Quarter and the areas below Skylight City. The outer belts are our responsibility. I'll do what I can, but where the Dreadnaughts go, the other factions will likely follow. Our focus needs to be on them."

"Assumin' we get what we need, can we fit that many people down here in Lyrinthum?" Ti-Leer asked.

"We'll make it work," Solan replied. "The more important issue is getting the citizens evacuated as soon as possible. I want them relocated from the outer belts before these fulcrum wars kick off."

"So, when and where do we start?" DiJinn asked.

"Soon," Solan said without hesitation. "And we may be away for a while. Take time to relax, because when we hit the recruiting trail, there will be very few breaks. This is a crucial time for everyone in the Skylight System. I feel it's inevitable that we're heading for civil war—"

"Pardon the interruption, but I may have found something else interesting." Cord stood and smoothed the eighth memoir on the table, then he flipped it over. He took his newly modified staff and shone the jewel's light on the paper. Some writing they hadn't noticed before was visible now. The spidery font of Albright's hand glowed like moonlight.

Everyone gathered around the table and leaned in. Cord read the strange language out loud.

~ EACH MEMOIR SHALL BE PLACED WITHIN ITS HOLDING CELL BEFORE JULY 4, A.D. 2286. ONLY THEN SHALL EACH COUNTDOWN INITIATE, TWO DAYS APART. THE FOLLOWING SEQUENCE WILL OCCUR: **7:2:6:3:5:4.**

~ WHEN A FULCRUM'S TIME REACHES ZERO, IT MAY BE IGNITED. THE FULCRUM'S POLARITY SHALL BE DICTATED BY THE ACTING HELIOGRAPHI.

~ ONCE A MEMOIR IS PLACED, IT CANNOT BE REMOVED. ONCE POLARITY IS ESTABLISHED, IT *MAY* NOT BE REVERSED.

~ ONLY A HELIOGRAPHI'S STAFF MAY IGNITE THE FULCRUM.

~ ONLY A PRIME VESSEL MAY IGNITE THE FIRST AND EIGHTH FULCRUMS.

~ WITHIN EACH VESSEL RESIDES THE ESSENCE OF A TITAN.

BLACK PRIME: REND-SHEAR

RED MINOR: ORION-LIGHT

ORANGE MINOR: URI-RAIF

YELLOW MINOR: MAL-FREER

GREEN MINOR: NOR-TRAI

BLUE MINOR: URI-LORN

PURPLE MINOR: MAL-TRIFE

INDIGO MINOR: ORION-DARK

WHITE PRIME: PORT-SHEAR

Cord fell silent just as everyone stood and began talking.

"What the hell are we supposed to make of that?" DiJinn asked.

"I don't understand," Kamber said.

Jet placed a hand on Cord's narrow shoulder. "A prime? A minor? Wonder what that means?"

Solan stepped away, her hands on the back of her neck, considering.

Cord stood and held out his hands, trying to calm everyone. "Allow me to speak." He waited for everyone to sit down. "To start with, it sounds like Albright's only giving a two-day grace period between each fulcrum war, starting with the seventh belt. It looks like the wars will alternate between the belts and work inward. The final two 'prime' fulcrums will bookend this entire saga."

"Cord," DiJinn said. "What do you make of this 'polarity' business?"

"That's a good question, Jinn. As usual, Albright's created something difficult to comprehend. We'll know soon enough."

"Wonder if these fulcrums require one of the new staffs to ignite them?" Jet asked.

"It doesn't appear that way. It states that only a Heliographi's staff is required."

"Polarity doesn't sound like armament. That part confuses me," Solan said.

"That's how it sounds," Cord agreed. "But if we've learned anything from Albright, it's to expect the unexpected."

CHAPTER 6
Port Loefi

AB Δ ΕΖ ΗΘΙΚΛΜ
<u>Ν</u>ΞΟΠΡΣ ΤΥΦ Χ ΨΩ

VAIL WAITED FOR nearly an hour within the dark cave system. Her legs were starting to cramp, and she stood to move around and stretch. She crossed her arms from the cool draft and thought about the last twenty-four hours. They'd coordinated with the Lucem, their mortal enemy, and defeated the Agency and Lybra to gain six of the nine memoirs. Against the odds, they'd managed to win the final reveal on the ninth belt, gaining the white memoir. General Dane had defected and commandeered nearly two dozen of the Agencies' war cruisers and numerous

41

frigates and jammers. Four of those battle cruisers were the largest in the fleet, including the SLS Armada, one of the most feared ships in the system. Vail was going to miss that particular part of their alliance with the Lucem.

And then the Atrum had betrayed the Lucem.

It marked the second time that had happened in their long history. Consequently, there would probably never be another such collaboration. That bridge had not only been burned, it had been incinerated. Such a shame, too. Together, they'd made a powerful force. Had it been Vail's decision, she'd have stayed.

For their combined strength, or because of Stroud?

Vail shook her head and kicked at a few rocks. They rolled down and disappeared into the darkness beyond, and the sound echoed into silence. She began to wonder if the Atrum had left her behind, or perhaps she was in the wrong cave system. Just as she was sitting down again, several pinpoints of light appeared in the dark. First, a pair of blue eyes that hovered in the darkness, then two, then three more pairs. Purple, violet, azure.

Vail stood and waited calmly, her hands behind her back. But inside, her heart beat slightly faster at seeing Mosstrom stroll toward her.

"What took you?" she asked as Joshia uncloaked and appeared in front of her as if by magic. Her cloak, like all the other Heliographi's, interwove protective graphene fibers and bent light around her form, rendering her practically invisible to most people.

"You still seem a bit uptight, my dear," Mosstrom said, his melodic voice drifting in the darkness. Its charm had led many unwary people to their deaths. She shut out its vibration and stepped past Mosstrom. Vail dropped the black bag in front of Joshia and waited.

Joshia nudged the bag open with her foot, searching the contents. Then she knelt and tossed each of the Atrum their staff. First Mosstrom, then Brit, Bofisto, Sojahn, Bo, Tetra and Myranda. But as she continued to search the bag, the corners of her lips turned into a snarl. "Where are the vessels?" Joshia's voice was calm and even, but Vail herd the rage just beneath.

Vail lifted her shoulder. "Stroud took them when he left the control room. I didn't have time to track him. I took what I could get and left."

"We need those vessels. Without them, the Lucem have a tactical advantage." Joshia crossed her arms and lowered her gaze at Vail. "The vessels may be the most important relic Albright has ever created."

"What did you expect me to do?" Vail shot back, but quickly brought her tone under control and held out her hands. "Joshia. Had I gone after Stroud and run into the other Lucem, I might not be standing here right now. I couldn't risk it."

"Are you sure, or do you have a soft spot for Stroud?"

Vail let out a long breath and clenched her jaw. "Seriously? Stroud? He means nothing, as do the other Lucem."

Joshia held Vail's gaze with her dark azure glowing eyes. Neither blinked as they faced off.

Joshia finally looked away. "We'll need those vessels."

"Why?" Vail said. "We have the memoirs. What could those jewels mean that's so important?"

"It's not your concern at the moment. Find a way. Get in touch with Stroud and use him to get the vessels back."

Once again, Vail wanted to snap back at Joshia and tell her to do it herself. *Why was she so insistent on her doing all of this?* "I'll see what I can do."

"Yes, you will," Mosstrom said.

Joshia turned and left with the other Atrum right behind her.

Vail waited, then caught up with Brit. He pushed his long brown hair out of his eyes and looked down at her. "What do you want?"

Vail shrugged. "What do you mean?"

Brit didn't slow as he looked away. "Every time you want something, you try to cozy up to me. So…what do you want?" Brit finally stopped and faced her.

Vail waited for the other Atrum to leave the cave. "What is it with Joshia?"

Brit gave her a strange look. "What? Do you mean the truce with the Lucem?"

"We had a good thing goin', don't you think?"

"Did we? Or did you and Stroud have a good thing going?"

"Is that what's bothering you?"

Brit held her gaze a few seconds longer, as if considering. "I know about that guy, Cutter. That was his name, wasn't it? I saw the way you reacted at the Century Eclipse. And now you're thinking about Stroud too much."

"That's not true, Brit. You know I hate the Lucem."

Brit continued to stare at her, then tilted his head. "Vail, you need to do some soul-searching. Because if Joshia figures you out, assuming Mosstrom hasn't already, she'll kill you without a second thought." Brit shook his head and left. "Figure it out, Vail."

N

Vail found a skiff in a faculty hangar bay and used her holopad to override its security system. Ten minutes later, she was leaving the first belt's air space and heading toward the seventh belt. The Atrum's base was in a secluded port named Loefi. In the crime-ridden port city, blending in was easy. Thanks to all the illicit activity, movement around the large port required less caution.

Even though the belt was less than two kilometers wide, it stretched out and along the outer surface for dozens of kilometers. Scores of rundown buildings littered the tight alleyways, which were poorly lit. It was a noisy place with dark markets and trading pits populating almost every square meter. Illegal weapons, armor and drugs were sold day and night. Like many areas of the ninth belt debris field, Loefi was one of the most dangerous port cities in the entire system.

Vail landed her skiff in one of the Atrum's private hangar bays, using a badge to gain access. She traversed dirty alleys and occasionally ran into local gangs. She could've cloaked to avoid the harassment. Instead, she used her alias to draw attention. These gangs would steer well clear of a Heliographi. But she welcomed the conflict. After all, a single girl of her age was a tempting target. Dealing with the harassment allowed her to dispense some angst.

Vail had always felt disadvantaged. During her years at Skylight University, she'd faced a fictional disease called ephebus mortem. A popular legend had her believe she would die before the age of twenty-four. Only after her induction into the Atrum had she discovered that to be a cruel hoax. Now, she was trapped in this twenty-two-year-old girl's body forever. She had forsaken her family and had no real friends, she supposed. Being immortal would be a dream come true for most people. But with no one to share that time with, what was there to look forward to? Though Vail's family still lived, they had disowned her long ago. Making contact with them would be dangerous. She never wanted to see them again, because…

…because she cared.

Just like she cared for Stroud.

And she hated herself for that. The thought of caring made her skin crawl. Stroud was a Lucem, and they should hate each other. But they didn't. She knew she had to keep that feeling buried deep.

Vail walked down an alley and turned a corner. She searched for the right storefront, which was an abandoned retail shop. Eventually, she found the right one and stopped in front of it. The shop still had racks along the aisles, but the front of the store had been busted out and ransacked long ago. As she moved into the shop, a group of vagrants fell in behind her.

A dozen men and women surrounded her and moved in. One of the women noticed the smirk on Vail's face.

"Something funny?" she asked and pressed closer to her.

Vail assumed this was the leader of the group. Her hair was cropped close in a buzz-cut. She was well built, with a heavy-set jaw and dark, brooding eyes.

"As a matter of fact," Vail said. She held up her hands in mock surrender. "But, please, don't hurt me. I'm just passing through."

The tone of Vail's voice caught the buzz-cut girl slightly off guard. "You don't sound too worried. Let's go ahead and empty our pockets, shall we?"

"If I do, will you promise not to hurt me?" Vail tried hard not to grin. She held a steady gaze, but the corner of her lips kept curling up.

One of the other men leaned in toward the buzz-cut girl and whispered to her. "Come on, Hearn. I don't like this!"

But the girl named Hearn continued to hold Vail's gaze. "What, you're afraid of one little girl? There're twelve of us. This'll be fun, Bogg." Hearn held out her hand. "Let's go, sweet cheeks. Hand over your goods."

Vail pulled out her compressed staff and slowly handed it over. "This is all I have, I'm sorry."

Hearn took the stick and held it up to the light, then looked back at Vail. "You've got more. We're not leaving until you turn out your pockets. If you don't, we'll search you, and it won't be pleasant, I promise."

Several of the gang members pulled out rail guns and leveled them at Vail.

Vail had had enough. Seeing the rail guns was the final line for her.

She grasped the compressed war staff back so quickly that Hearn didn't have time to react. The roundhouse kick broke her jaw and Hearn fell to the pavement, unconscious. In the same fluid motion, Vail tapped the staff onto the ground, and it unfurled and lit the dark alleyway in a turquoise light. It roared to life in multiple voices as she brought it down on another gang member's skull with a crack. She used the pointed end and thrust backwards, impaling the man standing behind her. Light poured through the staff as his body gyrated and convulsed. Electricity sizzled around his eye sockets. Vail held him off the ground as the other attackers dropped their weapons and fled.

Vail jerked the staff back, and the body thumped to the concrete, smoking and charred. Vail turned and stood over the man for several minutes, a rush of emotions flooding through her. She wondered what the man's name had been. She wondered if he had a wife or children. Maybe he'd been trying to scrounge up enough money for dinner? A pair of shoes for his kid, perhaps?

Vail felt a wave of remorse take her, and she dropped to her knees, letting her war staff clatter to the cold pavement. Sudden tears stung her eyes as she reached out and grasped the man's hand and squeezed. She could sense his lifeforce fading as she knelt there. She held him, witnessing the awful thing she'd just done. She could have knocked him unconscious and just as easily accomplished the same goal. She'd only meant to scare the attackers off. Instead, she'd lost control and committed murder...again.

I could have spared this man's life.

He'd have woken up with a headache and returned home to his family.

Was she starting to revert back to her old self?

Just a few days ago, being near Stroud, Brainiac and even Solan, her attitude had softened. Her thoughts had cleared. She had seemed to see things with her eyes open, not through a vision of rage and hatred. But being away from the Lucem, she sensed that something was happening. Not just inside her, but in the very air she breathed. It sounded odd, but it was the only way she could explain it. There was a sickness in the air, and if she felt it, she knew the other Heliographi felt it too.

CHAPTER 7
The Secret Meeting

ΑΒ Γ Δ Ε Ζ Η Θ Ι Κ Λ Μ
<u>Ν</u> Ξ Ο Π Ρ Σ Τ Υ Φ Χ Ψ Ω

VAIL FINALLY MADE it to the Atrum's hidden lair named *Hellfron*.

It had been the Atrum's base for a century now, since the creation of the Skylight System. It was a twisting, turning series of tunnels that formed a maze of rusted steel bulkheads and unused passages, not unlike the Lucem headquarters down in Lyrinthum. It was dark and foreboding, which she didn't mind one bit. The gangs that happened to know of Hellfron avoided it at all cost. Deep within, their fortress felt like a tomb. She could almost see the essence of previous Atrum wandering the corridors. How many had come before her, she didn't know. But if there was a haunted sector on the seventh belt, this was it.

Vail stepped into one of the many vast chambers, then made her way casually to her own quarters and undressed. Then she settled down onto her meditation mat and fell instantly into Vishmu.

Her experiences during meditation were bizarre, to say the least. Unlike the Lucem's, there were no stars and silly rainbows. For her, it was darkness and evil thoughts. Ominous clouds and lost souls that screamed and wailed. It sounded like those tortured souls were being folded and compressed into a two-dimensional world. If she had to guess, their sense of the third dimension was being painfully and forever extracted. She could barely endure those screams, and she wasn't the one experiencing it. Nonetheless, it was difficult to hear, even for an Atrum.

But if she wanted to recharge her Heliographi and survive, this was the only way to do it.

So, she sat cross-legged and drifted into the corridors of some ancient mind. A being out of time and dimension. She roamed those corridors, seeing things that made no sense, hearing whispered secrets that she had no business knowing. And every time she traveled there, she grew more powerful.

Gaining more power was worth the sound of the tortured screams. She had a chip on her shoulder, something to prove to others…to the Lucem and to Brainiac.

Often times, she wondered if she had finally surpassed him.

Ledbetter.

Leaving the Lucem behind did have the benefit of not seeing him every day. It was perhaps the one thing she *should* be happy about. Being away from that arrogant, skinny, smug…

…friend.

Vail's eyes snapped open in frustration.

What the hell was wrong with her?

First Stroud, who she should be trying to kill but had actually defended. Now, it was Ledbetter, who she had always detested.

Vail stood and grabbed her staff and cloak and wandered the halls of the Atrum headquarters, trying to clear her mind of Stroud and Ledbetter. She wondered if she might find Brit and try to pick up their conversation. She was somewhat worried about what he'd said.

What if Mosstrom *was* on to her?

Yet, she hadn't done anything wrong, not really. So, what if she'd left the Lucem staffs behind? Otherwise, they would have been doomed. *Stroud would have been doomed,* she corrected herself.

If there was one thing she was good at, it was deception. She could use her gift to fool anyone she wanted, including Mosstrom or Joshia. They wouldn't be able to crack through and probe her thoughts, as long as she stayed focused and kept her mind closed. Not that she was going to run off and join the Lucem or anything silly like that. She just couldn't afford to give away her true feelings, at least until she could do some soul-searching and figure it out.

Vail finally made her way to the inner sanctum of the Atrum base. It was a massive defunct reactor with soot-covered walls of thick steel plates. The center of the inner chamber was a series of grates that appeared like massive dragon's teeth, black and cruel looking. The high ceiling was topped by a large dome with stained translucent panels that lit the hall in a deep amber color. Joshia sat in the center on a steel ingot that looked to have been deformed by fire long ago. Her tall frame and broad shoulders were rigid as she sat with her eyes closed in meditation. Her silver hair fluttered in the breeze, the red accent barely visible in the dim light.

Joshia sat like that until all the Atrum were seated. Then her eyes snapped open, and she switched on a large hologram behind her.

Depicted was a detailed map of the ninth belt's debris field. It was an area that Vail knew little about, except the areas she'd recently been to called Cranium Nine, or C9. That area was also Lybra's stronghold, though she'd essentially taken control of the Agency base now. The map highlighted multiple areas, which Vail assumed to be territories run by gangs. Many of those factions had taken part in the hunt for the Heliographi Memoirs just recently.

Joshia stood to the side. "These are the various factions we're targeting. As you can see, there are four larger clans. It's understood that most of these gangs, if not all of them, will follow the Dreadnaught's lead. That makes an alliance with them crucial."

"How will we do that?" Bofisto asked. "The Lucem have the vessels. The Dreadnaughts respect power alone."

"I understand the situation, thank you, Bofisto," Joshia said in a mocking tone. "The system is heading for civil war. Alliances are how everyone will survive. The Lucem may have the vessels, but they are also on the opposite side of the system. How realistic is it for a group as large as the Dreadnaughts to simply move their entire organization?"

Joshia placed her hands behind her back and strolled around the chamber. Vail noticed how silent everyone was now. Brit, Bo, Sojahn, Bofisto, Tetra, Myranda and Mosstrom. All sat patiently.

"We have these," Joshia continued, motioning to the memoirs on the table before them. "They will have to do until we can attain the vessels. We'll recruit in groups. Each team will be assigned to a faction. Bofisto,

Sojahn and Bo, I want you three in the Orion Cluster of the debris field. Two of the larger gangs are located there."

Sojahn looked at Bofisto and Bo, then turned her glowing blue gaze back to Joshia and nodded. "We'll take care of it."

"Brit, Tetra, Myranda," Joshia said and indicated an area on the opposite side of the ninth belt. "Sector thirty-two. These are smaller factions. However, if we can get enough of them on board, it may sway the Dreadnaughts. Use whatever method works."

Then Joshia turned to Vail and gave her a twisted smile. "Vail. You're with Mosstrom. You're going to the Dreadnaughts lair."

Vail started to object. But she glanced at Brit, who gave her a subtle shake of his head. Vail crossed her arms. "And what about you, Joshia? Why are you not 'partaking' in all the fun?"

"Careful, Vail," Joshia said and placed her hands on the table.

Vail sat back in her chair, arms still crossed. She looked around the room, noting the other's expressions. Most of them didn't look her way, except for Mosstrom. She could almost feel him trying to read her thoughts. She quickly cleared her mind.

Joshia drew everyone's attention again. "To answer Vail's question, I'm working on an alliance with Lybra and the Tetrahedron."

There was a subtle shift around the room when she mentioned Lybra's name.

"Is that wise?" Sojahn asked.

"What can we offer her?" Vail added. "Lybra already has the troops."

Joshia nodded to the memoirs again. "Lybra has three memoirs, but not the ones she desires. We have those, and I imagine she would be willing to pay a steep price for them. I still have a few tricks up my sleeve."

But Vail had her doubts. Lybra was safe and sound on the ninth belt, and she had the numbers to overwhelm any faction in this war.

"I've discussed the memoirs with Sojahn and Bofisto," Joshia continued. "We feel that everything must go through the Atrum now, including the Lucem and Lybra. She will give up everything to gain control of the outer belts. Lybra has something we need badly as well. I will force an alliance with her to gain it. Some of you may not agree with me, but this is the way."

N

After their meeting, Vail waited outside and in the shadows.

She knew Joshia was up to something more. Vail's curiosity was driving her crazy, and it made her think of

Stroud and how he was that same way. *God, she was becoming more and more like him every day.*

But tailing Joshia *was* dangerous. If caught, Vail would be executed on the spot. She began to wonder why she even bothered with it. *Couldn't Joshia have her own agenda?* Why concern herself over Joshia's private matters? A curiosity like Stroud's was bound to land her in trouble sooner or later.

But tonight, Vail was following her instincts.

Ten minutes later, Joshia glided out of the shop and down the alleyway. Vail followed her through the streets, blending in with the vagrants and hoodlums. Strangely, Joshia was alone. Recently, Mosstrom had been glued to her. Whatever Joshia was up to tonight felt different.

Eventually, Joshia left the outskirts of Loefi and moved toward a boggy area. Vail was soon greeted by thick reed grass with foxtail plumes that were common to the area. The bald cypress trees gave way to marshland. The sound of treefrogs and crickets drowned out everything. The moon shone bright that night, with thick fog moving across the marsh, as if in a hurry to be on its way.

Joshia finally slowed and paused near a large willow tree; its wispy branches drooped low and swayed gently. Beyond the marsh was a vast expanse of water. There was a murky smell of stagnant algae in the sultry air. Vail found a stand of evergreens and settled in.

Soon, a shadow appeared. It was small in stature, a hood drawn over the person's head. Joshia knelt to one knee and bowed her head.

"You are late, Joshia," the figure said.

"Apologies, my liege," she replied.

"Do you have control of the memoirs? Are they safe?"

"Yes. They are in our possession, except for the three Lybra holds and one the Lucem still hold."

"Good. And the vessels?"

Joshia hesitated and seemed uncertain what to say. "Vail was unable to attain them."

"Wrong, Joshia. *You* were unable to attain them! This was your responsibility." The figure paused while Joshia stayed in a kneeling position, head still bowed. "We will stick to the plan. You will use the memoirs as collateral. The black vessel is all that matters. Do you understand?"

"But…the memoirs are—"

"The memoirs are of little use at the moment. We will reacquire them later."

"How? It will be difficult once they leave our possession."

"Calm yourself, Joshia." The dark figure's voice sounded like a hiss. "Trust in me."

Joshia paused, then squared her shoulders. "Of course. Always."

"Good. Now, repeat. I will take the memoirs and use them to attain the black vessel."

Joshia did so in an obedient tone. Vail had never seen her like this, and it shocked her.

"When you return next, you will have the black vessel, Joshia."

"Yes, of course."

"Remember. Lybra will ask for the Atrum's fealty, and you must give it. Let her make the decisions for now. Can you do that?"

Vail could see Joshia rubbing her fists in the dark. She sensed Joshia's defiance at that last command.

"Yes," Joshia said through clenched teeth. "I assure you it will happen."

"All is well, then. You will contact Lybra soon and make the offer. Once the Atrum team with Lybra, do not concern yourself beyond that. No one, not even the other Atrum are to know about this until the deal is complete."

"May I ask when you will return?"

The dark figure paused for a few seconds. "In due time."

Vail felt a sudden nervous anxiety then, as if an evil darkness permeated the night air. Or was her anxiety because she knew who the dark figure was? It was obvious, beyond a doubt.

Sybold had returned.

But why all the secrecy? Vail could only assume Sybold was waiting for the right moment.

Vail knew that Tyberius and Albright had assassinated Sybold a few years back. Somehow, the Atrum leader had found a way to short-circuit the normal process a Heliographi must take. After their human host passed on, that inner light would search out a new host at birth. The process would start over again, and the new Heliographi had to go through conversion within twenty-four years.

So, how had Sybold managed it? It didn't feel natural.

Vail had heard enough.

She snuck off in the opposite direction, not bothering to stay and hear the rest of their conversation. If she was smart, she'd bury that information deep and never tell a soul. Wisdom told her to forget about tonight.

Then again, her curiosity said otherwise.

CHAPTER 8
Private Time

ΑΒΓΔΕΖΗΘΙΚΛ<u>Μ</u>
ΝΞΟΠΡΣΤΥΦΧΨΩ

AFTER THEIR DAILY meeting in the control suite, Jet and Kamber raced out of Lyrinthum and into the Clipton Forest. Kamber was fast, but Jet had managed to keep up with her lately. She was a blur, moving quicker than humanly possible, thanks to her Heliographi. But he was too, and though she'd been a track star, he knew the forest paths better.

Kamber sprinted down the main trail in a cloud of dust. Jet veered off, taking a lesser-used path. It had more underbrush, but it was a straight shot to the hidden glen. He hurled fallen trees and skirted around large boulders, letting the morning sun light the way for him. Crickets murmured, then grew silent as he sprinted past, his cloaked form no more than a blur in the early light. Fog covered the ground, shrouding the area until he finally burst into Firefly Falls. He crashed through the thicket of trees and finally slowed to a stop just meters from the shoreline. A second later, Kamber crashed through the brush. She saw him, lowered her shoulder, and drove him into the lake. Then she took off her robe and dove in after him.

They both splashed at each other, laughing and yelling. Jet winced at his bruised ribs but smiled at her anyway. "You lost again, slowpoke."

She grinned back. "Did I? Or is there really a loser in this?" She swam closer, wrapped her arms around his neck and kissed him.

They treaded water as he stripped down and threw his cloak onto the rocky shore. They moved to a boulder beneath the waterfall, letting it cascade over them. Jet held her close, felt her warm embrace and let himself go. He thought back to that night when they'd spent the entire evening under the waterfall, under the stars, under the fireflies...

That night felt so long ago, yet only a handful of weeks had passed. It seemed that he'd lived a lifetime with Kamber since then. As he held her gaze, he noticed the pyramid shaped tomb near the shore and thought about his friend, Cutter.

Kamber sensed his mood change and paused. "What is it?" she asked. Then she noticed his gaze lingering on the shoreline.

Jet gave her another kiss, then pulled her with him to the shore and grabbed his cloak. They sat down on a large rock near the grave. Jet didn't say anything as he leaned back and looked up at the fireflies buzzing overhead. This hidden glen had been their secret retreat. In a time when there was so much death and destruction, it had been a godsend for him and Kamber.

She waited quietly for several moments, then leaned next to him. "Something's on your mind. Tell me."

Jet stifled a soft chuckle. "Where do I start? Cutter. The third phase of the Prism Effect. The upcoming fulcrum wars, and…"

Kamber looked at him expectantly. "And what?"

Jet looked up at the tree canopy and breathed deeply. "It just seems like something's wrong. It's hard to put into words. Do you sense anything odd lately?"

"I'm not sure I understand," she said. "Can you try to explain it?"

"It's like…like there's something on the air, or *in* the air. I feel something's wrong with the trees, the water, everything around me. I can't place it, and it's driving me crazy."

Kamber closed her eyes, like she was trying to tune into something. She listened, then shook her head. "Maybe…I don't know. Are you sure it's not some left over feelings from Cutter or Sylvant? That was pretty traumatic."

Jet considered for just a second. "No, this is something else. Something evil, something sick, I think."

Kamber looked at Jet's staff, which was propped up against an oak tree. The new vessel imbedded at the end of it glowed softly. "Maybe it's that thing," she said and lifted her nose toward it as if in disgust. "I don't like it. That thing gives me the creeps, Jet."

He glanced at the war staff, noticing how it seemed to be dormant, sleeping almost. "I know. Everyone, including me, seems to feel the same way. It's…not from this place, not part of our universe."

"One of Albright's strangest relics, I think."

Jet frowned. "I'm not sure it's one of his inventions, though. Maybe he brought it over from, well, I don't know. Another dimension, I guess."

Kamber shivered and wrapped her arms around herself. "Be careful with it, Jet. Please."

"It's okay. I don't think it's meant to harm me. I get the sense it's here to guide me."

She narrowed her eyes. "Guide? What do you mean?"

"Well, I'm not entirely sure," Jet said slowly. "I don't think it's ready to reveal its true purpose yet."

Kamber shrugged. "Let's change the subject, okay?"

"Yeah, alright." Jet leaned back, letting the sounds of nature sink in. He closed his eyes and felt the warmth of Kamber's skin against his. But soon she pushed back. Jet looked into her glowing eyes.

"Jet. It, uh…it sounds like we're going to be away from each other for a while. I think Solan wants me with her again."

Jet only nodded. He felt some frustration at that. Once again, Solan seemed to think he couldn't focus on his tasks with Kamber near, and to some degree, she was probably right. Although he didn't get as 'lightheaded' and silly around her now, he still felt a bit awkward at times. Though he didn't say it aloud, he had to admit that it might be for the best. "I think you're right, Kamber. We may be away from each other for a while it seems."

She hesitated again. "I wanted to ask about the ghost Lucem. You never explained all of it to me."

Jet took a deep breath. "That's a pretty heavy subject. You sure you want to hear about that right now?"

She slowly nodded. "I feel like I need to know what's happening. Is this all tied together somehow?"

"I think so, and I don't know why. I get the sense that Albright is sending me somewhere, a quest or something. I just don't know where or how to begin. I assume it will reveal itself when the time is right. I think these ghosts from my past, both Cutter and Brindall, are meant to help me."

"If you had to guess, what do you think this quest is?"

Jet paused, not sure if he should say anything. Deep down, he felt like he knew, but it frightened him to say it out loud. And if he told Kamber, she would only worry. "Kamber, let's not talk about this right now—"

She touched his arm. "Jet. I can handle it. Just tell me."

"It'll just make you worry, and you need to—"

She stopped him again. "Please. I need to know."

As he looked into her glowing eyes, he saw fear. But he also saw the same warmth and kindness that had drawn him to her from the beginning. The last few weeks had transformed Kamber, that was easy to see. She was no longer the wide-eyed freshman from Skylight University. She had been through multiple battles and seen death. She had saved lives. *What a difference a few weeks could make*, he thought. Kamber was ready now. She was a full-fledged Lucem and could take care of herself. He shouldn't worry about her. Yet, he couldn't help himself, and that would never change. Even though Albright had asked that he not tell anyone, Jet finally caved.

"I think Albright wants me to travel somewhere," Jet finally said.

She heard the concern in his voice. "Travel to where?"

Jet took a long steady breath. "Beyond this realm."

She smirked, but then gave him a serious look. "What, this is a joke?"

"There's something out there he wants me to find, Kamber. This has something to do with my gift. Just like you can see visions in your dreams. My gift is built for this quest. I just don't know what it is yet."

She considered, then nodded as if finally accepting what he'd told her. "We all have a purpose. If you feel Albright is sending you to do this, then you must go. And I will focus my dreams on you. Maybe I can help you. I think I can reach beyond this plane, at least, I will try."

Jet smiled and held a hand to her cheek. He leaned in and kissed her. "Thank you, Kamber."

She leaned on his shoulder as they sat silently on the rock.

Then Jet stood, let out a roar, and dove into the lake again.

Kamber giggled, dropped her own cloak, and dove in after him.

They spent the rest of that day swimming, talking and enjoying their time together. He tried not to think about the trials they might face in the near future. But that unsettling feeling lurked on the breeze. A sickness that seemed to permeate the glen, his thoughts, and everything around them. He couldn't seem to shake the ominous feeling from his thoughts.

Something evil was seeping into every corner of the Skylight System.

CHAPTER 9
A Monumental Mystery

ΑΒ Δ Ζ ΗΘΙΚΛΜ
ΝΞΟΠΡΣ ΥΦ ΨΩ

JET WAS BEYOND tired the next morning. He'd stayed out the entire night at Firefly Falls with Kamber. They'd made the most of what he perceived to be their last free day together, at least for the foreseeable future. It had, once again, been breathtaking.

At times, he just wanted to be alone with her and forget the struggles of their past lives. Being around Kamber was mesmerizing, like walking in a dream. The feel of her touch, the scent of her skin. Deep down, he wanted to believe that one day soon all of this fighting, questing, and hunting for relics would end and the Skylight System would return to normal. That one day, he and Kamber might be able to spend their days in peace and quiet.

But that wasn't likely to happen, being a part of the Lucem. Over the last four years, since his days as a freshman, things around the system had only gotten worse. He was reminded again of that recent feeling in his stomach. If this 'sickness' had a color, he imagined it to be a putrid green, blackened around the edges. He could feel it on the breeze at night and hear it in the crickets' murmur. Sometimes the birds chirping in the mornings grew hushed, as if nature sensed that evil lurking just around the corner. The cloud cover even seemed darker of late. A storm was coming, and it loomed on the horizon. That warning had persisted since the final memoir had been opened.

Jet found Cord in the chow hall, sitting in the corner, wrapped in his cloak. Ti-Leer sat across from him, babbling about his favorite ale. In front of them was a deck of playing cards. It looked like Ti-Leer was losing badly, though neither of them seemed to be into the game. As soon as Jet walked in, Ti-Leer quieted. Then he realized who it was and relaxed.

"Ah, lad. You gave me a scare. Thought you were DJ. You haven't mentioned anything about my magic flask, eh?"

"No, of course not, Ti," Jet said with a wink.

Cord seemed to wake, then stood and tugged at Jet. "A moment, if you don't mind," and they left Ti-Leer behind as he struck off on his own conversation.

Jet followed Cord into the dark corridor beyond, then waited for Cord to face him. Cord peered around to make sure they were alone.

"What's got you spooked?" Jet asked.

Cord spoke in a low voice. "I want you to come with me."

Jet gave him a curious look. "Where are we going?"

"Remember, Solan granted my request to search out the eighth fulcrum. Now that you've got the 'doom staff,' I figured you might come along."

"Why do you need my help?" Jet asked. "You're a stronger Lucem. Is there something else you want to tell me?" Jet watched Cord's expression and could see that he despised asking for help.

"Well, I sense there's something more now. I know you've felt it recently, too."

Jet furrowed his brow. "Yeah, actually. I didn't think anyone else had noticed it. There's something wrong, like…nature isn't well. Does that make sense?"

"Yes. It does. And you know the reason why."

"It's Sybold, isn't it?"

"Correct. I believe she's back. If I bump into her, I can't defeat her. I'm asking that you come with me."

"And you think I *can* beat her?" Jet asked and almost laughed. "Cord, I may have this powerful staff, but I have no idea how to use it. Going to the eighth belt seems pretty risky."

"We need to be prepared for the upcoming fulcrum wars. We can't do that if we just sit here. We have the eighth memoir in our possession. I get the feelin' we may not have it much longer. Let's go find this fulcrum and see what we're up against."

"You sure about this?"

"Frankly, it's the perfect time, and apparently Solan agrees," Cord said. "Everyone will be studying the memoirs. I feel like we should do this immediately."

As long as Jet had known Cord, he'd almost always been right. Jet trusted him as much as he trusted anyone. Rarely did Cord press an issue either. Based on his insistence, Jet could tell this was something he felt strongly about.

"Alright," Jet said and clapped Cord on the shoulder. "Any idea what region of the eighth belt we're headed?"

"Toward Goliath's Gate."

"You really want to get that close?"

"The fulcrum is somewhere near that particle collider."

"Okay, fine," Jet replied. "But tell me why you think we won't have the memoir for long."

"I sense that Solan may be forced to use it as a bargaining piece. If we want the inner memoirs, we may have to give up some of these vessels as well. Solan's main objective will be to protect the citizens, and there are a lot of them on the inner four belts. She'll want to 'circle the wagons,' as they say. Bring everyone in and set up defenses. Right now, we have a brief window to examine the eighth memoir. Let's go find it and see what we can learn. If we *can* locate it, my guess is the other fulcrums will be in a similar location on their respective belts.

M

Jet followed Cord in his own jammer, and twenty minutes later, they were working their way through the desert areas of the eighth belt. Jet was familiar with the bleak landscape, having been the one who attained the eighth memoir there. The howling wind pushed the two of them around as they waded through the dancing sand. Granules bit into his knuckles and peppered his cloak. Jet pulled his scarf tight across his face and secured his solar goggles.

At times, the relentless wind forced them to seek shelter in rocky outcroppings. On a few occasions, massive twisters roared past, sucking sand into the dark clouds. They had to stop several times and refer to the memoir. Before long, they entered a canyon, and the howling wind diminished. They hurried silently along the narrow rock passages that eventually turned into caves. It grew dark as they entered, and a cool breeze carried an earthy scent.

Cord used his staff to light the way. Soon, he stopped before a stone wall and searched the striated surface, looking at the memoir a few times. Then he pushed on a lower section, and it slid open.

They traversed downward, and the rock striations eventually changed to concrete and steel. Cord found a metal staircase and moved down it, Jet not asking any questions. There seemed to be hundreds of flights of stairs leading into the bowels of the hull. Through the open grate stairs, he could see distant lights below. The air grew still and muggy as they moved deeper. Thirty minutes later, they finally reached ground level.

They stood on a vast metallic field, which was the best way he could describe it. Above, there was some filtered sunlight shining through, highlighted in dusty god rays. The chamber was enormous, and the ceiling disappeared above.

As they trekked across the field, Jet noticed something in the distance. He could see the dark silhouette of what looked to be a pyramid. Large stone blocks, black in color, rose up from the metallic field and climbed perhaps fifty meters. Jet counted five massive steps, or plateaus, that diminished in size as they stepped upward. It was awe-inspiring and mysterious. Jet didn't know what to make of it. The strange Aztec-looking pyramid seemed so out of place in this steel jungle. Juxtaposed against the belt's bulkheads and metal walls gave it an unearthly feel, reminding him of the Hall of Vital Records.

When they reached the base of the black pyramid, Cord stopped and knelt in the shadows, pulling Jet down next to him. "We don't know who else might be around."

Jet glanced around the massive chamber and up the plateaued steps. "Well, I think we've found the eighth belt's fulcrum."

"I believe this is just a temple," Cord whispered. "The fulcrum must be inside."

Jet looked doubtfully at Cord. "Are you sure? I don't see a door."

Cord pulled out the memoir. "If I read this correctly, which I'm sure I did, then the fulcrum's inside."

"Then in we go," Jet whispered. "To the top, I guess?"

"Stay close," Cord said, and began scaling up the pyramid's tall plateaus.

Each one was perhaps ten or fifteen meters high, which they climbed easily. Jet and Cord hurried up to the apex of the large pyramid. From the top, Jet got a commanding view of their surroundings. What he hadn't noticed before was the pattern of large conduits and pipes that radiated outward from the pyramid's base and across the vast field. It looked like sunrays, almost. Or perhaps the conduits were an energy source that fed into the pyramid.

"Looks like some sort of energy node," Cord said thoughtfully. "That's intriguing. Might this be a power source? I wonder…"

"Come on, Cord," Jet said, pulling him by the shoulder. "Let's get on with it."

Cord referred to the memoir again, then located an area on the top of the large plateau. Hidden in the shadows was a small stairway leading down. Cord seemed to disappear as he walked down the stairs, and Jet followed close behind.

They wound their way around a four-sided staircase and into the heart of the pyramid. At the bottom was a spherelike chamber about twenty meters in diameter. Cord paused near it. He held his staff forward to light the curved wall, which revealed a mathematical language that matched the memoir. In the center of the clear sphere was some sort of glass pedestal.

"Looks like an altar," Jet said.

"I suppose that's one way to interpret it," Cord said. "According to the memoir, this is the inner sanctum. Let's have a closer look."

They stepped into the large sphere. The ground was made of stone blocks and near the glass lectern was a notch in the floor that reminded him of a large keyhole.

"I'm assuming the memoir goes inside this lectern," Jet said.

"Correct. It'll be on display for all to see."

"Like artwork," Jet mused. "Wonder why Albright did it this way?"

"Unknown. It doesn't seem like his style."

"What about this?" Jet said and nodded at the keyhole. He moved over and placed the vessel end of his war staff into it. It was a perfect match. "So, once the memoir is placed, a countdown begins. When it reaches zero, the staff is inserted, and the fulcrum ignites. Do I have that right?"

"Except the memoir mentions a code." Cord scratched his goatee. "Unless the vessels *are* the code. I think that may be it."

"I don't follow you," Jet said.

"Your war staff, or vessel, fit that keyhole perfectly." Cord walked over and tried to place his war staff into the opening, but the shape of it didn't match. "Remember, any Heliographi can ignite fulcrums two through seven. Only *one* and *eight* can be ignited by a prime. That would be you or Sybold. Perhaps that's the code the memoirs are referring to."

"Isn't it odd that Albright's not the prime?" Jet asked. "I mean, why me?"

"Like it or not, it's your responsibility."

"I just wish he was here to answer some of these questions. If Sybold really is back, we're in trouble without Albright. I just wonder how she did it. Albright and Tyberius killed her just two years ago. Somehow, she found a way to cheat the system."

"I don't know how she did it, but such a feat would require a great deal of power. Perhaps that's why she remains in hiding. She's regaining her strength."

K

Solan stood in the control suite and glared at the hologram in front of her. In the foreground was Joshia, her arms crossed and a devious smirk on her face. Her shoulder-length silver hair shone in the dim light, the prominent red accent unmistakable.

Solan shook her head at the hologram and fixed Joshia with her glowing eyes. "You can't be serious. You expect me to have *any* trust in you after what you just pulled?"

"I really don't care what you think. Right now, that's the offer on the table."

"So, I'm supposed to give you *all* the dark prisms? Is that right?"

"And the eighth memoir. In return, you get the first four memoirs back. You want those, I know you do, Solan. But it's going to cost you." Joshia shook her head and gave Solan a mocking smile. "Such a weakness, these citizens," she muttered under her breath.

Solan sat heavily at Albright's table, her arms crossed as she considered. Joshia had her in a tough spot now. Solan wanted to reach through the hologram and strangle her half-sister. She was barely able to control herself. Her hands balled into fists as she shook, though she tried to hide her anger. She didn't want to give Joshia the satisfaction of knowing how close she was to losing control.

"What does Lybra get?" Solan asked, steadying her voice.

"What she most desires, the eighth and ninth memoirs. In return, she will give the Lucem the red vessel and the first and second memoirs."

"How do you know she'll agree to this?"

"Lybra doesn't care for the vessels. She knows there's nothing to gain from them. The memoirs are more important to her. She can't afford to give up the outer belts."

"We don't even know what the memoirs do. Why does she want them so badly?"

"I think we can all agree they hold some special power. The outer belts are Lybra's territory. You do the math."

Solan lowered her gaze at Joshia. "And yet, you're just giving them to her? Why, when you were so adamant about keeping them out of mortal hands? I wonder Joshia, is there more?" Solan watched her, sensing a slight shift. *Oh, there was indeed more. But what?*

"It's really none of your concern, *sister*. Do we have a deal or not?"

Solan sat with her head bowed in thought. But she'd already made up her mind. It was the same logic Lybra had used—no one yet knew what the memoirs were meant for, but whatever it was, Solan wanted control of the inner belts. She couldn't leave millions of citizens exposed. "When and where?" Solan finally said.

"The ninth belt, at C9—"

"Absolutely not," Solan said immediately.

Joshia let out a long sigh. "Fine. Where do you propose we have this meeting of the three?"

"At a neutral site. The fifth belt. Tomorrow at mid-morning."

Joshia gave it a second thought, then nodded. "It's wide open, secluded. Very well. I'll notify Lybra, and we'll—"

"One more thing, Joshia," Solan interrupted. "You can tell Lybra not to get too comfortable. As for you, *sister*, I will never forget your betrayal."

Joshia tilted her head to one side and gave her another mocking grin. "Oh, I was counting on it, Solan. You never cease to amaze me with your *oath of honor*." Joshia snapped the connection closed before Solan could respond.

Of Memoirs and Titans

JET TOSSED AND turned in his cot that night. He'd been having a reoccurring dream for years.

Of late, that dream came more frequently. If he were being honest, it was more of a nightmare, though. During his days as a student, visions of this 'prophecy' had haunted him. *The Serpent and the Prism*, Tyberius had once explained. Albright had further clarified this 'vision' was actually a great war.

In his dreams, a large serpent would wrap itself around a prism, trying to crush it. Jet was always trapped

inside that prism with only his will to hold the walls intact. So far, the prism had never failed. Of course, this was just a dream, but he sensed that the real conflict wasn't far away. Whether it was a dream, a vision, or a war, still confused him. What wasn't confusing was the serpent, and who it represented. Sybold was back, and she was growing stronger each day. Just knowing that filled him with a sense of dread. That feeling had only intensified after he'd set the third phase of the Prism Effect into motion. Though he still didn't know what the third phase was, it worried him.

Unable to sleep, he woke and rubbed his eyes. Across his room and leaning against the wall was his war staff. *Port-Shear*, the memoirs had named it. The essence of a Titan, so they claimed, which meant little to Jet. As he gazed at it, the vessel glowed in a soft white light. It still seemed to be dormant, as if it hadn't fully awakened yet. The skull inside the vessel moved slowly; its hollow eye sockets appeared to elongate, and the toothy grin on its face whispered something to him. It kept repeating it, over and over. Jet watched its jaw as it clicked in unison with the ever-present whispering. As if caught in some cosmic loop that wouldn't stop, he sensed madness in that vessel if he watched for too long. He stood and draped his cloak over the vessel, trying to make the whispering go away. As he tried to drift off to sleep, he thought he heard the vessel laughing at him.

After another hour, Jet gave up and stood. He walked over, snatched his cloak from the staff and stared down at the skull. He grew concerned that he might go crazy listening to it. Surely, Albright wouldn't have given him such a thing if it were dangerous, right? Maybe there was a better way to communicate?

Jet finally bent down and picked up the war staff, careful not to wake it. Then he laid it across his lap as he sat on his rug. He closed his eyes and went straight into Vishmu.

In his meditation, Jet ignored his surroundings. The stars and galaxies whizzed by as his inner light charged off. This time, Jet let his Heliographi run and play and didn't follow it. Instead, he turned to search for his staff. Once he located it, he focused, and eventually, the staff materialized in his hand. He held it aloft and sent a thought.

The staff lit up almost immediately. A blinding white light erupted from the vessel, and the skull inside grew in size. Jet nearly dropped the staff as it expanded. It continued to grow until he was the one standing inside the vessel. It reminded him of the vision, and he grew concerned that the serpent might approach him.

But it was the skull that drew his attention. This being named Port-Shear dominated the interior of a vast globe. Jet stood before the massive figure, suddenly not sure if making contact had been such a good idea. The

thing looked at him, a floating head, its eye sockets glowing, its teeth chattering.

And it seemed to wait for Jet.

Jet wasn't sure what to do, but he assumed physical speech was pointless. He reached out again with his thoughts, using Vishmu to communicate. When he did, Port-Shear seemed to smile. Not the cruel, uncaring smile he'd seen several times already. This was a slow, approving smile, as if to say, *finally…you figured it out.*

An odd tingling overtook him. It was the strangest sensation he'd ever felt, and his entire body went numb.

…what are you… Jet asked.

…*prime…of the star-light…*

Jet recalled talking to Solan years ago. She'd mentioned something about other planes of existence, higher dimensions.

…why are you here… Jet continued.

…*guide…*

…to what…

…*to portal…*

Jet paused, trying to piece the strange conversation together. Port-Shear's language was hard to understand and came in fragmented thoughts. Jet imagined his attempt sounded childlike to it. But then he saw the vessel's light fade. Port-Shear flickered and suddenly disappeared.

Jet drifted alone, waiting to see if Port-Shear might return. He didn't know if there was a limit to their time together or if the entity had simply grown bored and left.

Jet turned and looked for his Heliographi, wondering where it had gone. He willed his being to roam the cosmos, calling out as one might for a lost child. When he finally located it, the light was stationary, frozen in place. Beyond, Jet saw what looked to be a portal of stardust. It swirled, and light seemed to cling to the edges of the whirlpool. Its interior was dark and lifeless, and he felt a moment of fear as he stared into the abyss. In all his time meditating, he had never witnessed such a phenomenon. He sensed that if he ventured too close, he'd be pulled in and never return. The voices he heard emanating from beyond that void were tortured and full of agony. He quickly corralled his Heliographi and pulled it with him.

When Jet awoke from his meditation, his staff was no longer on his lap. It was propped in the corner of his room, the skull staring at him.

M

Unable to sleep, Jet left and found Solan in the Clipton Woods. She already had a fire going and stood behind it with her arms crossed. The fire popped and cracked, sending shadows dancing across the tall pines surrounding her. A light wind whispered through the trees, and crickets chirped contentedly.

He stepped into the clearing and set his staff down gently, careful not to waken Port-Shear.

Solan gave him a quizzical glance. "Someone's had a rough night, it would seem."

Jet looked at her, then at his staff. "Yeah, well…I'm not sure how this is going to work out."

"You mean the war staff?"

Jet let out a long sigh. "I can't get this thing to shut up. I need to find a better way to communicate with it." Jet paused, then looked at Solan's staff. "Your staff got a vessel. Does it not talk to you?"

"Not that I've noticed. Maybe mine doesn't work that way."

"The memoirs said each vessel holds the essence of a Titan. I just assumed they were all the same."

Solan thought for a moment. "Your staff is special. A prime, the memoir claimed. It's something Albright meant for you alone. You need to discover that connection with it."

Jet took a seat and pulled his gaze from the staff and back to her. "Solan. Why are you really sending me alone to recruit the Dreadnaughts?"

"Simply put, I feel like it's time for you to take on more tasks by yourself."

"Is this coming from your father?" Jet asked. Not long ago, Solan had hovered over him like a mother hen.

Now, she seemed to be shoving him out the door with no guidance.

Solan shook her head. "No. I just feel the time has come. Soon, you may be faced with situations that will test your will. You must strengthen yourself without others' help. The white vessel belongs to your Heliographi, the timing is undeniable. Watching over you is no longer my responsibility."

Jet took the information in with a straight face, but inside, he felt nervous. The thought of moving on alone, especially in the days ahead, worried him. He felt suddenly reluctant to leave his comfortable place among the Lucem. But the whispering in the wind told him Solan was right.

Jet breathed deeply, then nodded. "I'm not ashamed to admit that I'm afraid. I used to hear the ghost Lucem Brindall and Cutter's voice guiding me. Neither seem to be around anymore. I wonder if this staff has scared them off or something—"

Solan furrowed her brow, then held up a hand. "Hold on. You've been seeing Cutter?"

Jet suddenly realized he'd accidentally let his secret quest slip. He slapped his hand to his forehead, then sat back. "I…wasn't supposed to tell you that."

"Well, you've said it, so out with it."

Jet huffed and clenched his jaw. "When I had that private talk with Albright, he asked me to unlock my gift, but to do it alone. I finally did that, at the Hall of Vital

Records. It felt like I was bending the rules, though. That's the best way I can explain it. Time seemed to stop when I was meditating. That's when I saw Cutter. It really was him, only different somehow."

"So, that's why you went to the Agency that night?"

"Yeah, and that's why I couldn't tell you. Albright intends for me to go on a quest of some sort, yet I don't even know where I'm supposed to begin or what I'm looking for?"

Solan gave him a wink. "Well, then I'm sorry too…for being so upset."

Jet waved it away. "Albright's reason that I do this alone was because my gift would protect me, where other Heliographi might be harmed. That's apparently why I am going alone. Your intuition is right. I need to do more on my own."

Solan slapped her legs and stood. "Well. Now that that's over with, I have something I need to share, and you're going to probably disagree with me."

Jet gave her a suspicious look. "Is this about the memoirs and vessels?"

"Yes. I assume Cord probably mentioned something about it?"

"Yeah. He guessed you'd be forced to trade the eighth memoir and the Atrum's vessels to get the first four memoirs."

"Nothing gets past him, huh? But he's right. Joshia contacted me and made the offer. We're meeting them tomorrow morning."

"We still don't know what the memoirs do," Jet said. "but…are you sure that giving the Atrum their vessels is wise?"

"I'm not willing to risk the safety of millions of citizens. If something does happen with the fulcrums, we need safe haven for these people. The inner four belts hold the vast majority of Skylight's population. We need those memoirs."

Jet thought but quickly agreed. "You're right, of course. We can't give up the interior memoirs. But giving the Atrum their vessels might make recruiting more difficult?"

"Agreed. But priority number one is the safety of the citizens. That's always been one of our primary directives. We'll just have to deal with the outcome."

"Where are we meeting?"

"At a neutral site on the fifth belt. There's plenty of secluded areas in case things do get out of hand."

"Are you concerned that the Atrum might betray us again?" Jet asked.

"That's why I need your buy-in. We *have* to be in lockstep on this."

"I hope we're bringing the whole gang with us."

Solan smirked at him. "Oh, most definitely. Stell, Dane and Linon. We're bringing out the firepower. Everyone is coming, and that includes our air fleet."

"A show of force?"

"Indeed. No one in their right mind would think about crossing us with Dane's air fleet hovering overhead."

Jet stood and faced Solan. "Let's go get those memoirs then."

M

The next morning, Stell, Dane, and Linon met with Solan and the other Lucem in the control suite. She faced the group, waiting for everyone to quiet down. "We've been approached with an offer, and I wanted to tell everyone that I've accepted it. That doesn't mean we can't change our decision."

"Let me guess," DiJinn said. "The Atrum are rethinkin' their motives. Those traitors want back in! That's a no vote for me, Sol."

"That's not what they're asking for, Jinn," Solan replied. "They are asking for a swap involving the memoirs and the vessels. Obviously, we must reacquire the first four memoirs."

"And in return?" DiJinn asked.

"We would have to give up the dark vessels and the eighth memoir."

DiJinn grunted and kicked her boots off the table. "Sounds risky. We saw what happened when we gave them the war staffs. These vessels increase their power; they'll misuse it."

"That's true, Jinn. But we're not sure what the vessels do yet. In fact, we don't even know what the memoirs do." Solan took a few seconds, then shook her head. "I don't want to risk it. I believe it's more important right now to protect the inner belts. Hundreds of millions of people are at risk if we don't get the first four memoirs. Whatever their purpose, we need safe haven for the citizens."

"That's why we're bringing citizens in from the outer belts?" Kamber asked.

"Exactly," Solan said. "The sooner we start, the better. People have been paying attention to recent events. Word is out, and everyone's nervous. I've spoken to most of the governors in the outer provinces, and they're preparing evacuations. Some of the more needy will require transport. We can provide that with our fleet."

"What if the memoirs do nothing?" Ti-Leer said. "We've moved a boatload of people for no reason."

"Regardless, we're mobilizing," Solan said. "We play it safe. If things work out differently, then we'll help relocate everyone."

DiJinn paced around the room. "Sol. Tell me about the proposal again."

"The Lucem will give Lybra the eighth memoir, and the Atrum get the dark vessels. In return, Lybra gives us the red vessel and the first two memoirs. The Atrum will give us the third and the fourth memoirs. Lybra gives the Atrum the black vessel and the ninth memoir."

"So, that leaves the Atrum with the fifth and sixth memoirs?" Kamber said.

"And all the dark vessels," DiJinn added.

"Along with the black vessel," Jet said. "That one worries me. I get the sense it's like the white one."

Solan placed her hand on Linon's shoulder and looked at General Dane. "Can you two prep the fleet?"

Dane grunted. "We'll be ready."

"Good," Solan said. "We leave in a few hours, and everyone is coming along."

CHAPTER 11
The Meeting of the Three

ΑΒΓ Δ Ε Ζ ΗΘΙΚΛΜ
ΝΞΟΠΡΣ ΤΥΦ Χ ΨΩ

JET TOOK IN all the activity as he strolled through the Lyrinthum hangar bay. Even at this early hour, there were training exercises on-going. They'd just finished a brutal battle for the ninth memoir, yet Dane was full steam ahead. Thousands of the elite recon troops were busy training the leftover prisoner army that Solan had freed from the ARC district.

Frigates were being prepped for that morning's meeting on the fifth belt. Solan wanted every available troop and ship there as a 'show of force.' Dane had commandeered a multitude of Agency ships during the ninth reveal. Four of those were heavy battle cruisers and, in fact, were the largest ships in the entire system. The SLS—an acronym for 'In Skylight's Service'— *Righteous, Stalwart, Vigilant* and *Armada.* The massive battle cruisers would be used for leverage and intimidation that day.

The flight to the fifth belt was slow, having their entire fleet in tow. The cruisers lumbered along at the center of the fleet. They were surrounded by hundreds of war frigates and destroyers, along with scores of jammers, which formed a protective ring.

Soon, Jet could see the fifth belt punching through the fog. It was primarily used for industry and refining, though its surface was still dense with trees. Vibrant green hues reflected from its surface in the morning sun and inundated the low clouds. There were vacant areas sprinkled across the belt where logging had been permitted. Like the sixth belt, this one also shared in carbon sequestering for the system, thanks to all the trees.

Dane's cruiser, the SLS Armada, led the way. Their fleet descended through the heavy cloud cover and hovered just above the belt's surface. They waited as the Agency and Lybra's fleet began to materialize through the clouds. The Agency fleet had taken a beating in their last battle for the ninth memoir. But it was the thousands of deadly jammer skiffs that drew Jet's attention. Since

Lybra hadn't slowed her production of the fighter ships, he knew that would be a problem for them in future conflicts.

The bay doors of the Agency frigates opened, and thousands of M-Class mechs dropped to the ground with a resounding thud. Even from his hovering jammer, Jet felt the percussive impact. Between the jammers and M-Class mechs, Lybra and Harok didn't really need an air fleet of cruisers and war frigates.

The two groups faced each other, neither moving until several black jammers uncloaked between them and settled to the ground. Jet watched as the Atrum, led by Joshia, hopped out.

Solan finally gave the order, and the Lucem, along with several platoons of the recon troops, lowered to the surface. Dane and Linon remained in the cruisers and stayed at the ready in case they needed any backup.

Jet hopped out of his jammer and followed Solan. Behind him was Kamber, DiJinn, Ti-Leer and Cord and they stopped in front of the recon army. Solan stepped to the front as Joshia walked over to face her. Behind Joshia was Mosstrom, Bo, Vail, Sojahn, Tetra, Myranda, Brit, and Bofisto.

"So glad you could make it," Joshia said in a mocking tone.

Jet watched Solan closely and noticed how tense she was. Her fists were balled behind her back, her brow strained. Solan stood silent for several seconds before addressing Joshia.

"I can't decide if I should greet you or strangle you."

"Please, Solan. I know you're optimistic, but what happened was inevitable."

"Yes, I suppose you're right. For a brief moment, I had hoped we could work together. Thank you for setting me straight. I owe you, Joshia. By abandoning us, you've signed your own death warrant."

"Have we though?" Joshia crooned.

"Lybra won't take you back, and we will never trust you again. Where will the traitorous Atrum go for shelter now?"

"Oh, don't you worry about us, sister. We can take care of ourselves."

Solan's expression turned rigid. Jet knew she struggled with the fact that Joshia was related to her. It was something she viewed as an embarrassment and had reluctantly agreed to let the Atrum into their inner circle. Yet had they not teamed up, all the memoirs would have been in Lybra's hands long ago. Unfortunately, the alliance had backfired when the Atrum had taken the memoirs, placing the Lucem in this mess. Though the Atrum had the smallest army, they held five of the nine memoirs now, giving them tremendous leverage.

Jet pulled his gaze from Solan and Joshia and found Vail. Once again, he noticed her tapping the nape of her neck—two taps and three lines. It was the same secret signal she'd given him last time.

Vail wanted to meet with him.

A platoon of the M-class mechs stepped forward and stopped. Cutting through them was a presidential skiff with Lybra and Harok inside. It slowed, then descended. Lybra and Harok stepped out, and she hobbled over, leaning on her metal cane. Jet watched as several of the Lucem tensed at seeing the old lady.

"Well, here we all are, yet again," Lybra chuckled and trailed off into a coughing fit. Jet noticed the disgusted look on Solan's face. Eventually, Lybra recovered and looked up at each Lucem, letting her gaze settle on Jet last. She hobbled forward and Jet saw the curved blade tucked in her belt. *She'd brought that on purpose*, Jet thought. She was trying to intimidate him. Lybra stopped in front of him and looked up.

"Mister Stroud. You're so clever, aren't you? How many times have you managed to escape me?"

Jet felt his skin flush. Lybra's ego was on full display, she couldn't resist the attention. The old hag was responsible for thousands of innocent deaths, including his friends…and she was within arm's reach. He could strangle her right there and end all of this in one swift blow.

But he knew he wouldn't.

And she knew it too.

Jet suppressed his feelings of hatred, having been through that scenario multiple times already. If he gave in and murdered Lybra, he would never be the same. His Heliographi would leave him, and he would eventually die.

"You're awful brave, Lybra," Jet said.

"No, you're simply weak. A stronger Heliographi would kill me right now. Why don't you just do it, Mister Stroud? Yes…get it over with. I'm…right…here." She held out her arms in an open invitation.

Jet felt his skin flush at the taunt and looked down at the curved blade again. Cutter's dried blood was still smattered along the edge. "Soon, I won't have to worry about you. Something else will take care of it for me."

"Is that so?"

Jet removed his war staff from his cloak and rotated it to face her. The yawing skull held Lybra's gaze then, and Port-Shear began to whisper. It was waking.

…let me show her…

Jet held the staff in front of Lybra. When she locked eyes with the skull, he sensed Port-Shear begin to laugh. Lybra's face turned pale. Her eyes grew wide in terror, then seemed to go blank. Jet knew from experience, Port-Shear had transported her to another dimension, and fear flooded her expression. Jet could see that she wanted to pull free and run. It took only a few seconds.

Then, Jet recalled Port-Shear.

…that's enough…

…No, it isn't youngling. Not for this one…

Jet tried to pull the staff free, but it seemed to be stuck in place. He gripped it with both hands and tugged as Port-Shear began to laugh with pleasure. It started as a low chuckle that turned into a fevered pitch, then a scream.

…stop…now…

Jet knew then that Port-Shear was trying to kill Lybra.

Several of the M-Class mechs moved in and trained their cannons on Jet. Without warning, they fired several rounds from their heavy railguns.

Then…everything seemed to move in slow motion. It was like Port-Shear had frozen everyone in place, like the others were in stasis.

Time seemed to suspend.

The mechs had managed to launch several cannon rounds, which had slowed to a stop.

Jet had asked Port-Shear to stop, yet the Titan had disobeyed him. *How was he to function like this?* If the staff continued to disobey his wishes, then it was no use to him.

Jet grew angry. He steadied his thoughts, then commanded Port-Shear again.

…stop this…

Suddenly, everything was back to normal. Lybra wasn't screaming, and the M-class mechs weren't firing rounds. It was as if time had paused, backpedaled, and reset.

But the look on Lybra's face was still pure terror. Jet could hear the unearthly laughter from Port-Shear and, apparently, so could Lybra. Jet knew that Port-Shear had shared her future, and Lybra had seen her own death.

With a last look at Jet, Lybra stepped behind her mechs and avoided looking at Jet or the war staff.

Solan also seemed to wake, and Jet began to wonder if the whole incident had been nothing more than a dream. Only, he knew it hadn't been. Somehow, Port-Shear had altered time.

Solan cleared her throat. "Let's get this over with. No sense in standing around insulting each other."

Lybra was still rattled. "Yes, I agree. Let's move on." Her voice was unsteady, and she stayed behind the mechs.

"Let's see the goods," Solan said.

Mosstrom moved forward and set a bag down. He opened it, and Jet could see the memoirs, all had been placed back into their protective cylindrical case. "As promised. The Ninth, third, and fourth memoirs. The Atrum will maintain the fifth and sixth."

Solan snapped her fingers and Ti-Leer lumbered forward with a bag and dropped it in front of Mosstrom. He glared at the dark Atrum, and his beard seemed to bristle. Then he knelt and opened the bag. Inside was the eighth memoir, along with the blue and indigo vessels. "We keep the lighter jewels," he said and stepped back.

Lybra clapped, and the lead mech marched forward. It stopped, and a compartment opened. A box dropped to the ground and popped open. Inside was the large black prism, along with two smaller vessels, red and purple. Jet could also see the first and second memoirs. "I keep the seventh memoir," Lybra trilled. "I require the eighth memoir from the Lucem. I have no use for the jewels." She gave a dismissive wave of her hand.

"I believe the deal was for memoirs one through four," Solan said.

"Yes. Which you will have in exchange for the eighth memoir, along with the blue and indigo vessels," Joshia said.

"And there they are," Solan said through clenched teeth.

Joshia walked forward, knelt, and looked into the bag. The glow of the vessels lit her face, and she nodded with a twisted smile of satisfaction.

Then Lybra stepped forward, along with Harok this time. She hid behind him, avoiding direct contact with Jet. She kicked cautiously at the bags, almost as if she were suddenly afraid to touch anything, and peered from behind the large M-Class mech. Then nodded. "That'll do."

Solan took the first four memoirs and the red vessel and then placed them in the bag. She handed it to Ti-

Leer, who grunted and tucked the bag under his arm and moved behind the other Lucem.

Joshia took the black, purple, blue and indigo vessels. She stood there with a lustful grin on her face as she held the vessels. It took her a few seconds to focus, then she handed them to Mosstrom, who tucked them into his cloak. Joshia dropped the ninth memoir into the box and stepped back.

Finally, Lybra knelt, her cane leaning against her hip. She examined the memoirs and picked them up. She held all of them up to the light with a gleam in her eyes. She smiled, seemingly back to her normal self. "Ah, excellent. Yes, are we all satisfied?" She thrust the memoirs into Harok's arms. Jet heard her whisper to him. "I own you now, Harok. You can thank me later for Goliath's Gate."

Harok seemed to be in a trance, as if he hadn't heard a thing she'd said. Lybra ignored him and continued. "Right," she trilled. "Colorful jewels, I hope they are worth it. We shall see, won't we?"

Jet felt an uneasiness settle around everyone. The three groups huddled separately with shifty eyes and hunched forms. If anyone was going to double-cross, they'd do it now. Just a few days ago, they had all been trying to kill each other. If a fight did break out, there was so much firepower surrounding the area that no one would survive.

But thankfully, that didn't happen, and everyone retreated with their spoils.

Obviously, Lybra only cared about the outer belts and the memoirs related to them. She had it all planned out, it seemed, and had been more than happy to give up the vessels. Jet assumed the eighth memoir had been at Harok's request. With the ninth memoir in hand, she would use it as leverage over all the factions, and there was a considerable amount of them located in the debris field.

But would they swear fealty to her, specifically the Dreadnaughts?

That remained to be seen. And soon, Jet would venture out to make his own pitch to them. Alone.

CHAPTER 12
A Late-Night Rendezvous

ΑΒΓΔΕΖΗΘΙΚΛΜ
ΝΞΟΠΡΣΤΥΦΧΨΩ

JET WAITED UNTIL 2 AM, then snuck through Lyrinthum to the Clipton Forest portal. He stole through the woods, cloaked and silent. The last time he'd met Vail in secret like this, they'd been at the cloister on Skylight University—the same place where she'd been converted to an Atrum. Back then, he thought Vail had been murdered and that E.M. was real. Of course, none of that had been true. The signal she'd just given him was Morse code for 3 AM.

When Jet arrived at the cloister, he waited in the shadows. The summer breeze was unusually crisp, with a hint of winter already in the air. The seasons moved fast in the Skylight System and the evenings were growing cooler, much faster than he remembered. Once again, he wondered if it had something to do with that sickness he'd felt.

Soon, Vail's blurry image appeared.

Jet braced himself.

He supposed he should be upset at her for stealing the memoirs and betraying them. Cord had warned him. Solan had warned him. Of course, Jet hadn't listened, wanting to believe there was still good in Vail. After all, she had left their war staffs behind. But lately, he knew she had struggled with her identity, with who she'd become. He held a glimmer of hope that he could save her, and he wasn't going to give up that easily.

Jet stepped into the moonlight and lowered his hood. Vail did the same and solidified, her arms already crossed and a scowl on her face.

"Here to berate me, Stroud?"

"Why would I do that," Jet said. "Besides, you're the one who wanted to meet."

"Seriously?" she retorted. "You have nothing to say about what we did?"

"What could I say that would make a difference? What's done is done. That's in the past."

"But you're upset."

"I'm disappointed, yeah," Jet replied. "How could I not be? We bled together to get those memoirs, and then you betrayed us. That burns a little. But let's move past that. You sent me the signal and here I am. So, let's talk."

Vail stood in the moonlight, letting it wash across her face. It highlighted her pixie-like features. Her nose and cheekbones dainty, her fair hair dyed turquoise at the tips to match her glowing eyes. Her pale skin cold in the bright moon.

"I…I just wanted to see how you're doing. Is that a crime?"

Jet tilted his head. "That doesn't sound like the Vail I know. What's really on your mind?"

Vail took a long second and rubbed her arms as if a sudden chill stole over her. "Have you felt it?"

Jet shook his head. "What do you mean?"

"You know *exactly* what I mean. That feeling is everywhere. It's in the air, on the trees…"

Jet took a deep breath. "Yeah, well, I guess…there's something different since the third phase. I think maybe I set something in motion. I assume you know about the second phase?"

Vail looked up to the moon, then took a seat against one of the stone pillars of the cloister. Jet sat next to her and waited as crickets murmured in the background.

Vail cleared her throat. "I know about the extinction event. Joshia seemed to know about it months ago."

Jet thought that strange. *How could Joshia know when Cord had only just figured it out?* Where was she getting her information?

"I assume you know what the cause is," Vail continued and settled back into the shadows. "Do you understand this *sickness?*"

"Yeah. Not sure what that means for us or for the Skylight System."

"What are you planning to do about it?"

"Vail, why are you sharing this information with me?" Jet asked and leaned forward. "Why do you care what happens to us? Sybold's return is a good thing for the Atrum, right?"

But the look on Vail's face was a mix of uncertainty and fear. He noticed her hands shaking slightly and felt a moment of pity. He knew that all Heliographi varied. Not all Atrum were purely evil. He sensed that Vail was morally gray, much like Cord. She was caught in the middle. Did Vail want out of the Atrum? Was that what this was about?

"The return of Sybold frightens you?" Jet asked.

"It should frighten everyone."

"Are you sure that's the reason you're here? To warn me, or is it something else?"

Vail threw up her hands in exasperation. "Can't I just get a thank you for wanting to help? Stroud. I don't care if you take the warning, if that's what you're—"

"Wait." Jet paused and leaned in close to her. "You…care about me. That's it, isn't it?"

Vail turned away as if to leave.

Jet reached out and touched her shoulder. "Vail. Look at me."

She turned to face him, and Jet noticed her cheeks were wet. "I hate this, Stroud. I hate it."

Jet moved in closer, his mind racing. Vail, with her defiant attitude and unapologetic personality, was barely recognizable to him. He'd only seen her like this one other time when they'd been students atop Apex. But this moment felt similar. Vail was struggling more than he realized. *He couldn't walk away from her in this state.* She needed some help. As far as he was concerned, they were still friends.

"What can I do?" Jet asked, his voice a whisper in the quiet cloister.

Vail gritted her teeth and straightened, then brushed a tear away. "I don't want your pity, Stroud."

Jet reached out and gripped her shoulder. "It's not pity, Vail. It's what friends do for each other."

"There's nothin' you can do to help me now."

"You could come with me, stay with the Lucem."

Vail smirked and nearly laughed out loud. But then her expression softened as she looked away again. "No, Stroud. That would never work, and you know it. The Atrum betrayed the Lucem, we will never be accepted again."

"So, what do you plan to do? Pretend? What'll happen when the Atrum figure that out?"

"No one does it better than me," she said. "I'll survive."

"But how long can you keep that up?" Jet asked. "Especially when Sybold returns?"

"At the moment, it's not her I'm worried about."

"Then who?"

Vail didn't answer, but Jet knew. There was one Atrum who had the ability to detect almost anything. One whose power nearly rivaled Sybold's.

"Mosstrom, right?"

"I can handle it." Vail stood, apparently done with the conversation.

Jet stood with her and reached out and took her hand. "Hold on, Vail."

She looked down at his hand in hers and stiffened, as if the action had taken her by surprise. Jet felt her tension but didn't let go. "I want to help, somehow. Please, let me."

"I don't know how, Stroud. I don't know where to start. This is new to me." Vail started to pull her hand away, but he held it tighter.

She smiled. It wasn't the sarcastic, cynical smile he was used to. This was genuine.

"You want to save everyone," she whispered. "Why?"

He shrugged. "I don't know."

Another long moment passed as they held hands. There was a sudden, strange feeling in his stomach, one that caught him completely by surprise. He sensed the same emotion in Vail as his heart skipped a beat, and his head swam. But then he thought about Kamber and finally pulled his hands away.

Vail's expression hardened, and she pursed her lips. "I came here tonight to warn you, nothing more."

Jet took a deep breath and straightened his shoulders. "Is that it?"

"One more thing." Vail moved out of the cloister and pulled her hood up. Just before disappearing, she whispered something. "I give you this information in reparations for our treachery. The Atrum are rejoining Lybra. Be prepared." Then she vanished into the night.

ΑΒΓΔΕΖΗΘΙΚΛΜ
ΝΞΟΠΡΣΤΥΦΧΨΩ

THE NEXT MORNING, Jet was officially on his way to recruit. Solan had insisted he start immediately after their meeting with Lybra and the Atrum.

He rose early but didn't bother to wake Kamber. He still didn't feel very confident about this mission. It was, in essence, his first *true* solo mission, and he was a bit nervous. Not frightened, just nervous. At first, he'd been shocked that Solan had planned it this way. After all, she had practically coddled him over the last four and a half years. Most missions, she had paired him with Cord, one of their top Lucem, primarily to protect and guide him. Truth be known, Jet understood that he wasn't the strongest Lucem and never had been. He had struggled throughout his time with the Lucem. But he *had* made strides. And now, he'd been gifted this powerful war staff. Apparently, an ancient being from another plane— a Titan, the memoirs had claimed. And maybe that's what bothered him the most. His new partner was one that he couldn't even talk to.

At times, the staff would light up in the middle of the night, and he could hear it whispering strange things. At other times, when he passed through the tunnels of Lyrinthum, the haunting voices grew silent. Not because of him, but from the presence of Port-Shear. Even those paranormal voices feared the war staff.

Jet's jammer was prepped and ready when he arrived at the hangar bay. Minutes later, he was rocketing toward the ninth belt debris field. His primary stop would be the port city of Harang-R. It was one of the largest ports in the ninth belt's debris field. The center piece was actually the third largest floating chunk left of the ninth belt with smaller satellites in the shape of the letter 'R.' Like some celestial constellation, it was home to several of the system's deadliest gangs. But it was the Dreadnaughts that Solan had tasked him to recruit. She was gambling that a show of force would persuade them, and his new war staff might just be the right tool for the job.

Jet entered the ninth belt's airspace and the debris field. The port city was near the far perimeter and soon he was navigating through the soupy wreckage. Steam and clouds blocked his view as smaller bits pelted his hull like hail stones. The sun cast a murky light across the debris, gray with a fine mist. Turbulence bumped his jammer about until he broke free and saw the busy port.

Much of Harang-R was dirty. Many of the outlying buildings were old and rundown from a past era. Having to pass through the atmospheric hole once a day, the entire region was exposed to outer space. In areas that were outside of the protective stasis domes, no trees or vegetation grew, thanks to the harsh conditions of space. But clustered around the tethered chunks were other areas with clear stasis domes. There were dozens of the glassy bubbles covering vast areas of land. Beneath them, nature flourished: trees, plants, flora and fauna.

Though Harang-R was the third largest chunk, it also tethered dozens of smaller chunks together with massive steel cables. To Jet, it looked like a free-floating spider's web, the smaller portions large cities in their own right. It was a cluster of islands with Harang-R at the center.

Jet watched as hundreds of frigates flew in and out of spiraling airlocks. When he flew closer, he could see more detail on the main island. Tall, castle-like buildings hopscotched up the sides of the steel and rock. Even the large cables seemed to be integrated into the buildings. It almost reminded him of some medieval castle with its primitive architecture, as if it had been repurposed from a different century.

Jet entered the access code given to him by Stell and settled his jammer in a private, long-term hangar bay. He switched into his disguise and moved down the stairs to street level.

He had to take sky ferries to get up the steep terrain and when he finally made it to the top, he stepped off with thousands of other people. Jet breathed in the chilly morning air, noticing the difference this far from the core.

Most of the locals seemed to be middle or upper-class residents and wore fine clothing. Mixed into the crowds were also traders, military personnel, and other less-savory folks. Jet didn't make eye contact as he worked his way along the cobbled streets and toward the fortress.

Before long, he stood at the front of the highest building. As he'd noted before, it looked like some fortified castle from another era. Its large iron gates were shut and locked with guards standing before them.

"Only invited guests may pass," one of the guards said. He brandished a light railgun in Jet's direction. "Unless you have council privilege, step aside."

Jet slipped his ring off, which immediately lowered his disguise. The guards gasped at seeing his glowing eyes. "I have an important proposition for your chief."

The two guards looked at each other, slightly flustered. The taller one straightened his shoulders as the other spoke into a holopad, then nodded.

"Come with me," he said.

Jet fell in behind him, slipping his ring back on his finger as he walked. "What's your name?" he asked.

They moved through a stasis field as it lowered, then snapped closed behind them. The guard faced him but didn't slow. "Name's Gerand."

He had a rough beard, worn graphene armor, which was partially hidden beneath his vest, and a compressed energy spear holstered in his belt. His dark eyes roamed the streets as he walked with long strides. Gerand kept pulling at his vest, trying to cover his armor.

"You been with this group long?" Jet continued.

Gerand didn't answer at first, as if considering how much he should say. Jet wondered if the Dreadnaughts were strict with their troops, maybe preferring they didn't speak to others.

"I've been with them long enough," Gerand said. "I'm finishing up my contract this year, then moving to Skylight City. I should have enough saved up to afford a small apartment for myself and my daughter."

Jet left it at that, assuming the man's wife had probably passed away.

Soon, they entered the lower wing of the large castle. Inside was a large concourse with thousands of people filtering by. Most of them were troops wearing the Dreadnaught insignia, but some appeared to be peasants or other nonessential workers. Jet followed Gerand as he stepped onto a vector accelerator. A stasis field surrounded them as they shot up several hundred meters, finally stopping near the top of a large tower.

Inside was a large antechamber with hundreds of people hurrying about. Large windows stood along one side and emitted hazy sunrays. As they moved deeper into the fortress, the traffic died down to a whisper.

Gerand stopped in front of a large pair of steel doors, then turned to face Jet. "Be careful what you say in here. Inside is the entire council, the chief, and all his deputies. These are some of the most powerful people in the region."

Jet took a deep breath and followed Gerand into the chamber.

The large room was circular in shape, about twenty meters in diameter. Ringing the perimeter was a short wall, then curved seating beyond. It stepped up in tiers, reminding him of an arena. Sitting in the bleachers were all manner of people, most dressed in the dark purple garb of the Dreadnaught Clan. At the twelve o'clock position sat a group of six people, which Jet assumed was the chief and his deputies. Jinn had referred to this man by the name Fritt. He wore a lavish robe that was intricately detailed with strange motifs. Fritt had his hood pulled low, making it difficult to see anything about his physical appearance or age. He stared at Jet from beneath the hood but said nothing.

Gerand brought Jet to stand in front of the group and stopped. "Show them your true appearance," he said.

But Jet waited as he continued to look around. The floor of what he knew now to be a gladiator's arena was covered with dried blood stains.

Then, a thought took him. This was a proving ground.

Jet removed his ring, revealing his true identity.

A gasp went up among the crowd. Jet continued to look straight ahead, though, not letting his gaze leave Fritt.

Finally, Fritt stood as the murmuring died down. Everyone waited silently.

"Tell me, Heliographi. Why do you seek us out?" Fritt asked, still not lowering his hood.

Jet placed his hands behind his back, trying to remain calm. "A dangerous time is coming. Soon, every group, faction, and citizen will have to decide who they will stand with."

Jet waited as Fritt remained silent. In the back of his mind, he could sense Port-Shear begin to stir.

…not now… Jet thought.

He couldn't afford to deal with the staff's insistent chattering.

…why so weak…youngling…

…stop it… Jet nearly yelled.

"What is your name," Fritt asked. "Your real name."

"My name does not matter. It won't change what's coming—"

"It matters if I say it matters," Fritt responded cooly. "Tell us."

Jet looked around the crowd, considering. He knew the legend about ephebus mortem was over—the Heliographi's identity was known. Jet shrugged. "My name is Jet Stroud."

Fritt took a moment as one of the advisors bent and whispered to him.

"Ah, I remember that name. The promising blaze player, Skylight University. What? Four years ago, I believe? A life cut short, some said. But that is the way of your clan, isn't it?" The man's deep voice seemed to fill the arena as he spoke. The crowd murmured as Fritt motioned to Jet. "Please, continue. What is so dire that the legendary Heliographi would seek our help? You hold most of the memoirs, if I remember correctly. Though our numbers are great, the Dreadnaught faction failed to gain even one."

"We believe that a great war is near. The system will be divided in half, and civil war will come. Any outside group that does not choose a side will be swept away."

"So, are you here on behalf of all Heliographi?" Fritt asked.

Jet hoped that no one yet knew about the Atrum's treachery. He decided to let that fact lay low for now.

He nodded.

"Well, it seems a bit inconvenient for us," Fritt continued. "Our stronghold is here within the ninth belt. I hear rumors that your base is located somewhere inside the first belt. It would take a great deal of convincing to move our entire operation."

"I understand your hesitation," Jet said and stepped forward. "I know the Dreadnaughts have a policy to remain neutral. But things are about to change in the Skylight System. The Dreadnaught army paired with the Heliographi would be a powerful force."

"Yes, true. But I prefer our place, right here," Fritt said, hands folded before him. "Is there anything more you can say that might sway me? Something more about the memoirs, perhaps?"

Jet wanted to tell Fritt the truth. But he couldn't give away too much, at least not now. Instead, he deflected the comment. "All we know is that the memoirs will bring a major change to the system. We believe that certain belts will offer safe haven for those who control them. I implore you to reconsider. If you don't pick a side, your people will not survive."

"We've survived many wars for nearly a century and have yet to pick a side. I think we will survive this conflict."

Jet took a deep breath, realizing that his current tactic was getting him nowhere. Fritt seemed to be dead set on remaining neutral. Then, Jet suddenly realized something. Fritt was pretending and had been the entire time.

"I'm not the first Heliographi to approach you, am I?" Jet asked.

"No," Fritt said. "And if you want our support, you'll need to do better than trying to frighten us into submission."

"I'm not trying to frighten you—" Jet stopped and started over. "Might I ask who has approached you?"

Fritt directed Jet's attention to a far door. From behind the partial wall, two cloaked figures moved forward. Jet watched them approach, their heads bowed. They stopped a few meters away. Then, the two Atrum looked up and met his glowing gaze.

CHAPTER 14
Trial by Intimidation

ΑΒΓΔΕΖΗΘΙΚΛ<u>Μ</u>
ΝΞΟΠΡΣΤΥΦΧΨΩ

JET STARED INTO the eyes of Mosstrom and Vail. He muttered under his breath as the two Atrum stepped up beside him and faced Fritt. Everyone waited.

Fritt folded his arms across his chest, his hands disappearing beneath his lavish robes. "What can you offer that they cannot, Jet Stroud of the Lucem?"

Jet began to wonder if this was all a game for Fritt. Was he playing them for entertainment? Would the Dreadnaughts really break their neutral stance? Either way, Jet had to be more convincing now that The Atrum were present. "We command the Recon army forces, the deadliest army in the system, led by General Dane. I assume you know that name?"

Fritt seemed to consider that. Dane was well known throughout the system and his name carried some weight. "I know of General Dane. He is a mastermind on the battlefield and a great warrior."

"Then you also know that he brought most of the Agency's air fleet with him. We now have the four largest battle cruisers in the system."

"Impressive. And what else?" Fritt asked. "Because I believe that Lybra and the Atrum have joined forces. Their combined resources favor them."

"Lybra and the Atrum will destroy the system. If they win, everyone loses."

"That seems unlikely. What proof do you have?"

Jet took a step forward and held out his hands in a plea. "Fritt. By now, you must know that the Heliographi are not of this plane. The one who leads the Atrum is coming, and she only knows death and destruction. She will destroy everyone."

Fritt shook his head, unconvinced. Jet knew he was on the verge of losing his support.

Mosstrom stepped forward and stood next to Jet. He held his staff forward, and Jet could see that he had placed the dark indigo vessel. Now he understood why the Atrum had wanted the dark vessels so badly. A more powerful staff in the hands of Mosstrom was an imposing sight.

"Master Fritt," Mosstrom began. "You are correct. We have joined with Lybra, who has access to the deadly Tetrahedron army. She commands a legion of the M-Class mechs and more jammer fighters than the Lucem. Might I add that we are near your base, a very convenient amenity, I believe. Why not maintain your current location while having the assurance of our superior army?"

Jet could almost feel the last nail being driven into the Lucem's coffin.

But Fritt continued to consider. Finally, he looked up. "You know how we settle these issues, I presume?"

Those were the words Jet had been dreading to hear.

He looked to Vail and Mosstrom. The dark smile on Mosstrom's face gave Jet chills. He had no desire to tangle with the ancient Atrum. But Vail didn't look at Jet, and he could see that she wasn't excited either.

"Trial by combat," Fritt said and held up his hands. The council began to stomp their feet and the thunderous sound drowned out everything.

Fritt quieted the council. He brought his hands together, then parted them. The arena floor slowly separated into smaller platforms. Below was darkness. Jet didn't care to guess how many unfortunate souls lie rotting down in those depths.

Vail brought her staff up, and Mosstrom did the same.

"Jet Stroud, he who needs to work on his abilities!" Mosstrom said in his deep voice, a malicious grin on his dark face. "Let us see if you are indeed prepared."

Jet hopped to a platform and steadied himself. His hands were shaking, his palms clammy as he stared at Mosstrom. Jet knew he stood little chance against him, let alone Vail too. But he wasn't going down without a fight.

...let me go, youngling...

Jet nearly toppled over in shock at hearing Port-Shear in his head. He knew what the war staff wanted. Yet, Jet felt a reluctance to unleash it. He had little control over the thing and Port-Shear was like a loose cannon, from what he'd witnessed so far. There was no telling what it might do, and he might not be able to contain it.

But the staff continued to whisper, its voice growing louder from beneath Jet's cloak. The bright white light began to show though and soon the congregation of Dreadnaughts was murmuring in confusion.

Jet shook his head. "This is about to get really interesting," he muttered and finally pulled the war staff from his cloak. He slammed the butt of it on the metal platform, then held it over his head. The staff roared to life and Port-Shear began to laugh at Mosstrom. The sound reverberated around the circular chamber and the light grew dim like a thunderhead passing before the sun. The only visible thing was the blinding white light of Jet's staff. The skull inside the vessel elongated and warped as if bending the fabric of time and space.

The murmuring from the crowd turned to gasps of panic and surprise. They dropped to the ground in fear and lay face down, afraid to look at Port-Shear.

Jet stepped forward, holding the staff aloft for Mosstrom to see. The Atrum had an uncertain look on his face as he stared back.

"This is what the Lucem have to offer," Jet said and turned to face Fritt. "This talisman is the key to our survival. It can protect us. That is why I'm here." Jet said this with as much confidence as he could muster. In reality, he had no idea if any of it was true. But it sounded good.

Everyone waited for Fritt to respond. Though Jet couldn't see his expression, the Dreadnaught leader seemed uncertain now. He finally motioned at Jet and the two Atrum. "Regardless. You will compete. This is how we decide."

Jet had hoped to avoid a fight but had no choice now. He turned back to Vail and Mosstrom.

But Mosstrom's hesitant look had changed to one of awe. "You should not invoke such methods, Jet Stroud. You risk much by freeing this entity in our realm."

"It chose me, Mosstrom," Jet replied and held the staff in front of him. Mosstrom's glowing eyes didn't leave the staff. It was then that Jet sensed his fear. Mosstrom's lips were tight, his knuckles white as he gripped his war staff in front of him defensively. Vail also avoided Port-Shear and hid behind Mosstrom.

Jet continued to wait, though. He had no intention of initiating combat—he would only defend himself. But it was clear now that Mosstrom's aggression had dissipated and there would be no battle.

Port-Shear continued to speak and apparently Mosstrom could hear it.

…Mosstrom…

Port-Shear seemed to be mocking the Atrum, as if trying to entice him into battle. The ethereal voice was accompanied by a laugh that echoed in his head.

…why do you wait…is your vessel ill…Orion-Dark…the indigo one…

Mosstrom went white as he faced Jet. Then he turned and bowed to Fritt. "We decline the Dreadnaught's support."

Jet nearly dropped his staff in shock.

The sudden surrender took everyone by surprise, and the entire arena went silent.

Mosstrom didn't wait. He turned and walked out of the chamber. Vail followed, not asking any questions but gave Jet what looked like a wink.

The pure white light of Port-Shear faded and extinguished with one last chuckle. Then, Port-Shear was gone.

Fritt faced Jet. "How long do we have to relocate our operations?"

K

Solan rocketed off in her jammer toward the ninth belt debris field. Next to her was Kamber. Solan had been so preoccupied preparing for the evacuations that she'd almost forgotten about Jet. Two days had passed when she'd finally got word that he'd managed to sway the Dreadnaughts into joining them. Though he hadn't gone into much detail, she sensed there was an interesting story to tell. And now that that hurdle was out of the way, it was their goal to evacuate citizens. They needed to transport as many people as possible from the outer belts. But first, they were heading to the Dreadnaught's port to meet Jet and hear what he had to say.

"So?" Kamber asked, folding her hands patiently onto her lap. Solan heard the concern in her voice.

She pulled her gaze from the console. "Jet only told me that he'd managed to secure the Dreadnaught's support. I'm sure we'll get the details soon enough."

"That's a big deal, right?"

"Yes. It's a game-changer."

"I sense you're not terribly excited," Kamber said. "What is wrong?"

Solan kept her gaze focused on the dark clouds along the horizon. "To be honest, the Dreadnaughts are somewhat unreliable. Of course, I knew this when I sent Jet. Don't misunderstand me, it's great news, and I'm proud of him. I'm just being cautious. I hope they honor their agreement."

"A bit of a rogue group, it sounds like."

"Very much so. But the fact that they're willing to relocate concerns me. They've spent decades in the ninth belt and lots of resources developing their port city."

"Is there something else on your mind?" Kamber asked.

"There's a lot on my mind these days."

"What is it that's bothering you right now?" Kamber pressed. "I see visions in my dreams, and you've been in them a lot lately."

Solan gave her a sidelong glance. "Your gift is *nocturnal consciousness*. It's rare, that one. But to answer your question, yes, there is something on my mind right now." Solan nodded her head toward the horizon.

Kamber turned her gaze to the stormy clouds in the distance. "What does it mean?"

Solan let out a long breath. "There's something happening in our system, and I don't know what it is. It's like…"

"…like something is constricting around you?" Kamber finished the thought.

Solan slowly nodded her head. "Exactly. Like a suffocating sickness is in the air…in the wind. Something is lurking out there—" Solan paused, then reset. "It's out of our control, whatever it is. We need to focus on the things we *can* control, which are evacuations now."

Kamber remained silent, her arms crossed, as if a chill had filled the cabin of the small skiff. "Jet mentioned the same thing. I don't like it either. It's been hard to ignore, though, in my dreams."

Solan gave her a quick smile, hoping to lend some encouragement. She could sense Kamber was uptight, probably because of Jet and his time away. She knew they were seeing each other, and so did everyone else. Their secret affair had been out in the open for a while now.

"Kamber, about Jet," Solan said.

Kamber's skin flushed. "What is it?"

"I know about you two. I don't think it's a secret anymore."

"Of course," Kamber chuckled. "As soon as Ti-Leer found out, then everyone knew. Is it wrong what we are doing?"

"No…that's not it," Solan said, getting her thoughts in order. "What I'm trying to say is…well, Jet has a lot on his plate, at least, he will soon."

"Don't we all?"

"Yes. But I sense that he has a challenging road ahead." Solan didn't want to alarm Kamber, but she also wanted to be honest with her. "I don't know an easy way to say this, so I'll just say it. Jet has an important task, a quest, I suppose. If he doesn't succeed, then many people may suffer. I can't explain why I know this. I just do."

Kamber wrapped her arms around herself and tried to hide the concerned look. "He told me about his quest, too, but didn't say what it was. He mentioned something about Albright. Whatever it is, I know he'll find a way."

"He has that ability, maybe that's why Albright chose him," Solan said with a wink. She laid a hand on Kamber's shoulder. "I just wanted to say that I'm glad you two are together. I think it's helped him. I didn't send him off to be away from you. I'm doing it to prepare him for what's to come. To be honest, I've been overly protective of Jet. I may have unintentionally slowed his development. I've always placed him with Cord or one of the stronger Lucem when I probably should have trusted him."

Kamber nodded and managed a weak smile.

Solan could still see her concern, though. "He'll be fine," she said, more to herself than Kamber.

"Yes, I hope so too."

Solan gripped the console tighter as she looked back to the storm clouds along the horizon.

CHAPTER 15
The Breaking of Rules

ΑΒ Γ Δ Ε Ζ ΗΘΙΚΛΜ
<u>Ν</u>ΞΟΠΡΣ Τ ΥΦ Χ ΨΩ

VAIL ACCOMPANIED JOSHIA and Mosstrom to the ninth belt debris field, wondering why she had been included. She was beginning to think it was simply to keep an eye on her, more than anything else. Their visit to Lybra's stronghold—which was more or less the Agency headquarters now—certainly didn't require her. Joshia and Mosstrom were more than capable on their own, probably two of the most powerful people in the entire Skylight System. Vail felt like a third wheel. And frankly, she didn't care for Joshia's company, and certainly not Mosstrom's. Though she was good at putting on a false front, Mosstrom was an enigma to her. His persona was dark, even for her liking. The elder Atrum had been around for millennia, according to Joshia. Though Vail didn't know all his abilities in Vishmu, she was particularly careful to guard her thoughts around him. Even though she didn't have much to hide, there was enough in her recent past that she didn't care to share, especially regarding her feelings about Stroud.

The three of them finally arrived at the Agency headquarters in separate jammers. It felt odd strolling through the headquarters, even in her alias. For nearly a century, this had been the center of Skylight's guardians. Now, it was the opposite, with Lybra in charge. They were once again allies with her. It made Vail anxious, and grumpy. She hated Lybra, and if she ever got the chance to be alone with her, she'd be hard-pressed not to kill her. They had accepted the deal with Lybra. Though the Atrum hated her, and Lybra disliked them, it was an alliance that made sense, for the moment. Once the memoirs had been placed, or the polarity of the fulcrums was set, Vail imagined that Lybra would turn on them immediately.

The three of them were escorted through the vast complex, along wide thoroughfares and hangar bays, where they were eventually seated in a large control room. They waited, Vail not speaking or looking at Joshia or Mosstrom.

The control room was like most of the others Vail had seen. High, open ceilings, multiple holographic screens along the perimeter walls broadcasting events from around the system. In the center was a large metal table and chairs.

A few minutes passed when an escort of troops marched into the room, followed by a dozen mech units with President Harok and Lybra Howling last. Harok and Lybra sat at the large table while the troops and mechs stood near the back of the room.

Harok stared straight forward, almost in a trance it seemed, while Lybra looked at them with a twisted smile of satisfaction on her face. She still wore the cerebral tiara—its wavelength disruption prevented any Heliographi from reading her thoughts. A nifty invention, though probably enormously expensive.

"Let me start by saying thank you for the memoirs," Lybra crowed. She stood and waved her hands around the table in a dramatic greeting. "I hope you are enjoying your jewels. But I suppose it's really just sharing, isn't it? What's yours is mine, now that we are a team again. I believe our agreement includes sharing intel too. Anything you discover must be disclosed. Yes, I do think you will do that."

Joshia sighed in annoyance but nodded and didn't say anything.

"Good, very well," Lybra said, then steepled her fingers slowly in front of her face. Vail could sense that Joshia was on the verge of losing control. Lybra had no idea how close to death she really was.

And that thought made Vail curious.

Between Joshia, Mosstrom, and her, they could likely wipe the entire room, along with all the troops in this base, especially with their enhanced staffs. How come Joshia *was* being so controlled? It made no sense to Vail. She knew Joshia too well. But then she recalled the conversation that night at the swamp. The dark figure had commanded that Joshia swear fealty to Lybra. *Of course, Sybold had a plan.*

"Now, I hear that we must begin preparations for the memoirs' placement, isn't it?" Lybra asked and raised an eyebrow. "Is that what we call it?"

Joshia nodded her head, almost imperceptibly. "Yes, placement is what we must do."

"And what happens after that?" Lybra asked, one of her eyebrows lifting so high that it nearly disappeared into her gray, tufted hair.

"Well, that's the question, isn't it?" Joshia said in a mocking tone. "None of us have ever placed a memoir, so it's all speculation."

"My dear," Lybra said, lowering her gaze. The tiara she wore glowed and the mech units standing around the room stood to attention, their armaments coming online. "I don't think I mentioned that my mechs have received an upgrade." She snapped, and one of the four-meter-tall units marched over and stood next to her.

Vail looked to see it holding a clear shield made of reinforced graphene. It also held a long energy spear that glowed a bright golden color. The tip was pointed down, burning a hole in the metal floor.

"Now, a little more respect, if you don't mind," Lybra said.

Joshia smiled. Then looked to Mosstrom and snapped her fingers.

Mosstrom stood from his seat so quickly that it caught everyone by surprise. He swung his war staff out, and it unfurled in one fluid movement. The first three mechs hadn't even moved before being reduced to a smoking pile of parts. Joshia backflipped over the table and had her staff at Lybra's throat before she could send a command to the other mechs.

"Yes," Joshia hissed, showing the whites of her teeth. "A little more respect for your elders, Miss Lybra Howling."

Vail stood at the ready, her hand on her staff as she looked at the other mechs. They stood at attention, but didn't move, Lybra holding them in place now. Harok sat stone-like, along with all the other troops. His skin was blanched white, a sheen of sweat on his forehead.

Lybra didn't flinch, though. She stared up at Joshia with her bright eyes and smiled. "Why, of course, my dear," Lybra mocked as she nodded her head. "Let's not get too far ahead of ourselves now. I don't think your boss would be happy about that."

Joshia lowered her staff and stood up straight. She sat down, joined by Mosstrom.

Joshia waved her hand as if nothing had happened. "As you were saying?"

Vail breathed a sigh of relief. Harok eased his grip on the table, and the entire room seemed to exhale.

"I need to understand what the Atrum know about these memoirs," Lybra said. "If we are to work as a team, we need to share these types of things."

Joshia tilted her head, as if annoyed. "What I can tell you is that the memoirs, once placed, will likely come on-line. I suspect a time and date will indicate when the fulcrum's polarity can be ignited."

"Do we know what this polarity is? Is that this so-called 'armament' the memoirs mentioned?" Harok asked. He'd finally found his voice and sat forward.

Joshia placed her war staff in her lap and leaned forward on her elbows. "As I just said, none of us have ever placed a memoir, so we have no idea what Albright has in store."

"Do we know about the other memoirs?" Harok continued. "What about the Lucem? What do they plan to do?"

"They will do the same," Mosstrom said in his dark, baritone voice. "They have one of the brightest Heliographi in a long time in Cord Ledbetter. He will crack the code. My guess is that he also knows the time and dates for *all* the memoirs, not just theirs."

"How could he know that?" Harok barked. "They haven't seen all the memoirs yet."

"Do not underestimate him," Mosstrom warned. "Do not underestimate the Lucem. I would advise that we prepare for opposition. When we place these memoirs, the Lucem forces may be there to oppose or gain the polarity."

"We *will* be prepared," Lybra said. "Besides, Harok, you need to attend to the final touches of your gate, I believe."

"Goliath's Gate, Lybra," Harok said in a somewhat irritated tone. "It's Goliath's Gate, for the thousandth time."

But Lybra waved it away. "Yes, yes. Whatever. Your gate is almost complete, I believe. Is it not? And with impeccable timing, I might add."

Harok sat back and took a deep breath. Vail watched his hand shake as he ran it through his dark hair. He straightened his tie and suit lapels. But Harok didn't seem himself, at least from what she knew of him. She thought he looked ill, almost emaciated in fact.

"It's nearly complete," Harok said. "We've had crews working on it around the clock for months now. Thanks to your refined rare-earth and funding, Lybra, we're almost there."

"I would recommend you be cautious, President," Mosstrom said and leveled a finger at him. Harok's face turned white as he stared into Mosstrom's dark glowing eyes. "You may find things you don't like in the depths of the universe and beyond. Shall I show you? 'Tis not a problem."

Vail watched Harok sit back in his seat before finally breaking eye contact with Mosstrom. "No…no, thank you. Of course, we are always careful. Tests will be conducted with great care."

Mosstrom smiled and gave a mocking bow of his head.

Lybra cleared her throat. "Yes, very well then." She snapped her fingers again and the doors opened. "Let me introduce my top General for this mission. He will see that the memoirs are installed in a timely fashion." She stood and held out a hand. "General Yune."

An older man, Vail guessed maybe in his early sixties with olive-toned skin and flecks of gray at his temples entered. He walked in and stopped between Lybra and Harok. The troops around the room snapped to attention and waited.

"We've missed out on the Dreadnaughts, it seems," Lybra said. "But who needs them? Yune, I assume you'll have the Agency troops and the Tetrahedron ready to go?"

"Yes Ma'am," Yune said without looking at President Harok. "We are awaiting your instructions."

Lybra stood and walked around the room as everyone waited, a twisted smile of satisfaction on her lined face. She stopped in front of a holographic map, one hand on her hip, the other clutching her metal cane. "Well, my darlings. Where shall we begin our domination of the Skylight System?"

N

Vail couldn't leave the Agency headquarters fast enough. Apparently, Mosstrom and Joshia felt the same way.

After sitting through the old hag's rambling praise of herself and what she had done for the system, Vail wanted to puke. She knew that Joshia also wanted to strangle her. Of course, Sybold had requested that Joshia stay her hand. But the question of why Sybold even needed Lybra still gnawed at her, whispering like some serpent in the dark corridors of her mind.

Vail was beginning to put together a theory, though. One that was becoming more evident with each passing day. The atmosphere in the system had changed, anyone paying attention would have noticed. Subtle at first but growing quickly. Something was coming. An event or perhaps a grand entrance. Sybold had returned, she'd seen that with her own eyes.

But the Atrum leader had been assassinated by Albright and Tyberius only a few years ago. Typically, a Heliographi's inner light had to reset by finding another host at birth. Which meant it should have taken decades before Sybold's return. Yet, the shadowy figure she'd seen near the swamp that night was a hale and youthful twenty-something host. Sybold had somehow found a way around the rules. Vail's theory was based around just that—breaking the rules had a price. And Sybold was still regaining her strength, even after two years. That explained why she'd commanded Joshia give the Atrum's fealty. She was simply using Lybra until she was ready to return. Once Sybold regained her full power, she'd likely kill Lybra.

Once they arrived back at Hellfron on the seventh belt, Vail left Mosstrom and Joshia without saying a word. She made her way to her quarters. But just before she got there, Vail stopped in the middle of the dark corridor.

Something held her back. She retraced her steps toward their central chamber and waited.

Soon, she saw Joshia and Mosstrom leaving. Vail considered, thinking about how her curiosity might not be a wise thing to follow this time. But a few seconds later, she cloaked and tailed them from a distance.

Like last time, they took the twisting trail through the swamp and to the old willow tree. Its bent and broken branches swayed in the moonlight like skeletal fingers, sweeping the ground mournfully. Vail paused a good way back and settled into the shadows.

The same cloaked figure moved out to greet them. Both Joshia and Mosstrom took a knee and waited until the figure bid them stand. "Did you bring the device?" the young lady asked.

"Why, of course, my love," Mosstrom said and held out something long and pointed.

"What of the alliance?" the girl asked.

"Lybra has accepted our offer," Joshia said through gritted teeth.

The girl smiled. "In due time, Joshia. I sense your anger, but you must wait a bit longer."

"I understand."

"Mosstrom. The staff."

He held out the staff.

"It's nearly time," the young lady said and looked up at the moon. Vail could see the edge of an outer belt aligning, and soon it would overtake the moon. Already, the light was changing, and everything was beginning to take on a sickly green hue. "The conversion is near. The time is now, Mosstrom. Have the black vessel ready."

Joshia pulled a bundle from her cloak and held it out.

"Mosstrom, first the conversion, then the staff. Joshia, the vessel must come last. We have only seconds while the staff is active. Do not fail me."

Seconds turned to minutes, which felt like an eternity to Vail as she knelt in the moonlight, waiting to see what would happen. She gripped the tree trunk so tightly it began to separate, sap oozing between her fingers like some sickly disease.

A sickness…in the air. Woven into the very fabric of the system.

Suddenly, the moonlight flickered, then faltered as if being snuffed out. The skylight eclipse darkened the surroundings to a deep shade of black.

Mosstrom took the large nail-looking device and slammed it into the girl's outstretched left palm. As soon as the metal pierced her flesh, a red light shot outward like a fiery beacon. As Vail looked on, the lady stared straight ahead, not saying a word. Her body went rigid, and Vail felt the pain from her own conversion four years ago. It had been so intense, she had passed out. Yet, this girl seemed to be enjoying the pain, relishing it, even. Slowly, the girl's eyes began to glow. Her pupils and iris flooded with a bright red. But just as quickly, they darkened a few shades as if blackness threatened to take over. The result was more of a maroon-colored glow, not the vivid red Vail had seen before.

The greenish light of the moon was starting to show through.

"Now!" the girl yelled. "The time is here."

Mosstrom pulled the nail like device away, and Joshia unwrapped the bundle of cloth around her hand.

Shining from the folds was the black vessel. Mosstrom handed the girl the war staff. She immediately slammed it to the ground, and it unfurled. The staff was long, over two meters in length. The wooden portion was glossy black in the moonlight. Glyphs and symbols surrounded the shaft, and the metal collars at one-third points pulsed with energy.

Then, the endcap of the staff opened as Joshia removed the black vessel from the cloth. She let it go, and the black jewel flew to the staff like it was magnetically charged. It settled into the end cap, which closed around the black jewel just as the moonlight flooded through. The skylight eclipse ended at that same instant with a thunderclap.

When Vail looked at the staff, it glowed in a black light, pulsing like dark matter. An aura seemed to surround the girl, who stared up at the staff with a twisted snarl of satisfaction on her lips. Then a shriek erupted from the staff as she held it over her head. It sounded like thousands of tortured souls waking from an ancient slumber. Vail held her hands to her ears, closed her eyes and tried not to scream.

When the shriek died away, Vail looked up to see Sybold, the Atrum leader, standing directly in front of her. The woman's gaze sent chills through her, and she nearly passed out in horror. Vail felt fear in that moment, one she'd never felt before.

As Sybold held Vail's gaze, she spoke to her. Vail began to waver, her vision faded, her legs gave out, and she felt weightless. Her body collapsed, and she fell to the mossy turf and knew no more.

CHAPTER 16

A Search for Fulcrums

ΑΒ Δ Ζ ΗΘΙΚΛΜ
ΝΞΟΠΡΣ ΥΦ ΨΩ

IT WAS SEVERAL days after their meeting with Lybra and the Atrum when Cord prepared to leave with Ti-Leer. Now that they had the first four memoirs, he had been tasked by Solan to locate each fulcrum, place the correct memoir, and document the event. But she had also asked him to locate the outer belts' fulcrums as well. *Go quickly with Ti-Leer and place our memoirs, then locate the other fulcrums, quietly!* Solan had said.

In his mind, Cord felt an urgency to place the memoirs now. It was also a race to understand each

fulcrum. According to Albright's plan, every memoir had to be placed before the July 4th date, which was less than a week away, and Cord didn't want to delay that. Once that was done, there would be a prescribed order to each fulcrums' ignition, according to the memoirs. Cord would start at the fourth belt and finish at the first belt. Once the memoirs were set, he would investigate their adversary's fulcrums. But he had to be cautious. He'd essentially be in enemy territory.

Cord had spent the night before tracking down and rummaging through each belt's architectural drawings. As one might expect, they were massive volumes of technical documents, ones that he found intriguing. He'd perused the technical plans with wonder and had to constantly reel in his fascination and refocus. Eventually, he had managed to locate several areas of interest on each belt. His quest would start there.

That morning, he could tell that Ti-Leer wasn't happy about the assignment, though. Ti-Leer had wanted to make the trip to the Dreadnaught's stronghold, probably in hopes that a scuffle might break out. Cord assumed that's exactly why Solan had sent him with Cord instead. However, the two of them were as different in personality as anyone. Cord was more detail oriented, where Ti-Leer was broad of mind and quick to temper. Not to mention that Ti-Leer would often babble on about nonsensical subjects, like the flavor of bourbon or the spices found in his favorite whiskey. Perhaps

Solan had felt their pairing would balance out, but Cord wasn't so sure. Over the four and a half years he'd known Ti-Leer, he'd had very little interaction with him. He personally preferred to venture alone, or at times with Jet, who he respected. But Jet had left a few days prior to recruit the Dreadnaughts, and he should be on his way back by now. Cord was as anxious as anyone to hear the news.

Regardless, Cord felt an excitement coursing through him. He would be traveling to places that very few people had seen. The underbellies of the belts were vast, with hundreds of levels and kilometers of unknown territory.

Ti-Leer hobbled into the hangar bay, stumbling into the other crew members. Cord could see he'd had another late night. "Oi, lad," Ti-Leer said and clapped him on his narrow shoulder. "We 'bout ready? Hold on a tick, remind me where we're headin' again? Seems I forgot. Oh, that's right…the fulcrums," he whispered, followed by a low belch.

Cord frowned. "You sure you're up for this?"

"I'm slightly offended, lad. Course, I am. Do ya think there'll be a pub where we're heading?" Ti-Leer shoved an oversized backpack into a compartment of his jammer, followed by a few boxes of whiskey. "Ah, fine. It was a joke. What, can't take a joke? Be that way, then. Let's move on!" Ti-Leer clambered into his jammer.

Cord shook his head and climbed into his own jammer and led the way out of the hangar bay.

Before long, they were entering the fourth belt's air space. Cord took in the surroundings. The rust-tinted cloud cover shrouded the tall talloons, which stood at attention along the belt's horizon. Their large spinning blades cut through the haze, casting ominous shadows across the thick cloudscape.

Cord piloted his jammer to an area near a disused block of factories. Even in the morning sun, the heavy clouds choked out the light and gave them some cover. Cord's main concern was avoiding any contact with the locals. Speed and secrecy were what they needed now. They couldn't afford word to get out about what they were searching for, though he imagined most citizens had already heard rumors about the strange fulcrums. But Albright had hidden them well, and most people wouldn't be able to find them in the depths, let alone venture down there.

He and Ti-Leer snuck through a vacant factory and found an old exhaust vent.

"Down the hatch, laddie," Ti-Leer whispered.

Cord bent the grill, and they moved into the belt's hull.

They followed the air duct into the bowels as the sounds from above faded. Soon, they were greeted by the sound of chugging equipment and the light grew dim. Cord smelled mildew mixed with the acidic odor of unused equipment. Twenty minutes later, he kicked through a rusty access panel, and they moved onto an open catwalk. It spanned about thirty meters above an open pit.

"Hope you're prepared for a hike," Cord said. "It might be a while before we find what we're looking for."

"I can walk for days," Ti-Leer huffed. His backpack was stuffed full and nearly as tall as he was. "I have the eyes of an eagle. I'll let you know when I see it."

I

Cord and Ti-Leer finally located the fourth belt's fulcrum. It was in roughly the same location as the one he and Jet had seen on the eighth belt, though that one had been much larger. Inside the stepped pyramid, they found the inner sanctum. The clear sphere was similar to the eighth belt's fulcrum as well with a glass lectern and keyhole.

"This is it. The inner sanctum," Cord whispered and removed the memoir from its protective case.

Ti-Leer inspected the glass lectern. "Odd, this place. Who thinks these things up?"

Cord made one more trip around the inner sanctum, hoping that he wasn't missing anything. Then, he walked over to the lectern. On the side was a panel that he slid free. Inside was a void about the size of the memoir. Cord unrolled the fourth memoir, smoothed it out, then placed it right-side up and stepped back.

The tiny microchips woven into the parchment latched onto the interfaces inside. The memoir seemed to suction to the void, and the clear panel slid back in place. Then the entire lectern seemed to melt into one solid block of clear graphene.

Ti-Leer looked around and held his war staff up defensively. "Something's 'bout to happen, I think."

Cord watched in awe as the parchment lit up. The insignia in the corner of the memoir glowed bright and the Roman numeral IV pulsed. There was a soft buzzing sound that whirred inside the globe. Then, the lectern's glass shone in a vibrant green light and projected forms onto the spherical walls of the inner sanctum. When Cord and Ti-Leer stepped outside, they could clearly see a countdown timer and date broadcast above in holographic fashion. It was large enough to see from anywhere inside the vast chamber.

"Suppose we'll have to return before that clock runs out. Am I right?" Ti-Leer asked.

"Correct," Cord replied. "And if we miss it, the polarity of this belt may be lost forever."

They quickly left the fulcrum, since there was nothing more they could do. Then they made the quick flight to the third belt and followed the same procedure. Cord was beginning to notice that all the fulcrums were basically in the same general location, with a few slight variations.

After the third belt, they moved on to the second and finally the first.

Like the eighth belt, the first belt's fulcrum was massive. It was almost identical, and there were power conduits radiating outward from the pyramid's square base like some Aztec god's maze or geoglyph. Cord documented everything in his journal, and they moved on to the next stage of their mission, which was exploring the outer belt fulcrums.

Thirty minutes later, Cord led the way across the dark skies and toward the seventh belt's airspace. Somewhere below the surface, they'd find the fulcrum; he only hoped they didn't run into any Atrum.

He felt more confident now that they'd placed the first four memoirs. Once placed, they could not be moved, only observed. But learning the locations of their enemy's fulcrums would allow Solan the option of contesting their polarity when the time was right. That decision would be hers alone. Cord knew one thing. Lybra and Joshia would certainly contest the polarity of the first four fulcrums, and he was betting they already knew the locations. The Lucem would have to decide how to approach the upcoming fulcrum wars. Would they defend or attack?

"Nearly there, lad," Ti-Leer's voice crackled over the comm link.

Cord slowed and let his jammer hover, then lowered into the clearing of a swampy marsh, still cloaked. He hopped out, Ti-Leer just behind.

"Ah, what a soupy mess," Ti-Leer hissed, kicking at a snake with his tactical boot. "How in blazes are we supposed to get down below?"

Cord nodded toward the horizon. "There should be a sequestration point just over that rise." He took out his war staff and used it to pole vault over large areas of water.

Soon he could see the small station, which had a tall security fence surrounding it. A few silos stood like thin turrets in the moonlight. There was a thick fog around the base from the nearby marsh. They slowed as they approached and hunkered down, looking for signs of activity. Cord saw one security bot and a few cameras, but nothing they couldn't handle.

Cord motioned to Ti-Leer, cloaked, and made his way toward the station. They hopped the ten-meter security fence and looked for the area Cord had noticed in the drawings. The interior of the station held dozens of methane storage tanks, but one of them was false. Cord found it and moved inside.

The interior was warm and poorly lit. They moved down a flight of stairs that dropped forever, it seemed. There was a vector accelerator, but Cord wanted to avoid notice.

After what felt like hours, they finally reached the ground level. They wandered between conduits and utilities as they snuck along. He could picture the schematics in his mind, using his photographic memory to pinpoint one of the three areas he thought might hold the fulcrum. It grew steamy and humid the deeper they traveled. Cord wiped sweat from his brow and knelt to the metallic floor. Like nearly everything else, it was rusty and flaking from the belt's internal environmental system.

"This the place, lad?" Ti-Leer huffed. He propped his hands onto his knees and sucked in air, trying to catch his breath.

Cord held up a hand as he scanned the area. "Quiet, Ti. Remember, we may not be the only ones here."

"Oi, right," Ti-Leer said in a lower voice. He took a knee next to Cord and pulled out his flask. "You think we might see some Atrum?"

"I hope not," Cord whispered back. "If we're lucky, we'll go unnoticed."

"Ah, but that's so boring. I thought you were more adventurous. At least, that's what Jet tells me."

"Priority number one is finding these fulcrums. Might be hard to do if we're fighting Atrum."

Ti-Leer took a sip from his flask, then pointed it at Cord. "Aye, but it'd be a wee bit more interestin', wouldn't you say?"

Cord turned to look at Ti-Leer. "Let's try to avoid that."

Ti-Leer chuckled. "Ah, fine." He sat back against a large steel column and closed his eyes. "Wake me when you find what you're lookin' for, won't you?"

Cord didn't answer as he continued to scan the horizon of the vast metallic chamber. It was littered with steel supports, cables, conduit and utilities. But nothing jumped out at him. It was large and open, but there were too many obstructions in the way, unlike the first fulcrum.

"I don't believe this is the right area," Cord said and turned to Ti-Leer only to see his chin on his chest, already asleep. Cord briefly considered leaving him and moving on alone. *It might be quicker*, he mused. But if he did run into resistance, it would be nice to have Ti-Leer around.

Cord nudged him with his boot, and Ti-Leer grabbed his war staff. He hopped to his feet and nearly tumbled over before steadying himself. "Give it back," he blurted, his speech a bit slurred. Ti-Leer patted his cloak and felt his flask, then relaxed. He took a quick swig, then placed it back in his cloak. "We 'bout ready then?"

Cord led the way out of the vast chamber. They meandered through narrow corridors and dark tunnels, Ti-Leer making quite a bit of a racket as they trekked along.

"You don't talk much, you know that?" Ti-Leer said.

Cord didn't slow but looked over his shoulder. "Quite frankly, I don't care to."

"Why?" Ti-Leer asked. "Trust me lad, sometimes it helps to get things out in the open. Take DJ for example. That lass will talk about anything, talks as much as me, in fact. You know what she once told me? She's never had a drink. Can you believe it!" Ti-Leer bellowed. "I mean, who goes through life without a drink or two?"

Cord shook his head. He tried to focus on the way ahead, the footing slick from the moisture. He held his war staff out in front to light the way, its yellowish glow reflecting off the silent walls.

"No sir, not me," Ti-Leer continued. "I want to experience everything. I'm not leaving anything behind when I go. You hear that? When my time comes, I can say I have no regrets…well, there is that one time. Aye, then the other time. Well, I guess there are a few regrets."

Cord eventually blocked out Ti-Leer as he focused on the way ahead. Soon, he recognized an area from the drawings. When they got closer, he turned to Ti-Leer.

"My apologies for interrupting your conversation, but I think we're nearing the site."

Ti-Leer looked confused at first, then he raised his eyebrows. "Oh, right. You want me to quiet down. No worries lad, quiet as a mouse."

Cord gave him a nod. "Let's stay cloaked, just in case. Staffs at the ready."

Cord moved through a narrow corridor that opened into a chamber. This one was larger than the previous one. It was also clear of obstructions like conduits and foundations. The ceiling seemed to disappear above and in the center of the open field was the familiar Aztec-inspired pyramid. Its geometry stepped up in a series of plateaus and narrowed toward the top. The stone was black in color, as if formed from volcanic rock.

"I think we've found it," Cord whispered over his shoulder. He moved to shadowy areas, approaching it cautiously. A stray bit of sunlight shone down over the pyramid from a nearby skylight well. It cast a golden hue across the metal alloys, giving the large monument an otherworldly feel.

At the foot of the pyramid, Cord stopped and listened. He could hear groans and creaks from the belt's hull. An occasional drip or chirp from some defunct equipment echoed from beyond. Otherwise, all was silent. Cord found the staircase that switched back and forth to the top entry. As he started to climb the stairs, Ti-Leer pulled on his cloak.

"What's the need of goin' inside? This is the right one. Let's be gone, lad."

Cord pursed his lips as he considered. There were still several more fulcrums to locate. He wanted to go inside and investigate, more for his own curiosity than anything else. Most likely, it was exactly the same as the other fulcrums. "Perhaps you're right. Let's move on."

They moved off the stairs and back across the field. When they reached an outcropping of some unused equipment, a light flashed through the top of the pyramid. It flickered, then solidified into the same holographic countdown timer they'd seen on the first four pyramids. There was a date and time, counting backward. Someone had just placed a memoir.

As they looked on, two blurry mirages exited the top portal. When they reached the edge, they uncloaked. An argument seemed to ensue, and one of the Atrum pulled out a war staff. When the dark-haired girl struck it to the ground, a black light erupted from the tip, and a loud thunderclap ripped through the vast chamber. Bolts of dark purple and black lightning spiked upward from the end of the staff and reached all the way to the top of the chamber. The other Atrum used its staff and managed to block the lightning strikes. The two Atrum sparred, their staffs lighting the dark like fireworks. But the dark-haired girl was too quick, too powerful. Cord immediately knew why. It was the black vessel, the one the Atrum had just acquired from Lybra. It was unique, like the white vessel on Jet's staff.

They were looking at Sybold.

The weaker Atrum faltered and slipped. With a powerful downstroke, the dark-haired girl brought her staff onto the other girl's head, and she slumped, unconscious. Then the dark-haired girl did something that shocked Cord. She lifted the unconscious Atrum's body and tossed it off the pyramid.

CHAPTER 17
Glass-Hewn

ΑΒΓΔΕΖ<u>Η</u>ΘΙΚΛΜ
ΝΞΟΠΡΣΤΥΦΧΨΩ

DIJINN, GENERAL DANE, Captain Linon, and Stell stood aboard the bridge of the system's largest battle cruiser, the SLS Armada. The three leaders—Dane and his Recon army, Linon and his prisoner army, and Stell with her spy syndicate named Vine—were helping the Lucem plan their next steps. Their goal that day was to start evacuating the outer belts. They had enough room to move thousands of citizens, though most had their own transportation. Solan had sent their entire fleet to help move some of the older and poorer people. *We have less than a week,* Solan had told DiJinn.

The hunt for the memoirs had just ended, and already they were racing to place them inside the fulcrums. But she knew that war would soon be on their doorstep. She brooded on that thought, wondering how things would play out. She felt impatient—she hated this calm before the storm rubbish. She preferred to get things over with, not spend time thinking about it. But Solan had a measured approach. She wanted to be prepared and strategize, much to DiJinn's dislike.

She glanced over at Dane. His hands were clasped behind his back, his muscular frame at attention, as usual. He scanned his troops from the bridge of the heavy battle cruiser. Following behind them were the other three battle cruisers: the Righteous, the Stalwart and the Vigilant. Those ships, along with scores of other war frigates and jammers, represented the largest air fleet in the system. She was thankful Dane had joined them, but he had forsaken his oath in doing so. Lybra Howling, the wealthy philanthropist, had taken control from President Harok. Somehow, she'd manipulated him and now, the system had no legitimate leader.

"Nearly there," Linon said, indicating an area on the holographic map.

Dane grunted and barked a few commands to his lieutenant. The Armada slowed and started its descent toward the seventh belt's surface. The area was a muddle of greens and browns, with marshlands mixed in.

"Did you make contact with the Mayor of Glass-Hewn?" DiJinn asked.

"Yes," Dane replied in a gruff tone, his gaze locked on the forward screen. "She's gathered up most of the citizens. We should be able to transport all of them."

"We'll be making multiple trips today," Stell reminded them. "We have about an hour, if we want to stay on track." She had replaced her old gray knit sweater with military fatigues. DiJinn had gotten so used to seeing the elderly lady in a homely outfit that she almost didn't recognize her.

"Set us down easy, Dane," DiJinn said. "Citizens should be arriving soon. I need to find the mayor."

The massive war cruiser settled down just outside of the small port town. DiJinn stepped out and found a dirt road into the province. Glass-Hewn was a picturesque town with tiny individual dwellings littering the nearby fields like a patchwork quilt. In contrast, the main town square was more of a piece of brutalist style architecture. The buildings were roughhewn blocks with swatches of glass poking through, which stood in stark contrast with the quiet countryside. Outside the city walls, she could see thousands of citizens streaming toward the ships. Families had packed everything they could carry, leaving most of their possessions behind. Watching the children leave their homes hit Jinn harder than expected. It suddenly felt real, now that she was seeing it in person. She pulled her gaze away and refocused.

The noise level increased when she neared the city walls. The gateway was guarded, but the officers greeted her with a wave. She no longer worried about wearing her alias. The secret of the Heliographi was over. The legend had been in place for over a century, but their secret had been leaked after the battles for the memoirs. People who had once questioned their existence now stared at them in shock. She'd forgotten how angry it made her, having been fifty years since her days as a student at Skylight University. It was a flashback that she tried to ignore. The citizens of the small city narrowed their eyes at her suspiciously. Here she was, trying to help these people, and still they regarded her like some outcast.

DiJinn finally arrived at city hall, which was a large building in the center of town. It was constructed of the same roughhewn blocks with large glass slag mortared in between. The different colored slag allowed the morning sunlight to filter through in a kaleidoscope of jeweled tones.

Inside was more of the same. The government building had an open, airy feel with a long thoroughfare and shops and offices off the main corridor. Above, the open atrium spanned through the top with some sunlight filtering in. It felt like a campus building, and for a split second, she was back at Skylight University. She placed her alias on now, not wanting to bother with the suspicious looks. In the center and off to one side was what she assumed to be the central business department. It was a large glassy box that appeared to have no structure holding it up. She walked in and sat in a lounge chair and waited.

A few minutes later, a man in a suit called for her. DiJinn followed him into an open office environment with clerks and assistants rushing around in a hurry. She realized that with the city shutting down in less than a week, there was a lot to cover. Things moved at a frantic pace, and she was jostled around before landing in another department. She was asked to sign in, then another manager ferried her to an enormous office.

She stood before a massive glass window that stretched dozens of meters high. It provided a spectacular view of the countryside beyond. She could see the line of citizens making their way through the city gates.

A lady behind a glass desk talked into a hologram as DiJinn waited.

"…I don't have the space, governor," the lady said in a raised voice.

"We have no choice, Claire," a man in a dark suit said. "Your port is the most centrally located. I'll send more troops to help, but it'll have to do. Good luck."

"Sir—"

But the man had already turned his attention to the next call and snapped the connection closed. The lady leaned against the desk and placed a hand on her forehead, then started rubbing her temples, unaware that DiJinn was there.

DiJinn sat forward and cleared her throat.

The lady sat up and held a hand to her chest in slight shock. "Goodness. You scared me."

"My apologies. I know you're busy."

"No. No, it's fine. Forgive me," the lady said. She was slim with pale skin and dark hair pinned to one side. She wore a business blouse and skirt, but dark circles clung below her eyes. "Please, come. Have a seat. We have a lot to discuss."

DiJinn stepped forward and settled into a plush leather chair. Then she shrugged and slipped her ring off, revealing her true identity. "Might as well get this out in the open. You need to know who you're really talkin' with."

The lady gasped and held a hand over her mouth as she stared into DiJinn's glowing eyes. "I…I uh. I'm sorry. I don't mean to be rude. It's Jinnie Dinn, isn't it?"

"It's okay, Claire. We don't have time for apologies. Please, Jinn will do."

"Jinn," Claire said, and moved to shake her hand. She smiled. "I'm so glad you're here to help. We really do appreciate your guidance. It's fascinating, though. I mean, getting to meet a Heliographi. I remember talking to my grandmother about the legend when I was young. I'm sorry, I hope that's not offensive."

DiJinn shook her head, then waved a hand. "I think we need to get on with it. There's a lot to cover and we need to stay on track."

"Yes, of course." Claire walked back around her desk and pulled up a hologram. "It appears we'll have more people than anticipated. Our port city is centrally located, and perfect for this mass exodus. I'd hoped just the surrounding areas, but I'm sorry to say there'll be more."

"We'll handle it. We'll be making multiple trips. It'll be a push to get everyone out by week's end, but no one will be left behind. Are you runnin' background checks, all that fancy stuff?"

"Yes. I have my best administrators on it. We're bringing as many resources as possible. We want to chip in where we can. I've sent everything to the location General Dane mentioned."

"That'll do," DiJinn said and stood to leave.

"Jinnie, I mean, Jinn." Claire stood and moved near her. "Is it true…President Harok, I mean?"

"What have you heard?" DiJinn asked.

"Just that…that he's been—oh, I'm not sure the best way to say it. Rumor has it that he's lost his mind. Has he gone insane?"

DiJinn could see the concern on her face. She tried to think of the best approach without alarming her, though she could already see that the rumors had spread. "The president is not himself at the moment."

"Then, it's true," Claire said. "Civil war will come to the system?"

"That I can't answer with certainty. This is a dangerous time. The Lucem will do what we can to protect the citizens. But we'll feel better after everyone's been relocated."

"There's something wrong, isn't there, Jinn. I can sense something is different. When I sleep, even when I'm awake."

DiJinn was a bit surprised. It was the first time she'd heard it from someone who wasn't a Heliographi. Perhaps the 'sickness' was growing? Just last week, she thought it had only been her overactive imagination. Apparently, that wasn't the case. "Prepare your people in the best way you can, Mayor. You need to remain strong and confident. The citizens will need that from their leaders. I suggest you hurry. We don't have much time."

ABΓΔEZHΘIKΛM
NΞΟΠΡΣTΥΦXΨΩ

JET STOOD NEAR the outskirts of Harang-R, waiting for Solan and Kamber to arrive. He'd spent the last few days hobnobbing with the Dreadnaught council members, doing his best to learn more about their newest ally. Though there was a lot on his plate, Solan had insisted he remain and continue to strengthen their relationship. In the evenings, he perused the port city, relaxing and talking to the locals. There seemed to be a much more relaxed pace in Harang-R. These people didn't care about the 'goings on' in the system and seemed to know very little about the tension that was building. In fact, very few had heard about the battle for the memoirs. He wondered if there was any news that reached the port city, or if perhaps the Dreadnaught's rule prohibited it, which he guessed was more likely.

Though it had only been a few days, he felt nervous all over again. He chuckled to himself. Considering everything that was happening right now, Kamber was still on his mind. The system was on the brink of civil war; the Atrum's leader, Sybold, had mysteriously returned; he'd just secured the Dreadnaught's alliance, and…he felt butterflies in his stomach because of Kamber. It was like their first night together at Firefly Falls all over again. But soon, they'd have less time together, and he needed to make the most of it.

Another twenty minutes passed as he paced anxiously around the busy port. Public transport skiffs came and left, ferrying thousands of locals across the tethered islands of Harang-R. Now that the Dreadnaughts had accepted his offer to join the Lucem, things had picked up around the port. He could still hardly believe what had happened. The Dreadnaughts were moving their entire operations to the innermost belt, though deep down, it made him suspicious.

Solan and Kamber's skiff finally appeared, and Jet walked over to meet them. Kamber hopped out and gave him a hug as Solan stood in front of him and stared, her arms crossed.

"Well? How in Skylight did you manage it?" Solan asked.

Jet shrugged, then held up his staff. It was dormant again, asleep. Jet nodded to it, then put it back inside his cloak, afraid he might rouse Port-Shear. "Mosstrom and Vail were here. This is going to sound strange, but the staff tried to provoke Mosstrom into battle. It was like this thing knew Mosstrom's staff, or vessel, I guess."

Solan lifted one cheek, considering. "Well, remember, these vessels carry the essence of a Titan, which is an entity from another dimension. Makes sense that some of them wouldn't get along. What did Mosstrom do?"

"Believe it or not, he actually bowed out of the competition. The Dreadnaughts offered us trial by combat, and he refused."

Solan grinned at that, but then gave Jet a serious look. "Just be careful it doesn't take control. The vessels may be able to sway the user."

"Really? I didn't think that was possible."

"I'm only saying it could be. Your vessel, this Port-Shear, is a prime, which means it possesses more power—"

Jet stopped her. "Hold on, Solan. How do you know some much about these vessels?"

"I've been doing some research since they showed up."

"But where? Is there an instruction manual or something I missed?"

Solan smiled and held out a hand. "I'll explain later. This isn't the time or place. Right now, we need to talk with Fritt. I want to discuss details about their relocation."

Together, the three of them made their way to the stronghold. Inside the dimly lit rotunda were all the chief's advisors, perhaps thirty in total. Jet, Kamber and Solan were seated near the center as everyone waited. Eventually, Fritt entered and sat on the deformed throne. He was still wearing the lavish robe with the hood pulled low. He gestured to Solan, and she stood and approached.

"Solan," Fritt said. "I knew your father, a great man. You resemble him in many ways. It's good to meet the new leader of the Lucem."

Solan bowed. "It's an honor. Jet tells me that we are to be allies in the dangerous time ahead. We are grateful for your assistance."

"We have been leery of the Atrum for some time," Fritt said. "It appears they have aligned with Lybra, who retains the Tetrahedron marauder army, some of our fiercest rivals. Our strife with them goes back decades."

"I understand. We have no love for them either," Solan said and placed her hands behind her back. "I sense there's something else on your mind?"

The chief nodded to Jet, then held out his hand. "Please, come forward."

Jet looked at Kamber, then Solan, but stood and walked to stand before the chief.

"You are special," Fritt said. "I have seen you in my dreams. Not many Heliographi have what you possess, save one other. Bring forth the starlight."

Jet looked at him, confused. He furrowed his brow. "I'm sorry, I don't understand."

"The starlight," the man said. "Your vessels are starlight. Yours is the brightest."

Jet blinked a few times, then took out his war staff and tapped it on the ground. It lit up, bathing the rotunda in a white light. Then it began to moan in an unearthly tone that made the hairs on the back of his neck stand up. Jet held the war staff in front of the chief as the other advisors looked on. A few even stood to walk over for a closer look.

It appeared that Port-Shear was asleep, though, perhaps occupied in another dimension, or whatever it was it did in its spare time. But the chief and his advisors continued to stare at the war staff in awe. Jet could almost envision a tribe of ancient warriors worshipping at the altar of some Aztec god.

Suddenly, the staff awoke, and Port-Shear erupted with light. An ethereal voice rang out and echoed around the large rotunda.

The men and women scattered and ran. Jet nearly dropped the staff.

The voice's echo faded, and Jet heard Port-Shear laughing in the distance as if he'd meant to give them all a good scare. It took twenty minutes for the chief and his advisors to reenter the rotunda. Jet couldn't blame them; the staff had scared him, too. The details about their relocation went much quicker after that. Soon, Jet, Solan, and Kamber were on their way back to the first belt.

M

When they returned to the first belt, Solan asked Jet to meet her in the control room that evening. "Enjoy these last few days," she'd said with a wink. "Before long, there won't be much free time."

Jet walked to Firefly Falls, anxious to spend some time alone with Kamber. When he entered the hidden glen, she was already there, sitting on her favorite boulder, legs pulled up and staring at the fireflies above.

Jet strolled over and sat down next to her and waited quietly. He sensed her pensive mood, and he wondered what she was thinking. He finally took her hand, and she faced him.

"What is it?" he asked.

"Just worried," she said and gripped his hand tighter. "You went alone. Solan and I spoke about it. I understand why she sent you by yourself. It just makes me nervous."

"I know she struggled with that decision. Since her father left, she's been under a lot of pressure. She's doing what she believes is right. Honestly, I think she's done just fine. But Solan is a perfectionist; she's too hard on herself."

"But it's dangerous, Jet," Kamber said. "Sending you out there with no others. We usually work in pairs. I…I just worry about you."

"I know, Kamber. But Solan feels that now is the time. I think she feels a bit guilty about not doing this sooner. Albright wanted me to figure out some of these riddles alone. Maybe Solan's intuition is telling her the same thing?"

Kamber stood and walked to the edge of the water, and Jet followed her. "Just promise me you'll be careful, Jet. Sometimes you do things that you shouldn't. Like going to the Agency the day of the final memoir. You shouldn't have done that. You nearly got yourself killed."

Jet gave her a weak smile. "Yeah. That was dangerous. And on the surface, it seems foolish. But I had to, Kamber. That was all part of this riddle, or quest, I suppose. Had I not gone that night, there are things I wouldn't know right now. If destiny is real, then you have to agree with me. I believe I was meant to go there, just like I'm meant to go on this quest, whatever it might be."

"Of course, you're right. We all have a destiny, a part to play in this. It's just hard for me to accept. I'm afraid of what's to come. I want to try and change it, but I know I can't."

Jet gave her a hug and held on to her. He wanted to stay with her at Firefly Falls, spend the rest of his life there, just the two of them. Safe, secure, happy. But he knew that was something that would never happen.

M

Jet spent the rest of the day with Kamber, mostly talking and trying to reassure her. Kamber seemed to understand that there wouldn't be much free time in the near future. Yet, Jet could tell that her concerns overshadowed their time together.

Later that evening, he found Solan in the control room, sitting in her chair with her boots kicked up on the edge of Albright's table. She had her head bowed in thought.

"Honey, I'm home," Jet said, hoping to lighten the mood.

Solan glanced up and gave him a weak smile.

"Before you say anything, I'd like to hear why you know so much about these vessels," Jet said and crossed his arms. "Have you been holding out on me?"

Solan sat forward and held his gaze. "That's not really why I asked you here, Jet."

"Okay. But why can't you just take a minute and talk about that? I feel like I need to understand these things better. I can barely control this…thing," he said, tapping the war staff beneath his cloak. "It might help me."

Solan sighed, clenched her jaw a few times, then clasped her hands together. "Years ago, just before Albright's assassination, my father shared some information with me, a passage in the Book of Vishmu. Though I think Albright didn't agree with his logic. They fought over it, and Tyberius finally convinced him."

Jet waited for her to continue.

Solan straightened in her chair. "These vessels are containers, that you already know. They hold the essence of higher beings known as a *Titan*. They are from another dimension, and each one has a different power or ability. A few are extremely powerful, like yours. Those are called primes, like Port-Shear. Its opposite is known as Rend-Shear, and you can guess who that one belongs to. The pure white light and the absolute absence of light."

"What about the other vessels?" Jet asked.

"There are twenty-four total, though only nine have been revealed: Albright, Tyberius, Cord, yours, and mine, for the Lucem. The Atrum's include Vail, Joshia, Mosstrom, and Sybold. In the document, there's a complete mythology behind them. Their lore is much older than the Heliographi."

"So, where is this passage? Can I see it?"

"Maybe later," Solan said and waved it away. "I'm not sure there's anything in there that will help us now, though."

"I'd still like to see it."

"I'll dig it up. But right now, we need to focus on the fulcrums."

Jet stopped and leaned onto one of the chairs. "What is she waiting for, Solan?"

The question caught Solan off guard. "I don't know, Jet. Perhaps Sybold's not ready, or, as Cord believes, she's still gathering her strength. All we can do right now is focus on the plan we have, which is preparing for these fulcrum wars." She stood and walked around the room before stopping near the front, where she brought up a holographic map of the system. Solan pointed to the seventh belt and an area along the portside. "Cord radioed me this morning. He's placed all four of our memoirs. Says they should be secured now, and we won't have to worry about protecting them."

"That's good, right? I mean, now we can focus on other things."

"I guess so, but there's more. He tells me when they were placed, a date and time appeared, apparently a countdown. When it reaches zero, the polarity of each particular fulcrum must be set."

"Okay," Jet said and sat down in his own chair. "Isn't that what's supposed to happen?"

"Yes, word for word, as stated in Albright's memoirs. Cord's managed to locate the seventh fulcrum, too. The Atrum have apparently placed that one. I've asked him to find the locations of the outer fulcrums. We may need to know their locations if we want to contest the polarity."

Jet leaned forward, placing his elbows on the table. "Seems dangerous. Lybra will have set up defenses, I imagine."

"She will, and yes, it will be dangerous. We'll make that decision when the time comes. Remember the sequence of fulcrum ignitions goes 7, 2, 6, 3, 5, and 4. That pattern fluctuates back and forth with the middle ground between belts four and five."

"What about the first belt?" Jet asked. "Did Cord mention that one?"

"It seems to be different, which means the eighth fulcrum probably is too. The ninth fulcrum, Cord wasn't certain. With that belt shattered into thousands of pieces, we may never know the fulcrum's location."

Jet walked over to the holographic map and nodded at the ninth belt's debris field. "Well, I suppose it isn't really a belt anymore, right? I wonder if that has something to do with it?"

Solan shook her head. "Perhaps the fulcrum was destroyed during the meteor storm a century ago."

Jet considered for a few seconds, then used the end of his staff to indicate the area between the fourth and fifth belt. "It seems like everything is coming together right here. That airspace is going to be very busy soon, assuming we lock down the polarity of our fulcrums."

"It will become the future battlefront," Solan said. "General Dane has mentioned civil war multiple times. The fourth and fifth belts are going to suffer the brunt of this war." Solan stood and strolled around the room. "Cord has indicated there are approximately two days between each fulcrum's ignition."

Jet shook his head in disbelief. "What is it with these countdowns? It's like Albright has everything on a tight schedule."

"And maybe he does."

"Yeah, but two days is barely enough time to regroup and organize for the next fulcrum."

"It would seem Albright had a plan," Solan said and shrugged. "Regardless, it's what we're faced with."

"The others aren't going to like it. We just finished fighting for the memoirs. That schedule took a lot out of everyone."

"No, they won't like it. And this schedule is much tighter than the memoirs were. This will test us all."

"When do you plan to tell them?"

"At our next meeting. The seventh fulcrum timer hits zero in less than a week. I need to talk with Cord as soon as he returns with Ti-Leer."

"Where is he now?" Jet asked.

"Last time he radioed me, they were near the seventh belt."

CHAPTER 19
The Riddle of Vail

CORD AND TI-LEER watched as the shadowy figure placed the seventh belt's memoir, started the timer, and left. The other cloaked figure had rolled down the side of the pyramid and lay unconscious on the ground. Before Cord could say anything, Ti-Leer charged across the metallic field, lifted the body, and hurried back. He gently laid the unconscious figure down. Cord looked on in disbelief.

It was Vail.

"It's the pretty lass," Ti-Leer said. "I like her. She's got spunk, don't ya think?"

Cord gave him a reproachful look. "Believe me, Ti. You don't want any part of this girl. I reckon she'd chew you up and spit you out."

Ti-Leer's eyes lit up. "That's exactly why I like her."

Cord shook his head, and Ti-Leer paused, then his face turned red. He kicked at the floor. "Well, we can't just leave the poor thing here."

Cord shrugged. "Why not? She can handle herself."

"Come on, lad. Where's your sense of empathy?"

"It doesn't exist."

Ti-Leer looked at Cord, then at the unconscious form of Vail. "Fine, I'll carry her myself." He dropped to a knee and hefted Vail over his stocky shoulder with ease. Cord sighed, but he knew it was pointless to argue now. Besides, deep down, he really did want to bring Vail along. He was more than curious to know what was going on.

"Alright, Ti. Best to keep an eye on her, though. When she wakes, she won't be happy."

"Right," he barked. "Where to now?"

They left the chamber in a hurry, Ti-Leer leading the way as he carried Vail's unconscious form with little effort. He began to chant as they marched. It was a low, guttural sound that reverberated softly through the metal corridors. Cord didn't mind at first. He was so lost in his own thoughts that Ti-Leer's chanting faded to white noise.

Cord was perplexed about a few things. Why had Vail been left for dead at the exact same time and place as he and Ti-Leer? Of all the fulcrums and places to be, why their location? The other dark-haired girl they'd seen had undoubtedly been Sybold. The black light of her staff was unmistakable. There had been rumors of her return, but how the Atrum leader had managed to respawn so quickly was of great concern. According to Solan, Albright and her father, Tyberius, had ambushed and assassinated Sybold years ago. They had done so for good reason. Albright had felt she was moving too quickly, which would throw off his schedule. Apparently, he had everything laid out on a very specific timetable. The other reason was easier to understand. Without a mature Albright around, Sybold would have little opposition and would wipe them all out. Right now, Albright was still a teenager, not ready for conversion just yet.

Ti-Leer slowed and let out a low whistle. "Would ya look at that, lad?"

Beyond was a vast chasm. "Are we taking the scenic route, Ti?"

Ti-Leer hefted Vail, then scratched his head. "Well, I thought we'd just take a shortcut, you know. I could've sworn this was the right...let me think." Ti-Leer held up his fingers and pointed in one direction, then narrowed his eyes and pointed in the opposite direction, then scratched his beard.

Cord knelt and pulled a holopad from his cloak. He found the location of their skiffs. "We're heading the wrong way Ti—"

Suddenly, Vail let out a groan and lifted her head. Ti-Leer nearly dropped her in shock. Vail took one look at him, and her glowing eyes went wide. She pushed up and then kicked her legs off his back. She flipped through the air and landed on her hands and knees and immediately pulled out her war staff. It unfurled to full length and bathed the chamber walls in a turquoise light.

Ti-Leer turned and faced her, pulling out his own war staff and hammered it on the ground. "Come on then, lass! I owe you—"

Cord moved in between them and held up his hands. "Hold on, Vail. Let me explain."

Vail was still a bit groggy, and her brows arched as if trying to recall her surroundings. "What the hell is happenin'? The last thing I remember…was…" Vail didn't finish her thought, but her eyes grew wide in terror, and she seemed to lose her focus. "Why am I here? How did this happen?"

"You tell us, lass!" Ti-Leer chuckled. "We're doin' research, and the next thing we know, your sassy little—"

"That'll do, Ti." Cord didn't want to hand out any information about their mission until he found out what had happened to Vail. At the moment, he was still trying to decide whose side Vail was even on. She was tricky, and he knew she could be mischievous. He'd witnessed as much over the four years he'd known her. She was good at it too, one reason he'd kept such a close eye on her during their recent collaboration for the memoirs.

Vail relaxed and stood up straight, rubbing at the dried blood along her brow. "Where're the other losers, or is it just you two?"

Cord ignored her. "What's the last thing you remember?"

Vail hunched forward and leaned on her staff. She slowly shook her head. "I…I was at the…what belt was it, I don't know—" She paused in mid-sentence and her eyes grew wide again. Her skin seemed to blanch in the dim light.

Cord waited a few seconds longer. "Go on."

"She's back, Ledbetter," Vail said. He detected a genuine waver in her tone. Vail was clearly afraid.

He took a slow breath. "Yeah, I know."

There was a long pause between the three of them in the narrow corridor, each processing that thought. Though Cord had known all along, hearing it out loud was unsettling.

Cord turned to Ti-Leer. "I feel that one of us should return to base and notify Solan about Sybold."

Ti-Leer gave Cord an indignant look. "Oi, so you get to stay with the pretty lass, and I have to trek my fat—"

"Hold it right there," Vail said, a confused look on her face. "Ledbetter. What are you proposin'? 'Cause if you really think I'm spending any time alone with you, you're wrong."

Cord ignored her. "Ti, just do it. Trust me."

"And what do you want me to say when I get back? That you're spendin' some time relaxin' with the pretty girl while the rest of us prepare for battle?"

Cord pulled Ti-Leer aside and out of earshot from Vail. He lowered his voice. "I want you to tell them about Sybold only, Ti. Not a word about Vail to Solan or Jet or anyone till I figure out what's happened to her. Something doesn't feel right, and I mean to get to the bottom of it. Not to be rude, but I need to have her alone to figure this out."

"Ah, you think this is some sort of conspiracy, do you? But it ain't. You saw what happened. That other girl knocked her on the head and left her to die. What mystery is there to be had?"

Cord wasn't so sure, though. He was confident he could get the truth from Vail. But he also didn't want Ti-Leer unintentionally giving any of their plans away. "You should get going, Ti," Cord said and draped a thin arm over Ti-Leer's broad shoulders. He guided him toward the far corridor. "Remember, not a word about this, not to anyone."

"Ah, fine," Ti-Leer said, which sounded more like a pout. "I was hopin' for a little more action anyway."

Cord gave him a crooked smile and a gentle shove in the right direction. Then slowly turned to face Vail. He crossed his arms and lowered his gaze at her. "We should talk now."

Vail glowered at him as Ti-Leer stomped off, muttering to himself. Vail waited until he was gone before addressing Cord. "What is it you want to know, Brainiac? You think this is some conspiracy, a riddle that was custom-made for you alone to solve. The true Skylight Fallout, come to save the day?"

Cord held her gaze, ignoring the sarcasm. A wry smile stretched across his face. "This should be interesting, no?"

Vail rolled her eyes and bent down to lace her boots. She straightened and tucked her staff into her cloak. "I assume I won't be needin' this, right?"

"Not at the moment, it appears. You gonna answer my question?"

"What is it you want, Ledbetter?"

"A little honesty would be nice, for starters. I know that's a high bar for you, but let's try."

She flared her nostrils at him, her pixie-like features contorting into rage. "I think my memory's been wiped clean, okay? I don't remember much of anything over the last day or so."

"You don't know any fulcrum locations?" he asked.

"What did I just say?"

There was an uncomfortable pause as the two faced each other. For a moment, Cord thought she was going to take out her war staff and swing it at him. He felt his fingers twitch with excitement and almost relished that notion.

But Vail blinked and sighed. "Are we marching off on some grand quest?"

"Yes. I am. I assume you're homeless now?"

Vail didn't answer at first. She crossed her arms and looked off, avoiding his gaze. Her turquoise-dyed hair fluttered in the low breeze that hummed through the cavernous space.

"You need help," Cord continued. "I imagine that's a tough pill to swallow, having to ask for assistance, after what you did."

"After what I did?" she blared. "What the hell is that supposed to mean?"

Cord smirked. "Oh, I suppose those memoirs just walked off on their own?"

"You don't know that," she shot back. "There're half a dozen other Atrum—"

"Vail. You can drop the act. Why did you leave the Lucem? Better yet, I'm curious why you left our staffs behind. Was it a moment of weakness, perhaps?"

"Mind your business, Ledbetter, and I'll mind mine."

"I wonder why you're really here?" Cord asked in a low tone.

"Believe me, it's not because I want to be."

"That *was* Sybold we saw. Odd that she just happened to drop you off at the very moment we were here."

Vail rolled her shoulders, then held up her hands. "What do you want me to say? I have no clue why the Atrum evicted me."

"The better question is, why didn't Sybold just kill you?"

That seemed to catch Vail's attention, and Cord saw the look of concern cross her face. He sensed that Vail was wondering the same thing. Given Sybold's nature, Vail *should* be dead right now. Yet, here she was, alive without a home instead. Sympathy wasn't a part of Sybold's nature.

Cord continued to watch her reaction closely. She had a knack for shielding her emotions, and perhaps that was her gift. But was it powerful enough to fool him? *Powerful enough to fool Sybold?*

The reaction he witnessed from her in that split second seemed to tell him otherwise. Vail *didn't* know what was happening. She seemed as confused about it as he was. Regardless, he'd get to the bottom of it. He had plenty of time to pick at her until she slipped. He would soon find out how tricky Vail really was, and, perhaps, how good at cracking riddles he was. He smiled at that.

Cord turned and started walking in the direction of Ti-Leer. "Skiff's this way. If at some point your memory magically returns, let me know, won't you?"

Vail pursed her lips in frustration and fell in behind him.

Cord knew Vail would never admit when she needed help. Asking for assistance was something counter to her very being. But right now, the fact that she was coming along with him spoke volumes. Vail was either frightened by what had happened, or she was very confused…or both, perhaps.

It took twenty minutes to reach his jammer, and Ti-Leer was gone when they arrived. Cord hopped in as Vail stood in front, trying to decide what to do.

"We don't have all day, Vail." Cord powered up the engines and checked his gages, not looking at her. "If you want a ride, I advise you to hop aboard."

"I'm not sure this is a good idea, Ledbetter."

"Oh, it is undoubtedly *not* a good idea. But of course, we both know that."

"Where are you heading, anyway?"

"I'm hunting fulcrums. Are you coming with me or not?"

Vail looked up at the dark skies above and dropped her arms in resignation. The wind kicked up, and the air was filled with mist that swirled around the jammer's engines. The trees in the clearing swayed and groaned as Cord waited for her. He gave it another few seconds and shrugged.

He was about to close the cockpit's windshield when Vail finally climbed aboard, muttering under her breath. She pushed back in her seat in frustration as the jammer lifted and rocketed off toward the sixth belt.

Cord suddenly realized it was the first time they'd ever been alone together in the four and a half years he'd known her. It was an odd feeling, to say the least. They'd always been at odds with each other, their personalities on opposite sides of the spectrum. Where Vail was hasty and unapologetic, Cord was more thoughtful and patient. She cared little for the finer details and how things worked. She said what was on her mind with little regard for others' feelings, which Cord actually didn't mind.

"I suppose you're lovin' this?" Vail said, breaking the silence. "Helping me out…lending me some assistance?"

"Why, whatever do you mean?" Cord replied, a crooked smile on his face. He was indeed enjoying himself.

"You've been getting' under my skin since Skylight University. It had to be you, of course! I can't seem to get away from you. Why couldn't it be Stroud?"

"What about Jet?" Cord asked.

Vail shot him a glance, then shrugged. "What about him?"

"I would recommend you keep your distance. We may have been aligned for the reveals, but those days are over. Stay away from Jet."

"Or what?" Vail crossed her arms and lowered her gaze at him. "Are you Stroud's bodyguard or something? Like he needs your protection."

"Perhaps."

Vail chuckled. "You still think you're better than me, don't you? You're so arrogant, Ledbetter. Besides, I don't think Stroud needs your help anymore."

"All the same, keep your distance."

"I suppose you think you can protect him from Sybold? Don't kid yourself. She's beyond…" But Vail stopped and looked back out the window as the moonlit clouds shot by.

Cord narrowed his eyes at her. "Something you'd like to add?"

She waved her hand, dismissing it. "It's…it's nothing."

"It appears you're no longer aligned with the Atrum. They've obviously abandoned you. Like it or not, you're now closer to the Lucem than them. If she intends to harm Jet, help us understand. Or has that slipped your memory as well?"

But Vail remained silent, and Cord sensed she was struggling internally with what to say. The look on her face was subdued, but he sensed anger just beneath the surface. At least, that was the vibe he was getting. Then again, perhaps she was simply trying to deceive him.

There was no more talk for the rest of their trip. When they hit the sixth belt's air space, Cord cloaked his jammer and moved into a busier skiff lane. He followed it down and toward the surface. Cord had noticed the increased traffic over the last week. With the fulcrum wars all over the news, citizens were relocating by the millions. The luckier ones had relatives on the inner belts. But the less fortunate citizens were left searching for a place to weather the storm. Though Solan had plans to relocate and evacuate as many people as she could, Cord knew there would be some leftovers caught up in the war.

The sixth belt was a dark emerald tone in the moonlight. Cord settled into an outcropping that was covered in vegetation. They were a good distance from the nearest province named Horvin, which was primarily a tourist resort. Most citizens who ventured this way were on expeditions or safaris, of which there were very few these days, with all the evacuations taking place. The tension around the system was at an all-time high.

Vail followed along behind Cord as they cloaked. Using his holopad, he located a secluded portal that led them down to the inner hull. Like all the other hulls, the interior was hot and steamy from the environmental system that helped maintain the surface temperature.

"Any idea where you're goin', Ledbetter?" Vail asked when Cord paused to look around.

"At the moment, no. But if this belt's fulcrum is built like the others, I believe it'll be approximately thirty-two levels down and just portside of the twelve o'clock position."

Vail sighed. "I knew I shouldn't have asked."

Cord continued to work his way down as Vail shadowed behind him. About an hour and several complaints from Vail later, they entered another large chamber. The unmistakable stepped pyramid loomed beyond, with some stray moonlight spilling in from a nearby skylight well. The two made their way closer but stayed hidden in the shadows. Once they made ground level, Cord paused and held up a hand.

He pointed beyond. "There, at the base," he whispered. "See it?"

Vail squinted, then smirked. "Yeah, I do."

Several blurry shadows walked around the base of the pyramid. Lined up behind them were ranks of troops with about a dozen of the M-Class mech units. Floating above the top of the pyramid was a huge holographic image displaying a time and date for all to see. The clock was counting backwards.

"Those mechs look different," Vail hissed.

"Lybra's added a few more weapons, it would seem," Cord said.

"What are they doin'?" she asked and settled back. She laid her staff across her lap and leaned against one of the rusted bulkheads, rubbing her forehead as if still tired.

"It would seem they've set up a base of operations. They're already fortifying this fulcrum, even though it won't be ready to ignite for quite some time."

"A bit premature, don't you think?"

Cord shrugged his narrow shoulders. "It's a smart move, actually. They have the numbers to do it. That's going to make things more difficult for us."

"Shouldn't be a problem for you," Vail chided as she looked on. "Well, you have what you need, right? What are we waiting for? Let's go."

"Not so fast, Vail." Cord pulled at her sleeve as she tried to stand. "I want to know exactly *where* that fulcrum is inside that pyramid."

Vail let out a sigh. "Are you insane? You'll never make it in there without being noticed."

"I didn't say that I would."

Vail settled back in again. "Then what *are* you saying?"

"We're getting inside that pyramid, one way or another."

"We?"

"Correct."

She shook her head, her lips curling at the corners. "Good luck, Ledbetter. That's a suicide mission."

"Not if we wait for those Atrum to leave. And I'm itching to try out this new staff, I'm sure you are, too. We can cause a disruption while we're at it. That should be right down your alley." Cord held up the war staff. The end of it glowed dully in the dark. Cord felt the new power coursing from the ancient vessel. Though it wasn't as potent as Jet's war staff, it would do. He felt the need to understand this new version. *For research purposes*, he told himself.

"And I thought I was the crazy one," Vail muttered.

"You are," Cord quipped.

"I'm not the one trying to take on half the Agency forces."

"You're coming with me, Vail."

She dropped her head and muttered, "Why did I do this to myself? Okay, fine, Ledbetter. But when we go down in flames, don't say I didn't warn you. What's the plan?"

"For the moment, we wait."

CHAPTER 20
Ti-Leer's Secret

NOW IS THE TIME!

Jet awoke and sat up in his bed, his heart racing. That voice still lingered, like a fading cosmic echo. It was a voice that he knew.

It had been his old friend who'd been murdered atop Chroma the day of the Century Eclipse. Cutter Jade.

Over the last several months, he'd theorized that Cutter was out there somewhere, trying to communicate with him from a great distance. But of late, his voice had gone silent, along with Brindall's voice too. He had a feeling it had something to do with his modified war staff, Port-Shear. But much of that was still a mystery. He only knew that his own 'gift' was a part of the riddle. Albright had tasked him with *figuring it out*…alone.

Jet had recently unlocked something at the Hall of Vital Records, just before the ninth reveal. He could now communicate with others who had passed on from this plane of existence *without* being at the hall. He also had a sneaking suspicion that he was on a quest beyond this realm, a quest to find clues or perhaps to recruit an army. While the Lucem were building an army here, had Albright sent him to do the same from beyond this realm? As ridiculous as that sounded, it was beginning to make more sense. The fact that he'd been gifted the war staff and vessel, which coincidentally held the essence of some otherworldly being, only reinforced that theory.

Okay. So, what *if* that much was true? Then how was he supposed to begin? He wanted desperately to ask Cord, knowing this was exactly the sort of thing he excelled at.

But Albright had requested that he do this alone.

It may harm others, even Heliographi, Albright had said. *Your gift is designed to protect you in this quest and you alone.*

And it was apparent that now *was* the time. That voice was suddenly urging him to move. But he just didn't know how to start this task. He needed help and hoped a sign would emerge soon.

He got out of bed and meandered to the mess hall. Ti-Leer was there, probably recovering from a hangover, Jet assumed. Ti-Leer spooned at his gruel halfheartedly, one hand propping up his chin.

"Ti," Jet acknowledged as he sat down next to him. "What's wrong?"

Ti-Leer ignored him at first, staring vacantly at his food. "You have a mission to attend to, don't you, lad?"

Jet sat there, facing Ti-Leer, unsure what to say at first. "What mission are you talking about?"

Ti-Leer set his spoon down and turned to look at Jet. "I know about your secret mission. Go on, ask me how." Ti-Leer crossed his stubby arms across his barrel chest.

Jet continued to look at him in stunned silence. He waited for Ti-Leer to continue, but he didn't. "Okay, fine," Jet said. "How did you know Albright is sending me on a secret mission?"

Ti-Leer chuckled, then belched. "Oh, because he told me. 'Bout fifty years ago."

Jet waited a few seconds, still trying to process how in Skylight Ti-Leer was tied to all of this. "Ti, if you have some insight, I'd certainly like to hear it."

"Oi, he said as much, Albright did. Can you believe that? He asked that I keep it all quiet," Ti-Leer said in a low voice, a slight grin on his face. "Albright knew exactly what you'd say to me, even fifty years ago. It's like something guided you to the mess hall while I was sittin' here, eating this crap. How can someone know all that? Aye, it's beyond me, that's for sure—"

"Ti," Jet interrupted him and grasped his shoulder. "Please. This is important. I need to know what's going on. Many lives may depend on this—"

"You don't think I know that?" Ti-Leer said, raising his voice. But he quickly calmed himself. "I know, lad. I've carried Albright's secret for longer than you've been alive, youngster. And I had to wait until the right time. He made me promise." Ti-Leer took out his silver flask and held it up to the light. "Fifty years is a long time to carry a secret, you know that? I had to engrave the date on me flask, so I wouldn't forget. Something I'd see every day. Well, I can keep a secret, except for Cord's. I think he's makin' a big mistake—"

"Hold on," Jet said and narrowed his eyes. "What does Cord have to do with this?"

Ti-Leer's eyes grew wide, then he waved it away. "Ah, nothin'. Forget I said that—"

"Come on, Ti!" Jet said, barely able to contain himself now.

"Can't you give me a moment in the limelight? I was just startin' to enjoy myself. Maybe we can play twenty questions? Wouldn't that be fun? No? Ah, fine then."

Jet calmed himself and waited patiently.

Ti-Leer huffed. "It's like I said, you already know. I'm a bit disappointed you hadn't figured it out yet."

Jet threw up his hands. "Obviously, I don't!"

Ti-Leer wrinkled his nose. "Where'd you meet your girlfriend, eh? Where'd ya bury your mate, Cutter?"

Jet sat back, stunned. Then slapped his forehead. *Of course, that was it! Cutter's resting spot…he should've known!*

Jet stood and grasped Ti-Leer by the cheeks with both hands and kissed his forehead. "Thanks, Ti. I owe you!" He turned to leave, then stopped. "You should probably still keep this a secret."

Ti-Leer smiled and blushed. "A new bottle of bourbon should settle it."

But Jet was already sprinting down the corridor and out of the control suite. He bumped into Kamber on his way out.

She grasped him by the shoulder to keep herself from falling over. "Jet. Where are you heading in such a hurry? I thought we were still organizing evacuations today? Solan wants us in the control suite this afternoon."

Jet held her gaze, but he was thinking about the hidden glen at Firefly Falls. "I…yeah, just let her know I had something to see to."

Kamber tilted her head. "What are you up to?"

Jet shrugged, hearing the slight concern in her voice. "I—" Jet paused, scratching his head. "Kamber, just let Solan know it's important, okay? I'll talk to you later. I promise."

Kamber took his hand. "Jet. Whatever you're doing, promise me you'll be careful. Promise me."

Jet held her hand and gave it a squeeze. "Of course. I'll talk to you soon."

Jet let her go and hurried down the corridor.

It was still early morning when he exited through the Clipton Woods portal. He hurried along the gravel trails and jogged to Firefly Falls. He entered the hidden glen through the heavy underbrush and found the pyramid-shaped tomb. He slowed as he neared it and stood at the foot of the barely visible grave. He looked around the high tree canopy, noticing the fireflies and the brief rays of morning sunlight that managed to penetrate through. There was some lingering fog around the rocky shore and the roaring of the waterfall flooded his thoughts.

So, what was he looking for? Ti-Leer hadn't gone into detail, and Jet had been so excited that he hadn't thought to ask more questions. He'd been to this site a hundred times and had never noticed anything special.

Jet took a seat at Cutter's grave, crossed his legs and placed his war staff across his lap. He closed his eyes, trying to focus.

But nothing came to him. No voice, no hints, no epiphanies.

What was different now? Was there anything new about this place since he'd buried Cutter?

He slowly looked down at his war staff. The only difference right now was the presence of Port-Shear.

The white vessel.

Jet stood and picked up the staff. He held it out in front of him, and the white vessel began to glow.

He sensed that Port-Shear was waking.

The vessel glowed brighter when he turned to face the lake but dimmed when he turned away. *Okay, that's new*, he thought. He followed the vessel when it glowed brighter, and it led him along the rocky shore and closer to the waterfall. He found a rocky pathway near the shoreline and hopped across it, the war staff glowing brighter and brighter as he followed it.

Eventually, Jet stood behind the waterfall and felt the cool, misty spray. The rock he stood on was covered in moss, and the lighting had a turquoise tinge to it. His war staff glowed with such intensity now that he could clearly see his surroundings. One particular rock caught his attention, and he stepped into what seemed to be a cave. He moved deeper inside, the sound of the roaring waterfall diminishing. Eventually, he noticed a symbol carved into the rock. Jet knelt to examine it, and his war staff started to pulse. He heard Port-Shear begin to whisper, a low moaning that caused the hair on the back of his neck to stand up straight.

The small engraving in the stone was a Heliographi symbol, one he was familiar with.

It was the letter M, his own symbol.

Jet lifted Port-Shear and pressed the vessel end of it to the symbol. The stone rock shuddered, then rolled aside. He stood at the brink of the opening, excitement coursing through him. But there was also fear. He was on the edge of his quest, one appointed to him by Christian Albright. One that might determine the fate of the human race. He felt nervous anxiety race through him as he stepped inside. The stone boulder slammed shut behind him as Port-Shear's laugh reverberated through the chamber beyond.

CHAPTER 21

Town Hall
July 1, 2286, A.D.

SOLAN HAD WORKED with General Dane and Captain Linon to ferry the majority of citizens to the first belt, at least the ones who had no other place to call home. Stell and her crews had also worked around the clock to retrofit the inside of the first belt's hull to accommodate the influx. There was little room left on Skylight City now. Most of the housing there was occupied by citizens who could afford the higher rent. Solan was mostly concerned with housing the young and needy.

At first, she didn't know how it would all work out. She was afraid there just wouldn't be enough room. But Stell was a magician, and her crews had the first belt's hull ready in record time. This meant that the Lucem's operation was out in the open now, but it didn't matter. Since the Heliographi were no longer a myth, there was no reason for hiding anything. Most citizens knew there was something going on beneath the first belt anyway.

Solan had always known this conflict would disrupt normal life. That included most citizens' work and routines around the entire system, not just those on the first belt. All that said, things went on as normal at Skylight University. Classes continued, and students enrolled. But Solan wondered how long that would last. It was up to the Lucem to prepare the governors, senators, and city mayors for what was to come. *The sooner, the better*, she thought. For those citizens who remained on the outer belts, she assumed they would eventually regret not taking her warning. Change was inevitable now.

On the third day of evacuations, Solan toured the first belt's internal operations. Stell had already set up a vast social network. Makeshift sleeping areas had turned into pop-up cities. It was becoming a town of its own. Stores, shops, schools, and work. Hospitals, pubs, emergency crews…Stell had thought of everything. She seemed to know everyone and had brought in the trades or specialties most needed.

Later that evening, Solan called for a town meeting in the largest space she could find. There was a massive chamber where the first memoir reveal had taken place. This 'inner globe' was a perfect sphere and ideal for large meetings. It was about a kilometer in diameter and had enough tiered seating for almost everyone under their protection now. A makeshift stage was set in the middle on a floating platform. With Solan was Stell, Dane, Linon and the other Lucem, except for Ti-Leer and Cord, who were still away on their mission. She'd searched for Jet but hadn't found him. According to Kamber, he'd had something important to do earlier that day but wouldn't say what it was.

When Solan arrived, the spherical amphitheater was filled to capacity. Stell had set up holographic screens and a sound system around the space as well as in the overflow areas. Every citizen would hear her announcement. Solan stood on the floating center stage, looking out at the sea of people above and below her. She stepped up to the podium and waited for the crowd to quiet.

"I want to start by welcoming you all," she began. "I know this isn't convenient. It's not what anyone wanted. Our system is heading into a dangerous time. Before any rumors start, I can tell you that we don't know what will happen in the coming days and months. A war is coming, but we have managed to secure four of the memoirs, which we feel will provide shelter for citizens closer to the inner belts."

The crowd began to murmur at that, and it was loud enough to drown out her voice. Solan gave it a few seconds, then held out her hands.

"Please, stay calm." Solan waited until the noise died down. "I know you are all concerned. I promise you that we will do everything we can to protect you and your families. Many of you are not familiar with me. My name is Solan Alexander. I was a student at Skylight University almost fifteen years ago. I was also diagnosed with ephebus mortem. As some of you know, that disease was rumored to kill its victims before the age of twenty-four. As you can see, I am beyond that age now. The fabled disease was made up to hide people like me. I am part of an organization known as the Heliographi, more specifically, the Lucem. Our group is sworn to protect the Skylight System and its inhabitants."

Another murmur moved through the crowd, and she heard doubtful whispers. Solan let the murmuring calm before continuing. "I hope that you will trust me, though I understand your hesitancy. This is an unprecedented time in our history." Solan motioned to Dane. "Though many of you don't know me, you've probably heard of this man next to me. General Dane is the most decorated soldier in Skylight history. He has served and protected the system for decades."

Solan stepped aside, and Dane moved to the podium with DiJinn next to him. Dane gripped the podium and looked out at the crowd. Several people began to clap, and before long, there was loud chanting. The entire amphitheater seemed to erupt with cheering and praise. Dane finally held out his hands and spoke.

"Let me start by verifying what Solan has already told you. She and the Lucem are friends of the system and have sacrificed to protect you all. They have secretly and selflessly done so, while taking no thanks for themselves, all while you and your families have remained safe. But a new danger has arisen, one that will push us all to our limit soon. Our system President, John Harok, unfortunately, is under some influence. Because of this, I have decided to leave my post and work alongside Solan and the Lucem. I implore you to trust the Lucem. Please, treat them with respect."

The crowd clapped and started cheering again.

Dane continued. "I promise you that I will defend you and your families with every fiber of strength I possess. What I cannot do is organize this operation alone. That will take the cooperation of every one of you. Next to me is a lady named Stell, who has worked tirelessly to set up a social network. Life will go on as it has. There will be work, chores and school. You will pay your bills, and you will earn your keep. There will be no looting, fighting or illegal activity here."

Again, the crowd clapped. Then Dane motioned to Stell.

Stell took the stage and selected a hologram. As it expanded, she went over the different districts and rules every family would be assigned to. Solan stood back and listened, thankful for her team's help. Without Stell, Dane and Linon, she knew none of this would be possible.

The town hall meeting lasted late into the night, as many representatives had questions from their constituents. When it ended, Solan was ready for a quick meditation and bed. But on her way out of the arena, Linon approached her.

Solan stopped to look at him and stifled a yawn. "Yes?" she asked, trying not to sound too annoyed.

DiJinn and Dane stepped up next to Linon. He scratched at the stubble on his chin. "Solan. I hate to bother you. I know you're busy, but I have a favor to ask."

Solan blinked a few times. "Sure. Let's hear it."

"I need to return to the ARC district."

Then Solan remembered that Linon had a son who'd been taken captive by the Tetrahedron. "You want to search for your son, I take it?"

Linon nodded, and she could see that he was slightly uncertain then. "I'm sorry. I know this isn't a great time. But I'd like to bring him home before things get too dangerous around the system. Something tells me there's a window right now, and I need to take advantage of it."

Solan gave him a quick smile. "What can we do to help?"

"Just give me your blessing to go after him. I may bring a few of my troops. I know you're busy, so I won't ask for any more resources. This is something I can handle."

Solan chuckled. "Yes, I have no doubt you can. Please go with my blessing."

General Dane stepped forward and faced Solan. "I would like to accompany him."

That caught Solan off guard, and she immediately began shaking her head. "I don't think that is wise, Dane."

But Dane continued to stand in front of her, unflinching.

Jinn stepped up next to Solan. "Maybe it's not a bad idea, Sol. I can go with Dane and make sure Linon will make it back—"

"Absolutely not," Solan said, giving DiJinn a long stare. "I'm not sending both of my top commanders away this close to the first fulcrum war, even if you go with them."

Jinn took Solan by the arm and pulled her aside. They moved to a corner of the room, and DiJinn lowered her voice.

"Sol. Please. Dane needs this."

"Why?" Solan asked. "Jinn, it's not going to happen."

But DiJinn continued to hold Solan's gaze, their glowing eyes illuminating the dark corner as they faced off.

"Dane senses something. And frankly, so do I." DiJinn said.

"Really? Then enlighten me," Solan replied.

DiJinn blinked a few times. "I sense that Linon's son might be a valuable asset."

"In what way?"

"I don't know yet. I can only sense that we need him. Sol, you could command Dane to stay, but this is what he lives for. Let him go, he can handle himself, you know that. You can't micromanage everyone."

"I never said that I was," Solan snapped. But deep down, she knew Jinn was pointing out the truth. It was a weakness: she was guilty of managing others too closely sometimes. She didn't like the idea of sending Dane, Linon and Jinn on this little mission. But what if there *was* a valuable asset down in the ARC borough?

"I'll watch over them, I promise, Sol," DiJinn said. "I'll bring them all back."

"Jinn. You know that Dane is perceived as our leader. These citizens still don't trust the Lucem, which is fine with me. In time, they might, but right now, they need a figure they can rely on. That makes him extremely important."

"I understand that," DiJinn said.

Solan let out a long sigh. "Fine. But you must hurry. The first fulcrum war begins in three days. We need to be at full force by then. I can't do this without you three."

"I'll bring them home safe and sound," DiJinn said.

Solan took another long pause, looking at the others. She finally gave Jinn a nod, knowing that she needed to trust in her friends. Giving them the okay to do this mission ran deeper than her concerns about something going wrong just before the first fulcrum war. It was a vote of confidence, and the others needed this from her. But deep down, she already had her doubts.

PART TWO

THE MISSING DAYS

CHAPTER 22

A Court of Titans and Stars

JET PAUSED JUST inside the large cavern. He felt a bit unsettled at the ominous sound of the cave's portal closing so abruptly behind him. He held Port-Shear in front of him defensively, searching the darkness with its unearthly glow. The interior of the cave was large, and embedded in the ceiling were sparkling rocks that shone back at him like glitter—a plethora of multicolored minerals and pyrite that helped define the dimensions of the chamber. Golds, ambers, and greens flickered in his staff's white light. Jet could sense that Port-Shear was wide awake now. It hummed in his hands, whispering in his head—that soft chuckle, or a knowing smile, perhaps.

...wait for what comes next... he could almost hear it say.

The cave seemed to stretch on for kilometers. Jet understood that he was meant to follow. This was how his quest was to begin: the next step in his journey. All those years of Brindall speaking to him. Those decades of Albright preparing the different phases of the Prism Effect. Albright's Key, the war staffs and vessels, the death of Hanely Hurse, Shiloe's paintings, maybe even the Book of Vishmu. All of it was tied to this moment in time, and what would follow after. It was the chain of events, progressing as fate would have it.

Step by step, Jet moved deeper into the chamber, letting Port-Shear guide him now. Soon, the cave began to slope downward, and the air grew cold. Jet could see his breath in the light of the staff, small puffs of steam that seemed to float in place. The smell of earth stung his nostrils, a pungent, earthy fragrance. The weight of the darkness descended around him, pressing in, trying to snuff out the light of the staff. The gravel beneath his boots crunched, scattering echoes in multiple directions.

The cave eventually narrowed to a pinch point and dead-ended into a spiral staircase. It was carved of stone, rough and rudimentary, as if some blind mason from eons past had chiseled it from a massive stalagmite.

Jet stepped cautiously onto it, gliding down into the depths slowly, wondering where he was being led. The deeper he went, the stranger he felt. It was like a session of Vishmu, yet different. The connection was more intense, more central to his being, perhaps. He sensed entities around him now as he ventured farther.

When he neared the bottom of the spiral staircase, he could see a light ahead. It was a warm, golden light coming from an expansive pool of water. Above, water dripped from stalactites, perhaps from the Clipton River. The sound echoed around the pool's chamber, a soft pitter-patter like rain droplets in a spring thunderstorm. Jet stopped at the edge of the golden pool and knelt. There was steam coming from it, bubbling up from the depths like some natural artesian well. He dipped a hand in the water, and it was warm to the touch. It felt soothing, alluring, *deceptive*.

"What now?" Jet muttered.

…immersion…

Jet nearly jumped as Port-Shear whispered out loud. *Immersion?*

…yes…

Jet stood near the pool's edge, considering. It sounded like Port-Shear was urging him into the water.

…salvation… Port-Shear continued.

But Jet wasn't sure. He felt he needed to understand more before he just hopped in some strange well.

He sat cross-legged on the wet stone shelf above the pool, closed his eyes and laid the war staff across his lap. He went into meditation almost immediately. The vibe was alive here, amplified, like the Hall of Vital Records had been, only stronger. He stepped outside of his being and stood. All around him were gossamer wisps. It reminded him of the first time he'd seen Brindall, the ghost Lucem. There were hundreds, maybe thousands, of entities floating around the well. They phased through the rock and floated across the water. Some of them even stood upside down. When he looked closer, he could see they were all wearing Lucem cloaks, too. *These must be past Heliographi.*

Jet set his inner light free. It moved from his being, just like in his normal meditations. But this time, it moved into his own ethereal being as it stood there. Now, Jet *was* a ghost Lucem, but with his Heliographi light still inside.

…bring me…

Jet's ethereal form reached down and took the war staff from his lap. He held it, his ghostly hands translucent and cold. Then, Jet did what Port-Shear had asked.

He waded into the illuminated well of golden water.

Even in his ethereal form, the water was warm. It was a spiritual kind of experience. As he walked farther into the center of the vast well, steam rose around him, and ghostly figures wandered aimlessly past. When Jet made it to the center, he looked down and saw the source of the golden light. It was a portal of sorts, from what he could make out.

…stand…

Jet moved to stand directly over the portal.

With Port-Shear in hand, he waited.

Seconds passed. Then minutes passed.

Suddenly, the ground began to vibrate. Water fizzed, bubbled, and frothed around his ghostly figure. The other Lucem ghosts moved closer and surrounded him, as if noticing him for the first time. They began to moan, an unearthly sound that rose to a howl. The noise turned to a fevered pitch as the quaking ground intensified. The light grew brighter; the portal spun rapidly, creating a whirlpool. Lightning flashed from beyond, and Jet felt his being, his Heliographi, begin to stretch. Starting with his feet and extending up through his legs, then his waist, and torso.

It was as if time slowed down to a crawl.

The quaking increased, and the ground, the entire belt, and everything in the Skylight System began to disintegrate. Like a vortex of dust and sand, he was being erased from existence.

He began to panic.

He heard the ghosts around him speaking words of calm. But Port-Shear howled, an unpleasant-sounding laughter that Jet tried to drown out.

When the whirlpool reached his head, Jet managed one last thought.

What have I done?

M

When Jet awoke, he was still clutching his war staff.

He floated in limbo, at least that's what he assumed. He was still in his ghostly form, but there was nothing but darkness and space everywhere. Behind him was the vortex, only now it was a spinning light that bent around the core of the whirlpool, sucking it in, then spitting it out. Matter and antimatter zipped in and around him at light speed, yet to him it seemed to move in slow motion. He held out his hand and caught a bit of starlight in his palm, then released it and watched it move into the spinning void.

What was he? *Where was he?*

Jet felt another moment of panic. He didn't have a physical form, yet the laws of physics didn't seem to apply. And somehow, he knew this. Somehow, he knew he could go places and do things that he couldn't while meditating. During Vishmu, laws still applied, at least, he thought they did. But here, he sensed he could do more. If he thought of a place, he could go there.

…to guide you…

Jet heard Port-Shear speak, its voice boomed around the cosmos as if on cosmic waves.

Help me! Jet pleaded. He felt dismembered, dispersed…barely able to control his fear.

…*calm*… Port-Shear spoke.

Jet waited, eased, then let his thoughts relax.

In the blink of an eye, he was standing on a grassy field. The sky above was black. Clouds moved past so quickly that he could barely see them. The tall grass was gray with gold flecks, something from his dreams, or maybe his nightmares. There was no real definition to the stalks, but he could see them with great detail. The longer he stared, he could see movement from the cosmic winds pushing the steles around, mesmerizing him. Inside each stalk was a fractal pattern that continued to split and morph, like everything else around him. Golden sections, infinite possibilities…a maddening landscape of inexplicable geometries. It was beautiful in a way he could not explain. His human perception was baffled and unable to comprehend what he was experiencing. Yet, if he focused on his ethereal essence instead, it all made sense…perfect sense, in fact. He was in a different dimension now, a higher dimension. He understood that much. His ethereal form matched the thousands of other forms around him, and soon, the expansive field was crowded. The steles of cosmic grass continued to shift and contort. They extended up and grew into tree-sized spikes, each one carrying a galaxy of stars and planets. From one infinite possibility of laws, rules, and universes to multitudes of beings and civilizations. As each stele expanded beyond view and reach, the field quadrupled, and the entities surrounding him grew to cosmic giants. Through all of it, Jet was suddenly aware of Brindall and Cutter's presence. He felt them at his side now. Jet held on to Port-Shear with a death grip, barely able to contain his fear.

One stele twisted and multiplied in fractal patterns toward him. From one of the millions of patterns, three giant figures stepped out and stood on the field of stars. The other beings gathered around, shrinking in size, and waited.

Of the three giants, the one on the right held out a hand and gestured. It spoke, yet there were no words or sounds. It wasn't even a thought. The best Jet could comprehend was a feeling. Yes, it was a feeling that carried emotions, and somehow, he could understand it. The giant—which Jet realized now was a Titan—was asking for his purpose here.

It took Jet a minute to comprehend the language. He vaguely understood how he should reply. He used his empathy for the people he loved on Skylight. He thought of Solan and the other Heliographi. His love for Kamber, Dane, Linon and the millions of other citizens. He shared the dangers they faced, the thought of how everyone might be erased—an entire civilization lost to a war of hate, if Sybold had her way.

The Titan in the middle brought a light forward, then handed it to the one on its right. That giant took the light, a clear prism-like jewel. Then held it into its being, and more feelings flooded through Jet's form. It was asking why they should intervene on his behalf.

Jet was beginning to understand now. Port-Shear had transported him here. Cutter and Brindall had been waiting here to represent him. Jet was pleading his case before a cosmic tribune, a court of Titans and Stars.

If he had to guess, Sybold was probably doing the same thing in some other dimension, perhaps.

Jet looked at Brindall and Cutter for help, but neither seemed to be invited to speak.

Jet used his empathy again to respond. He thought about how his love for those people might be lost if he wasn't strong enough to protect them. He sent feelings of joy and happiness he felt when he was around his people. Then he sent feelings of sadness and loss, thinking about how he would feel at losing them—how he'd felt when he'd lost Cutter. But he needed more, and he dug deeper, using Port-Shear to amplify his sorrow. The staff emitted pulsing white light that flooded the field and the court of Titans. Port-Shear screamed pain and sorrow. It was having an effect now. Jet could sense the emotion in the Titans. Their empathy reflected back toward him. The central figure took the prism back and placed it within its own being, and the vessel abruptly disappeared. The Titan stood, towering into the stars and galaxies beyond. It seemed to cover the entire universe with its gesture of acceptance. Then the Titan brought cosmic rays of light together, bathing the court in starlight. Jet felt a love he didn't know existed. The feeling was too much, and he began to slip.

He fell from the court, plummeting past planets and stars and galaxies.

He passed through time and watched it warp and stretch and tear.

His vision continued to distort and morph until he felt water bathing him. The golden warmth of the well surrounded him, and he felt grounded again, back to his ethereal form. But when he stood, he could see the silhouette of his physical form still sitting at the well's edge, legs crossed, and eyes closed.

…rejoin… Port-Shear moaned.

Jet moved through the water and toward the ledge, already missing its warmth. He wanted to stay in that soothing water forever. He wanted to leave behind his old world of misery. He wanted to be away from the pain and hate of this place. He wanted to go back to the Titans, to the everlasting love he'd just experienced from that prism of starlight.

…soon…not yet…rejoin now…

Jet stepped reluctantly from the water. As soon as his ethereal form touched the wet, stony floor, it settled back into his physical being, and he awoke.

CHAPTER 23
The Burning Lands

JET SAT WITH his legs crossed, Port-Shear across his lap. It took him several minutes to feel like he was back within his own being. He could still hear the vestiges of his conversation, or feelings perhaps, with the Titans. But he could not visualize the events. He wondered if his mind simply wasn't able to comprehend such things and had blanked out. All he could recall was the simple plea he had made as he stood in the Court of Titans and Stars, a plea on behalf of the beings of this plane of existence.

What now?

…patience… Port-Shear chortled.

Jet looked down and thought about tossing the war staff into the glowing well beyond.

He eventually stood and stretched, wondering how long he'd been sitting like that. His back ached, and he could barely straighten his legs. He scratched his face and nearly let out a scream when he touched his cheek. He had a full beard, thick and flowing.

He rubbed at his face, suddenly in shock. *"What in Skylight?"* he muttered.

"Oh no!" he yelled and turned and raced up the spiral staircase. He slipped and tumbled a few times, his legs still stiff. A sense of dread shot through him as he sprinted up the stairs. How long had it been? What had he missed?

When he reached the stone door, he rammed his shoulder into it. He heard the stone crack at the impact, but it didn't budge. He kicked at it and pounded with his fists, before realizing that Port-Shear was the key. He tapped the vessel to the middle and the boulder rolled aside.

When he stepped through the stone portal, he stood atop a pyramid, one that hadn't been there before. Everything around him was on fire.

The Clipton Forest was a smoking ruin beyond. Trees had been burnt to a crisp, and the smell of charred ash filled his nostrils. Heat flared against his face as he looked up above him. In the distance, he could see the outer belts, glowing bright with fire. Most of them had been broken or split and floated in different directions. The air felt heavy and suffocating, like the oxygen had been extracted and replaced with methane. Near him, and arcing from the tip of the pyramid, was a massive black lightning bolt. He could hear it searing the air as it raced along the horizon and toward the second belt.

Jet turned and raced down the pyramid and along the gravel paths back to Lyrinthum.

He could barely breathe as he ran and had to use his cloak to cover his mouth from the free-floating ash that clogged the air. He could see the Clipton portal now, but there was no vegetation left to cover it. Everything that had once been green and blue and beautiful was gone, replaced with shades of red and black and gray.

He kicked the portal open and dropped into the tunnels. Inside, he felt the haunting voices immediately attack him. He was bombarded with evil thoughts of anger and hatred. He focused, holding Port-Shear in front of him as he sprinted along the corridors.

When he burst into the control room, it was empty. The chairs and equipment were in disarray, as if the space hadn't been used in years. In the center, Albright's table lay in ruin, hacked to pieces, and scattered across the rusty floor.

Jet sprinted to the sleeping quarters, yelling Solan's name. Down in the hangar bay, it was a complete ghost

town. There were no ships, jammers, or frigates. There was no sign of Dane or Linon or the recon troops. The entire base was empty.

Jet found a holopad and powered it on. He checked the date…

…and dropped the holopad to the ground.

He sat heavily on the cold steel floor and placed his head in his hands and felt tears sting his eyes.

The date on the holopad read January 18, 2287, A.D.

His trip to the mystic court of stars had only felt like half an hour at most. *In reality, he had been away for half a year!* His quest to recruit entities from beyond had, in fact, been a waste of time. It had cost him everything, it appeared. He'd missed the fulcrum wars. He'd failed everyone he loved.

Jet sat up and grabbed the holopad again. He tried to think through the haze of shock—*what had Cord said?* The first fulcrum ignition had been on the seventh belt. He thought he could remember how to get there. Maybe it wasn't too late?

But inside, he knew it was pointless. He could clearly see what had happened. The Lucem army had failed, the system had burned. Still, he felt the need to go and understand, at least. After that, he had no clue what he was going to do.

Jet tried to block out the alarmed voice inside as he explored the hangar bay. Surely, there was a skiff or something. He stumbled around in a trance, eventually meandering back outside and into the smoking ruins of the first belt. He ran aimlessly, trying not to panic. He was alone. No one was left, that he could sense, on the entire belt.

When he reached Skylight University, it was barely recognizable. War had taken place everywhere, it seemed. Nothing had been spared. The buildings were toppled, the ground was cratered. He recognized the signs of mortar rounds and railgun blasts around the once-beautiful campus. He stumbled past the destroyed Crux Stadium, climbed over the remains of Apex. Whatever had happened, this seemed to have been the epicenter of the final battle. He searched the wreckage, not sure why. He felt the need to dig. Jet lifted large blocks of stone and steel and hurled them in anger. He finally found what he was looking for.

A hand protruded through the rubble. When he removed the debris around it, he recognized who it was.

He'd found the body of Solan.

Her staff had been shattered and lay in pieces next to her lifeless form. A scream ripped from Jet's throat as he pounded the ground. Tears stung his eyes, and he wept until he passed out.

K

Solan stood next to Kamber as they looked out over the busy hangar bay down in Lyrinthum. Once again, she sensed Kamber's anxious mood and knew she was thinking about Jet. Solan felt a growing concern for him now. He'd missed their last meeting, which wasn't like him. According to Kamber, he'd had something 'important' to take care of. Perhaps her Heliographi was warning her. Whatever it was, she sensed Jet's fate was out of her hands now. She only hoped that he would return soon and that the powerful war staff would protect him.

Solan reached out and placed a hand on Kamber's shoulder. "He'll be fine."

Kamber stood stonelike, her arms crossed and didn't look at Solan. "He's gone. I can feel it."

"Then we focus on our own fate, here and now. I need you, Kamber. These citizens need you."

"Of course," Kamber said. She cleared her throat and took a deep breath. "You're right. It's what Jet would expect of me."

Solan gave her shoulder a squeeze. "Let's go find Stell and see about the rest of these citizens. I have a final visit with the Dreadnaughts and you're coming with me."

The two of them found Stell, who was in the middle of a small group of governors, giving directions and organizing the hundreds of thousands of homeless people now. They had divided into color-coded neighborhoods, housed in the hull of the first belt and sprinkled tightly around its circumference.

When Stell was done, Solan greeted her. "Thank you, Stell. You're an angel, you know that?"

Stell tugged at the sleeves of her moth-eaten sweater and shook her head. "No, Solan. You are. These people may not realize it now, but they will eventually. They owe their lives to you and the Lucem. I feel that when this battle begins, the system is going to buckle. Let's hope it doesn't break."

"Yes, let's hope. We're going to need all the help we can get, which means Kamber and I are heading back to the Dreadnaught's base. I was hoping to take one of the cruisers."

Stell gave her a worried look, her hands fidgeting with her hair and tugging at the bun. "Why would you need one? Are you worried?"

Solan gave her a long look, her lips pushed to one side. "I don't know yet. I'm getting some strange vibes, but I don't know what it means yet. I want to get back out there as soon as possible. We need their support. I wanted them to relocate quickly, before they changed their mind. And yet, they've sent nothing over. Fritt is a smart man, but he's also a mercenary, which means he thinks like one too."

Stell nodded. "I know the type. Mercenaries are unreliable. Please, take any of the cruisers, I'm sure Dane won't mind."

"Speaking of Dane, how did it go?"

"He left early this morning with Jinn and Linon. They took a small detachment of top recon troops. They left in disguise. Dane felt it best to work undercover."

Solan didn't like the arrangement but understood Linon's concern. She knew it was important for him to bring home his son and that had been part of their deal anyway. But taking Dane was concerning. These citizens needed his presence. Solan prayed that Jinn and company would all return safely. It was up to her to protect them, especially Dane, though she knew he could take care of himself. He was a fox, if ever there was one.

H

DiJinn worked her way closer to Dane as their small frigate bumped along. He was busy directing his troops around the cramped cargo bay. He'd elected to bring just a dozen of his finest soldiers along, feeling a covert operation would draw less attention. Linon stood near them, looking on thoughtfully, though DiJinn could tell he was a bit antsy. She also sensed Linon's feeling of guilt. Of course, he knew this little side mission to bring home his son was a burden on their main goal. Being prepared for the upcoming fulcrum wars was paramount. Just like the memoir reveals, these fulcrums were the next big event in Albright's wild chase. The free will of the Skylight System hinged on the strange devices. She'd heard Cord describe one of the fulcrums as some sort of mythical-looking pyramid buried deep within each belt. He had, in fact, painted the picture quite well, what he'd explained as a doomsday furnace that each of the memoirs would ignite. But what exactly did that mean, and what would they ignite?

Dane barked at his troops as they neared the earth's troposphere.

Linon walked over and gripped Dane's shoulder. "Thank you, again. I can't tell you two how much I appreciate your help."

"Thank me when we get back," Dane replied in his gruff voice.

"We have just a few days," DiJinn said. "Solan can't afford any more than that. Can you get us around the ARC district in that time?"

Linon scratched at his chin, the dark stubble peppering his face already gave him a rougher look than just a few days ago. "I think so. I assume my son is in an area known as the 'Collusion Block.' That's littered with shops and black markets. I've been there a handful of times before I was imprisoned. It's not a cheerful place. We need to be cautious."

Dane only nodded as he looked out of the front window of the frigate. "Let's buckle in. Once there, we change into our disguise. You're leading the way, Linon."

It took thirty minutes to punch through the troposphere and into the storm known as the Unbalance. Turbulence pushed their frigate around, and lightning crashed outside the small portal windows. Eventually, they neared the massive domelike bunker nicknamed the Pit. Jet had often referred to it as the 'hellhole' and for good reason. The subterranean borough he had been raised in was not a kind place. Citizens there lived in constant fear of slavery and starvation. DiJinn knew he'd grown up in a harsh environment, and he'd somehow made it out alive. Considering his condition with ephebus mortem, she could only imagine the torture he'd endured. And now, Linon was leading them down into the Pit to rescue his son from those same conditions.

They found a private hangar bay and paid the exorbitant fee. Privacy was a factor now. The crew changed into their uniforms, which was a mixture of ARC citizen garb. The recon troops wore local militia uniforms, dark brown and striated camouflaged fatigues. Dane, Jinn and Linon dressed in typical citizen garb: torn trousers and stained canvas shirts with worn boots. They all wore hats to prevent dirt from building up on their scalps.

"Lead the way, Linon." Dane gritted his jaw and nodded.

With the recon troops on either side, Linon led them into the main thoroughfares and under the large, vaulted ceilings of the ARC district. The mining town gained most of its profit from rare-earth minerals and other precious metals. But mining operations took place far below the main city. Linon led them across and through the vast markets, which were loud and boisterous with yelling and trading. It was crowded, and DiJinn kept an eye out for any Tetrahedron troops.

They stayed close, careful not to get separated. Dane and DiJinn were positioned in the middle, and the recon troops encircled them. It was midday, though there was no sunlight through the clear dome above. The area was lit by the bioluminescent shale ferns that clung to the rock walls and ceilings.

They moved into another area when Linon paused the group. "Ahead is a secure district. Remember, this is considered a privileged area designed for upper-class citizens. As you can see, we don't fit in. We need to make it to the lower areas quickly, where we will blend in. We want to be in the sublevels. That's where I think he'll be."

"Linon," DiJinn said, and reached out to him. "Just in case we get separated, what's his name, your son?"

"Patrick." Linon gave her a smile, then turned and led them through the district's portal.

CHAPTER 24

Stranded in Time
January 18, 2287, A.D.

WHEN JET AWOKE, he stood and screamed at the fiery red sky. He lifted Port-Shear and swung it against collapsed structures and stone blocks, obliterating them into tiny pieces of debris. Power rippled and warped the fabric of space and time, sending shockwaves out and decimating everything around him.

He finally dropped his war staff to the ashen dirt and fell to his knees. He began to dig through the smoking ash, his hands burning from the charred remains of the buildings. He ignored the pain, and several minutes later, he had freed Solan's body. He lifted her and held her in his arms as tears rolled down his face.

Jet sat like that for what seemed like hours, forgetting about his surroundings and everything else. He could only look into Solan's eyes. Her normal yellow-greenish glow was gone, replaced with a dull-white and vacant stare. Her face had cuts, and her body was broken.

Eventually, he laid her down and sat next to her. He felt despair set in and had no idea what he was supposed to do next. Albright had tasked him with completing this quest, which he'd assumed was meeting with the Titans. He'd followed his instincts and used Port-Shear to get to the alternate plane. There, he'd pleaded his case before a court of higher beings. And now, he had returned to his own plane only to find it a smoking ruin. *Where did he go wrong?* He should be back, fighting alongside his friends, alongside Kamber. He could only assume he'd spent too long at the Court of Stars. He hadn't realized how slowly time flowed there. Otherwise, he would have moved quicker to be back in time for the fulcrum wars.

What now? Jet thought. *What now!*

...now we work...

Jet sat up and looked at the war staff. Port-Shear was glowing. The clear vessel that housed the skull shimmered and pulsed. Jet crawled over to it and lifted the staff.

"What?" he asked it. He could hear the hysteria in his voice. "What do you mean?" he said, anger rising up. "Should I follow you to another dead end? To another failure?"

…now we work…

Jet took the staff and stood. He thought about bringing it down onto his knee and throwing it into the flames.

As he stood there, he began to consider, though.

Maybe being here wasn't an accident after all? What if Albright had meant for him to see this future apocalyptic world? Had wanted him to see something *specific?*

Jet felt a sudden urge to move, like there was still time to make a…

…difference… Port-Shear whispered.

"Just tell me." Jet gripped the staff and felt anger and frustration set in again. *Why was it always so difficult to communicate with this thing?*

He waited for Port-Shear to respond, but the staff had gone cold again; the light had faded. Jet could only shake his head as he subdued his frustration. He looked up to the clouds above and watched as the ruined belts in the distance floated across the red sky. The glowing chunks moved randomly as he racked his brain, trying to think of what he should do next. He did sense that time was a concern now. If he was somehow locked into this futuristic world, did that mean his friends were still alive in the past world? One that he could perhaps return to and make a difference?

Jet didn't know. He only knew that he needed to move. If he *was* looking for something here, he wouldn't find it by standing around. He needed to find a way off the first belt, what was left of it at least. But part of the problem was that nothing looked the same.

Jet knelt to Solan and gripped her hand, taking a moment to say goodbye. Clutched in her balled fist was a metallic object. Jet took it and held it to the fading sunlight.

It was the lead badge for the Lucem. She'd mentioned it to him once but had refused to wear it for some reason. Jet wondered why she'd been holding it, though. If there had been a battle here on the first belt, why had she made an effort to hold onto it of all things? He flipped it over and noticed a digital imprint on the back, which looked like a code. He stuffed the badge into his cloak.

Even though he was in a hurry now, he couldn't leave Solan's body lying atop the ashes. He found a flat piece of wall and broke it down. Then scooped smoldering embers over her body until it was buried beneath and already turning to ash. Jet felt another wave of grief and guilt hit him. But he brushed the tears from his cheeks and left the ruins.

There were thousands of private hangers below the university. As expected, most of them were empty. He imagined that citizens had panicked during the war and fled. There were signs of battle everywhere he went. Holes in walls, rounds of ammo on the floors, pitted ground from mortars. He continued to race between the empty hangars until he finally found a ship.

But it wasn't just any ship.

It was the massive battle cruiser called the SLS Armada. General Dane's pride.

Jet found the entry and tried to board the ship. But the keypad prevented him from lowering the gangway. He grew frustrated again until he remembered Solan's badge. He placed the digital imprint to the keypad. It beeped, and the gangway lowered. Jet could only shake his head at Solan's foresight.

Once aboard the main bridge, Jet engaged the artificial intelligence system, hoping the engines would still fire. They did, and he slumped in the captain's chair, breathing a sigh of relief.

He maneuvered the massive battle cruiser out of the university hangar and soon he was rocketing away from the wreckage of Skylight University. As he crested the first belt, he noticed the black bolt of energy again. From this vantage, he got a better view of it. The strange bolt emitted a black light that seemed unnatural. It rose perhaps a few hundred meters above the first belt, then bent horizontally toward the second belt. He set the coordinates for the second belt and followed the bolt.

Jet couldn't stop thinking about his friends as he sat in the pilot seat. It was almost too difficult to think about Solan. She had been his mentor and the first Lucem he'd met. She was responsible for his conversion into the Heliographi and had looked after him like the parent he'd never had, though he'd thought of her as a friend. But all the other Lucem had been just as close: DiJinn, Ti-Leer, and Cord, who had been his closest friend over the years after losing Cutter.

Then there was Kamber.

His heart ached all over again.

It ached because he knew if Solan was gone, then Kamber was too, buried somewhere on the first belt beneath the ash and dust.

Just thinking of her not being a part of his world sucked the air from his lungs. He'd only just met her, but in that short time had felt a kindred spirit. Someone he could have shared his life with and been happy till the end.

But what had he expected? He'd known this war was coming and that death would follow. He just never thought it would happen like this, stranded in some future world far from home. A world that burned because of his failure.

He stood and walked around the bridge, unable to sit still. The computerized beeping of the systems faded into background noise as he tried to clear his thoughts. Jet had put so much trust in Albright, and he'd done what he thought was right. He had followed his intuition. In the past, that 'intuitive voice' had rarely led him astray. He thought it strange that the voice was missing now. The ghost Lucem named Brindall had guided him from beyond this plane, aided by his friend Cutter recently. It appeared his new guide was Port-Shear, who had replaced Brindall and Cutter. Jet wasn't sure he liked that arrangement.

He continued to pace around the empty bridge and finally decided what he should do next. He would visit each fulcrum. Perhaps there, he could find some answers.

He settled the Armada onto the second belt, not far from the black energy bolt, and stepped onto the ashen landscape. This belt had once been the civic center of Skylight. Now, it looked like something from his nightmares. Jet pulled his cloak over his mouth and nose as he hurried to find a path down below. As he raced around, sweat poured down his face from the heat of the ground. There was a sickening feeling in his mind, one that reminded him of the past Skylight world. Only this was much stronger.

Jet finally found a deformed mechanical vent and kicked through it and dropped down. The heat lessened only slightly, but there was no breeze, and the humidity was almost unbearable. Each belt's hull was vast, and he began to see that it might take years to locate each fulcrum. Though they were large, he didn't have the time to search for each one like this.

He took a knee and held the war staff upright. He sent a thought to Port-Shear, willing it to direct his way. It was always random, Port-Shear's responses. Whether laziness, diffidence, or because of the great distance, Jet didn't know. But this time, Port-Shear woke, which surprised him.

…lead… Port-Shear whispered, and the white vessel began to glow.

Jet stood and held the staff in front of him. The end glowed brighter when he made a correct turn and glowed dimmer when he guessed wrong. Within an hour, he was standing in the vast chamber that housed the second belt's fulcrum.

The entire chamber was a wreck.

There had been an epic battle here, based on what he was seeing. Burn blasts on the walls, cratered out floors, conduit hanging from the upper reaches of the ceiling. The amount of dead bodies made him feel nauseous. The large metallic field was littered with corpses, all stacked on top of one another.

But it was the black lightning bolt that drew his attention. It rose up from the center of the stepped pyramid and out through an opening above. It resembled the one on the first belt, and forked and jutted out, licking the steel structures nearby in an electric frenzy.

Jet moved cautiously across the floor and began to climb the stepped pyramid, silently working his way up. When he reached the top, he stopped to catch his breath. Jet peered over the edge and down into the opening where the lightning bolt emanated. It was dark below but appeared vacant. He hopped down some twenty meters to the rusty metal grate and let his eyes adjust to the dimmer light.

Inside, the pyramid looked much the same as it had on the eighth belt. The inner sanctum was like a large globe, made of clear walls and a glass lectern off to one side. In the very center was the large stone fulcrum. Suspended inside the glass case of the lectern was the memoir. The parchment glowed, having been activated now. The glyphs etched into the paper had expanded and projected in holographic fashion. Slumped against the backside of the lectern was the dead body of DiJinn.

IF THIS IS *the future, am I altering my former past?*

Jet couldn't stop asking himself that question as he stood aboard the Armada, trying not to think about DiJinn.

Was being here—seeing this future apocalyptic world—creating a new narrative? One that might possibly change the fate of his friends like Solan and DiJinn? He hoped beyond hope that was true. If Jet *could* reset all this misery, he would only find out by returning to his own world. Seeing Jinn had unsettled him just as

much as seeing Solan. It broke his heart all over again, seeing her lifeless body, propped against the fulcrum. If he had to guess, Jinn had sacrificed her life defending the memoir.

The more he thought about it, the more he felt that this *was* part of Albright's plan. Perhaps he hadn't made any mistakes after all. If that were true, then Albright *had* left him a return ramp home, right?

Right?

And *IF* there was a way home…then yes, he felt certain he was rewriting the past.

Kamber wouldn't agree with that philosophy, though. She had always felt that fate was predetermined. No matter what one did, their story had already been written. Jet wasn't so certain.

The ramifications made his head spin, though. Cord would be much better suited for this task. But Cord was in some past world doing who knew what. And Kamber…

Jet wondered what she was doing at that moment. She had been with Solan when he'd left.

And when he thought of Solan, all he could see was her vacant stare. That milky white haze of a dead Heliographi. But that was in this world, and he didn't linger on the thought. If he wanted to prevent this burning hellish nightmare, he needed to get busy and figure it out.

Below the Armada was the third belt. It glowed a bright red and parts of it had deformed like molten lava. Fire burned in random places, and Skylight City was almost unrecognizable from the utopian landscape it had once been.

Jet settled the battle cruiser down to search for survivors.

He stepped onto the ashen ground, and puffs of black flakes fluttered from beneath his boots. It was difficult to breathe, as if the heat had sucked the oxygen from the air. Like the other belts, the vegetation and trees were charred and blackened, and the smoke choked out the sunlight. Jet hurried along, Port-Shear held before him, lighting the way.

He moved into what had once been the populated areas. The buildings were mostly toppled and collapsed. A great war had taken place here, too. Like the last belt, he recognized the telltale signs of railgun rounds in the building facades. Glass windows were blown out, and the streets were pitted. Death and ruin were everywhere.

Jet moved into the buildings and searched through the wreckage. He yelled, calling out for survivors, and eventually heard someone calling for help. On the ground floor of an office building, Jet saw a woman. She looked to be in her late twenties with reddish-blonde hair. Her leg was pinned by a steel beam from an upper floor. He raced over to help.

"It's okay," Jet said as he knelt.

The lady was calm, considering the situation. She had managed to clear out some of the lighter debris around her, but the beam had pinned her to the ground.

"Are you hurt?" Jet asked.

"Only my leg," she said, then gasped when she looked into his eyes. "You're a Heliographi."

"No time to explain," Jet said. "Let's get this off—"

"The beam is too heavy," she said.

Jet ignored her and looked around to see half the building resting on the beam. "Be ready to crawl under, alright?"

"I can help," she said.

"It's okay. I should be able to move it. Just be ready." Jet gave her a quick nod. Then he gripped the hot beam and used his legs to hoist it up. The girl crawled under and limped out of the building. Once she was clear, Jet let the beam drop and raced from the building. The entire second floor crashed down and buried the area in a cloud of dust and ash.

Jet took a knee to catch his breath, then turned to look at the lady.

"I'm alright, I think," she said and looked at him with one eye squinted. "What are you doing here? I thought all the Heliographi were dead?"

Jet froze and stared into her eyes. "What did you say?"

"The Heliographi. All of them died in the war. Except for one."

Even though Jet had assumed this, his stomach lurched at hearing it. He felt suddenly lightheaded and used his staff to steady himself. He remained silent for a few more seconds, then held out his hand. "Tell me more as we walk. Can you stand?"

She nodded and got to her feet. "I'm okay, really."

"Alright, follow me."

Jet wanted to search through the other buildings but decided to return to the battle cruiser instead. Once aboard, he helped the lady into a seat and sat across from her. She seemed remarkably healthy, showing little effect from the heat or lack of oxygen.

"What's your name?" he asked and took his cloak off.

"I'm Sember." The lady held out her hand and smiled. "Thank you for helping me."

"My name's Jet," he said and shook her hand. "I didn't see any other survivors. How did you manage to stay alive out there?"

Sember scratched her head, considering. She was average height and had an athletic build. Her blonde hair had a reddish tinge and was matted with dirt and soot. There was an odd, iridescent shimmer to her eyes that sparkled when she tilted her head. Her face was rounded and kind with dimples at her cheeks. Her expression remained vacant, though she seemed a bit rattled. She wore some sort of military uniform, and it was ripped and torn with the stains of battle.

Jet waited for her response. She seemed hesitant to speak at first. "I…I'm a…what they call a genie."

Jet narrowed his eyes. "I'm sorry? I don't think I understand."

"A genie. A human with genetically modified genes. You've never heard about us?"

Jet slowly shook his head. "Can't say that I have. Can you explain?"

Sember looked out the window. "Shouldn't we be on our way? The heat might damage your ship."

"Not this one," Jet said. "We'll be safe on board. But you're right. We should move." Jet stood and sat in the pilot seat. Sember followed him and settled into the co-pilot seat. Once they were off the ground, Jet set the autopilot to cruise around the third belt to get a better look. Then he turned to face Sember.

"Can you tell me what happened here?"

She gave him a funny look. "What do you mean? Were you not part of the fulcrum wars?"

Jet didn't really care to explain his situation to her at the moment. It would be difficult, and besides, she might think he was insane. "Yeah, well…I was preoccupied when it all happened. Missed most of the action, I guess."

She continued to look at him suspiciously but lifted one corner of her mouth. "The memoirs were found and split amongst the three groups: the Atrum, the Lucem, and Lybra and the Agency. The Atrum joined Lybra, which tipped the scales in their favor. When the memoirs were placed, the countdown for each fulcrum was set into motion. Each fulcrum war was fought for control. The Lucem won several of the inner fulcrums but lost the final battle. Eventually, all the Heliographi were killed." She stood and walked around, stretching her leg, which Jet noticed was already starting to heal.

Jet remained silent until she returned. "What more can you tell me about this?" Jet motioned out to the horizon and the fire storm around them. "You said you watched the Heliographi fight and die. Were you there, helping? Your uniform is one I recognize. Part of the Agency, right?"

"I was a part of the Agency but defected after Lybra Howling took control from President Harok. I helped with the local militia when the fulcrum wars began and ended up on the third belt. One by one, the fulcrums fell to our enemy. There were a few victories, but we couldn't hold on. It seemed a never-ending retreat inward to the smaller belts. I managed to flee when the first belt fell and ended up on the third belt. I found low areas and survived the aftermath."

"What about the Heliographi?" Jet asked. "Did they say anything to you?"

Sember shook her head slowly. "I never got a chance to speak with any Heliographi. I just saw them on occasion, leading the armies."

Jet leaned back and crossed his arms in thought. "What do you know about these lightning bolts?"

"Not much, really. Something about polarity." Sember nodded out the window. "Keep going, and you'll see it soon."

Jet piloted the Armada just above the third belt's wreckage, which had once been Skylight City. A few minutes later, he saw it. Arcing along the horizon was the same massive bolt of lightning. It pulsed from an opening in the belt and tore through the smoke and clouds. The bolt bent horizontally toward the fourth belt, and connecting to it were the first two lightning bolts. They all intertwined and coupled in a sequential way, each bolt growing broader and greater the farther out it traveled.

"It's just like the first two, only larger. But what is it?" Jet asked.

"From what I gather, each one comes from a fulcrum. I believe they are a transmitter, perhaps. Can you not feel the sickness all around us? It's in the air. Hate and fear, like poison. It has something to do with these bolts and fulcrums. When each fulcrum was ignited, the sickness, or bloodlust, grew worse. It was like a snowball effect, and it gained momentum as each fulcrum fell to the enemy. It was awful to watch. You saw the victims on the first belt, I assume? The white eyes, the bloody ears, the look of fear on their faces—"

Jet waved her off. "Yes. Thank you, Sember. I remember. I don't think I'll ever forget." Jet felt anger and grief run through him at the image of Solan's face again. Not only had they lost, they had been decimated. "I had hoped we'd put up a better fight. Cord, Solan…Dane and his fleet. We had a lot of good people. I just wish I could talk to one of them."

"It was the sickness," Sember turned away and looked out the window; a strange spasm overtook her momentarily. "The bloodlust. I believe it's a power the remaining Heliographi wields. The fulcrums amplify that power. They were designed to do so, at least, that's my guess. Maybe they are receivers, the fulcrums, not transmitters? Once they were ignited, the memoirs gave them power, but the polarity was set by the Heliographi. The first belt and the eighth belt…that's where the main signal comes from, or so I hear."

"That's why they are different," Jet muttered, remembering what Cord had noticed. "The first and eighth were larger fulcrums."

"That bloodlust permeated the fabric of our system, leading up to the war. The fulcrums have made it worse. That's why it seems to be everywhere…in the ground, in nature, in the very air we breathe."

"I sensed it before I left, though it wasn't this bad," Jet said. "I think the other Heliographi did, too. We just didn't know what it was."

"The Lucem were somehow able to fight the effect for a longer period than others. But eventually, they also fell. Everyone went insane. The survivors had no choice but to move to the ninth belt. Thanks to my genetics, I've managed to survive. Now everything is ash and ruin." She gave him a thoughtful look. "I wonder how you're able to handle the bloodlust when the other Lucem couldn't?"

Jet thought about what Albright had told him. *Your gift will protect you when it might be dangerous for others.* He looked at his war staff, thinking they were probably connected, working in unison somehow. "Honestly, I'm not entirely sure. I know that each Heliographi has a special ability. This might be part of mine."

"Everyone had to swear fealty to the remaining Heliographi. All survivors now live on the ninth belt, under her rule."

"Her…" Jet said and knelt in front of Sember. He grasped her hands. "Tell me about her, Sember."

"I don't know her name. I only know that her presence, her effect, has turned the Skylight System to ash and ruin. The only place to go is the ninth belt and live under her rule. That is your only choice, if you want to survive."

CHAPTER 26

An Alliance on the Edge

SOLAN AND KAMBER stood next to each other aboard the bridge of the SLS Armada. They were on their way back to the ninth belt to check on the Dreadnaughts and their preparations to relocate.

In the back of her mind, she knew something had gone wrong, though. The Dreadnaughts were deceptive, she knew that. Though they had pledged their allegiance to the Lucem, Fritt was no idiot. Moving their entire operations would be no easy task. She had a feeling he was rethinking his commitment to them. If the Dreadnaughts *were* defaulting on their deal, she didn't know if she could sway them back, either.

Solan had only asked for a minimal crew to come with her, hoping the SLS Armada would fill the gap in troops. The twenty or so jammer escorts surrounding them gave her some additional confidence. Solan felt certain that another show of force would do little if the Dreadnaughts were indeed intent on backing out. But she had to know for certain and wanted to meet Fritt in person. If the Dreadnaught's support was off the table, she needed to rework her plans now.

The battle cruiser wasn't exactly fast, thanks to its heavy armor. It took nearly an hour to reach the ninth belt. But soon, they were punching through the debris belt. Solan glanced over at Kamber and placed a hand on her shoulder. Kamber smiled up at her.

Solan gave her a wink. "Steady, Kamber. We're only here to check on their progress."

"Then why the Armada?" she asked.

"Just in case," Solan replied.

They were hailed over the intercom, and an air controller gave them clearance. "Welcome, SLS Armada. Proceed to boarding platform ten."

They docked the Armada, and a few guards escorted them to the stronghold. Solan followed, with Kamber and a half dozen recon troops beside her. She walked confidently but felt for her war staff tucked under her cloak. She hoped she wouldn't need it today. Still, she gripped it tightly, her senses on full alert as she followed the guards.

Soon, they were standing in the main court of the Dreadnaught's stronghold. The stone walls spanned up, and light filtered from a clerestory high above. A few birds had even made their way in and had built nests in the rafters, their soft chirping stood in contrast to the tense mood. She recognized the dark splotches around the floor as dried blood. Solan understood this was a proving ground, but Jet had already faced that challenge.

The elders seated around the rotunda looked on with narrowed eyes and tense faces.

Fritt stood, his robes draped around him as he gestured to her and Kamber with welcoming arms. The stocky man's face was hidden behind the hood of his lavish robe, as was typical. She often wondered if anyone had truly seen Fritt's face. "Solan. Leader of the Lucem, replacement to the great Tyberius Alexander," Fritt said in a regal voice.

Solan bowed, somewhat stiffly and quickly straightened.

"What brings you back to my court so soon?" he asked.

She relaxed her grip on the war staff and held her hands in an open gesture. "Chief Fritt," she acknowledged. "Thank you for the warm welcome. I thought I would offer our help in your relocation. There are pirates that patrol the air space between the outer belts." This, of course, was an ice breaker to her bigger concern of 'why the Dreadnaughts had not started moving their operations.' The Dreadnaughts would have no problem fending off pirates, as most steered well clear of them. Fritt was smart enough to know that she knew this, too. But…he played along with the charade.

"Thank you, my good Solan. You have plenty on your plate as it is. I'd hate to pull from any of your resources. The safety of the citizens and their relocation is paramount and should come first."

Solan nodded. "Yes, of course. I would be remiss had I not at least offered, considering you've committed so much to our cause. Let me again express our gratitude. It means a great deal to the Skylight System and its citizens."

Fritt waved it away. "Please, it's of no concern," he said tersely and took a seat on the malformed throne. "But I must ask, why have you really come to see me?"

Solan held his gaze. "Isn't it obvious by now?"

"The last Lucem to visit us was Mister Stroud. I assumed he was your emissary. Why not just send him again?"

"I felt it wiser to attend to this myself, considering the importance of the matter."

Fritt seemed to consider from behind his hood, his purple and golden robes glinting in the smoky sunlight. "Are you certain? Why do I sense there is more? My good Solan, if we are to be allies, there must be *only* the truth between us. So, why not Mister Stroud?"

Solan felt her skin flush. She heard the condescending attitude in his voice. Of course, Fritt would know something was wrong. She wanted to retort back and ask him the same—*why should he not tell the truth about their alliance?* Solan held her temper in check, though, and steadied her voice. "Let's just say that Jet has a very important matter to attend to."

"Important matter…or is he lost?" Fritt asked. "Without his war staff, I wonder how the Lucem will fare in the fulcrum wars to come?"

Solan looked on, wondering how in Skylight Fritt had known Jet was missing. "He is on an important mission. That is all I can say. I hope you can appreciate my discretion at the moment."

"Solan. Without Heaven's Staff, the Lucem are of no use to us. And right now, I sense that it is lost."

Solan wrinkled her brow at that. *Heaven's Staff?* It was the first time she'd heard that term. She felt a bit of panic set in—the Dreadnaught's support was slipping away right in front of her. Originally, her intent was to use Jet's war staff as leverage only. But she had underestimated its importance to a clan like the Dreadnaughts. Of course, the Dreadnaughts would worship such a relic. That was the main reason they'd even pledged their support. And somehow Fritt knew

that Jet was missing…*or had the Atrum slipped that information to Fritt?*

She realized then she should never have come. Being here without Jet spoke volumes, she saw that now.

"Return with Mister Stroud in three days' time, or we will be forced to go our separate ways, Solan Alexander."

Solan didn't bother trying to convince Fritt or his council. She bowed, turned, and marched off with Kamber right behind her.

"What just happened?" Kamber hissed, quickly stepping next to Solan.

Solan glanced around her, then lowered her voice. "Fritt somehow knows that Jet is missing."

"How is that possible? We just found out ourselves."

"Something tells me that Joshia is behind this." Solan could only shake her head. Without the Dreadnaughts, the fulcrum wars were going to be a lot more difficult. The Lucem had the Recon army and the prisoner army, who they'd freed from the Tetrahedron. Stell's intel was irreplaceable, and Dane's air force was crucial. But they just didn't have the troops to compete with the Agency, Lybra's M-class mech army and the Tetrahedron soldiers. And if the Atrum were indeed aligned with Lybra again, that made the Dreadnaught's alliance even more crucial. Even with more of the upgraded war staffs, it probably wouldn't matter. To top it all off, Jet was missing. It put her in a grumpy mood, and she stepped up her pace, anxious to get back to the Armada now. They *had* to locate Jet in three days if they wanted Fritt's support. But deep down, Solan had a growing suspicion that Jet was beyond their reach. She worried that he might not return at all.

"Why did Fritt refer to Jet's war staff that way?" Kamber asked. "He seems to know more about it than we do."

"What?" Solan asked, distracted by the rush of troops around her now.

Kamber pulled at Solan. "Heaven's Staff. What did he mean by that?"

Solan shook her head as they finally made it to the proper boarding platform. "I don't know. I need to find answers and I think I know just the place."

"Which is where?" Kamber asked.

"I have some documents. I may find some answers there. I just need to find some time."

"What about the citizens?" Kamber asked. "We still have some evacuations."

Solan was desperate to find answers, though. But even half a day at this point was crucial. She could bring the material with her, of course, but the constant distraction would drive her crazy. No. She needed time alone to think and sort things out.

Solan gripped Kamber's shoulders and faced her. "That's why you're going to organize the remaining evacuations."

The look on Kamber's face was pure shock. "Me? Are you joking?"

"No, Kamber," Solan said. "You're ready, and these people need you. You'll do fine."

Kamber took a deep breath. "Yes, of course. I understand."

Solan could see the concern on her face and gave her a gentle shake. "I'm sure he's fine. Whatever Jet's up to, I sense it was destined for him alone. I'll do my best to find out what I can."

K

Just after midnight, the SLS Armada made the first belt's airspace. They'd ferried what citizens they could from Glass-Hewn on the seventh belt. When the battle cruiser docked inside the main hangar bay, the citizens were greeted by Stell's team and given food and water.

Solan turned to Kamber. "It's your duty now. Get as many people evacuated as possible."

Kamber looked tired but eager. She took control of the bridge. As soon as they were fueled, her crew immediately turned the large cruiser and the rest of the fleet and set a course back to the outer belts.

Solan felt worn, too. But she was anxious to start some research. She hurried to her quarters and found an extra sweater. Then she grabbed something to eat in the mess hall. There were plenty of people there, but thankfully, no one pulled her aside. Soon, she was hurrying through Lyrinthum and toward Skylight University. She found the proper passages and approached the basement, locating the bookshelf. Solan pulled the brass lever and stepped onto the staircase, the shelf closing behind her.

Down the steps and she stood in the stacks of the library's basement. Throughout her career as a student, she'd spent plenty of time down in the stacks. It had become a home away from home for her. The solitude and quiet nature had helped provide some peace in dealing with ephebus mortem. That had been nearly fifteen years ago. The stacks had also proven to be a great place to hide things. Down in the dusty, forgotten wing, she'd stashed the final painting by Van Saint called *The Verification*.

Solan moved through the large vaults of the stacks and found an unused air vent. She pried the grill open to reveal an old leatherbound book, which was one of the few surviving copies of the Book of Vishmu. She brought it over to the old claw and ball table, then lit a few nearby candles. She settled into the old wing-backed chair as the haunting breeze crooned through the space, threatening to extinguish the candles.

She scanned through the ancient codex. The book was old, some parts dating back several thousand years. Inside it was the mystical practice that the Heliographi used known as Vishmu, something only immortals could achieve. But it was complex, and though she'd studied it for the last decade or so, there were parts of it that she would never understand.

Within the ancient book was information about their race, which the Heliographi had passed down through the millennia. The old parchment was littered with notes, lessons, and experiences. Each Heliographi class had shared in the documentation of knowledge, from the Alpha to the Omega: both Atrum and Lucem alike. But no Heliographi understood all of it, not even Albright. Much of the archaic language was coded in a mathematical dialect of charts and sketches, which made it difficult to translate.

What she was looking for now was something her father had mentioned some fifteen years ago. She'd followed up on it recently and found some documentation within this copy of The Book of Vishmu. They were tiny sketches which she understood now, after seeing the vessels.

She flipped through the pages, searching line by line as the night deepened in the chilly basement. It wasn't until she had almost finished the book that she finally found the passage.

CHAPTER 27
The Panther

DIJINN, DANE AND Linon, along with the dozen recon troops, entered through a rusted, circular grate. It was some ten meters in diameter and groaned in protest as it was swung open. There was a loud, unison chant echoing from beyond. DiJinn checked her ring, making sure her guise was in place. There would be a bounty on all Heliographi now, and word had likely spread to the subterranean districts on earth as well. Backed by Lybra, Jinn assumed the bounty was large enough to entice mercenaries to take the risk to capture, or kill, a Heliographi. She had to be on guard in unfriendly places like this. The last thing she wanted was to place the mission or troops at risk because she'd been careless.

The chanting grew louder as they entered the underground district. Ahead, she could see the pit fights. Prisoners faced off against each other as bets were placed. She tried to ignore the barbaric nature of it all as they passed, though her temper flared. She knew that most of these people had been raised from a young age to be pit fighters by guardians or parents. It was disgusting, in her opinion. Solan and the Lucem had recently freed thousands of prisoners, but that had only been in one sector. Apparently, there were hundreds more used for different purposes down here. This area had been unknown to them before. They were definitely in the 'darker' side of the ARC district, and that was saying something.

But DiJinn didn't have time to get sidetracked. She needed to stay focused on finding Linon's son, Patrick, and get him out of this hell-hole. They had work to do back in the Skylight System.

Linon led their group past the pits, ignoring the fights. Soon, they found several wide, stone staircases leading down. They followed them, wedging themselves between all the yelling citizens. It seemed to take forever as they pressed through the raucous crowds. DiJinn noticed that most of the people seemed to be part of the pit fights and wondered if anything else took place down in the bowels of the ARC district.

Ahead, Linon stopped and stood in front of one cage. It was a large rusty box that was perhaps a dozen meters on all sides. Inside were a dozen men and women. They all wore ripped clothing and wielded iron clubs. Around them, other citizens screamed and hollered at the pit fighters. There appeared to be two sides, with six fighters on each side. They all circled, waiting, it seemed.

DiJinn moved closer to Linon with Dane near her. "Let's move on, Linon."

But Linon seemed to be in a trance, his gaze on one of the young men. He nodded toward the cage with his chin. "That's him. That's my son in there."

DiJinn and Dane turned to face the cage as the pit fighters began to advance on each other. The thin man had dark hair and a curly beard. He was tall, like Linon, and his wiry muscles rippled as he seemed to prowl around the cage. DiJinn could see by the way he moved he was an experienced fighter. Patrick seemed to be directing the others on his side. DiJinn watched as he hefted the iron club and moved with ease. The others leapt and fought near the middle of the cage. Iron spikes surrounded them, forcing them to stay near the center and in close contact.

The fighting was brutal, with half the fighters being knocked out in the first few seconds. They went down and didn't move as the quicker men and women faced off. Patrick had brought two opposing fighters down without a scratch. Near the far side of the cage, there were children watching, and she realized they belonged to the fighters. How cruel it seemed that they were forced to watch as their parents fought to the death. She gritted her jaw in anger and had to look away. She felt her eyes sting as she turned to face Dane, who had a stoic look on his face. But she knew he also felt the same emotion.

The bellowing continued as the remaining fighters battled. It was then that DiJinn understood what the crowd was chanting. *Panther!* That must be Patrick's nickname, and he looked every bit as deadly.

Patrick dropped two more, and the final opposing fighter faced the remaining four on Patrick's side. He turned away, knelt, then bowed his head, refusing to watch or look at the children beyond as they screamed. The other four moved in on the middle-aged woman.

Then it was over, and the crowd cheered wildly.

The keepers moved in and chained the remaining fighters and led them out. But Patrick was led in a different direction.

"Let's move," Linon said.

DiJinn followed Linon but caught a glimpse of Patrick's face as he wedged between the crowd of chanting citizens and saw the tears on his cheeks.

They followed at a distance, careful not to draw attention. DiJinn kept her eyes open as they moved slightly upward along gravel paths. The roaring began to fade, and ten minutes later, Patrick was loaded into an iron crate with stone wheels. Half a dozen slaves pulled the crate toward a castle-like building that was carved into the far cliff face. It was darker the farther back they traveled, and the crowd thinned out as the noise diminished to a whisper.

Linon moved to a dark niche between some stone hovels and paused the group. "That must be the Pensioner's keep," he whispered, pulling everyone down with him. "These pit fighters, especially the better ones, are sought after. Only very wealthy citizens can afford them. My son just fought in one of the central arenas, which is reserved for top fighters."

DiJinn looked from Dane to Linon. "Any idea when his next fight might be? If there's enough time in between, we could break your son out. We'd be airborne within the hour."

"The better fighters draw larger crowds, so they'll want him fresh. My guess is he'll fight again tomorrow."

"Well, what are we waitin' for?" DiJinn said.

"Hold on, Jinn," Dane said. "We need a plan. There're only nine of us."

"There are thousands of pit fighters in those cages back there," Linon said. "Why not use the same tactic as last time and free them?"

DiJinn gave him a doubtful look. "We need to be quick, whatever we do."

"It's not a bad idea," Dane said. "There's not much of a Tetrahedron presence here with the fulcrum wars ahead. I don't think I saw any in that crowd, just local militia. If we can free your son first, then he can help us with the other pit fighters."

Linon didn't consider long. "If I know my son, he's not leaving these people behind anyway. Besides, he'll know this place much better."

They decided to wait till the guards' shift had changed. Then the group ambushed the patrol and switched out clothing. DiJinn assumed this wealthy Pensioner had his own personal guard, but nothing they couldn't handle. The bigger challenge would be freeing the pit fighters.

Linon led the way once they'd all changed. DiJinn stayed near the front, her staff at her fingertips. Dane had a few recon troops hang back at the entry gate as sentries.

The keep towered up the cliff side as they approached. It had dozens of levels and was carved deep into the rock face. The area was relatively quiet, being at the end of the district's lower level. There were no vector accelerators, so they split up and took different stairs. Dane and the recon troops moved to the far end, while she and Linon took the nearby stair tower.

When they hit the mid-level, they paused.

"Doesn't seem to be anyone home," DiJinn whispered.

Linon answered over his shoulder. "We'll know when we get near the top. Keep your eyes open."

She followed Linon. But a few steps up, she sensed something was out of place. DiJinn grasped Linon by the shoulder and pulled at him. "Something's not right," she whispered. "Let me scout ahead. Wait here."

DiJinn pulled her cloak over her head and disappeared. She moved up the flights, the tip of her staff barely visible in the dark. Waiting at the top of the stairs were eight or nine guards. Too late, DiJinn realized that her staff had given her away.

The guards rushed in and pressed her against the wall. One had a knife and thrust it into her torso, but her cloak bent the blade back. She twisted away, and the knife clattered to the stone floor. DiJinn lowered her shoulder and shoved the men off. The guards flew through the air and onto the upper plaza. DiJinn sprang up the remaining steps and brought her staff down. A bolt of lightning erupted from the ground and stunned several men. They hit the wall with a crushing blow, then lay silent. The remaining two guards backed away and were about to turn and run. She flipped through the air and landed between them, twirling her staff and knocking them both unconscious.

DiJinn searched the rest of the upper plaza to make sure it was clear, then whistled down to Linon. Across the large room, she saw Dane and his troops finishing up another group of guards. They all met in the middle of the plaza.

"They had advanced warning, Jinn," Dane said in his gruff voice. He'd taken a blow to the head, and blood caked his brow. He wiped at it with his forearm. "If this Pensioner is home, he likely knows we're here."

"Let me move ahead," DiJinn said. "This is gettin' dangerous. My cloak should shield me from any security systems. I'll get an idea of what we're facing."

"Be careful, Jinn," Linon said. "They may use Patrick as leverage, if they know we're here for him."

DiJinn stood and cloaked.

She floated up the stairs silently. Like an apparition, she made her way to the top level and the main living quarters of the luxurious keep. The upper floor had a huge balcony with an intricate stone balustrade along one end that provided a commanding overview of the lower district beyond. The lights twinkled, lighting up the underside of the vast cavern's ceiling. Muffled sounds from the fights beyond filtered down into silence as she crept across the cobbled deck. Beyond was an entry door into the stone mansion.

Inside, it was dark and silent. Obviously, a trap, she thought to herself. She lived for this—it made her feel giddy. The challenge of breaking and entering, especially when she *was* expected, made it all the more exciting.

The mansion was perhaps seven or eight levels and topped just beneath the underside of the cavern's ceiling. She leapt to the second level with ease, her form shrouded and blurry. Mounted to the stone walls were heat and motion sensors, which was actually a pretty advanced system, she noted.

Once she reached the top level, she moved in through a window and into the master suite. She tiptoed down wide hallways, which were filled with fine art and sculptures. The Pensioner's mansion was impressive. In this destitute underground world, it wasn't hard to see who was making all the money from the pit fights.

Downward she moved, thoroughly searching each level. Yet there was no one home, even at this late hour. She was a bit surprised. Surely, a butler or servant would be around. Someone sleeping or having a late-night snack. That's when a realization hit her.

This wasn't a trap. It was a decoy.

DiJinn shot back toward the window and hurled through it. She hopped over the balustrade and landed on the ground floor some twenty meters below. She raced to the stairs and back to the place where she'd left her team.

Lying on the stone paving were the recon troops, blood pooling around them.

There was no sign of Dane or Linon.

CHAPTER 28

Of Ash and Desecration
January 18, 2287, A.D.

O F COURSE, JET knew who Sember was referring to.

Only one Heliographi had survived, and it certainly hadn't been him or any of the Lucem.

Sybold had come. But how she had cheated their ancient progression system was a mystery. She would have reset after Tyberius and Albright's assassination of her only a few years ago. Sybold should be a toddler at best.

But according to Albright, she had unknown powers, and apparently, she must have used them.

Regardless, she was back. Though the full legend had yet to reveal itself, Jet knew that it would culminate in a war, one Albright had referred to as 'The Serpent and The Prism.' Jet knew that he was the Prism and that Sybold represented the Serpent. At the moment, he didn't feel very heroic about the prospect of facing her again.

"Jet?"

Sember sat in the copilot chair, looking at him with her hands on her lap, fidgeting. She nodded out the window of the Armada. Jet turned just in time to avoid a free-floating hunk of the third belt. He managed to bring the battle cruiser back in line and eased his grip.

They continued to orbit around the third belt's airspace. Everywhere they looked were toppled buildings and collapsed structures. Jet scanned the wreckage, hoping to find survivors. But everything was ash and desecration. The entire system seemed to have been consumed by a great firestorm—a biblical scene come to life.

"Sorry. I'll pay closer attention," Jet said. He felt somewhat sick to his stomach. His hands shook slightly and Sember reached out to steady him.

"I know it's difficult to see," she said and gave his hand a squeeze.

Jet took a deep breath and let it out slowly. Then he faced her. "So, you said your body can withstand the sickness or bloodlust, was it?"

"Yes. My body is genetically enhanced, including my mind, along with strength, immunity, reflexes. Not at your level, of course. Not nearly as deadly."

"Any side effects? I mean, there must be something? Sorry if that sounded insensitive."

"No, it's fine. Probably my emotions, I'd say. At first, I wasn't tied down to any. I used to be more outgoing and confident. That's all changed now. Suddenly, I feel…vulnerable, or fragile? Maybe depressed is a better word. I think the bloodlust has affected me, but not in the same way as others. Since I'm the last of my kind, I don't have any way to verify that."

"Mind if I ask what happened to your family?"

"No idea. Whoever they were, they died ages ago. The Genie program was developed well before the Skylight System was completed."

Jet narrowed his eyes at her. "Exactly how old are you, Sember?"

She leaned her head, doing some quick math. "At least a century, maybe a century and a half? I stopped keeping track a while back."

Jet raised his eyebrows at that. "You don't look a day over twenty-five. It's just odd that I've never heard of the program."

"There was a handful of us. Given up at birth, used as test subjects, and kept highly secret. The Agency felt citizens wouldn't approve or that the technology might get abused. It was shut down prior to the Territory Wars."

"Right. The Territory Wars," Jet said. "Something about the war for Skylight, right?"

"Before the Skylight System, the districts below the earth's surface were offered a contract by wealthy elites. The North and South fought along the 37th parallel of North America. By the winter solstice of 2186 A.D., whoever held the most territory would win the right to populate the Skylight System. The Agency, a secret organization formed by Christian Albright, vowed to prevent that."

Jet had never heard the full story, though he really hadn't asked about it, with everything else going on.

"I can see that truth still hasn't made it around the system," Sember said. "It's a pity. Many innocent lives were lost to uncover the truth. But it's not important now, I suppose."

"I knew a man who fought in those wars. His name was Brindall, my predecessor."

Sember sat forward in her seat, a bit of excitement in her tone. "You knew Brindall?"

"Well, kinda. He died right before I was born. His symbol was the 'M'."

She sat back. "Of course. I keep forgetting about the way Heliographi work."

"Sounds like you knew him," Jet said. "What was he like?"

Sember gave him a subdued smile as she leaned her head back and wrapped the blanket around her. "Brindall. He was brave and honest and caring. A leader…and a good friend. I miss him. My only regret is that we didn't get to spend more time together after the wars. But when he was brought into the Agency by Gorgan Freemantle, I saw very little of him after that. Then he died on a mission, delivering some secret device. That was the last I heard of him."

"Sounds like he was a good man. I only know him through Vishmu."

She gave him a confused look. "Can you still speak with him?"

"It's complicated," Jet said.

"Would it be possible to send him a message?"

Jet stared at Sember, wondering what their real connection had been. "I suppose I can try. But lately, I haven't been able to find him."

Sember gave him a slow nod. "Well, if you do…just…tell him I miss him."

"Do you remember any of the other Heliographi?"

"Of course. Quite a few of them. We fought side by side," Sember said, but her voice was monotone again, unflinching.

Jet sat back for a moment, giving his head a rest. He could see the burning belts on the horizon, and the sight still shocked him. "I just need to understand why I'm here, Sember. If I ever want to make it back to my past world, then—" Jet stopped himself midsentence and closed his eyes in frustration.

"Hold on." She gave him a suspicious look. "Make it back to your 'past' world? What is it you're not telling me, Jet?"

Jet lowered his head. "It's a long story. Besides, you'd probably think I'm crazy."

"I've been around Heliographi too long. Go ahead, try to surprise me." She raised her chin and waited.

"I'm from the past, I don't belong here, and I don't know why I'm here," Jet said bluntly. "How's that for starters?"

She gave him a half smile. "Sounds kind of normal these days. Go on."

Jet settled in and let out a long sigh. "I guess it all started when the Heliographi got these." Jet held out the war staff and pointed to the white vessel.

Sember leaned in and looked closer. It was the first time she'd noticed it. "I know a little something about them. Brindall carried this one, though not the staff, just the head piece."

Jet frowned at her. "Really? That's interesting. Albright never mentioned it. Anyway, this is called a vessel. It's said to hold the essence of a higher being known as a Titan. These grant special powers. I think this one might be enhancing my own ability. I was asked to go on a quest, which took me to another plane. On my way back, something must have happened. Now, I'm stuck here and don't know how I'm supposed to get back, if I even can."

"Okay…" Sember said, her brow furrowed. "That's a lot to take in."

"I can only assume that I need to find something in this future world, and then return home."

She seemed to consider, her mind running through the ramifications. "Of course, I'll help with what I can. You saved my life. But…I've told you all I know."

Not sure what to say, Jet turned his attention back to the console and the third belt, which continued to solidify through the smoke. They hadn't seen the larger portions of Skylight City yet, and Jet grew concerned at what he would see. Finally, the main skyline appeared, and he gasped. The once majestic metropolis was a mass of burning steel and ruin. The tall skyscrapers reminded him of some giant's skeletal remains. The steel frames were deformed and glowing red from the heat.

Jet piloted the large cruiser down to the surface and landed it on one of the wide thoroughfares. He grabbed a mask, and Sember followed. They stepped into the streets and walked in a daze. It all felt like something from a dystopian nightmare. Lying in the streets were husked-out armored vehicles and dead bodies. The war-ravaged landscape was difficult to take in. Beyond, and along the horizon, was one of the tallest buildings. Lancing up through it was the black bolt of lightning. It arced up through the smoke and collided with the other black bolts before racing off toward the outer belts.

Sember stared at it, a blank look on her face, then turned to him as if waiting for his reaction. Jet ran toward the building, and she fell in behind him.

Minutes later, he was working his way through the lower levels of the building and into the belt's inner hull. There was a large, square staircase that encircled the opening the bolt shot through. He kept moving down and toward the source of the bolt. Soon, he could see the familiar pyramid. It was like the others, an Aztec-inspired shape with stepped plateaus that tapered up into smaller squares.

When they reached the bottom, he found the hidden switchback stair that led up to the apex of the ziggurat. They burst into the upper chamber and stood looking over the guardrail at the bolt. Jet sensed a darkness in that energy source now, stronger than the ones before. It was hard to look at, like there was evil emanating from it. He sensed that Sember wanted to leave. But Jet continued down inside the pyramid and searched the stone base. Glyphs were etched into the clear domelike structure surrounding the inner sanctum. Like the first two, the third memoir was encased in a clear box.

The memoir glowed as energy coursed through it. The parchment pulsed and fluxed, and he could hear a humming in the air around them. It sounded like a dark dialect, an ancient language long forgotten. Barely audible was a chanting that sounded like millions of voices. The memoir was the real source of the bolt. But what was on the other end of that bolt?

Jet took Port-Shear and held it over his head. Then he channeled all his energy into the staff, and it glowed white with unearthly power. Then he hammered the clear casement of the memoir. When the staff struck it, there was an explosion that rocked the interior chamber, blowing him and Sember backwards and into the glass wall of the globe.

It took several seconds to regain his bearings. Jet stood and looked for Sember. She lay on her side, unconscious. He quickly rushed over to check on her. She was fine, just stunned. He turned back to look at the memoir.

The clear case didn't even have a crack in it.

With all the power his staff could generate, it had done nothing to the memoir.

"I don't think you can stop it like that."

Jet turned to see Sember sitting up on her elbow. Another one of the strange spasms shook her body, and it seemed like she lost consciousness for just a split second. Then she was back, blinking at him.

"How do you know that?" Jet asked.

"It's a guess. Whatever's on the other end might offer a solution, though."

Jet sat down next to her and leaned against the glass wall of the inner sanctum. He let the war staff drop as he slouched and took in a long breath. "Yeah. That's what scares me."

CHAPTER 29
Humility and Trust

ΑΒΓΔΕΖΗΘΙΚΛ
ΝΞΟΠΡΣΤΥΦΧΨΩ

CORD AND VAIL continued to wait for the majority of that day, down in the belly of the sixth belt. He could tell the day was waning, based on the shadows cast from the nearby skylight well. The sunlight filtered, reflected, then refracted down through the well in a multitude of reds and rust-colored tones. He remained calm as Vail patted her leg. She was growing impatient, which wasn't new.

Cord leaned back against one of the rusted pillars, ignoring her insistent tapping. He kept one eye trained on the pyramid beyond, and the other on Vail. He still wasn't sure what to make of her situation. Yet, he could sense that she was different somehow. Not long ago, she had been dark and brooding—maybe even malicious. It was the cost of being in the presence of the Atrum. That was simple to understand. Though he didn't necessarily object to all of the Atrum's viewpoints, many were beyond his limit. For example, Mosstrom. He was one of the eldest and most powerful Atrum. In Cord's vision, Mosstrom's soul was black. His dark essence was pure evil, and there was no limit. But some of the other Atrum weren't as bad. He had even sensed moments of empathy, even kindness at times. Like Bo, who had offered to help save Jet when he'd been captured by Lybra. Vail had done the same.

So, was Vail changing?

Was she beginning to turn over a new leaf? Was she really starting to show signs of clarity, guilt…forgiveness?

Or was it all an elaborate hoax?

Vail was gifted at deception. Her ability might even rival his own at cracking riddles. Which one would prevail?

Cord turned to look at Vail. She had her knees pulled up to her chest, her black cloak covering her. Laid before her was the war staff, the colorful jewel-like vessel a greenish turquoise. Vail had been one of the nine

Heliographi to receive a staff upgrade. It made him wonder again how she would fare against him in a dual.

"What are you starin' at," Vail huffed, looking at him over her shoulder. "Tryin' to figure me out again? Keep guessin', Brainiac."

Cord gave her a crooked smile. "I doubt you'd understand, Vail. I don't see any point in trying to explain it."

"You're so arrogant, Ledbetter. But while we're on speakin' terms, mind tellin' me why you're not here with Stroud? You two seem to go everywhere together."

"Why would I share any intel with you? That would be a tactical error."

"Oh, but we *are* a team again, it appears."

Cord frowned at that. "It seems that way for the moment. But are you still here because you need a support group, or are you sticking around because of Jet?" Cord watched her reaction closely and witnessed a split second of hesitation. There was indeed something involving Jet. "Why so concerned about him lately?"

"Who said I was concerned?" Vail huffed but left it there and looked back toward the pyramid.

"If I didn't know any better, I'd say you were worried about him."

Vail shot him a glare in the dark. "What the hell would you know about that?" she said in a low hiss. "Ledbetter, you've never been concerned about anyone besides yourself. Don't lecture me."

"But it's so obvious, isn't it?" Cord said, seeing he'd hit the mark, and he wasn't about to let it go now. "Since when did you become so concerned about him, I wonder? Are you having a change of heart now that the Atrum have abandoned you? Or does this go deeper? Are you finally starting to trust someone other than yourself?"

"It's really none of your business," she said. "But while we're on the topic of *self-improvement*, you could be a little more sympathetic."

Cord narrowed his eyes at her. That didn't sound like the Vail he knew or had known over the years.

Vail continued, a snarky grin on her face now. "The infallible Cord Ledbetter, lecturing me on empathy. I never thought I'd see the day. Your arrogance has no limits. Do you truly think you're above me? You have no idea what I've been through."

Cord sat with his arms crossed and recalled his conversation with Jet. He'd felt Sybold's presence had had a detrimental effect on the Atrum, who had gone missing for the last several years. During that time, the Atrum *had* seemed more cooperative throughout their hunt for the memoirs. But that collaboration had collapsed immediately after the final memoir, just as he'd predicted.

"I'm not judging you, Vail," Cord said.

"Seriously? You expect me to believe that? You don't have the ability to sympathize with anyone. While you're beating me up over my 'shortcomings,' maybe you ought to take a look at yourself for once—"

A loud bang echoed around the vast chamber, and they both sat up.

Beyond, several loading mechs had dropped a crate and were scrambling to pick it up. Cord counted all four Atrum rush over to inspect it, and he wondered what might be inside the crate. Several minutes later, it was hoisted up the side of the pyramid and into the top opening.

Finally, the four Atrum moved out of the chamber and left the area. It was just after dusk, and Cord waited another ten minutes to make sure they were gone. Then, he and Vail cloaked and moved in.

Cord held his war staff within the folds of his cloak to keep it hidden. But he also knew that the M-class mechs could see into other spectrums. They had to race between equipment and across the expansive field to reach the foot of the pyramid. Its base was large, and the hidden switchback staircase was difficult to locate. It wound up the pyramid's large plateaus and toward the apex. But Cord elected to bypass the stairs and simply vault up the large plateaus with Vail right behind him.

Hundreds of troops continued to move supplies and weapons into the pyramid. Cord intended to verify what he needed first, then destroy those supplies. He needed to get inside and make certain the fulcrum matched the others. He wasn't taking any chances. He only hoped Vail would stick with him.

They reached the top of the pyramid, then snuck inside and settled in for a look. It was just as he suspected: this fulcrum's layout matched the others almost exactly. Square shaped floors ringed the inside of the ziggurat with a four-sided staircase spiraling down. At the lowest level was the fulcrum device, and surrounding it was the inner sanctum—a clear spherical-shaped room. Projecting above the fulcrum and over the pyramid was the countdown timer. Crews of mechs and troops marched around inside and barked commands at the loaders. There were hundreds of crates with weapons, armor, and other supplies. Food rations had been brought in along with some larger vehicles. It looked like they were planning to camp out for a while. Cord began to think that the Lucem army should start considering the same thing but didn't know if they could spare the troops.

He settled back and gave Vail a nod. *Time to get to work,* he sent the thought to her.

She gave him a wicked smile, and her eyes glowed a bit brighter.

Cord dropped from his perch and immediately began hammering the M-class mechs, who posed the greatest threat. Vail followed suit and before long the entire area atop the pyramid was in chaos. Troops yelled and ran around, unaware of what was happening. The mechs below fired their propulsion systems and flew up to assist. Cord guessed there were forty or fifty of them. But with their new war staffs, Vail and Cord were making quick work of the units.

The opening into the top of the pyramid was narrow, and they were able to pick off enemy units as they entered. Soon, there was a pile of parts lying around, making entry even more difficult. Cord had noted the new array of weapons the mechs possessed and was thankful for his new staff.

The war staff's EMP pulse was broader and more powerful. When he used the blunted end, it had a greater punch to it. He also seemed to have better awareness around the battlefield now, like there was a voice inside the vessel, warning him of potential dangers. He could see why the Atrum had wanted the vessels so badly, even more than the memoirs. It was a new power, one that could sway the flow of battle if used wisely.

Vail's upgraded staff seemed to be the same, and she handled the opposite side of the entry with similar ease. Ten minutes later, more troops started pouring in. Cord backed up and bumped into Vail. Both were breathing heavily, and Cord felt a bit weak. Though the new staff was more powerful, it also drained his Heliographi quicker, it seemed.

"Let's finish this and get out of here, Ledbetter!" Vail said, trying to catch her breath. "If word gets back, the Atrum might return."

They lifted the crates of supplies and heaved them over the edge of the platform. The weapons, armor, and supplies crashed down to the floor below with a loud bang. They cloaked and hurried from the pyramid as reinforcements showed up, along with more M-Class mechs. But Cord and Vail were already across the field and into the shadowy recesses of the bulkheads beyond.

CHAPTER 30

A Prophesy Unrealized

SOLAN HAD FINALLY located the passage she was looking for. The sketches in the Book of Vishmu were almost too small to see. On the page were the strange crystal looking vessels, hand sketched like some architectural blueprint. Each one was slightly different. Next to them was an avatar, which she assumed was the essence of the Titan it contained, granting each Heliographi their gift. Why Albright had chosen to include only nine vessels in this hunt was a

mystery. Perhaps those were the only ones meant to play a part in his plan.

Below the sketch was a basic diagram of the war

staff. The rudimentary drawing looked like a schematic of sorts, an exploded diagram that showed the vessel attaching to the top of the staff, almost like a headpiece. In fact, the vessel itself was like a small club, or mace perhaps. It appeared that Albright had meant for the two to go together.

But Solan was filling in gaps, guessing at most of it. She felt like she was reading a book with every third word missing. Regardless, from what she could decipher, the jewellike vessels looked like weapons. Two of the vessels caught her attention, though. The white one, which was Jet's, and the black one, which had gone to Sybold. Those two were known as 'primes.'

Solan spent hours poring over the tomb in the candlelight. She searched desperately for information about the staffs and finally found something that drew her interest. Each vessel had been given a name, which she assumed referred to that particular Titan. Jet's staff had been named Port-Shear. The diagram near his staff showed what looked to be an opening…a portal, perhaps. Not long ago, she'd sensed that Jet was a great distance from them now. Was that because he was in another plane of existence?

Or was he on another timeline altogether?

Somehow, she felt that might be the best explanation.

At first, he'd refused to talk about his quest, stating that Albright had asked him not to share it. Could it be that his gift and his vessel were working together somehow?

She rubbed her eyes and sat back, craning her neck, and rubbing it. Solan checked the time to see that she'd been in the stacks the entire night and dawn was near. She lifted the book, flipping it over a few times and wondered if she should bring it to Cord. He'd already scanned through one copy of it, but maybe this one was different? This was, after all, the one her father had given her. But Cord had his own duties, and she didn't want to distract him. Besides, she didn't even know when he'd return.

Regardless, she had to get up and move around. She'd spent too long in the stacks and needed some fresh air to clear her thoughts and think.

Before she left, Solan pulled out her holopad and snapped a holographic image of a passage she'd found on one of the pages. It was in reference to the old legend about *The Serpent and The Prism*. Then she hid the book and finally left the stacks.

Using her alias, she walked out through the front rotunda. Its large stone columns greeted her, and the top façade cantilevered out like wispy feathers. The light mist swirled around her, though the familiar ringing of

Chroma was missing, thanks to the Century Eclipse. The sun was coming up as she walked down the large steps of the library.

There was a different mood around the campus now. It was obvious that strange things were happening around the Skylight System, and even the students and faculty felt it. Though life continued to move on as normal, things weren't normal. Perhaps the faculty felt there was some comfort in a structured schedule or routine. Perhaps it helped keep the students' minds off what might be coming—which was a civil war. Many students had in fact dropped out, or their parents had elected to hold on to their money. It wasn't difficult to see that an education might not be the most important thing right now, and she couldn't blame the citizens for thinking that. Regardless of all the upheaval, Solan still found the campus to be one of the most comforting places. She always enjoyed opportunities to return to Skylight University, as it set her mind at ease.

Solan reflected on her days as a student as she strolled thought the manicured lawns and tree-lined malls. Her time here had been complicated, if not stressful. Like the other Heliographi, dealing with the legend of ephebus mortem had been traumatic. Making it through Skylight University had been like a trial by fire. That ritual had toughened her up in preparation for what she was facing right now, though. Oddly enough, she found herself missing those days.

Solan took her time as she walked the campus, making a few pitstops along the way to ease her troubled mind as she thought about the prophetic passage in the Book of Vishmu.

She eventually found a secluded table near a large oak tree and sat down as students hurried to class. Even though it was still July, the weather was cooler than normal, and it felt like fall might come early. She pulled out her holopad and opened the holographic passage. As she read it again, it was easy to see that this was another prophesy—another riddle.

When the Primes are cradled within the keyhole, the daylight or darkness shall fall to protect or desecrate the meek. One of true intent shall initiate and hold at bay the opposite. Know that a Future without the chosen will render this plane decrepit. Only one can there be. The Serpent Effect will take hold, lest Heaven's Shield initiate and lo will ruin follow the remaining days.

Solan sat back after rereading the passage a few times, her brow furrowed. She switched off her holopad and rubbed her forehead. She felt pressure set in as she thought about everything she'd read in the last twelve hours, and here was this strange riddle to top it all off.

She understood the first phrase. Jet and Sybold had attained the two prime staffs. That part of the prophecy had come to fruition already, thanks to the memoirs being unearthed. The second part of that sentence, she thought might be referring to the fulcrums. Cord had mentioned that any Heliographi staff could ignite a fulcrum, but this passage made it sound like only a prime could set something in motion. Was that referring to something much larger though?

But it was the third phrase that caught her attention. The word 'future' stood out because it was capitalized.

The Future…

She thought again about Port-Shear. Jet had been sent on a quest by Albright, he'd told her as much. So, where was he? Or perhaps the better question was, *when* was he? Once again, her suspicion was telling her what she had already guessed. Jet was on another timeline.

However, it was the fourth and final phrases that sent a chill through her.

Only one can there be. The Serpent Effect will take hold, lest Heaven's Shield be initiated and lo will desecration follow the remaining days.

Only one…

That, she guessed, was a reference to the great war of The Serpent and The Prism.

If ever there was an ominous omen, here it was. She didn't have to read between the lines on that. Though she didn't know what the Serpent Effect was, or

Heaven's Shield, both appeared to be tied to the primes, Jet and Sybold.

If Jet was in another plane, or timeline, maybe there *was* something she could do to help him. A sudden inspiration took her, and she rifled through her cloak and brought out the Lucem badge. She held it to the sunlight, a look of disdain on her face. She'd never wanted it, but her father had forced her to accept leadership. Now, she would use it to send what help she could. Solan felt pretty certain now that Jet would not be back in time to meet Fritt's deadline. And if he didn't return, she wouldn't have much need for the badge anyway. On the back, she plugged in the digital code for the one thing she knew would survive an apocalypse. It was also the one thing that might help him achieve his goal, whatever that might be.

K

When Solan made it back to the control suite, Ti-Leer was slumped forward, his head on the old table and he was snoring. Solan bumped the table, and Ti-Leer sat upright, pulling his mop of hair back and out of his lime-green glowing eyes.

"Ti." Solan nudged his chair. "Why aren't you with Cord? How long have you been back?"

Ti-Leer took a second to orient himself. "Oh…let me see." He started counting on his fingers, then subtracted a few. "One…no, two days. Hold on a tick—"

Solan held up a hand. "Why aren't you still with Cord?"

"Well, he…uh. He booted me in favor of that pretty lass. Can you believe that!"

"What? Are you referring to Vail?" Solan asked, her eyebrows coming to a point.

"Aye. She was dumped at that fulcrum. Was it number two? I think it was number two. Speakin' of number two, I need to take care of something—"

"Ti," Solan said, trying to calm her frustration. "There's no time. Just tell me what happened."

Ti-Leer lowered his voice. "Well, mind you, Cord asked me not to say anything."

Solan waited, her arms crossed.

"Of course, neither of us were certain. But it sure looked like her."

Solan leaned in, placing her hands on the table. "Who? Vail?"

Ti-Leer shook his head several times.

Solan held out her hands impatiently.

"Sybold," Ti-Leer whispered and looked around suspiciously.

"You saw Sybold? Are you positive?"

"Listen to me, lass. I got the chill in me when I saw that shadow. It was her, by the hair of my beard…it was Sybold. She's back."

Solan brought a hand to her brow and rubbed her forehead. "Did Cord say what his plans were with Vail?"

"Not really, but he wanted to be alone with her. He had somethin' on his mind, maybe a little R & R with the pretty lass. I know it's what I'd—"

"No. He's trying to figure out what's happening."

"Yeah, maybe that's it, too," Ti-Leer said.

Solan shook her head again then counted on her fingers. "Cord's chasing fulcrums with Vail. Jinn's with Dane and Linon and we haven't heard a peep from them. Kamber's overseeing the rest of the evacuations. Jet's missing, and without him, we will lose the Dreadnaught's support." Solan sat down, her head in her hands. She tugged at her dark hair and tried to remain calm. Everything had gone to hell in a handbasket, it seemed. She felt a moment of panic, those old insecurities of poor leadership suddenly hit her. But she pushed the moment of weakness away and balled her fists.

"Ti. Do me a favor," she said.

Ti-Leer hopped anxiously to his feet, then steadied himself. "What can I do?"

"Let's see if we can help Jinn. I feel like she's the one who'll need it the most. I don't think we can do anything for Jet at the moment. I have no idea where

Cord is, but he can handle Vail. Kamber should be fine, I hope. But we need Dane back here. His leadership in the upcoming wars will be crucial. Plus, these people see him as their natural leader, not me. Go find them but stay in your guise. Got it? I'll follow up with some transports later."

"I'm on it." Ti-Leer turned and marched out but stopped and looked back at her from the doorway. "Solan, what're you planning, if you don't mind me askin'?"

She held his gaze, not sure if she should say anything just yet. "I'm…staying here, in case someone needs me."

Ti-Leer lowered his eyes at her. "Lass. I know you too well. Be honest with me."

Solan let out a long sigh, then nodded. "I'm going to find my half-sister, Joshia."

CHAPTER 31

The Prize Fighter

DIJINN KNELT IN the dark, both fists on the paving as she stared at the dead recon soldiers. She wanted to scream. She'd fallen for the oldest trick in the book and left her team. Now, these soldiers had been killed because of her. Worse yet, it seemed that Dane and Linon had been taken captive. She'd never forgive herself if Dane ended up dead, and neither would Solan. Dane might be one of the most important people in their camp at the moment. The fulcrum wars were already tipped against them.

She lingered a moment longer, wishing she could at least give the men and women a proper burial. But she didn't have the time. Instead, she gave them a moment of silence, then slipped back into the shadows. Now, she was going to be forced to use every bit of her ability to figure a way out of this. She was on her own now and couldn't afford any more mistakes.

Her first order of business was to find Dane. Maybe Linon would be with him if she was lucky. It was likely that she would miss her deadline now. Solan was going to be furious.

DiJinn worked her way back down the cliff face and toward the lower ARC district. When she reached the main thoroughfares, she used her disguise to blend into the markets. The bartering was loud and raucous, even at this late hour. She returned to the arena district and scanned the cages. Since the pit fights ran nonstop, no one bothered to ask any questions as she browsed through the fighters. This underground district seemed to never sleep, and she had lost all sense of time. She was tired and stressed, after what had just happened. But the thought of Dane in shackles angered her, and fresh adrenaline gave her a boost. Dane would be forced to fight to the death, of course. A man with his background and experience would be placed in the pits immediately.

H

Hours passed, and DiJinn found no leads. There were hundreds of arenas in the lower district, maybe even thousands. She felt a moment of despair set in. The adrenaline had worn off, and now she was just plain tired. She needed to step aside and do some meditation and recharge her Heliographi. But there was no place with any privacy, and she doubted she could fall into a trance with all the commotion anyway. But as she continued to think about Dane, she realized he would likely be placed as a prize fighter. His notoriety alone would draw a huge crowd. Even down here and away from the Skylight System, Dane was well-known, and his accomplishments were legendary. DiJinn felt that if he had been traded off, any wealthy petitioner would make a fortune placing him in top fights.

She needed to find the more affluent pits. There had to be a VIP arena somewhere. She stopped into a market, found the sales booth, and propped an elbow on it. She found a cheap knife, which was more of a sharp piece of metal and slid it across the counter. The storekeeper eyed her, his gaze lingering on her a bit too long. She noticed something oozing from one of his eyes and frowned in disgust.

"Anything else for ya, sweetheart?" the man asked.

DiJinn pushed the knife closer to him. "Yeah. Where can I find the prizefighter pits, the good ones?"

The man chuckled and took the knife. He scanned it. "Lass, I don't think you can afford the cost of admission. Now, I can direct you to the right place to make some extra credits, maybe some favors, if you like?"

"I can cover the fee." She slid a hundred credits over to him to pay for the cheap knife and watched his eyes grow wide.

"Right then. You want to head down the main thoroughfare. At half a kilometer, take a hard right and follow the lights. Ya can't miss the main arena."

DiJinn reached for the knife. The man slapped his hand over hers and held it tight. "Where'd ya get so many credits, love? I wonder…" The man licked his lower lip as he ogled her.

She wanted to reach out and strangle the middle-aged man. "That's really none of your concern. I'd advise you to keep your hands in your pockets, where they're safe and warm."

The man held her gaze, narrowed his eyes, then smiled. "Of course, love. You be careful out there. It's a rough place."

DiJinn gave him a wry smile, which drew a leer from the man as he turned to the next customer in line.

DiJinn left the store, dropping the knife in the trash as she stepped onto the busy street. She followed the man's directions, realizing that it would take her at least twenty minutes to walk the half-kilometer distance, thanks to the dense crowd. She was also aware of the group of thugs following her. Once she turned the corner, she ducked into a side alcove and vanished. It killed her to do it, though. She felt her frustration boiling over. She was upset about her situation, the storekeeper's attitude, losing Dane and Linon, and of course, the murdered recon troops. She wanted— *needed*—to release some frustration, and these thugs deserved a few broken arms. A fight would set her at ease.

But she couldn't afford to draw attention to herself right now. Maybe later, she could return and teach them a lesson.

The six thugs passed by her location, returned, and seemed confused by her sudden disappearance. She waited a few minutes until they finally gave up and left.

DiJinn continued on and finally noticed the bright lights ahead. There, she could see a huge arena constructed of iron and stone. It *was* hard to miss, just as the storekeeper had said. Large steel gates crossed the front and stone walls on the sides, which funneled the long lines inside. The clientele here was definitely a step up. Nicer clothing, highbrow hats, clean-cut hair and faces. She made an adjustment to her alias and matched the 'snootier' garb. At the gate, she paid the twenty credits and moved toward the main entrance. There was another admission fee to the box seats, which she paid.

Once inside, she scanned the schedule of fights. Sure enough, she saw what she had suspected.

Dane was one of the top bills.

The arena and surroundings were crammed with spectators. It was like some ancient coliseum from the past. She found a seat and settled in, trying to devise a strategy as the fighters faced off below her. The brutality disgusted her, and she had a hard time sitting through it. She felt instant pity for the men and women. Like the fight she had witnessed with Patrick, only blunt weapons were given. Some matches were just bare knuckles.

She wanted to leap into the arena but doubted she could take on so many people. Though there weren't many troops she could see, there were enough bouncers to prevent her from just leaping in and freeing the fighters. There were hundreds, maybe even thousands, with guards mixed in as well. That would be a suicide mission. If she had three or four other Lucem, perhaps. She was going to have to think of something else.

An hour or so passed when the announcer's voice boomed around the large arena. The crowd erupted and stood to their feet. She looked toward one of the entryways and saw Dane being pushed in. His shirt had been ripped away, showing his broad shoulders and the scars down his back and chest. The tattoos and insignias from his military service seemed to glow in the ruddy light. There was no mistaking who he was, and it appeared that word had spread rapidly through the underground district. These wealthy citizens were here to see Dane.

He stopped in the center as a huge man was brought in. He had a club in one hand and appeared to be a crowd favorite. The announcer bellowed, welcoming the crowd. Dane was cheered when his name was announced. DiJinn felt her heart drop again at seeing him in such a state. She hated these people for cheering as Dane stood there, his head bowed and shoulders slumped forward in defeat. Her eyes stung as she watched, but inside, she was screaming. She wanted to rush to his side and help him.

A gong sounded, and the large bruiser of a man began circling Dane. But he stood like a statue, ignoring the man. DiJinn felt her heart leap to her throat when she understood what was happening.

Was Dane planning to sacrifice himself?

Was it because of his murdered troops? Was he blaming himself for their deaths?

It was all she could do to settle herself and watch what happened next.

When Dane finally looked up, he smiled at the large man and said something.

DiJinn's worried expression slowly faded, and then she grinned. *Like hell Dane was giving up*. She should know better.

Dane held out his hands in a plea for calm as the other fighter sneered at him. He was at least twice

Dane's size and much broader. They circled each other among the cheers from the crowd.

But Dane's offer was ignored. The man moved in and tackled him. Dane rolled expertly out of the way, slipping deftly from the slower man. DiJinn found herself watching with some amusement now. At first, she'd been worried by Dane's body language. Of course, that had been a decoy.

She had very little concern for Dane at this point. He was a seasoned fighter with a mental fortitude very few humans could match. He had decades of hand-to-hand fighting. He'd survived some of the harshest conditions of war one could imagine. As far as humans went, Dane was one of the deadliest men she'd ever met. He would be a champion in this environment; she might even have trouble convincing him to leave. Her concern now was for the other man in the arena. He was simply a slave, captured and probably tortured into fighting, though she could see he was enjoying it. If Dane grew too upset, he could end this citizen's life in a matter of seconds. She didn't want that, and neither did Dane.

The fighter moved in again, rushing clumsily with his head down. Dane threw his first blow, but even she could see he was holding back. Still, that blow stunned the large man and would likely have incapacitated an average fighter. The first look of fear settled on the behemoth's face as he stood slowly and shook his head. Then his face turned red, and he charged again. DiJinn caught the hint of a smile on Dane's face as he clasped his hands together and hammered on the man's collarbone. There was a loud crack, and the man fell forward in pain. Dane wrapped an arm around his neck and applied enough pressure to render him unconscious as the crowd roared in glee.

DiJinn turned, a slight grin on her face. *Oh yeah, Dane was having fun.* He'd be fine until she could return. Now she could focus on finding Linon and his son, Patrick.

H

DiJinn considered waiting to see if she could make eye contact with Dane. But he was immediately whisked away by an armed escort.

Instead, she returned to the holding caverns beyond. Thousands of rusted cages sat stacked and packed tight with other pit fighters. DiJinn slipped the gatekeeper a dozen credits and walked in. She didn't know exactly what she was looking for, but followed her instinct and it led her through the labyrinth of cells. Eventually, she turned down a dark, dead-end row. At the end was a cage set apart. Inside was a man with long dark hair and a matching curly beard. He lay propped against the bars, head bowed. DiJinn approached and tapped lightly on the cage, trying not to startle the man. His head snapped up, and he focused on her instantly.

"Patrick?" DiJinn whispered.

The man nodded with one eye narrowed suspiciously. "What do you want?"

"I'm a friend of your father. I'm here with him to set you free."

Patrick lunged forward and gripped the bars of the cage. "My…father? I thought he was dead. Is this a joke?"

"He's here. We came to rescue you."

"Why isn't he with you?"

DiJinn paused for a split second. She still didn't know if Linon had survived the ambush. "We got separated. I wanted to let you know he's here. I'll get you out. I made a promise to your father."

"Is my father in danger? Who are you?"

DiJinn removed her ring, and her alias faded. A look of shock and awe stole across Patrick's expression. He gasped as he stared into her glowing eyes.

"So, it's true," Patrick whispered. "The Heliographi are real. That must mean…that my father is involved in the search for the memoirs."

"That search is over. War is beginning up top, and we need his help. That war will soon bleed over into all corners, even down here. I need to find him and get you out. That was our agreement."

"Can you tell me your name at least?"

"My name is Jinnie Dinn. You can call me DiJinn."

"DiJinn. I'm grateful for your help. But I'm afraid I can't leave."

She let out a heavy sigh. "Why is that?"

"These people are slaves against their will. I'm their unspoken leader and won't leave them behind."

Great! DiJinn thought. *Why can't things ever be easy?* "Patrick, we don't have time. I need to have you and the others up top by day's end. The first fulcrum war begins soon—"

"These people may be able to help you. There are hundreds of thousands of hardened fighters here. They'll listen to me."

A slow smile eased across DiJinn's face. "History has a way of repeating itself."

"What do you mean?"

"We went through the same thing with your father. He refused to leave his people behind as well. We'll need a plan."

"I have communications with everyone. We talk through code. I can have word sent out and be ready within the hour if need be."

"Our biggest issue is gonna be transporting everyone."

Patrick considered. "There are so many fighters, we can easily overwhelm the militia. In fact, there's been a decrease in their presence lately. We just need out of these cages. Most of the prime-time fights take place tonight. If you can wait until then, we should get an eight-hour window."

DiJinn held his gaze in the dark. "Send the word out. I'll have the transports ready. But I still need to find your father, and I have no idea where to start."

Patrick smiled. "I think I might. When I was a child, there was a playground he used to take me to. It's at Peripheral Heights, along the upper rim—"

There was a commotion in the next row over. DiJinn saw guards moving between the cages, checking the locks. She pulled her hood over her head and disappeared as the game wardens moved in, cuffed Patrick, and led him away for his fight.

CHAPTER 32

A Clue Amidst the Madness
January 18, 2287, A.D.

JET HAD A CLEAR GOAL NOW.

He needed to discover what lay at the other end of the strange energy bolt. What he might find there frightened him, though.

Jet stood and walked around the clear globe of the inner sanctum one more time as Sember sat quietly.

"Well, we might as well get started. I want to stop at each belt along the way. I need to see each fulcrum."

"I don't understand," she said. "So far, it seems like they're all identical."

"I can't explain. It's just a feeling I get," Jet said. "Besides, They're on the way. Maybe there's a clue I'm meant to see."

Sember stood to her feet and nearly fell down again. Jet steadied her. "That blast caught me off guard."

"Yeah, sorry about that," Jet said and helped her up the stairs. "Probably could've given you some warning."

They made the long trek to the belt's surface. He used the Lucem badge to enter the Armada and set a course to the next belt.

Jet slumped back in his seat as the battle cruiser rose steadily over the ruined skyline of the third belt. He was glad to be moving on now. It was sad to see the once-tall structures reduced to rubble. The pride of the Skylight System had been erased and would never be rebuilt in this world.

Jet and Sember said little on their trip to the fourth belt. His mind was preoccupied with questions. At least he knew where he was going, but he still wasn't sure what he would face. He laid his head back and closed his eyes as that question swirled in his thoughts.

What would Cutter do?

Jet drifted off. In his dreams, he thought about the sickness—*the bloodlust*. He had felt it back in the present-day Skylight as well, though it hadn't been as powerful then. Now, it was almost unbearable. He felt an impending doom in the air, and it was growing worse the closer he got to the outer belts. He could hear low frequencies surrounding him, barely perceptible. Little vibrations that screamed and clawed at him. They passed through his body, darkening his soul and mind. In his dream, these demons brought pain and madness. Behind them, looming on the horizon, something evil lurked with searching red eyes. The same red eyes he'd once seen as a student four years ago, yet that red was now a sinister shade of midnight, a bottomless well of malice.

Jet sat up, and his eyes fluttered open. Sember was standing near him, shaking his arm.

"Are you okay?" she asked, but with little emotion.

Jet craned his head and rubbed his neck. "How long was I asleep?"

"Ten minutes, maybe." Sember tossed a packet to him and a bottle. "I found some rations and water. The ship seems to have been stocked with food by someone. Lucky us, right?"

"Yeah, lucky," Jet said, thinking again of Solan. "You seem to be an expert at surviving. How?"

"I'm designed for it. I require less food when I need to hibernate, so I can go long periods without sustenance. But my abilities are dulled when I do."

"Is it like flipping a switch?"

"Yeah, something like that."

He opened the ration and sniffed it. He should be starving, but he wasn't. Everything felt congested, like his mind was shutting down or something. Was it the sickness setting in? Maybe it was finally having an effect on him, just slower than others? He could only assume that his gift was protecting him, keeping him on life support perhaps. Or maybe he was simply experiencing depression from all the death and destruction? In the back of his mind, he couldn't stop blaming himself. If he'd only made it back in time, maybe he could have prevented all of this. He was beginning to wonder what to believe, though. Surely, Port-Shear wasn't just for transporting him to alternate planes of existence.

Sember seemed to notice his mood and laid a hand on his shoulder again. "We're approaching the fourth belt. Where should we land?"

Jet pointed out the front window of the Armada and at the black bolt of lightning. "At the source. Let's see if anything's different here."

They landed near the opening in the belt where the bolt arced upward. It was in one of the smaller port cities. Jet's holopad read, *Hominee.* He pulled on the respirator mask and stepped onto the charred ground of the port city. Blackened tree stumps lined the streets and cottages glowed red from the flames. Jet led the way, eventually finding a route down into the belt's hull. The heat diminished as they traversed down, but it was replaced by an oppressive humidity. He felt sweat soak his clothes as they walked down hundreds of flights of stairs.

Eventually, they found the black bolt and followed the light from it. Soon, the silhouette of the stepped pyramid loomed in the distance like some grimdark nightmare. As they crossed the battlefield of metal and steel and dead troops, Jet began to feel nauseous. Smoking craters and husked-out vehicles clogged their way, forcing them to reroute numerous times.

Jet felt like he was sleepwalking at times. He was tired, but there was something sinister clouding his vision now. He could only assume the 'bloodlust' was growing stronger with each step he took closer to the source.

Twenty minutes later, they topped the pyramid and were about to enter when Jet stopped. He dropped to his knees in shock and grief.

Lying face down was Ti-Leer.

Jet pulled at him and turned him over. Ti-Leer's face was like Solan's—a vacant white stare, his body bruised and broken. Jet buried his face in Ti-Leer's cloak and screamed in anger.

Sember stood next to Jet, silent.

He sat there for a long time, not wanting to leave. Sember finally knelt and sat across from Jet, a blank look on her face. He could see that she was uncomfortable and not sure what to say or do. Jet lifted Ti-Leer's body and walked down to the bottom of the pyramid, where he laid him down. When he set Ti-Leer on the metal floor, his silver flask tumbled out.

Jet picked it up and smiled and wiped his cheeks. "Ti-Leer's flask, password protected, of course." Jet held it up to the light, the bolt illuminating the cold walls of the orb-like sanctum. On the front of Ti-Leer's flask was a date etched into it: *July 1, A.D. 2286*. Jet chuckled, remembering that Ti-Leer had done so to prevent himself from forgetting Albright's directive. Jet tucked it into his cloak. Then he lifted Ti-Leer's body and tossed it over the rail and into the lightning bolt. The body was vaporized instantly, a cloud of ash swirled upward in the warm air current and floated out of sight.

Jet leaned heavily on the railing, feeling the weight of the events bear down on him. He already knew his friends were dead, but seeing them was difficult. In the back of his mind, he worried that he might see more of them as he visited each fulcrum. He hated to think about seeing Cord or Kamber now and tried to push the thought away.

As he stared at the clear globe of the inner sanctum below, he noticed something. Near the area of the memoir was a symbol he hadn't seen before, mostly because it was so large. It was partially hidden behind the other glyphs and symbols surrounding the sanctum, almost as if it had been designed to blend in unnoticed.

"What is that?" Jet said and leaned over the rail and pointed at it. The symbol was large and etched into the glass in Greek. "I think it's the Greek letter I."

"Not sure I see it," she said. "Are you certain?"

"Yeah. I've been converting Greek since I joined the Lucem." Jet hopped over the rail and dropped down five meters, with Sember making the leap right behind him. He reached out and traced the emblem with his hand. The Greek symbol was about a meter tall and etched into the ten-meter spherical wall of the inner sanctum. The letter 'I' seemed to be highlighted among the other engravings now that he focused on it. Yet it was composed of the other tiny etchings surrounding it, like some cryptic collage. This explained why he hadn't noticed any of the others before. There was clearly some significance to it.

"What do you make of it?" Sember asked. "It's pretty obvious, now that I see it."

But Jet could only shake his head. "I assume we just missed the others, since all the fulcrums are similar."

"Should we go back and check?" Sember asked. But he could tell that she didn't want to.

"No, I don't think we have time." Jet glanced up. The lightning bolt shot straight up through the surface of the belt's hull some three hundred meters above. The sky's foreboding red and unearthly flames made him feel even more anxious. They were getting closer to the source. Something was feeding those flames. Something ancient and evil.

"Are you okay?" Sember asked.

Jet leaned on his staff, a moment of weakness took hold and he had to steady himself. A sudden realization hit him then.

He was dying.

"This place—" Jet paused and straightened. "I can't sustain it, Sember. I'm not meant to be here."

She looked at him, seemingly unfazed. But he sensed her shock and confusion. "I thought you said you were meant to be here?"

"I was meant to *see* something here. But I feel out of place in this future world. I know it now. I've already died once in this timeline. Somewhere out there is my body lying in a field of ash. I don't know how long I have, and I don't know how I'm supposed to get back." He took a deep breath. "Come on, we need to move. Time is running out."

M

They boarded the Armada and moved out of the fourth belt's air space. The heat increased as they moved toward the outer belts. He was constantly in a deep sweat, it seemed, like a fever was setting in. He slouched in his seat, unable to get comfortable. Sember gave him concerned looks as she took over the piloting.

Before long, they were approaching the fifth belt. It had been used for carbon sequestering, once resplendent with trees and forests to balance the synthetic atmosphere.

Jet roused himself and stood slowly as the Armada settled down on the belt's surface. When he stepped through the gangway, a heat wave hit him in the face. He struggled to take in a sharp breath through the mask's respirator. The temperature had indeed increased, and he braced himself as he pushed through the oppressive heat. They located the black lightning bolt on the horizon and hurried through the charred remains of the once-green forests. Some of the old lumber mills stood silhouetted in the blackened landscape like skeletal remains.

It took twenty minutes to find access to the hull below, and Jet walked as quickly as he could down the metal stairs. He could feel his strength fading as they worked their way below. Sweat poured down his forehead as the smell of burning materials filled the air. Black smoke made visibility difficult. Eventually, they located the fulcrum.

Jet stood next to Sember as they looked over the railing. Beyond and just above the encased memoir, he made out the Greek symbol of the letter 'R'.

M

It was a struggle for Jet to make it back to the Armada this time. It took twice as long, and he leaned on his staff as they trudged through the ash and ruin. Once aboard, Sember set a course to the sixth belt. Jet settled into his seat and wrapped himself in his cloak. He was shivering now, and his fever was getting worse. His dark hair was soaked with sweat and clumped to his forehead and neck.

Jet slept during the flight to the sixth belt. He was trusting in Sember and thankful that he'd found her now. Otherwise, he wouldn't have made it much farther. He found himself wondering if fate had aligned their paths.

When they made landfall on the sixth belt, he could barely stand. He took several minutes, closing his eyes and meditating, trying to find the strength.

"Jet," Sember said and gripped his arm. "Why don't you let me do this? I can go verify the symbol. Don't force yourself to—"

"No, Sember." Jet sat up and used his staff to push out of the chair. He wavered, and she steadied him. "I need to see it. I feel like this is something I need to do. Besides, if I don't keep moving, I may not be able to later. I need this."

She nodded and opened the gangway of the Armada. She tried to help him, but Jet held up a hand. "Let me try, please."

Like the fifth belt, this one had also been part of the Skylight System's carbon sequestering. It broke Jet's heart to see the destruction when he stepped off the ramp. There was so much red and black choking the horizon that it seared his vision. The sickness he felt in the air was mentally suffocating. As his fever had increased, so had the feeling of doom. He began to wonder if he would survive long enough to even see what this 'source' was. As they moved closer to the source, his struggles continued to worsen. But this was no longer about him. It was about those back home who were counting on him to survive. Though he wanted to collapse and just wait for the end to come, he couldn't let them down. That thought strengthened his resolve.

Yet, he also wondered why his gift was failing to protect him now. Why was he feeling so weak? Yes, he was a being out-of-place, and yes, the real Jet Stroud was likely dead in this future world. Right now, he was an imposter, an unnatural deposit in this apocalyptic world. But he didn't think any of those were the real cause of his sickness. There was another reason, one he knew he'd find if he could make it to the source.

CHAPTER 33
Partners in Crime

CORD AND VAIL raced from the sixth belt's fulcrum and up one of the stairwells as M-class mechs began to flood into the area. Their ambush had caught Lybra's forces completely by surprise. Soon, they were in Cord's jammer and rocketing toward the fifth belt.

Cord plugged in the coordinates. If the Atrum and Lybra were already setting up bases at their own fulcrums on belts five through eight, then he wondered if they might be trying to secretly do the same at the

Lucem's fulcrums one through four. At the very least, the Lucem needed to consider the same tactic. Cord was kicking himself a bit—he should have been thinking ahead like that. But he was too focused on finding the fulcrum locations right now.

Vail let out a heavy sigh.

"Something on your mind?" Cord said. "You obviously want some attention. Let's hear it."

"Isn't it obvious?" Vail said. "If we're hunting another fulcrum, you can expect the same resistance, especially after our little raid," Vail said. "Why bother lookin'?"

"Nonetheless, we will continue. If we plan to challenge the fulcrum's polarity, we need to know their locations."

"Please, Ledbetter," Vail huffed. "You think the Lucem actually stand a chance of stopping anything?"

"Quite frankly, I do."

Vail glared and gave him a side smirk. "Well, that's adorable. But let me tell you something. I know what they have; I've seen Lybra's inventory. You are overmatched, especially with the Atrum joining the Agency now. It'll be a bloodbath, and Sybold hasn't even shown her face yet. My advice is to conserve your troops and defend your fulcrums, 'cause you're gonna need all your resources. Just let the Atrum have their fulcrums."

"I don't believe they'll settle for just theirs. Sitting back and waiting seems ill-advised. Mind if I ask when you became a military tactician, though?"

Vail rolled her eyes. "I've *seen* her forces, Ledbetter. The Lucem can't win if they attack."

"I don't agree with your philosophy, Vail."

"Listen to me, you arrogant fool. You need to prevent Solan from attacking."

Cord noticed the hint of desperation in her tone, which was something new.

"Do you want to see more death and destruction?" she continued. "We've had enough of that questing for the memoirs."

Cord gave Vail a long look. "Am I really talking to the same Vail Hart? You've changed, there's no denying it now. Why do you care what happens to us?"

Vail's skin flushed a bright red and she immediately turned away. Cord had never seen Vail act this way. She was actually embarrassed *because* of her concern, and considering she'd sworn an oath against the Lucem made it even more intriguing.

"I appreciate the fact that we're not friends, Vail. We've never been close. You dislike me, and I don't care for your company. That said, you *can* talk to me."

"And what good would that do? You have no sympathy, empathy, or ability to console me. You wouldn't understand."

"Perhaps we can help each other then."

Vail narrowed her eyes at Cord. She smiled at him, then started laughing. It was a low giggle at first, then it turned into a full belly laugh. Cord didn't know how to react at first. He gripped the controls tighter, looked from her to the flight gauges, then back to her. Soon, Vail was in tears.

"Mind if I enquire what the *hell* is so funny?"

Between gasps, Vail managed to eke out a sentence. "You…you think you can…help me? You actually think…you could understand my problems?"

Cord simply shook his head and looked away. "Why do I even bother?" he muttered.

Eventually, Vail's laughter settled down and she wiped her eyes. "Can I just be honest with you, Ledbetter?"

"I'd prefer it no other way," Cord said, not looking at her.

"Fine. I can't believe I'm even sayin' this, but…"
Cord faced her. "Go on."

Vail took a moment and wiped her eyes again. She cleared her throat as if pressing into a more serious mode. "Well…you're right. I have changed. I'm not sure when, but…I guess I do care about—*some* of you, that is."

Cord shook his head and chuckled. "Another game of yours? We really don't have time for this, Vail."

"Truth is, Ledbetter, I *do* care about my friends. Yes, you heard me—my friends! That includes Stroud and

Bo…and you. I realized something the day Cutter was murdered. They say that the light of a Heliographi exists along a spectrum. Some of those lights are morally gray, while others exist along extremes, like Sybold and Stroud. I feel like mine and yours aren't so different. I may be on the darker side, but I can do things that other Atrum can't. I realized that I *can* care for others, and that I *can* feel emotions like sorrow and regret."

Cord listened to Vail but held his expression in check. Inside, he was shocked that Vail was actually admitting this to him, of all people. Since he'd known her over the last four and a half years, she had never shared anything personal with him. It was something he thought he'd never witness.

"Go ahead!" she snapped. "Act like you didn't just hear me. But I know you did. And you *know* I'm right. Our Heliographi are similar in nature."

Cord was still at a loss for words, something he wasn't used to. He felt suddenly out of place—shy and nervous as he sat next to her. Was this yet another trick from Vail to gain his trust?

Why was Vail really here? Sybold should have killed her.

Cord straightened in his seat. "I'm not sure what you want me to say. You claim to care about your friends. Am I to suddenly believe after all the things you've done that you've switched sides?"

"I was under an influence, one that's grown lately. I know that's hard to get through your head, but it's true.

Sybold's back, and she means to rend this system apart. Maybe my Heliographi has decided to fight that impulse? Maybe *that's* why Sybold really dumped me and left me for dead—"

"Negative, Vail," Cord said. "There's another reason Sybold released you. She's waiting for something."

"Fine, Brainiac. What's she waitin' for, then?"

"The right time," Cord said, his voice unwavering. "Sybold is waiting for the right time to let you die."

Vail didn't respond at first. Her eyes grew wide, and her skin blanched slightly. Then she sat back and rubbed her forehead. "Forget it, Ledbetter. I thought you could help me figure this out."

"What you're saying does make some sense. Maybe we can do some more research back at our base."

"So, you're okay bringing me back to the Lucem?"

"What did you think I would do?" Cord asked. "Abandon you right here with no place to go?"

"I would expect no less," Vail said with a familiar hint of sarcasm.

"Well…perhaps we're both changing," Cord muttered. "Not sure I'm agreeable with it, though."

"Yeah. Me neither," Vail retorted, but there was a different tone in her voice this time."

Cord kept his gaze locked straight ahead. He didn't think he could look at Vail at that moment. He was feeling something he'd never experienced before. But he was still leaning toward caution.

"What about the fulcrum wars?" Vail asked.

"What about them?" Cord said, his walls up again. He wasn't ready to share any secrets just yet.

"What do you think will happen?"

"Exactly what one would expect with war: death and destruction. Not a pretty picture."

Ahead, they were approaching the fifth belt. Materializing through the thick mist, the outline of it solidified. Early morning sunlight gleamed through the clouds, and tiny prism effects lit their surroundings.

"One last fulcrum," Cord muttered and slowed his jammer.

The fifth belt was forested and thick with trees. Though it was really a transitional belt, having a modest population, there were pockets of activity sprinkled about. Port cities and resorts were sparsely woven between the rivers and forest.

He found a clearing and settled down. Nearby, a large exhaust vent poked through the lush green carpet of grass. Vail followed him inside and down. Daylight punched through some areas of overgrown vegetation but grew dimmer as they dropped through the levels.

Fifteen minutes later, Cord found the fulcrum. It was similar to the others, and Agency troops marched around. He felt they'd made it there before any alarms had been set off from their last raid. Fortunately, he didn't see any mech units or Atrum. "Let's go before reinforcements arrive," he said.

They slipped in unnoticed, then scaled up the side of the pyramid and to the top. Cord dropped about twenty levels and stood near the fulcrum, inspecting it closely.

"Looks the same, Ledbetter," Vail chided. "Nothin' out of place here. Let's be off." But then she backpedaled and moved closer to the fulcrum. "Wait. What's this?" She leaned in for a closer look.

Cord took his war staff and placed it in the keyhole in the floor. It glinted in the dim light. The end of his war staff was a perfect fit. "This is what will ignite the fulcrum, in theory. Any of our staffs will work on fulcrums two through seven."

"What about the other two? One and eight?"

Cord gave her a long look. "It appears that those are special, reserved for your esteemed leader or our good friend, Jet."

CHAPTER 34
The Honest Truth

ΑΒ Δ Ζ ΗΘΙΚΛ

ΝΞΟΠΡΣ ΥΦ ΨΩ

AFTER SENDING TI-LEER off to find Jinn, Solan sent a message to Joshia using their 'backchannel.' It was one they'd established during their hunt for the memoirs. Solan hoped that Joshia had maintained it, assuming she'd even answer her.

Joshia had maintained it, and she did answer.

They both agreed to meet at the wreckage site of Chroma, which was still under repair from its collapse during the Century Eclipse. Solan felt safer meeting

349

there. She didn't think Joshia would try to harm or capture her. Then again, she didn't know what to expect, now that Sybold was in the mix. Joshia was her half-sister, but still an Atrum. Solan was placing a lot of trust in the fact that they were sisters, especially considering the Atrum had just betrayed them. That had set the Lucem back considerably, all because Solan *had* 'trusted' the Atrum.

Solan left the control suite and stole through the passages of Lyrinthum. Twenty minutes later she neared the construction site of Chroma and slowed. She cautiously made her way to the area where she'd first made the agreement with Joshia to join forces. Had she known the Atrum would betray them and take the memoirs, she'd never have made that deal. But that was in the past, and she needed to focus on the present.

Solan didn't have to wait long. Soon, Joshia's cloaked form dropped from a ruined catwalk above. She moved closer, blurry and shrouded, then materialized in front of Solan. Her stature and appearance were similar to Solan's due to their shared lineage. She was tall with tapered shoulders and an athletic build. Her dark skin stood in contrast with her glowing azure eyes. Her silver hair was highlighted by a red streak and fluttered in the breeze of the wrecked chamber.

"Well, hello, *sister*," Joshia mocked and bowed low.

Solan ignored the sarcasm. "Tomorrow, we start the fulcrum wars. What have you to say?"

"Am I to assume you're here to caution me or frighten me off?"

"Why would you assume that?" Solan crossed her arms as she held her sister's gaze.

Joshia returned her stare. "Shall we cut to the chase? Why did you call me here? Surely not to talk about warnings or intimidation."

Solan gave her a wry smile. "We still haven't resolved the issue facing our race. We're dying off, Joshia. Our inner light is no longer respawning."

Joshia only shrugged. "What do you expect me to say about it?"

"Should I assume that your leader might have something to do with this?"

"What makes you think Sybold is back?"

"Spare me, Joshia," Solan quipped. "I'm not that blind. Why deny it now? We all feel it, her stench is everywhere."

Solan watched Joshia closely, but she remained silent with no expression on her face.

"Do you have anything to say about your betrayal?" Solan continued. "I accepted your offer in good faith. I even brought you the war staffs."

Joshia finally cracked a smile. "It's who we are. You should have known better than to trust us. I do appreciate the war staffs, though."

"Do you have no concern about our Heliographi not respawning?" Solan asked again. "Do you not agree we should work together to fix this at least? It's in both our interests."

Joshia's defiant look finally softened, and she looked away. Solan caught a split second of hesitation. *So, she did know something.*

"Tell me what you know, Joshia," Solan said. "If not for me, then future generations of Heliographi."

"You've heard the legend, I take it?"

"Are you referring to the Serpent and the Prism?" Solan said. "Yes, I know of it."

"It's to be the final war and it's almost upon us. Your so-called leader, Christian Albright, set all of this in motion, along with Shiloe. We tried to find out why she set the Prism Effect in motion—"

"So that's why you held her for so long?" Solan said, her fists balled. "A century of torture to get an answer out of her!"

"Shall we end this conversation now?" Joshia said, raising her voice.

Solan felt enraged. The torture of Shiloe Van Saint *would* not be forgotten. But Solan took a deep breath and lowered her gaze at Joshia. She held out her hand for her to continue.

Joshia began pacing the wreckage, her arms crossed. "I could gather only a few things from Shiloe. Somehow, Albright was able to manipulate the light of our Heliographi in a way that would allow another Heliographi to *collect* it, *not* extinguish it."

Solan narrowed her eyes. "Are you suggesting that Albright and Shiloe worked together to *combine* our Heliographi?"

"That's exactly what I believe."

"And you base this on what? The tortured responses of Shiloe Van Saint?"

Joshia only shrugged. "I didn't start the whole thing; it wasn't my decision to kidnap her. But you can take the information or leave it, sister."

Solan shook her head, trying to think through her disbelief. "It makes no sense. Why in Skylight would Albright do such a thing?"

"Think, Solan," Joshia held out her hands. "You say you've felt it. It's everywhere, in fact. A sickness in the very air we breathe."

Solan understood then. It was like a thunderclap that hit her upside the head.

The final war with Sybold would come soon…

…and Jet Stroud was too weak to face her.

That's why Albright had engineered the second phase of the Prism Effect—to extinguish *all* the Lucem so that Jet could collect their Heliographi. Which meant the same had to be true for Sybold, and Joshia knew it. *Albright was allowing Jet to become a demigod!* But Sybold would be given the same opportunity. Somehow, Albright had known it was the only way Jet would stand a chance against the Atrum leader.

"You're afraid that Sybold knows this?" Solan asked.

"Yes, of course, I'm afraid," Joshia hissed. "You see, Solan. There is no escape for us. The run of the Heliographi finally comes to an end. Our family tree—our lineage and bloodline—stops here. Only one will survive this, and that one will collect *all* twenty-four Heliographi in the end. The lone survivor of our race will become a god."

Solan took a deep breath, then shook her head. "There must be more to it."

"You're wrong, Solan," Joshia said and gripped her shoulders. "This system and this entire plane of existence will be destroyed by the final war. There is no hope for any of us. Christian Albright has doomed us all with his actions. He's a fool for setting the Prism Effect into motion! He's a fool for believing in Jet Stroud! No one can defeat Sybold now."

"Then why are you helping her?" Solan asked, gripping her sister's arm. "If you already know the outcome, why help her?"

Joshia held Solan's gaze, and a tear ran down her cheek. She gave Solan a weak smile. "Because this is my role to play, just like the one you must play. The laws of the universe prevent me from doing otherwise."

K

Solan left Chroma that day with a bittersweet feeling in her soul. Joshia, as conflicted as she was, had told her the truth—she knew that much. Perhaps it was payment for the Atrum's treachery. Stealing the memoirs and war staffs had weighed on Solan since that day. She'd kicked herself for not keeping a closer eye on her half-sister and the other Atrum. But there was no point in worrying about that now, with so much about to happen. At the start of the day, her biggest concern had been tomorrow's war at the seventh belt's fulcrum. The Lucem army would do their best to prevent the Atrum from setting the polarity of the fulcrum. But after talking to Joshia, the fulcrum wars paled in comparison to this news about Jet and Sybold.

Who should she share this information with?

No one, she thought. No one except Jet, if he didn't find out on his own. That was assuming he ever made it back.

Besides, what would it matter? They were all destined to die someday. Her greatest sorrow was that their ancient race would not continue on, though. Albright had indeed taken a big gamble on his design of the Prism Effect. The first phase had shown each Heliographi's true color, dividing them out individually. The second phase had caused the Heliographi *not* to respawn. The third phase would allow the two 'primes' to collect deceased Heliographi souls. But what would the fourth phase bring?

Regardless, she would hold on to this information for as long as she could. As a leader, was it the right thing to do? *Maybe.* Didn't the others have the right to know? *Probably.* But if fate was moving, there was nothing within her power to stop it.

Solan had to play her part in this game and focus on the things she could control, which was preparing her forces for tomorrow's battle. But with Jet, Cord, Jinn, Dane and Linon all missing in action, she didn't know what to expect. They had lost the Dreadnaught's support, she assumed. She only hoped that some of the others would return, because things weren't looking good at the moment.

Solan finally entered the Lyrinthum passages through the Clipton Forest portal. She decided to stroll through the hangar bay and check on preparations and offer what encouragement she could. Most of the troops were training or readying their weapons and armor. All four of the massive battle cruisers were fueled and ready, including the SLS Armada. Its presence would help with morale, but most of the fighting would be inside the belt and around the open field surrounding the fulcrum. The cruisers would be too large to fit into the belt's hull, though the jammers might.

It was growing late when Solan got word of Cord's return. She met him in the control suite and gritted her teeth when she saw Vail standing there with him.

She placed her fists on her hips as she faced the two. "I hope there's a good explanation for this."

Cord gave Solan a sheepish grin and shrugged his shoulders. "I know it looks odd, but maybe you should have a seat so I can explain."

"No, I'll stand." Solan held out a hand, ready to hear what Cord had to say.

Cord retold the story. When he got to the part about the shadowy figure dumping Vail, she paused him, her hand held up. "Wait. You believe that Sybold herself did this?"

"Yes, I do," Cord replied. "Both Ti-Leer and I witnessed it, though we can't completely verify who it was."

Solan turned to Vail. "What's your story?"

Vail gave her a snarky grin and leaned against the rusted bulkhead. "Isn't it apparent that Sybold doesn't want me around?"

"She should have executed you," Solan said. "Why didn't she?"

"Well, we did discuss that," Cord said in his slow drawl and leaned against Albright's table. "Vail seems to believe—"

Solan held up a hand and stopped Cord. She looked directly at Vail. "Why don't we let our new *guest* tell us?"

"Fine," Vail said, but Solan noticed a difference in her tone now. It wasn't the same snarky response she was used to hearing. "It *was* Sybold," Vail continued. "She's back. And to be completely honest, I don't know why she allowed me to live. I guess she didn't kill me because it wasn't the right time."

Solan narrowed her eyes at Vail. She could sense in that instant that Vail *had* changed. "Wasn't the right time? What do you mean?"

Cord spoke up. "I believe that Sybold is waiting. I don't know why just yet. It's a feeling I get."

Solan thought back to her conversation with Joshia that evening, and how she believed that only two Heliographi would be able to collect souls. *Did that have something to do with Vail?*

"So, why should we allow you back?" Solan asked.

Vail shrugged. "Do you not believe me?"

"It's more about what you did recently. I gave you my trust, and you broke that. What do you have to say?"

"What would you have me do?" Vail asked. "If I went against Joshia's order, she would have had Mosstrom kill me, which he would've gladly done. I had no choice."

"Alright. Then what do you propose?" Solan asked.

Vail shrugged again, but she could see the girl's skin flush red. She was embarrassed, maybe even ashamed at that question.

"Solan, if I may," Cord said, breaking the tension. "I propose we allow Vail to join us. If she betrays us again, I will track her down and kill her myself."

Solan and Vail both gave Cord a shocked look.

"Don't look so surprised," Cord muttered. "Yes, you're right to be suspicious, but I feel that Vail is being honest, for once. Killing her shouldn't be necessary."

Vail huffed. "Come on, Ledbetter. I've told the truth before."

"Anyway," Cord continued. "I think it's what Jet would want."

"I never thought I'd see the day where you'd be defending Vail," Solan said with a grin, despite the situation. "Alright, Vail. You're in. Better prepare yourself for the other Lucem, though. They're not going to be happy. Cord, she's your charge now. You'll be responsible for her actions."

"Speaking of Jet, where is he?" Cord asked. "I need to talk to him immediately."

Solan crossed her arms as she sat back. "Well, that's a really good question, Cord."

Cord's eyebrows knit upwards into a point. He brushed his dark hair back, a bit nervously, Solan thought. "What exactly do you mean, Solan?"

"Jet's gone missing, and we have no idea when he will return."

A strange look stole over Cord's face, and Solan knew he had already figured it out.

"You already knew about his so-called quest, I see?" Solan asked, and Cord nodded.

"He'd briefly mentioned something to me," Cord said.

"All we can do now is wait for his return and hope he is fine." Solan turned to face Vail. "Don't cross me again, or I'll make sure Cord carries through on his promise."

CHAPTER 35
The Midnight Riot

ΑΒΓ Δ Ε Ζ <u>Η</u> Θ Ι Κ Λ
ΝΞΟΠΡΣ Τ Υ Φ Χ Ψ Ω

DIJINN MADE HER way to the rim-top neighborhood Patrick had mentioned. She'd thought about sticking around to watch his pit fight but decided against it. It was apparent that he could handle his own affairs, and locating Linon was more important. It was a long shot, but if Linon had managed to escape, she hoped she might find him up here.

DiJinn moved up a narrow switchback trail and checked her coordinates. There were three rim-top neighborhoods that fit Patrick's description, but she'd narrowed it down to two. When DiJinn arrived to the first one, she hunkered down in a dark alcove and surveyed the site. It was high up on a stone ridge that ran perhaps three hundred meters along one side, creating a rim. Below was an impressive vista of the ARC's lower district and just above was the milky white stasis dome. She was so close to it that she could hear the storm beyond. The rain hissed as it pelted the dome and dissipated into a static pop.

DiJinn found the park nestled into the center of the neighborhood like a town square. It was designed for children, with swing sets and a merry-go-round. She assumed this was probably one of the wealthier suburbs, based on the size of the stone houses. She settled into the shadows and watched the kids running and playing as neighbors chatted on benches. It was a completely different environment from the one down below where the men and women were forced to fight for their lives. This area of the ARC district seemed to be separated from reality.

She waited for several hours as nighttime approached, and the neighborhood activity subsided. By the clock, it was near midnight, though one would never know, thanks to the cloud-covered moon. She saw a lone figure walk across the empty thoroughfare and sit in a swing. DiJinn watched the silhouette and knew that it was Linon by his tall, rigid gait, though he had a slight limp. He'd found or stolen some clothing and a hat.

DiJinn gave it a few more minutes, then walked casually out and sat in the swing next to him.

"Nice of you to join me," Linon said without turning. He seemed to be in a different world, though, his tone flat and devoid of emotion.

"What happened?" DiJinn asked.

"They knew I would come for my son. They knew we were there and waited for you to leave. Please tell me I haven't lost my son a second time."

"He's alive," DiJinn said. She was nervous and felt exposed, sitting out in the open like this. "Come with me. We need to find cover. I know where Patrick is."

The look on Linon's face was relief. He let out a sigh and leaned forward in the swing, a slight wince on his face. "Of course, I knew if you could find him, he'd lead you here. I used to take him to this park when he was a child. We couldn't afford such a place, just liked to pretend. I'd hoped he would remember."

"He did. You've raised a good man. I can see that much by the way he cares for you." She glanced at him, noting his expression again. "You're in pain. What is it?"

Linon shook his head and waved it away.

But DiJinn was persistent and knelt before him. "Linon. If you're hurt, I need to know."

Linon looked into her glowing eyes, then set his jaw. "I didn't escape the ambush without a fight. Dane took most of them himself. Seems they didn't care as much about me. Dane sacrificed himself so that I could flee. If

I had to guess, they were targeting him specifically." Linon opened his cloak to reveal a blood-soaked tunic.

DiJinn gasped and moved the fabric aside. "Linon!" She looked at the knife wound, which was a slash just below his ribs. He'd wrapped it, but the gash was too wide and hadn't completely clotted. It looked badly infected. "You've lost a lot of blood. We need to get you back to the frigate now—"

Linon gently pushed her hands away. "No, Jinn. There's no time. I know there's a window right now. We have less than eight hours. This is our chance to free my son *and* strengthen our forces. We won't get another chance before the fulcrum wars start. I know my son— he won't leave these people. If he has a plan to bring them, we need to take that opportunity. I won't abandon him again."

"Linon," DiJinn said and placed a hand on his shoulder. "You can't go on. I know, believe me."

"I can manage," Linon said. He stood, holding on to the swing.

DiJinn stood and gave him a doubtful look. She could tell it was pointless trying to convince him. Linon was here for his son, and nothing would change his mind. She only hoped he could stick with her. Things were going to move quickly now. "Alright. Let's move. We need to leave this place."

Suddenly, an alarm blared from the next street over. DiJinn helped Linon across the thoroughfare. She'd assumed that two people alone in an upscale park would get someone's attention. Just as they made the shadows, several military police entered the park and searched the area. DiJinn draped her cloak over both of them, and they huddled together and waited.

It took nearly an hour for the guards to leave the area, and silence returned. DiJinn led Linon back down the narrow switchback stairs, and soon, they were in the busy market areas. She led them back to the arena district and paid for access to the pits. Linon pulled his hat down as low as he could while she loaded her alias. Another forty credits got them access into the cage area, and she moved down the same aisle. But Patrick's cage was occupied by a different man now.

She cursed under her breath. "They've moved him."

"They move the fighters around constantly, depending on what time their next match is," Linon huffed, holding his side. "If he's in the area, we need to find him."

They hurried around but didn't split up. DiJinn wasn't letting Linon out of her sight in his condition. They asked several of the caged fighters as they went. Everyone knew Patrick and was happy to help. Eventually, they pieced enough information together to locate him.

When they finally found Patrick, he was sitting with his back to them, leaning against the bars. There was blood on his jerkin, but she couldn't tell if it was his or from his last opponent.

Linon was about to rush across the aisles to him. But DiJinn grabbed his cloak and pulled him back. She gripped his shoulders. "Linon, no!" she hissed. "Just wait, he's not goin' anywhere just yet."

Linon gritted his jaw, then closed his eyes and relaxed. "Sorry Jinn. You're right. What's the plan?"

"Take my cloak and let me scope out the area first. Don't move, okay? I'll only be gone a few minutes. If we free your son now, we may not have enough time to get to Dane. Let me find his cage."

"Then what?"

She smirked. "I think we're 'bout to start a riot. You up for that?"

Linon winced but managed a smile. Then he handed her cloak back. "You're going to need this more than me. I'll be fine this time."

"Give me five or so minutes," DiJinn said and took her cloak. "Don't move. I'm serious, Linon. We do things my way, alright?"

Linon nodded. "It's your show, Jinn."

She cloaked and left Linon in the shadows.

DiJinn did a quick sweep, looking for any stationed troops or guards. There was no trap this time. She ran by the cages, looking for Dane. Several minutes later, she found him. Dane was chained to a wall, in sight for everyone to see. They were parading him as a prize fighter. That made her blood boil. *Someone was gonna pay for that.* But she calmed her temper for the moment.

Now, she had to time everything perfectly. But she didn't know if she'd be able to free enough of these pit fighters quickly enough to arm them before military police arrived. But what option did she have? She had to get back to Solan tonight. They would all be needed for the first fulcrum war in the morning, and it looked like she was bringing some friends with her. A lot of them.

DiJinn turned and ran right into a cloaked figure who grabbed her and placed a hand over her mouth.

H

"Easy, lass!" Ti-Leer whispered.

DiJinn let out a sigh. She wanted to yell at him but managed a terse smile instead and gave him a hug. "Ti!" she whispered and gripped his shoulders. "You're just in time."

"Aye, Solan thought you might need some help. I assume you've got a plan?"

"Kinda," she said, and ran through everything with him.

"I see Dane," Ti-Leer said and nodded in his direction. "I can get him down and make sure he's fine—"

"Actually, I'll get Dane and Patrick. I could use your help freeing all these slaves, though."

"*This again?*" Ti-Leer cackled and tugged at his beard. "Didn't we just go through this with Linon?"

"Yeah…well, looks like we're in the business now. Our biggest problem will be gettin' 'em out of here. Apparently, we're not leavin' anyone behind."

"Solan thought of that too, lass."

"What do you mean?"

"We've got the Armada and the rest of the air fleet standin' by. It's enough to transport most of these people. The leftovers can hijack some frigates, I don't care."

DiJinn almost kissed Ti-Leer. "I owe Solan for this—"

"Oi, what 'bout me?" Ti-Leer said his arms held wide open.

"You too, Ti," she said and clapped his arm. "Let's move before things fall apart."

DiJinn ran back to Linon while Ti-Leer began quietly ripping the locks off the cages. Soon, there was some commotion, and the pit fighters were able to get a set of keys. DiJinn ripped the door off Patrick's cage and Linon grabbed his son and gave him a hug.

"We're 'bout to start a riot, then we make for the loading bays," DiJinn said as she sprinted off to Dane.

Ti-Leer helped guide the fighters down the thoroughfares and toward the loading bays. All was going well until the military police showed up.

DiJinn left Ti-Leer behind. She was only concerned about Dane now. She reached the wall and scaled up it. She grasped the chains and ripped them out. Dane was fine and able to walk on his own. Soon, they were sprinting alongside Ti-Leer and the other pit fighters. There were thousands littering the aisles and marching from the arena now. They easily overwhelmed the guards and roared when they saw Patrick leading the charge. He pumped his fists in the air as the thoroughfares flooded with fighters, who took up arms along the way.

When they reached the hangar bays, the Armada and hundreds of other ships were there, waiting. Within minutes, they were filled with arena fighters and moving out of the ARC district's airlocks and into the turbulent night sky.

CHAPTER 36
A Democratic Vote

JUST A FEW hours after midnight, frigates began pouring into the Lyrinthum hangar bay. There were crews of people, led by Stell, rushing around in preparation for the flood of ARC citizens. The massive SLS Armada was the first to arrive, and the gangway opened to emit a smattering of rough-looking fighters. Solan recognized the look and dress of the men and women. These were pit fighters, used in slum areas of the black market for entertainment. She'd had no idea what Jinn would bring back, but she wasn't expecting this.

Throughout the night, ships continued to arrive. Some belonged to Dane's fleet, others were obviously stolen or hijacked. Either way, she could see they'd have more mouths to feed. The majority were men and women, but there were also thousands of children. Stell's team immediately flew into action and began attending the weaker ones. Nurses and physicians took them to triage, and additional cots were set up. Food and water were brought in, and before morning, everyone had been offloaded and assigned to a living quarter. The Lucem army had just received a boost, but at what cost? Solan was beginning to worry about their supplies now but pushed the concern from her thoughts to focus on the first fulcrum war, which would take place that morning.

"How many?" Solan asked DiJinn and Ti-Leer as they settled into the control suite to discuss tactics. Cord was there with Vail. Kamber had finished evacuations early that morning and sat in her chair. Near the back stood Dane and Stell.

"Hard to say, but in the hundreds of thousands," DiJinn said in an unusually soft tone. She ran her fingers through her tangled red hair anxiously, and Solan could see she wasn't herself.

"Hundreds of thousands?" Solan replied, the shock evident in her voice. "Are you certain?"

DiJinn shrugged and turned to Stell.

"It's a lot, but we'll manage," Stell said. She wore the same gray sweater with holes in the sleeves and hair pinned into a bun.

Solan dropped her gaze to the table and considered. "The first fulcrum will be ignited today at noon. We need to get into position within the hour. I wanted to wait for everyone to show up. I'm glad you all made it."

"Sol, should we consider skippin' this one?" DiJinn asked, a bit uncertainly. "I mean, everyone's tired and we have a lot to do with the new arrivals. It's a lot to take in right now."

Solan took a deep breath and looked around the room. She held up her hands. "This is now a democracy. I assembled this team as representatives for all of these people. Dane, you speak for the Recon and the air fleet. Stell, your team looks after the troops and the people under our care. Jinn, Ti, Kamber and Cord. We represent the Lucem. My word isn't the final say anymore. Let's take a vote."

"Wait," Kamber said. "Where is Linon? He represents the prisoner army."

DiJinn leaned on the table. "Linon was injured trying to free his son, Patrick. He's in triage right now."

"How bad is it, Jinn?" Solan asked.

She shook her head. "He lost a lot of blood. I don't know."

There was a silent moment that was broken when Linon's son, Patrick—the man nicknamed *The Panther*,

and to Solan, he looked like one—stepped into the room. Everyone glanced up at him.

They all waited, not sure what to say.

"My…father sent me to stand in his place," Patrick said. "I am here to represent our people now."

"How is your father?" Solan asked.

Patrick didn't answer at first, which was enough for everyone to understand that his situation was dire. "If it's alright with you, may we talk about it later? I understand the urgency. My father fought to save me and my people. It is his wish that I take over his spot and lead them. I'm here to do that."

"I'm sorry to hear about your father. I hope his condition improves," Solan said. "He is a good man." Solan took a moment, then folded her hands in front of her. "We're discussing today's battle. We need to decide if we will move to attack or wait until we're in a better position. As leader of your group, you have a voice."

Patrick bowed his head, considering for a few seconds. "I realize that my people are now under your care, which I am grateful for. For our part, I will gladly defer my vote to you, Solan. Without your help, we would not have this freedom."

"I appreciate that, and we welcome you, Patrick," Solan said. "We are glad to have you in our time of need. That said, I really do want your opinion. In the days ahead, we will need a united voice if we are to make good decisions for our system."

Patrick leaned forward and took a long breath. The young man still wore his pit fighter garb, which was stained and bloody. He ran a hand through his dark hair, his black curly beard tangled with dirt and gore from the recent riot. But Solan found a calm confidence in him and understood why so many had taken him as their leader. Like his father, Patrick had the same hallmarks of charisma and level-headedness. "Thank you, Solan. Not long ago, I thought the Heliographi was a myth. Now, I find myself representing a large group of people who have no home, and we're in the middle of a war I know nothing of. Much of my life has been spent living in slavery." Patrick took another brief pause and glanced around the room. "If I may be candid, most of my people are tired and need some time to adjust before we go off to war. These are hardened people, and they know how to fight. Still, a little time to adjust would be a good thing. If you need us today, then we will happily fight under your command." He stepped to the back of the room and bowed his head.

Solan looked at Dane with a wink. "I hope you had fun in the lower ARC district. What say you, General?"

Dane grinned, but it was brief. "I am always ready for battle, as are the Recon. It's what we do. Our air fleet is prepared. If these fulcrums are as prophesied—and the side who holds the most of them will rule the system—I don't see what choice we have. That doesn't mean we can't approach this with caution, though."

Solan nodded. "Duly noted." She looked to Stell.

"I, too, am grateful for the Lucem, Solan," Stell said. "You have graciously funded our operations over the years and provided a safe haven for needy children, many who now serve under our operation, Vine. But I fear that we may be rushing into this first fulcrum war, given the recent flood of new immigrants. Perhaps we should avoid a catastrophe and reserve our troops for the next fulcrum when they're ready? As always, I await your decision and will back you without question."

Solan once again nodded and looked at the Lucem sitting around the table. "Cord, Jinn, Ti, Kamber?" she said and leveled her gaze at them. "For the Lucem, what do you think?"

Cord looked at DiJinn, then stood. "I'll speak first because I see the rationale in both arguments. Dane is right; losing ground right away seems like an unforced error on our part. Then again, if we barrel into this war, distracted and uncoordinated, we might lose too many troops, diminishing our chances at the next fulcrum. We are outnumbered already. And let us not forget that one of our most powerful assets is missing with Jet not here. All that said, I believe we should make an attempt."

Kamber stood next to Cord and placed a hand on his narrow shoulder. "Sorry, Cord. I'm not so certain. Without Jet, and the power his war staff might bring, we will be hard pressed. I vote we sit this one out."

Ti-Leer stood next to Cord and Kamber. "Aye. If Sybold's back, and she shows herself at the first fulcrum, we gonna be in a world of hurt."

"Is that a yes or a no?" DiJinn quipped.

"I'm with Dane on this one, lass!"

Vail cleared her throat, and everyone turned to face her. "I know it's not my place to speak—"

DiJinn leaned forward in her chair and placed her elbows on the table. She leveled a finger at Vail. "Sol, why is this traitor even here? How can we trust that she isn't—"

Solan held up a hand and DiJinn went silent. "What is it, Vail?"

"I was there when Sybold returned. She's not at full strength yet. If she's at the fulcrum today, then I'm guessin' she won't engage. Still, I would advise against an attack. I've seen what Lybra has in reserve. More M-Class Mechs. More jammers. Let's not forget about the Dreadnaughts."

Solan held Vail's gaze a few seconds longer, then motioned to the group. "A show of hands. Should we go to battle today? Yea or Nay?"

DiJinn, Ti-Leer, Cord and Dane raised their hands. Kamber, Stell, Patrick and Vail remained silent.

"You're the tie breaker, lass," Ti-Leer said to Solan and stifled a soft belch with the back of his arm.

Solan paced the room, then pulled up the three-dimensional map of the seventh belt. It showed a section cut through the belt's hull and the strange pyramid that housed the fulcrum. She knew that Lybra and the Atrum forces had already set up defenses around that pyramid, according to Cord. As much as she hated to sit one out, she knew the wise thing to do was just that. Without Jet's help and Lybra's forces already dug in, it would be a tough offensive maneuver.

"We sit this one out," she finally said and looked around the room. "However, we will send in a reconnaissance group to observe. I want to see how this happens. Perhaps we can gather some intel and prepare for the next one. We'll take this time to set up our own defenses around the second belt's fulcrum. Dane, I want you to handle that with Patrick. You two represent our armies now. We'll take the same approach as our enemy and set up early defenses. Each fulcrum event will occur just two days apart. Things are going to move fast now, and we won't get a break for a while."

"I noticed that the first, eighth and ninth belt fulcrums aren't involved in this," Kamber said. "Do we have any more information about them?"

"I have some insight on that," Cord said. "While I was doing research, I noticed there isn't a ninth belt fulcrum. I searched through all the blueprints. Among the thousands of floating islands, none possess an internal void similar to the other belts."

"Yet there is a ninth memoir," Solan said.

Cord cracked a crooked smile. "Albright strikes again. I have no solution at this time. If I were to wager a guess, though, I'd say the first and eighth belts will come into play *after* the other fulcrums are ignited, and only then. Though, I could be wrong."

Solan took another moment. "All we can do now is focus on what's in front of us—one fulcrum at a time. Stell. Continue working with the new arrivals. Dane and Patrick. We need a battle plan to defend our fulcrum in two days' time. Cord, Vail, you're observation team number one. Ti-Leer and Kamber, you'll be team number two. I want you all to scout the seventh belt's fulcrum as it's ignited. Take no action. Are we all clear?"

Ti-Leer stood and saluted her, then steadied himself as DiJinn looked on in frustration, shaking her head. "Are you sure that's a wise grouping, Sol?"

"It'll do," Solan replied. "Jinn, hold back for a moment, won't you?"

Solan dismissed everyone as DiJinn stayed seated with her boots kicked up. After everyone had cleared the control suite, Solan closed the door and looked at her.

DiJinn grinned back at her. "By the look, I'm guessin' you've got something dangerous cooked up?"

"During the seventh fulcrum's ignition, I have a mission for you."

DiJinn gave her a devious smile. "Let's hear it."

"We need to know what happened to Jet. If you can get to the Hall of Vital Records, we'll know if he's still alive. I didn't want anyone else to know, especially Vail."

That made DiJinn sit up. "Why'd you let that snake back in?"

"Because I don't sense a malicious motive in her now. She has a part to play in all of this. I'd rather have her close where I can see her, not roaming out there somewhere."

"Doesn't mean I have to like her, but I understand why you're doin' it now. As far as Jet, of course he's still alive. He has to be…"

But Solan heard the hesitation in DiJinn's voice as she trailed off. She stepped over to her and gripped her friend's shoulders. "We need to know, Jinn. It's the only way to find out for sure. Most of Lybra's forces will be on the seventh belt, so it should give you a window."

"Sol. If Stroud is dead, or whatever, we won't survive what's coming."

"Yes. I understand."

"Do we really want to know if he's dead?"

"We *have* to know. As much as it stresses me to do this, we need to find out as soon as possible so we can plan around it. Please, go quietly and do this. I think you're the only one who has the ability to get in and out of that place now."

DiJinn smirked. "It's gonna be a hornet's nest, tryin' to get in there now. But yeah, I can do it."

"Just be careful, Jinn," Solan said, then gave her a hug and held on to her for a long moment. She felt an uneasy knot in her gut as she embraced her best friend. She only hoped she wasn't sending DiJinn on a suicide mission.

CHAPTER 37

Missing in Action

JULY 4, 2286, A.D.

ΑΒΓΔΕΖΗΘΙΚΛ
ΝΞΟΠΡΣΤΥΦΧΨΩ

LATER THAT MORNING, Linon fell into a coma and, within a few hours, passed away.

The group was there at his bedside but later gave Patrick time alone. Solan and the others tried to focus on their duties and distract themselves from the loss. But it was a harsh reminder of the danger facing them. Linon had brought his son home and given his own life to save him. Now, Patrick would step into his role and lead the freed ARC citizens, which many were now referring to as the *Freedom Army*.

Solan noticed Dane chatting quietly with Patrick just afterward. He gripped the young man by the shoulders and seemed to be offering some guidance. Solan thought Dane would make a good mentor, and perhaps that's what he was doing. Linon had been Dane's second-in-command, for the short time he'd been with them. And maybe Dane felt it was his duty to look over Linon's son now.

Solan took a few minutes to go over everything with DiJinn before she left to the Hall of Vital Records. Solan could see that she was excited about the mission. DiJinn excelled at subterfuge and if anyone could find out if Jet was alive, it was her. Cord and Vail left at daybreak, followed by Ti-Leer and Kamber. According to the memoirs, the seventh belt's fulcrum could only be ignited at noon by a Heliographi's war staff. The polarity, though, would be determined by an Atrum or Lucem. They were essentially giving Lybra the fulcrum for free, and it drove Solan mad.

But deep down, Solan was relieved that they were sitting this first battle out. Their forces weren't ready, a result of all the side missions that had taken longer than expected. Having the new ARC troops was great, but it had also thrown off their plans.

Now, Dane and his team had two days to plan their defense of the next fulcrum, which was in their own territory on the second belt. She felt in her gut that if the Lucem couldn't claim all four of their own fulcrums, the

Skylight System was doomed, which was one reason she wanted to try and take one of the Atrum's. But with Jet missing in action, she didn't know what to expect. She could only control what was in front of her.

As the teams left the Lyrinthum hangar bay, Solan decided to stay behind and wait for news. As much as she wanted to be out in the thick of things, she needed to direct traffic. Soon, she'd get her chance at a little action.

I

Cord looked across the cockpit of his jammer. Vail sat with arms crossed and eyes closed. Behind him was Ti-Leer and Kamber in a separate jammer. They would also observe the fulcrum event, but from another vantage point.

Cord was now responsible for Vail's actions. Ironically, he had done the one thing he thought he'd never do—vouch for Vail Hart. She was impatient and unpredictable at times, and he wondered what the hell he'd been thinking. She was his exact opposite in so many ways, yet he felt different around her now in a way he couldn't explain. While hunting fulcrums, he'd felt somewhat out of sorts being near her. At first, he was only helping her because that's what Jet would expect of him. Now he wasn't so certain. He didn't like this new feeling because he couldn't rationalize it, and maybe that's what bothered him. What he was feeling shouldn't make any sense.

"Something wrong, Brainiac?"

Cord glanced at Vail, then back at his console. "Seeing as I'm responsible for you now, I recommend that you control your emotions, especially where we're heading."

"What do you think I'm gonna do, Ledbetter? Run off and announce our position? I'm not that stupid."

Cord could sense that she wanted him to respond. Arguing was her way of dealing with uncomfortable situations. But he didn't have the desire at the moment and ignored her.

A few minutes later, Vail sighed. "Solan says Stroud's missin'. What do you think happened to him? I know you have a theory; you always do."

"Unknown."

"Well. If you're not gonna tell me, then I have one."

"I'm listening."

"Did it ever cross your mind that his new war staff might be the cause of his disappearance?"

Cord turned to Vail. "Yes. The thought has crossed my mind. But I don't have any evidence. Do you?"

"I don't have any proof, no," she said. "It's just a hunch. Joshia presented the black prism, and it bonded to Sybold's war staff. There's a lot of power in that relic.

If Sybold's vessel is like Stroud's, then there's no telling what either are capable of."

Cord raised an eyebrow. "Precisely. A lot of mystery surrounds the war staffs. Goes without saying."

"I was there that night. I overheard Joshia in the swamp near our base. Sybold's taken control of some poor soul: a girl about our age. But she didn't seem right. Unnatural may be the best word. Joshia converted Sybold to an Atrum that night. Not sure how Sybold managed it since she was assassinated several years ago."

"She's found a way to break the rules, it would seem," Cord said. "These strange happenings with Sybold and Jet are obviously centered around the new vessels."

"It strikes me as odd that Albright fought so hard to make things equal for both our clans. I mean, why the hell would someone give their enemy so much?"

"I've considered that on multiple occasions," Cord replied. "I do find it peculiar, but perhaps Albright was held to a higher set of rules that are unknown to us."

"Or maybe he was just an idiot?" Vail chided but sighed and held up a hand. "Apologies. Anyway…I…" She paused and looked out the window. "Just worried about Stroud. That's what I really wanted to say. I feel a connection with him. I've never been able to explain it."

"He has a girlfriend, you know that."

Vail shot him a dark look. "It's nothing like that, Ledbetter. What if there's a connection between our Heliographi? Does that make any sense?"

"Actually, you two are next to each other on the spectrum. Your two symbols might just be connected. There is a fascinating theory called duality. Back in the early 1900s, a French physicist named Louis de Broglie conducted some groundbreaking work in quantum theory. He believed that the wave-particle duality—"

Vail held up a hand. "Let me stop you right there, Ledbetter. I really don't care about all that."

Cord tried to continue, and Vail plugged her fingers in her ears. "Stop it. I'm serious, Ledbetter. Can we just skip all the mumbo-jumbo?"

Cord paused with a subtle grin before looking away.

Vail crossed her arms and turned in the opposite direction.

Ten minutes later, Cord settled his jammer down nearly a kilometer from the entry into the seventh belt's hull.

"Can't you get us a bit closer?" Vail asked, her grumpy tone back.

"Not unless you want to be seen. We're on foot from here. Can't take any chances."

Cord led the way through the forest and to the same remote vent he'd used last time. They had to use extreme caution now, since the entire area was filled with troops and patrolling mechs. If they were caught this far behind enemy lines, they'd never be able to battle their way out.

Vail followed Cord's lead, and he was secretly thankful for her company. Though he hadn't completely bought into her return, he admired her prowess. Vail was a deadly Atrum, and her skills might match his own now. They were a formidable duo. He only hoped they wouldn't have to prove that today.

Eventually, they found a perch among the defunct conduit and pipes some two or three hundred meters above. It gave them a perfect view into the pyramid and no visual obstructions to the fulcrum inside the inner sanctum. Cord noticed that the fulcrum was surrounded by M-class mechs. Blurry shapes marched back and forth around the base. Cord could clearly see that every Atrum was there for the event. Lybra wasn't taking any chances.

H

DiJinn rocketed off in her jammer. She pushed the thrusters to their limit, trying to make up time. she wanted to infiltrate the Agency headquarters, Flotsam, while the seventh fulcrum was being ignited. With so many enemy troops at that location, it would mean minimal guards at their headquarters. She could only imagine the shocked look on Lybra's face when no one showed up to dispute the fulcrum's ignition.

She made the ninth belt's airspace in record time and landed her jammer in a remote area to avoid attention. She initiated her alias as she walked into the museum, which was practically vacant of visitors. There was much less public activity around the system now, especially with all the evacuations taking place. Many port towns and resorts felt like ghost towns. It was a depressing sight to see.

DiJinn found the back areas and cloaked. As she had suspected, it was mostly vacant. But she assumed the area near the Hall of Vital Records might be guarded. She reached out with her thoughts, checking areas as she glided along. She kept her staff at the ready but beneath her cloak to avoid detection. It appeared Lybra had installed new safety measures. Cameras and heat and motion sensors, which wasn't an issue for her. But soon, she heard the sound of mechanical clicking, which she recognized immediately as M-class mechs. These can-cans had been the bane of her existence lately, and they had been upgraded with additional weapons. She wished her staff had received one of the upgraded vessels. *No matter,* she thought. She'd make do. Ten minutes later, the noon hour was upon her. At that moment, Lybra and the Atrum forces were setting the fulcrum's polarity, whatever that entailed. She needed to hurry.

She found the Hall of Vital Records. There were a handful of mech units guarding the entry, which she quickly dispatched. Now, she had five or so minutes until reinforcements arrived. She took a deep breath and moved around the Hall of Vital Records.

She found Jet's meditation chamber and entered. At the threshold, she noticed the avatar—a skull encased within a turquoise prism. Inside, there was a large stone carved wall that stretched up toward the tall ceiling, topped by a skylight. The stone column seemed out of place in the metallic chamber. Etched into it was what looked like a family tree, which aligned all the previous Lucem that had born the symbol of the letter M. She crossed her legs and settled in, dropping immediately into a deep meditation. She let her inner light race off, and it galloped across the cosmos. DiJinn didn't really know what she was looking for but soon felt a presence near her and grew frightened. A chill descended around her, and she heard something whisper her name. She focused on that presence and thought she recognized it. *Was it Stroud's old friend, the young man named Cutter?*

Then, she saw it. A turquoise light that zigzagged randomly. But it was a great distance, perhaps light years beyond. She began to understand that Jet was still alive, but his Heliographi was weak, growing dimmer, in fact. The real reason they couldn't find him wasn't because he was lost. It was because he was in another timeline in an alternate universe.

391

Cord used a pair of binoculars as he surveyed the inner sanctum of the fulcrum. Across from him, on the opposite side of the vast chamber, he could barely see the blurry outline of Ti-Leer and Kamber perched high above in the shadows. Surrounding the pyramid were thousands of M-Class mechs. Beyond them were tens of thousands of troops. Cord made out the Dreadnaught's banner amongst the Tetrahedron troops. Solan wouldn't be happy to hear about that, but of course, they'd known that would happen.

At ten minutes till noon, a long black skiff settled down near the base of the pyramid. He saw Lybra, followed by President Harok, step out. Then, a figure cloaked in black appeared magically from the shadows. It seemed to glide along the riveted metal floor. Behind the figure was Joshia.

The small detachment walked up the narrow stairs to the top of the ziggurat, then down the internal stairs. Soon, they stood next to the clear graphene encasement, and the figure dropped its hood. A dark-haired girl, who Cord guessed to be in her early twenties, held a war staff with the black vessel on one end. The young lady's eyes glowed a bright red. It was indeed Sybold. She'd been missing in action so far, and he wondered when she would fully return.

Just before noon, the roof portion above the pyramid began to slide open, and daylight poured into the space. Chunks of grass and trees fell from the opening and crashed down around the pyramid's base. The apex of the fulcrum began to glow in a nondescript color, which he found difficult to describe. The sunlight beamed in, and soon, it was projecting down at a perfect angle and right above the fulcrum. Then the black-haired girl took the memoir and placed it in the clear case. She held the war staff above her head and said something, then slammed the glowing staff into the keyhole Cord had noted before. Seconds later, the ground around the entire pyramid began to quake. The glowing light at the fulcrum's apex turned black, and a bolt of lightning shot up through the opening above. Cord and Vail watched as the bolt continued skyward and up through the synthetic atmosphere, disappearing into outer space.

So it Begins

SOLAN STOOD AT the portal of the vast Lyrinthum hangar bay, arms crossed and waiting for the observation teams to return. She was also growing concerned for DiJinn.

Surrounding her was a hubbub of activity. Stell and Patrick were busy coordinating all their troops. The prisoner army was seasoned now, having faced multiple battles. Of course, Dane's recon troops were some of the deadliest soldiers in the system. However, the newly acquired pit fighters that Patrick had brought from the

ARC were used to a different type of combat. Though they were numerous and helped increase their numbers, getting them coordinated was proving to be a challenge. Before leaving, Dane had charged his recon commanders with training the pit fighters, and they were busy working through exercises.

A few hours past noon, Solan saw a vapor trail and then Cord's jammer materialized. It maneuvered into the hangar bay and settled down. Cord and Vail hopped out. Seconds later, Ti-Leer and Kamber followed. Solan didn't bother leading them to the control suite as they all sat down right there on the hangar bay's floor to chat.

Cord detailed the events with Vail adding thoughts along the way. "Sybold was there," Cord stated. "She ignited the fulcrum herself. Some sort of energy bolt emitted directly from the fulcrum. The direction was straight skyward and out of the system's atmosphere. I'm not sure what to make of it."

Solan thought for a moment, leaning back against a crate. "Was there anything else you noticed?"

"Just that she placed the staff in the notch next to the memoir. As I believe, any staff should work, though I'm sure Sybold wanted the glory herself," Cord said. "There was a large force protecting the fulcrum. If they're planning to set up and defend each fulcrum in the same manner, it's going to be a tough road ahead, Solan."

"I hear you, Cord. But if we can claim just one additional fulcrum, it may be the tipping point we need."

"The same goes for our enemy," Cord reminded her. "Before today, I felt the same as you. Given their larger numbers now, I wonder if we should reconsider our strategy, though. Even with our forces ready for the next fulcrum, we may be wiser sticking to a defense."

Another jammer uncloaked and entered the hangar bay. DiJinn hopped out and greeted everyone, giving Solan a hug.

Solan smiled and gripped her shoulders. "What did you find?" she asked as DiJinn settled into their circle and crossed her legs.

DiJinn paused for a second, glancing around at each of them. She gave Vail a doubtful stare, then looked to Solan. "You sure this is a good idea?"

"It's okay, Jinn," Solan said and nodded. "What did you find out about Jet?"

DiJinn drew in a deep breath. "It's complicated. But I can say that he's alive, though his lifeforce seemed weak. I'm not sure what it means."

"Anything else?" Cord asked.

DiJinn closed her eyes, as if trying to recall something from a distant memory. "I sat in his chamber. I sensed there was another presence nearby. It was odd, like it could only communicate with emotions. I think it was warning me."

"Jet has mentioned the same presence to me a few times," Cord said. "A former Lucem named Brindall. Perhaps he's aiding Jet, wherever he is."

"Is that it?" Solan asked.

The look on DiJinn's face cycled through multiple expressions. She glanced sidelong at Kamber, perhaps uncertain if she should speak her mind. She took another deep breath. "I sensed that he's lost and doesn't know how to return."

"Lost?" Kamber said, raising her voice.

DiJinn shrugged. "I think…he's in a future timeline, if that makes any sense."

The entire group began muttering at that.

"Fascinating," Cord said.

"How the hell is that even possible," Vail barked.

DiJinn sighed again and held up her hands. "At least we know he's still alive."

The talk died down; everyone lost in thought.

Eventually, Solan stood and paced around the group. "Let's keep our focus. I need all of you to come with me."

"Where we goin'?" Vail asked as she stood.

"To check on General Dane," Solan said.

K

It was a short flight to the second belt. Now that the memoir had been placed in its special encasement, Solan noticed that a small opening had appeared just above the mysterious pyramid. To her, it resembled a robotic iris, the metal edges like some strange airlock that had spiraled open. *An oculus to the gods,* she mused.

DiJinn was able to pilot their small frigate through the opening and between the hull's infrastructure. The piping, conduit and foundations proved to be a challenge, but soon DiJinn settled the frigate down in the vast field surrounding the pyramid.

Beyond, Solan could see Dane directing the multitude of troops. They were busy setting up defenses in and around the pyramid's large base. Missile batteries, trenches and spiked barriers littered the area. It was amazing that he'd managed to set up so much in just a few hours.

They climbed the stepped ziggurat and greeted Dane at the apex. Jinn gave him a hug and hung on his shoulder.

"What can we do to help?" Solan asked.

Dane gave her a brief nod and grunted. "I think we have it under control."

"You feelin' good about it?" DiJinn asked.

"We'll be ready." Dane led them around the pyramid and laid out his plans. The field around the pyramid was half a kilometer in all directions. Most of it was filled with trenches and barriers. "We'll have snipers on high ground. Inside the pyramid will be our last line of defense, just in case," he said.

Solan could see a few heavy tanks and bunkers surrounding the inner sanctum.

"Let's hope it doesn't get that far," Solan said as they walked down the stairs and inside the pyramid. "What'll be our biggest challenge?" she asked when they stopped at the base of the giant fulcrum device.

"I have a few concerns," Dane said. "We're currently outnumbered. By my best estimates, Lybra's forces outnumber ours by a three-to-one ratio. But we have the benefit of defending, which gives us an advantage. My other concern is timing. We'll need to break down our assets as soon as this fulcrum is ignited. We'll only have two days' time to relocate, assuming we go with an offensive approach. That'll push us to our limit."

"Stell's crews can help with that, General," Solan said. "Lybra will have the same problem. Even with her larger army, she can't afford to overextend her forces to multiple fulcrums. It would probably spread her too thin."

Dane rubbed his chin. "I believe that you're correct. We've run some simulations to see if she can defend two fulcrums at once. Each time, we come out on top. Still, we shouldn't make any assumptions. I'm not taking anything for granted."

"Out of curiosity, do you think she might try to set up an early defense at one of our fulcrums?" DiJinn asked.

"No. I don't," Dane replied. "Lybra and her generals have access to the same artificial intelligence we do. I Imagine they've run their own simulations and have come to the same conclusion we have. Even with her larger army, she cannot defend multiple fulcrums—she knows that would be an error. If she did, we'd simply set up at one of hers. My guess is that she'll want all of the outer fulcrums and *hope* that she can take one of ours by attacking. Regardless, we have scouts in place to warn us if she tries that."

"I think you're right, Dane," Solan said. "Lybra won't risk giving up any of her four outer fulcrums. I sense that she'll want plenty of cushion around her stronghold *and* Goliath's Gate."

Dane nodded. "I don't need to tell you this is going to be a costly war, especially if we attack a fortified fulcrum. We need to pace ourselves if we want to reach the end."

"I understand, Dane. But we can't let her go undisputed on every fulcrum. We've already let one go."

"I'm not saying we should," Dane said. "I just want you to understand the cost if we do."

К

The next few days seemed to fly by quicker than Solan cared for, and still, there was no sign of Jet.

Dane finalized his defenses the night before and immediately ordered their forces into position.

Back at their base, Solan noticed the unsettled feeling. She sensed the anxious mood in the air as citizens flashed concerned looks and whispered in the corridors. Groups huddled together and held vigils. Through it all, operations continued as normal down in Lyrinthum—at least, as normal as could be, considering their situation. Stell ran a tight ship and could be seen meeting with governors and representatives, trying to calm their fears of civil war.

Solan decided to call another town hall meeting early the following morning. It was held at the same venue as before, and the globelike arena was filled to capacity. The event was broadcast to all areas of their base for those who couldn't get a seat. Solan opened by trying to reassure the anxious citizens. She gave a brief overview of what to expect, feeling that transparency was the best approach. In her opinion, being honest and blunt about what could happen was crucial. She preferred the 'rip the band aide off' approach—good bedside manner had never been her strength. Solan's plan was to deliver the bad news and take the heat. Then, she would turn it over to Dane and let him rally the crowd and leave on that note.

General Dane took the stage among cheers and a standing ovation. He gave a rousing speech, and the mood shifted from doom and gloom to hope and triumph. His charisma lifted the crowd, his words rang out like a battle hymn. Solan looked on with a smile. Dane seemed to carry an aura that instilled confidence in those around him.

An hour later, Dane and Solan boarded the SLS Armada. Hundreds of thousands of people cheered as the massive battle cruiser led the fleet out of the hangar bay. Solan stood near Dane and Kamber on the bridge as they made the short flight toward the second belt's airspace.

"You doing okay?" Solan asked Kamber as they gazed out the forward window.

Kamber shrugged, then nodded, her arms crossed tightly. Solan noticed the dark circles under her glowing eyes.

"Just focus on your part," Solan said and placed an arm around Kamber. "It'll help take your mind off Jet. Something tells me that he's playing out his part in this. I know you believe in fate, and fate isn't done with him. He'll be back soon enough."

"I hope you're right, Solan. I had dark dreams last night."

Solan knew that Kamber's gift was seeing prophesies through her dreams, which almost always came to fruition. "What did you see?"

Kamber shifted and turned away. Solan could see that she didn't want to talk about it.

"I saw fire," Kamber whispered. "This world, the Skylight System, was on fire. Everything burned. Millions were dead."

Solan continued to stare out the forward window but remained silent. In her gut, she felt suddenly nauseous. For a split second, she was at a loss for words. "Perhaps your dream was more symbolic? It happens to me sometimes—"

"No, Solan. Everything we know and love will be tested. Before it all ends, we will be tried by fire—"

"Make the call, Solan," Dane interrupted and nodded out the forward window.

The air fleet had stopped and hovered over the fulcrum's location.

"Let's deploy," Solan said, and the air fleet lowered to the surface. Thousands of troops, vehicles and supplies hit the ground to join the forces already in place.

Solan marched with Dane, Kamber, and a detachment of recon soldiers. The smaller ships that could fit into the oculus filtered in. The larger battle cruisers and war frigates remained airborne and would provide resistance to any ships trying to enter the hull. It would help slow down Lybra's forces a little, and they would need all the help they could get.

Once they hit the battlefield, Solan tried to convince Dane to stay atop the pyramid and direct traffic. But he insisted on being at ground level and closer to the battle, which worried her. If they lost Dane, it would be a devastating blow. Be he wouldn't take no for an answer. "I need to be close to feel the rhythm of war, Solan. These troops need to see me. It'll be fine."

In the end, Solan agreed, though she vowed to stay near him.

When Dane entered the fulcrum base, every troop rallied around him. Hundreds of thousands of soldiers began moving into position and the inside of the vast chamber was alive with motion.

Solan checked the time as she took up a position near the base and settled in with Ti-Leer, Kamber, DiJinn, Cord and Vail. They waited anxiously for Lybra's forces to arrive.

CHAPTER 39

A Fever of Bloodlust
JANUARY 18, 2287, A.D.

JET FELT LIKE HE WAS DYING.

He sensed that some unnatural power was the cause of his strange illness. Jet was beginning to understand that this *bloodlust*, as Sember had called it, was the real reason, and its source was lurking somewhere in the outer portions of the Skylight System. If he wanted to survive, he needed to move on and leave these belts and their sickness behind. But he was bound to physically seeing each fulcrum before he left, even if it killed him in the process.

The two of them made their way into the bowels of the sixth belt. The steamy environment felt like the inside of a furnace, and Jet had to lean on his staff as Sember propped up his other arm. It took a full hour this time to descend into the lower areas and reach the open field around the pyramid. Sember helped him over the railing to stand next to the clear encasement for the memoir. Near it was another Greek symbol of the letter 'C.'

Jet felt it, letting the hot stone burn his fingertips. The fulcrum radiated heat and seemed to suck in the air around them.

Sember fought off another of her strange spasms, then pulled at him. "Come on. Let's go. I don't like this."

Jet was too weak to argue and leaned against her. It felt as though he'd aged fifty years since first stepping foot in this dreadful world. He was even beginning to forget the details and wondered how long he'd actually been in this dystopian nightmare. *Yet…it had only been one day, hadn't it?*

Sember led him up the stairs and back across the burnt field of ash and trees. She helped him into the seat of the Armada and found a blanket. Jet passed out almost immediately, falling into a restless sleep as Sember set the coordinates to the seventh belt. The Armada rose and followed the black lightning bolt along the red horizon.

As Jet curled in the seat, his dreams grew worse. Darker somehow. A sense of death filled his every thought. He remembered that same feeling when Cutter had died. But this felt ten times worse. He tossed and turned in his fever dreams, sometimes sitting up and screaming. Sember stood nearby, speaking words of comfort to soothe him. She found a damp cloth and laid it across his brow.

It felt like days later when the Armada finally made the seventh belt's airspace. Sember shook Jet awake.

"We're here," she whispered.

Jet roused himself from slumber, thankful to have an excuse to leave his dreams. He reached for his staff and propped himself up. "What day is it? How long have I been here?"

Sember shook her head at the question. "Jet, it's still the same day. Nine hours since you found me, maybe." She stood in front of him. "We should leave this place. Let's skip these last two belts. Please, I don't like this…something doesn't feel right."

But Jet stood, leaning on Port-Shear and waved her away. "No, Sember. I have to. I need to see the letters. Please, help me. Don't leave." He reached out and gripped her arm.

"I won't leave you. I promise." She helped steady him.

When they stepped off the gangway, Jet heard a noise in the air. It was a mournful hum, as if thousands

of ancient voices moved with the wind and ash blowing around them. It was a haunting sound, reminding him of the Hall of Vital Records. When he'd first met Brindall, the ghost Lucem, he had heard something similar. These haunting whispers were in an ancient dialect, one that chilled him to the bone.

Sember tilted her head. Apparently, she heard it too and moved to stand near him. "What is it?" she whispered.

They stood stonelike near the ramp of the battlecruiser, frozen. Jet felt adrenaline begin to course through his veins as Port-Shear began to thrum. The war staff glowed dully in the dark air, as if waking from some distant plane. Jet held it in front of him, watching the glow from the white vessel pulse in rhythmic waves. Sember moved behind him, still gripping his arm.

Jet could see the source of the voices now. Floating in the air, mixed in with the ash and dust, were thousands of free-floating bodies. Shades of white and gray slivers that had no form or shape moved in quick, swirling motions. It was like stained rags of some bleached robe, torn and rendered in battle perhaps. Intertwined in the masses, he could make out faces that periodically formed, then vanished just as quickly. They grinned and laughed at him, taunting screams from the depths of the ground below. The spinning masses made him feel sick, nauseous, and disoriented. But everywhere he looked, the air was choked with the unearthly white streaks.

Sember clung to him, her eyes wide with terror as the apparitions buzzed near them.

"Stay close," Jet whispered, and held Port-Shear aloft. The war staff's vessel created an orb-like shield that surrounded them, preventing the 'sheet-demons' from getting too close. Jet could hear Port-Shear speaking in the same language as if warning the evil spirits to steer clear.

"Let's go," Jet said.

With Sember glued to his side, Jet found the strength to move forward. Whether the sudden shot of adrenaline, Port-Shear, or his desire to protect Sember, Jet wasn't sure. Perhaps it was a combination of all three. Regardless, he moved quickly to an old exhaust vent and found a staircase leading down and into the belly of the seventh belt.

After what felt like hours, they finally reached the bottom. Jet pulled at Sember as he rushed across the field and toward the pyramid. He felt a moment of fear as the sheet-demons bounced off Port-Shear's aura. If the Titan decided to leave them now, he had no doubt they would be overwhelmed. Whatever protection his gift might offer, it wouldn't be enough. He only hoped the fickle war staff wouldn't grow bored and leave.

Jet wrapped a cloaked arm around Sember and felt a moment of guilt for dragging her into this. He could see that she was on the edge of a breakdown. Sember's genetically modified mind wasn't equipped to handle this. Jet suddenly understood why Albright had asked him to do this alone. He was seeing it first-hand.

Before long, they stood inside the inner sanctum.

"Hold on, Sember. We're almost there." Jet searched the stone wall with his hands, looking for the letter. He wiped sweat from his brow and tried to calm himself.

Sember began convulsing with the strange spasms, and she was about to pass out. The heat was also starting to affect his vision. But finally, he found it. He stepped back to see a large Greek symbol of the letter 'A.'

Seconds later, they were sprinting up the stairs and back across the field. Jet pulled Sember as she screamed in agony. She stumbled along behind him, her eyes shut and tears pouring down her cheeks. The sheet-demons seemed to sense her pain and flew at them with renewed intensity, as if feeding off her fear. Port-Shear's shield began to buckle from the fury but held.

"Almost there!" Jet yelled as he pressed the war staff forward, punching through the thickening demons. They howled as Jet led the way, Port-Shear roaring back in warning. He sensed that the Titan was ready for a fight. But Jet's only goal was getting Sember aboard the Armada.

Sember finally stumbled and passed out. Jet lifted her over his shoulder while still holding his war staff. His lungs burned from the heat and ash. He could barely see a few meters in front of him now as the demons tried to prevent them from leaving. Jet was so disoriented that he didn't know which way to go. He felt another surge of panic hit him. He spoke to Port-Shear, willing the staff to lead him. The white vessel glowed brighter when he moved in the right direction. Jet followed it, sprinting along the seventh belt's ruined surface. He stumbled and crawled through pitted fields and cratered thoroughfares until his boots finally hit the Armada's gangway.

Once inside, Jet laid Sember on the floor and closed the gangway. He held the staff out like a torch, preventing any of the demons from entering the battle cruiser. When the gangway slammed closed, Jet dropped to his knees and released the staff. He ripped the respirator off and almost gagged.

"Sember!" he yelled, though it was little more than a croak. His throat was so dry he could barely speak. He pulled her respirator off. Her face was pale, her hands cold. Jet checked her vitals, then held her in his lap, trying to warm her. He did the only thing he could think of and dropped into Vishmu.

Jet let his inner light race off as he searched for Sember. He called out to her, willing his Heliographi to search for her soul. Soon, he found her light. It was dim, but he recognized the color, an auburn-gold tone. He floated near her, calling to her. Her light grew a bit brighter as he neared, and Jet used his Heliographi to envelope her. He lent her some of his light and led her with him. Like a ray of sunlight, her light began to pulse.

He held on a second longer, then released her and awoke.

Jet steadied himself and looked down at Sember. The color in her skin was returning, and he cradled her head. He smiled down as her eyes fluttered open.

"It's alright," he said, his voice still hoarse. "We're back. We made it."

Sember sat up and looked around, her eyes still wide. "Well, I never want to go through that again." She stood and steadied herself on a seatback. "How did you manage that? One moment, you're nearly dead. The next, you're fighting off those…" She shook her head again. "Well, I'm not sure what those were. But…how?"

Jet took a deep breath. "I had some help from Port-Shear—"

Sember raised her brow. "That thing has a name?"

"Odd, I know. It's a long story. Anyway, it saved us."

Sember took a seat. She held a hand to her forehead, still weak. "I'm sorry Jet, but if you want to see what's on the eighth belt, you're on your own."

Jet nodded and placed a hand on her arm. "I wouldn't ask you to go through that again. I'm sorry. Had I known, I would have gone alone."

"You saved me," Sember said. "I was gone. Felt like I was floating, like I was in limbo or something. How did you do it?"

"Honestly, that's the first time I've ever done it. I used Vishmu. It's an ancient practice."

"You…brought me back. Thank you."

Jet felt his skin flush and shook his head.

Sember leaned back and closed her eyes. There was a quiet moment, the dull roar of the Armada's thrusters filled the bridge with white noise as he sat there on the floor.

Jet reached up and took her hand. "Sember. I've been meaning to ask you about something."

She gave him a thoughtful nod, though somewhat strained. "Anything."

"I've noticed something about you. It worries me."

She frowned. "The spasms, right? I was wondering when you might say something."

"Are you okay?"

Sember let out a low sigh and slowly shook her head. "I'm not sure. It began just before you found me, right after the building collapsed. I've never experienced it before. They're random, and when they happen, I seem to black out for a few seconds."

"Is there anything I can do?"

Sember only continued to shake her head. "I just don't know. Maybe it's this sickness somehow affecting my system? I hope it stops once we leave these belts."

There was a silent moment, Jet wondering what he might do if something bad were to happen to her. He tried to convince himself that she would be fine and everything would simply return to normal.

"Your staff," Sember said, nodding at it. "It has something to do with all of this, right?"

"Do you mean the fulcrums?" Jet asked, thankful for the change in topic.

"And the wars, yes."

Jet considered. "It has a part to play, just like the Atrum's leader. Her staff is also powerful. A black vessel, similar to this one." Jet lifted the war staff and gazed at the clear jewel. The skull inside was quiet now, dormant. Perhaps recouping its energy.

"If that's true, and her staff is equally powerful then she would have overwhelmed the Lucem because—"

"Because I wasn't here," Jet finished for her. "I wasn't in the past either. Everything you see is because of me. The human race lost the fulcrum wars because I chose to go on a mission that I thought would help. Instead, I'm stuck here in limbo, it seems."

"If this is limbo, maybe we're in their world."

"You mean those demons?" Jet tilted his head. "Maybe. I hadn't really thought of it like that."

Sember's skin turned pale for a split second. "Why didn't we see any on the inner belts? It's like they're concentrated on the outer belts. What's the difference?"

"We're closer to Goliath's Gate," Jet said, more to himself. "That's the particle collider inside the belt's hull. There must be a connection."

"They're not of this world," Sember continued. "If they spread, they'll destroy everything. You said you're here for a reason. Maybe that's it. Maybe you were meant to see all of this?"

"I can't prevent it, unless I make it back," Jet muttered and rubbed the back of his neck. He stood and paced the bridge. Sember had a point. Perhaps this was one of the reasons he was here. But he had a feeling it wasn't the 'only' reason. There was a lot he needed to understand about this future Skylight.

Jet sat down again and gazed at Sember. Even though he'd known her for less than a day, there was a bond developing already. After all, they had survived a near-death experience together, and he had a feeling there was more to come. Sember was caring and brave; he could already see that much. She reminded him of Kamber…and how much he missed her. He tried not to think about the fact that in this future world, she was dead. He clung to the hope that he would return to her soon.

"Did you have anyone special here?" Jet asked.

Sember shook her head. "No. I've outlived everyone I knew. I made a conscious decision long ago not to get attached."

"Sounds lonely," Jet said.

"It's easy for you. You have—*had*—other Heliographi."

"I had human friends, too," Jet replied. "But you're right. A good friend of mine died, and it hurt to let go. It still hurts." Then a thought hit him. "Hey, if I ever get back, why don't I look you up? You could join the Lucem, if you want."

Sember seemed to perk up at that. "Brindall was a former Lucem and a good friend. He was always kind to me. If your friends would allow it, then I'm sure I would enjoy that."

"Consider it done, assuming I make it out of here alive."

The Armada's console beeped, and an automated voice warned that they were entering the eighth belt's airspace. Jet let his gaze follow the black lightning bolt as it bent along the horizon. But this time it was different. Unlike the others, there was just one exit point for the bolt. All along the eighth belt, the bolt seemed to inundate its entire surface. It was bathed in an electric surge, like the belt was generating the energy. The surface seemed to shift and dance in the energy storm. It was like a vibrant cocoon surrounding the belt's surface.

Jet glanced at Sember, and she returned his gaze with wide eyes.

"I think we found the source," Sember whispered.

"We need to get through that," Jet said and took control of the ship. "Hold on."

Sember buckled in as Jet pushed the controls downward. The Armada plunged into the energy storm, its insulated hull protecting them from harm. Still, Jet held tight to his harness as the battle cruiser punched through. Eventually, the turbulence died down, and Jet and Sember let out a gasp.

As the Armada lowered, Jet got a clearer picture of the surface. It was charred beyond recognition, more so than the other belts. Every opening in the belt's hull coursed with electricity. Teeming around the desert surface were millions of the sheet-demons.

The Second Fulcrum

ΑΒΓΔΕΖΗΘΙ<u>Κ</u>Λ
ΝΞΟΠΡΣΤΥΦΧΨΩ

SOLAN'S GRIP TIGHTENED on her war staff, *Mal-Freer*, as the time grew near.

She steadied her breath and mentally prepared herself. The yellow glow of her staff lit the surrounding area—rusty steel plate floors and hardened stone walls at the pyramid's base. She glanced around at the troops and sensed their anxiety, too.

Beyond her were countless vehicles, ships, and weapons of war. Dane had created a series of trenches surrounding the pyramid. Spreading out from its four

sides were hundreds of trenches that zigzagged across the rugged metallic field and out of sight, like some prehistoric maze in an alien landscape. Howitzers had been anchored to the sides of the pyramid and were trained on the trenches. Floating around the vast chamber were the deadly jammers and a few of the smaller frigates. Unfortunately, their entire air force wouldn't fit through the opening above. But it gave Solan some satisfaction just knowing that the heavy cruisers were patrolling the airspace overhead. It would create a problem for Lybra's army if they deployed too close to the site. It would slow them down and perhaps prevent some of her larger weapons from being deployed.

All they needed to do was defend the pyramid's inner sanctum until the fulcrum's timer reached zero. According to Cord, any Heliographi staff could then set the polarity of the fulcrum. Once that was done, nothing could change it…that they knew of. They were free to leave and prepare for the next event. Solan only hoped that casualties would be minimal. But she felt Dane knew what she did. This was going to be bloody.

She had spread the other Lucem around the pyramid's base, trying to bolster support to all four sides. She hoped the Lucem's presence would also boost the troops' morale. She'd placed Kamber inside the pyramid. *We need a Lucem there to ignite the fulcrum, Kamber,* she'd told her. Solan could see she wasn't happy about the assignment. But it made the most sense. Kamber was the least experienced Lucem, plus, she would provide a final backup in case everything else failed. But personally, Solan wanted to keep her as protected as possible.

An hour before the scheduled noon ignition, the ground began to quiver. Solan reached out to steady herself and looked up to see hundreds of smaller airships dropping through the tinier vents in the hull above. Swarming across the metallic field were thousands of vehicles and troops.

The fight was on.

"Steady," Solan hollered to the troops near her. "Hold your ground."

The sound of battle echoed throughout the vast chamber. Railgun rounds and tracers lit the air and men and women hollered orders. The trenches slowed Lybra's vehicles as troops flooded ahead. From his perch nearby, Solan heard Dane barking out commands. The mounted howitzers boomed, pummeling the enemy forces on the ground below. Aerial dog fights erupted around them. Jammers and smaller frigates engaged the enemy, while Solan caught glimpses of the air battle on the belt's surface above.

Their snipers rained fire on the enemy front line. Some portions of the trenches suddenly opened, dropping enemy troops into pits far below, a trap Dane had set. Tanks moved in from the shadows beyond, circling in behind the enemy's flank, and complete chaos

ensued. Lybra's foot soldiers managed to reach the base of the pyramid. Solan felt her staff begin to hum, ready for war. It whispered to her, speaking an ancient language. A smile creased her face as she brought it down into a platoon of mech units, scattering them in an explosion of mystical energy. The buzz of war took hold as she charged forward, leading a group of recon troops.

They engaged the enemy as the flood of mechs slammed into them. Soon, they were being forced back and against the sloped sides of the stone pyramid. Adrenaline coursed through her body, and she lost track of time. *Had it been five minutes? Ten minutes…an hour?* She managed to hold her side of the pyramid, hoping the other three sides were secure. The constant sound of Dane's voice above, directing the battle gave everyone encouragement, though. If he was still directing the war, that was a good sign.

After what felt like hours, Solan sensed the rhythm of war begin to change. In the distance, she could see platoons of enemy mechs heading in the opposite direction. Lybra's transports dropped in behind enemy lines to load up troops and evacuate. The flood of bodies pressing on her began to diminish. Solan felt like she could breathe again. She took her first break, leaning on her staff, and glanced around.

The metal and stone walls of the pyramid were blackened and smoking. Husked-out vehicles sat mangled across the chamber. Fire burned in several locations where a few frigates had been shot down. Solan stepped around the damage and then saw the bodies. Mixed in with mechs and equipment was the gore of battle. Dead troops, both enemies and allies, littered the ground. Many of the newest troops had taken the brunt. Solan tried to ignore the vacant stares as she rushed around to check the other sides of the pyramid.

But before she could reach the portside of the pyramid, the ground shook violently, and the section of hull directly over the pyramid's apex opened wider. The larger oculus allowed daylight to spill into the chamber, bathing everything in a golden hue. Then, a noise echoed around the space, something that sounded like thunder roaring beneath her feet. Solan looked up to see a pure white light rip from the apex of the pyramid, reminding her of a bolt of lightning. The sound of it sizzled as it arced upwards through the oculus and into the sky. The low-lying clouds parted as it zipped past. It felt like the air around her was being sucked in, like the bolt was gathering all the energy.

She watched in awe as the remaining enemy soldiers raced from the chamber in a full retreat now.

"We've done it," she whispered.

The second fulcrum's polarity had been set.

She took a knee as the troops roared in victory.

As soon as she caught her breath, Solan raced up the narrow stairs on the side of the ziggurat and then down inside the pyramid. At the bottom, and next to the fulcrum, she saw Kamber pulling her war staff from the keyhole.

K

The Lucem army lingered inside the pyramid, studying the inner sanctum and fulcrum.

"Cord," Solan said. "Are you certain the polarity can't be reversed once we leave?"

DiJinn stepped closer and tapped the clear graphene case of the lectern. "Let's hope that's true, 'cause we can't afford to leave any troops behind."

Cord leaned in to get a closer look at the memoir. "From what I've gathered so far, once placed, the memoir can't be removed. The polarity is set, and it can't be changed either…at least, that's how I read the memoirs."

Solan wiped her brow with the back of her arm. "Well. I guess there's no sense in sticking around. We need to prepare for the next fulcrum immediately." She turned to Dane and placed a hand on his broad shoulder. "How bad is it?"

Dane clenched his jaw; otherwise, his stoic expression remained intact. "I estimate we lost ten percent of our troops. Most were the newer soldiers, unfortunately. Vehicle damage was a little less. Having the air fleet above probably saved a lot of lives. We managed to prevent almost half of the enemy from entering the hull."

Solan glanced at the group around her, the people who she considered their leadership council. There were some cuts and bruises, but otherwise, everyone looked fine. She felt a moment of pride standing there with them. Winning their first fulcrum was a great accomplishment, considering the odds against Lybra's larger army. But there were six more to go, and based on their current losses, the pace didn't seem sustainable.

But what could be done?

This was the path before them, and she knew none of them would quit or give up. The fate of the Skylight System, and perhaps the human race, lay in the balance. The only factor left that might sway the outcome was Sybold and Jet. Why Sybold hadn't been present today was a mystery, just like the strange disappearance of Jet.

K

Back in the Lyrinthum base, Solan gave everyone a few hours to recover. The Lucem, Dane, Patrick, and Stell met in the control room later to discuss their next move.

"The next fulcrum event will be on the sixth belt in two days' time," Solan said. "What do we know?"

"A head-on assault doesn't seem wise," DiJinn said. "Even Lybra's forces felt that."

"Aye," Ti-Leer said. "And if they get there first and set up defenses, which I'm sure they're already doin', that makes it all the more difficult,"

"We should reconsider our tactics," DiJinn said.

"I'm open to suggestions," Solan said, leaning against Albright's table. "But we've already discussed this. We chose not to challenge the first fulcrum because our forces weren't ready. I think we owe it to ourselves to try at least one offensive."

"Solan," Dane said. "I wanted to see how our first defensive campaign would go. All things considered I'd say it was mostly a success. We have no idea how an offensive campaign will work out. If we do decide to attack, I strongly suggest a fallback option."

Solan faced Dane and held his gaze. "What would be our fallback?"

Dane crossed his arms. "I've been doing this for decades. What I saw from our forces today was encouraging. The troops are starting to work together as a unit, though the newest ones need a bit more training. Still, we lost roughly ten percent of our forces. An offensive maneuver will cost more resources."

"In plain terms, what are you suggesting?" Solan asked.

"I'm on board with an offensive campaign. If things aren't going well, we pull the plug. We only get one chance at this. If it fails, then we only defend for the rest of the fulcrum wars."

"And we simply 'concede' the rest of the enemy fulcrums unchallenged?" Solan said.

"That's correct," Dane said. "That is my advice."

"Sol," DiJinn said. "I hate quitting as much as you. But I feel that Dane's opinion aligns with what I saw today. Hell, Lybra's army is three, maybe four times our size now with the Dreadnaughts. And they were forced to retreat against a much smaller army. That's tellin', no?"

Solan glanced around the room. Then held up her hands. "I don't like the idea of simply letting Lybra claim fulcrums uncontested. But we are a democracy now. Let's give this one shot and if things go awry, we retreat with no shame. Then we'll focus on defending fulcrums three, four and one."

"Solan," Cord said and waited until he had her full attention. "You are aware Sybold will return to the battlefield soon. When she does, we have no way of stopping her."

J. Wint

CHAPTER 41
The Sixth Fulcrum Gambit

ON THE EVE of the sixth fulcrum war, Solan planned to spend the day meditating and recharging her inner light. She was starting to feel some of the stress set in. Overseeing the operations with so many peoples' lives in the balance hadn't really hit her till now. But when she strolled through the hangar bay and noticed that several familiar faces were missing, the reality of war weighed heavily on her.

That evening, she made her way out through the Clipton Woods. She breathed in the crisp, fresh air, letting it calm her nerves. She could feel the hint of cooler weather ahead, despite the fact it was still July in the system. It seemed unnatural, as if something was causing the seasons to accelerate. In fact, winter might come early, and the trees were already starting to change color. Normally, she loved fall and watching the colors change. It had happened so abruptly that she hadn't even noticed. But lately, she'd lost track of everything, it seemed. She couldn't enjoy the simple things with her thoughts always turning to dark outcomes. It had all started with the loss of her younger sister. Things had gone downhill quickly after her father had left. He'd given control of the Lucem leadership to her, something she hadn't wanted. Then had come the hunt for the memoirs, followed by the loss of some of her closest friends. The Atrum betrayal had been the icing on top. And now, this war for fulcrums had her tied in knots, along with Jet missing, and…

…and the extinction of the Heliographi.

The Lucem had yet to talk in great detail about this—about their ending. She assumed that none of them cared to, that they wanted to focus on the 'here and now.' The prophecy that Cord had recently unearthed tumbled around in the back of her head. *How in Skylight was this all going to work out?* She'd always known she would die someday, perhaps in battle or on some crazy mission. She had assumed her inner light—her Heliographi—would continue on with someone of her own likeness—had assumed her memory would live on, reincarnate through the next in line to carry her symbol. She would have never guessed their ancient line would be erased because of the Prism Effect.

Joshia had known the truth for years, though. And all that time, Christian Albright hadn't even shared his plans with his closest friends. Because he knew the consequences if he did. That others might not play out their part if they knew the truth. Deep down, she understood why Albright had set everything in motion now. If this was the only possible way to prevent the downfall of the human race—and the Lucem had sworn to protect them—then Solan would do her part to see it through. It just all felt so morbid.

She had to trust in Albright's foresight: that was his gift, after all.

All of this brought Sybold to the forefront. What was her part in this and when would she make her appearance? Then she recalled the conversation she'd had with Kamber the day before. It was one that had concerned her, though they hadn't finished talking, with the fulcrum war at hand.

I saw fire, Kamber had said. *This world, the Skylight System, was on fire. Everything burned. Millions were dead. Everything we know and love will be tested.*

Solan continued her stroll through the forest as she thought about that. Kamber's dreams weren't to be ignored. But was her dream meant to be taken literally?

The light of the moon and the gravel paths finally revealed the clearing in the pines. She stepped through the evergreens and stood by the stone-circled firepit where her sister's ashes lay, along with the other Heliographi who had died. She kicked at the rocks, watching them scatter across the ground. Standing there, looking at the ash in the firepit was too much for her to handle at that moment. She had wanted to do some meditation but decided to move on and turned and left the clearing.

Solan followed her intuition as she walked through the Clipton Woods. Soon, she pushed through the underbrush and into Firefly Falls. She let her eyes adjust as yellow and green fireflies buzzed overhead. The roaring waterfall cascaded over the cliffs some thirty meters above. Near the rocky shoreline and at the foot of a mound of stones sat a cloaked figure.

"Evening, Kamber," Solan said.

Kamber sat on a large boulder, her knees pulled up. "Solan," she said, her eyes still closed. It was the briefest Kamber had ever been with her.

Solan tried to relax but felt a bit uptight as she sat down next to Kamber. "I thought I might find you here."

Kamber finally looked at her. The light of the fireflies matched her glowing gaze. "I know he's alive, I can feel it. But he's in trouble, as Jinn said. And I'm not there to help. Just knowing that kills me inside."

"Jet's one of the most resilient people I've ever met. He'll be fine."

Kamber only nodded but said nothing.

Solan leaned forward and crossed her arms. "I…wanted to follow up on something you said yesterday, and we never finished our conversation."

"You want to know more about my dream?"

"You said the world burned. That everything was on fire. I'd like to know more."

Kamber closed her eyes again, trying to recall the dream. "It's fading already. I only remember the destruction and ruin. There were dead citizens everywhere. A great war had occurred."

"Did you see any of the fulcrums?"

"Yes. I do remember seeing them. They were all lit with a black lightning bolt, like the one on the seventh belt."

"All of them were like that?"

Kamber nodded.

"Yet, the one we set yesterday on the second belt was a white bolt. I wonder if your dream represents one possible future?"

"Or maybe it's the one Jet's in now?"

Solan considered that. "I don't know what's happening, but I think you might have seen one possible outcome of a great war, one prophesied by Albright."

"The Serpent and the Prism," Kamber said. "Jet had mentioned it to me in passing."

"That's right. Jet believes differently. That the future isn't set, and that fate *can* be changed."

"Let's hope he's right," Kamber said.

"Yes. Let us hope."

K

The entire hangar bay was alive and swarming with activity at five A.M. the next morning.

Solan worked with Dane and Linon to get their air fleet prepared and ready. The sixth belt was only a thirty-minute jaunt, but getting everything in place would slow things down. The other Lucem went ahead to scout the area and make sure there were no ambushes along the way. Solan knew that Lybra's forces were already in place. After licking her wounds from the loss just a few days ago, Lybra probably wasn't going to hold anything back.

Their goal that day was to 'test' the waters. Once the fighting began, if they started losing too many resources, Dane would make the call to retreat. Solan hated giving up on a fulcrum. The last thing she wanted was to give Lybra a free pass. But she understood that they had to conserve their troops for future battles. Attacking a fortified position, especially with fewer troops, would be a greater challenge than defending. And not being able to utilize their most lethal asset—their air force led by the four massive battle cruisers—put them at a bigger risk. Hopefully, Sybold didn't decide to make an appearance today.

Around nine A.M., Solan received a call from DiJinn that the way was clear. Lybra had *all* of her forces in place, of course.

The sixth belt held an emerald tone in the morning light. Trees clogged the surface, and finding enough clear space to drop troops and vehicles took time. But eventually, they made the transition and ground forces found various avenues into the belt's hull. Solan cloaked and moved to the front, helping scout the way. Ahead, a reddish light could be seen, and she stepped into the massive chamber.

The sixth belt's pyramid looked the same as the others. The stepped plateaus narrowed inward and upward toward the ceiling high above. Like the other fulcrums, there was an opening overhead, but it was too small to allow any large ships inside.

Surrounding the pyramid's four sides were thousands of troops, vehicles, trenches, and cannons. Solan felt her stomach turn at the sight. It was an impressive display of power, and she considered calling off the attack right there. But she'd known Lybra had a greater force. They had to try, at least.

The Lucem army continued to file into the vast chamber, and the noise level grew to a fevered pitch. Shouts echoed across the hardened steel walls. Lybra's forces stood statue-like around the pyramid as Solan and crew aligned their troops. Once again, several of the smaller war frigates and jammers were able to fit through the opening above the pyramid. They took positions behind the troops and hovered in place, waiting for orders.

Solan found the other Lucem, Dane and Patrick. She nodded to Dane, then checked the time. All their forces were in place with just under an hour till noon.

"Your call, General," she said.

Dane grunted and scanned the battlefield with a pair of binoculars. He didn't answer for several minutes, and she could tell he was uncertain. "Lybra's brought in more troops," Dane finally said. "That changes the situation."

"Don't tell me we came all this way to miss out on the fun?" Ti-Leer said.

But Dane continued to grit his jaw. "I don't like it, Solan. But there might be a chance if we can get some of our smaller frigates into position above that pyramid. If we can fight from top down, we'll have the higher ground. But there's also a risk. We could lose everything if we don't keep a close eye on the battle."

Solan crossed her arms as she considered. Dane was nervous, which made everyone else nervous. "Let's stick to the original plan. We're going to do this. Dane, keep a close eye on the battle. If you see anything that you don't like, order the retreat. If we can manage to get the frigates into position, then let's do it."

Dane nodded and pulled Patrick aside. They began relaying orders to the platoon leaders with word about the plan.

Solan checked the time again. "Let's get on with it. Jinn, Ti-Leer. Take the far flank. Cord and Vail. Starboard side. Kamber, you're with me again. Remember, if we can get inside that pyramid in time, any staff will ignite the fulcrum. Listen for the retreat and protect the troops if that happens."

Solan and the Lucem moved into position.

The enemy line began to shift, seeing the Lucem army preparing for battle. Solan felt her heart pounding as she and Kamber made their way to the front line. Their presence had an immediate effect on the foot soldiers around them. Solan took a few minutes to hurry along the line, speaking encouragement.

"Stay near me, Kamber," Solan said and cloaked.

Kamber nodded and gripped her war staff.

Tension was high as both sides yelled and screamed across the battlefield at each other. She could see Tetrahedron and Dreadnaught sigils sprinkled into the crowd of troops. Mixed in with the enemy front line were also the deadly M-Class mechs, which would be the Lucem's main focus.

Dane finally gave the order, and the Lucem army marched steadily across the field. Heavy vehicles led the way, sweeping the metallic floor for mines or traps. Their war frigates and jammers trained their rail guns and missiles on the M-Class mechs. The front line seemed to crawl forward in slow motion. With ten meters left, the enemy line suddenly flooded forward, and the clash was deafening. Solan used her staff to block incoming fire while dismantling mechs. She dropped EMP blasts, which stunned the vehicles and mechs. Above, the jammers moved in and attacked. But graphene shields covered most of the enemy lines, and anti-air rockets found their mark.

Solan tried to keep an eye on Kamber, but she was swept away in the battle. Solan fought through dozens of M-Class mechs as she charged ahead. Her upgraded staff was much more powerful than before, but the number of mechs seemed endless. Her staff blazed, its unearthly glow slicing through vehicles and mechs, creating a path for her troops. The minutes seemed to turn to hours, though, and they made very little headway. Solan stood on a pile of mechanical parts and dead bodies. It seemed that enemy troops just kept appearing, and it didn't take long to sense that things weren't going well. Throughout the battle, Solan kept wondering one thing.

Where were all the Atrum? Lybra was accomplishing everything she needed to do, and she wasn't even using one of her deadliest assets. Solan knew if Lybra was purposely holding them back, it would also infuriate Joshia too.

Solan turned to briefly look behind her. She could tell they were losing too many troops. Somehow, they'd lost ground. In her earpiece, she heard Dane barking orders. It wasn't long until he signaled for a full retreat. Solan found the platoon leader and relayed the order. She held her ground in front of the retreating soldiers. Not far away was Kamber, her greenish-yellow staff lit the area like wildfire. Solan worked her way toward her, and they stood side by side, giving their soldiers enough time to board the transports. She thought she could see DiJinn's staff on the far side. Their air fleet, what was left of it, flew in the opposite direction.

"Let's move!" Solan roared and pulled Kamber with her.

A few minutes later, the ground vibrated like an earthquake. The interior of the chamber lit up with sunlight as the oculus above slid open. A black lightning bolt ripped through the opening and pierced the cloud cover.

Solan guided Kamber ahead of her as they raced for the surface. Eventually, they found a vent and soon pushed through the thick green vegetation near the belt's surface. They sprinted toward the extraction area, Solan hoping they hadn't been left behind. The sky was filled with transports and skiffs making their way back to the first belt. A skiff dropped in low and hovered in front of

them. Cord and Vail waved and helped them board the ship before rocketing off.

CHAPTER 42
Revelations

JET GRIPPED THE chair's arms tighter as turbulence pushed the Armada from side to side. But it quickly died down as they breached the storm surrounding the eighth belt. The electricity dissipated the lower they dropped. What little sunlight there was filtered in and gave the sky a strange hue. Jet piloted the ship around the circumference of the belt but remained beneath the storm's fury.

Soon, they had found the source of the storm, and not just for that belt, but all the belts.

It was the same pyramid as the rest—a stepped ziggurat in Aztec fashion. But this one was much larger and had heaved up and through the opening in the surface. The steel and terra firma had buckled around it, like some volcanic eruption. The desert landscape had been shoved aside to make room for the massive pyramid. Arcing from the steps of the pyramid were thousands of black lightning bolts. They coursed up to the lightning storm above and circled it. One thick bolt, which connected all the other belts, poured in and straight down through the middle of the giant pyramid.

As they hovered above the barren landscape, the sheet-demons they'd noticed earlier had thinned out and disappeared altogether in the blowing dust. It was as if the howling windstorm had pushed them away, at least, for the moment.

Jet lowered the Armada and settled it onto the sandy dunes of the desert.

"I need to go see this one, Sember," Jet said as he knelt in front of her.

Sember seemed to consider, then moved the blanket and tried to stand. "Let me come with you then—"

Jet forced her back into the seat. "No. You're staying here. I can handle this alone."

"Jet, you almost died on the last one."

"I'm feeling better. Just…let me handle this. I think this is one of the reasons I'm here."

"What do you mean?"

Jet stood, reaching for his respirator. "To face this challenge, alone."

Sember sat back and curled into her blanket just as another spasm shook her body. She gave him a weak smile. "Just be careful."

"I'll be back before you know it." Jet hurried around the bridge, gathering his staff and cloak. The respirator hung loosely around his neck as he knelt again and gripped her arm. "Thank you, Sember. Thank you for getting me this far." Jet lowered the gangway and stepped out into the billowing heat.

As soon as the ramp slid closed, Jet was hit by the same weakness. Whatever strength he'd gained was almost instantly sapped away. When he turned, he could hear the low, moaning voices in the distance. Just on the edge of perception were the white sheet-demons, swirling like some massive tornado and waiting for him to venture deeper into the cursed landscape. The sand scattered around him, kicked up by the heat-fueled wind. The black light from the electrical storm beyond colored the skies a dark azure color. The large dunes and blowing sand were soaked in a dark indigo. Occasional flashes ripped across the ominous sky with red flames licking the horizon. The heat seemed to claw at his cloak, threatening to burn his flesh.

Jet readjusted the respirator and pulled his cloak tighter. The blowing sand disoriented him as he struggled to maintain his footing. He could see the outline of the large pyramid on the horizon, backlit by intermittent flashes of black lightning. He hunched forward and trudged over sand dunes as tall as skyscrapers. Jet felt his strength leave him with each step.

He was beginning to understand something now. The entire Skylight System was under this dome, or perhaps it was a sphere generating this unnatural effect. That's what had driven everyone mad with rage and hate…to the point of death. The *Serpent Effect*, created by Sybold, was a sphere of existence. And he knew he had to make it through this to see the final letter. In fact, he sensed it was imperative to his quest to see it.

Soon, he could see the white sheets with greater clarity. The demons seemed to be focused around the massive pyramid, which loomed large now. They churned in all directions like a ghostly vortex. When Jet drew near the entrance, he mentally prepared himself for spiritual warfare. He'd experienced some of that on the seventh belt. He had a feeling this would be much worse.

The dark portal into the pyramid gaped at him. It seemed to taunt him as he held Port-Shear, the tip glowing pure white. The war staff hummed as if in preparation. He heard it begin to whisper. Jet took a deep breath, then stepped into the opening and the darkness beyond.

M

It felt like he'd phased into another dimension.

His footing was soft, spongy almost. The heat intensified, and his heart rate increased. The noise of the demons grew which sounded like tortured souls from some nether region. But Port-Shear's protective aura surrounded him in a pure white orb as he walked down a massive set of stairs.

Below, he could see a huge opening in the belt's hull. The lightning storm outside seemed to be an extension of the internal belt. The energy inside matched the same intensity, and tiny snakes of energy snapped and hissed around him. Down he went, circling the large four-sided staircase. The deeper he ventured, the greater the pressure built inside his head. He felt weak and drowsy, like everything was a fever dream. The sheet-demons flew around him like a swarm of banshees, the pestilence bouncing off Port-Shear's light. Jet focused on his footing, noting that his weakness increased as he went deeper.

He thought about his friends as he descended, and it seemed to ease his anxiety. Thinking of Cutter, Cord, Solan, and Kamber, even Vail. That preoccupied him and gave him some conviction. But the wailing and fear and hate continued to grow around him, nonetheless.

Finally, Jet reached the bottom of the staircase and paused. He took a knee to catch his breath while still holding his war staff aloft. He could hear the anger from the demons, screaming to get through to him. Not just physically, but mentally too. He had to maintain his sanity if he wanted to survive. He was facing one of his greatest challenges right now, and failure meant instant death.

A thrumming drew his attention, and he stood and moved in that direction. He passed through a small opening and into an area he recognized. It was the tubular chamber of the particle accelerator called Goliath's Gate. The project had been at the center of many conspiracies over the years. The insane amount of money and secrecy surrounding it he'd never understood. But now it was starting to make sense. President Harok had been a man possessed, trying to finalize its construction. And now, it appeared to be fully functional…with impeccable timing, no less. Its circular chamber followed the curvature of the belt and allowed scientists to conduct experiments. Smashing atoms together at light speed revealed secrets of the universe's origins. The collider on the first belt had proven too small and had been decommissioned in favor of this one. Goliath's Gate had promised greater speeds and hidden secrets…*perhaps a portal to other dimensions.*

Jet could see now that the source of the black bolt *was* Goliath's Gate. There was no doubt that it had been designed for this purpose. It had been developed under the guise of a particle collider, and perhaps it did function as one. But its true purpose was much more, as he could clearly see now. It was generating that energy that connected *all* the belts. The accelerator was powering the pyramid that linked the other belts' pyramids, in fact.

Jet felt a moment of clarity then, one that nearly caused him to fall to his knees.

Goliath's Gate had been created as a weapon, right beneath their very noses, in fact. It was the vehicle that had been designed to generate the Serpent Effect.

This had all been planned out more than a century ago. If Goliath's Gate had been developed as some sort of weapon, then Albright had certainly known about it. He should have countered that with his own weapon, *right?* After all, Albright had always been the defender of equality. Jet was starting to wonder if that was Albright's true purpose on this plane of existence. *The arbiter of balance.*

Regardless, the answer had been in front of them the entire time.

The Lyrinthum Particle Accelerator…

…*Project David.*

It was smaller, much smaller. If it was also a transmitter, like Goliath's Gate, then the other pyramids were nothing more than receivers. Whoever controlled the polarization of the belts' receivers would control the system. And what Jet was seeing now told him everything he needed to know. In the past Skylight world, Sybold had won the battle for the receivers. Probably because no one had ever realized that the first belt's accelerator was also a transmitter.

But that wasn't entirely true.

The other piece to that was because Jet hadn't been there to ignite it with Port-Shear.

He had needed to see this with his own eyes. Now he understood how it all worked.

Jet moved down the curved path of the accelerator's loop. It was slow going, though. His moment of clarity had provided a quick boost, but his energy was fading again. The way ahead was blurry from the thick sheet of demons now. Soon, there were so many that he could barely make out his surroundings.

He finally made it to the Fulcrum's large base. It glowed red like some Titan's fiery forge. The floor quivered as he walked up to it. He used his staff to shine some light on the side of it. On the outside of the fulcrum was something he hadn't noticed during his first visit with Cord. There were glyphs etched in stone like some ancient tapestry of an untold story. Below that was a new bronze plaque that read:

PROJECT GOLIATH'S GATE
CONCEPTUALIZED JULY 4, 2186, A.D.
COMPLETED JULY 4, 2286, A.D.

The plaque verified what he had assumed. This project had been planned out long ago—a century in the making. But it hadn't been completed until just recently, the day of the first fulcrum war, in fact. Impeccable timing indeed.

But it was the large Greek symbol that drew his attention. It was the Greek letter 'S'.

He stayed just a minute longer before hurrying out of the inner sanctum.

When Jet set foot on the long staircase, he felt his strength wane. He glanced up to see the air filled with thousands of white sheet-demons. Sweat poured down his body, and his hands shook as he held the staff up like a beacon. The evil spirits immediately surrounded him as if they sensed his moment of weakness. Their whispering grew to a scream and Jet forced his way through them and began the long climb.

A quarter of the way up, he lost his footing and tumbled backward several steps, somehow managing to hold on to Port-Shear. He stood and leaned against the stone balustrade for a few minutes, trying to catch his breath. His resolve slipped just slightly, and the demons howled in excitement. Jet knew he couldn't hold out for much longer—he needed to muster his strength.

He began climbing the stairs again.

But at the halfway point, Jet had to stop again. His breathing came in quick gasps, though the humidity had lessened somewhat, being closer to the top. But he knew as soon as he stepped through the portal, the heat would get worse. He still had a long trek back to the Armada.

Jet willed himself to keep moving. He placed one foot in front of the other and tried to drown out the haunting screams in his head. Soon, his vision swam with the white sheets, their faces leered at him through hollow eye sockets and toothless grins. Like before, he thought he knew those faces, perhaps citizens who had died in past conflicts. Citizens who now resided in this godforsaken limbo world—people he *wouldn't* be able to save.

Jet couldn't see the top of the stairs through the evil spirits, but he sensed he was near. Just a few more steps and he reached the portal. But his strength was nearly gone now, and he was tripping over his own feet. His entire body was drenched with sweat. The heat seemed to suck the air from his lungs, and the spirits continued their relentless attack on his psyche.

He knew then that he'd never make the long trip back to the ship.

Sember would sit there, waiting for him, and she wouldn't leave. *She would die waiting for him.* Yet another person who'd sacrificed their life for him. The thought of Sember waiting on his return caused the last bit of strength to course through him, and he pushed through the pyramid's portal and into the howling desert wind.

M

As soon as he exited the portal, Jet ripped the respirator off and breathed in some air. But he was forced to quickly replace it due to the blowing sand and ash. He stumbled about a hundred meters, but the heat was simply too much. He dropped to his knees, then fell flat on his face. Jet lay in a dreamlike state as sand began to pile around his body. He still grasped Port-Shear, though. Its protective aura surrounded him as the spirits renewed their attack and crashed down on it. Jet tried to clear his mind, but a thick fog blurred his vision and confused him. He didn't know if he was alive or dead or somewhere in between. He felt disoriented, not certain which way was up or down. His body and mind were disconnected, as if floating in opposite directions.

…rise, youngling…

The voice of Port-Shear roared inside his head, grounding him in reality.

The Titan forced its will on him, and somehow, Jet managed to stand to his feet. He meandered through the desert for several more minutes before collapsing again.

Dark dreams filled his mind. The demons swirled around Port-Shear's light, waiting. As soon as Jet lost consciousness, the light would fade. He heard their taunts, mocking his weakness. Jet could feel his lifeforce fading along with the war staff's protective orb. His breathing slowed, his pulse faltered and finally stopped.

Then, the demons flooded through.

In Jet's dream, he could see Port-Shear standing between him and the demons. The war staff transformed into some huge prism-like being. The facets of its body glinted in multiple lights—arcing and searing the sheet-demons that tried to pass. But the Titan moved and blocked them. Port-Shear roared so loud the heavens shook as Jet watched in awe.

But eventually, they overwhelmed Port-Shear and, one by one, began to filter through. He heard the Titan roar one last command.

...rise, youngling...

Jet felt the ground rumble; the sand vibrated around his form. He drew in a shuddering breath, his heart pounding, his ears ringing.

Jet grasped the staff, the white light ignited again, and the demons fled. He pushed onto his hands and knees, trying to clear his blurry vision. Hovering just ahead of him was the Armada. The massive battle cruiser settled down, and the sheet-demons scattered. The gangway lowered, and a girl sprinted out and lifted him in her arms. Jet looked into the eyes of Sember just before passing out.

CHAPTER 43
The Costly Mistake

THE BATTLE FOR control of the sixth fulcrum had been a costly campaign for the Lucem army. Solan sat on the bridge of the Armada with Dane and Patrick. It was a quick debrief to go over their mistakes, but she could tell that no one was interested in rehashing the events.

"Numbers are still coming in," Dane said. "It's an estimate, but we lost nearly twenty percent of our forces."

Solan felt her skin flush. *Twenty percent!* She wanted to kick herself. It had ultimately been her call to pursue the sixth fulcrum. Hindsight told her how foolish that had been.

She stood with her arms crossed, not sure what to say, but inside, she wanted to collapse to her knees. Dane seemed to read her thoughts and stood in front of her. "We had to try, Solan. Now we know our next course of action. It'll be defense from here on out, and we can focus on that."

Solan clenched her jaw. "Lybra will walk in unchallenged on belt five, and you can bet she'll still oppose our fulcrums as well. We can't afford to make any mistakes now. She'll challenge us because she has the troops and doesn't care about loss of life."

"And we'll make her pay for it," Patrick said. It was the first time he'd really said much since the wars started. Solan noticed the cuts and bruises along his face. Like his father, Patrick preferred to be in the thick of it with his troops. But she also knew his people had taken the brunt of the last assault.

Solan clapped his shoulder. "Yes, Patrick. We'll make her pay."

Dane held Solan's gaze, then looked at Patrick. "May I make a suggestion?"

"Of course," she said with a dismissive wave.

"I'm concerned about timing. The fulcrum wars are moving closer together and farther from our base."

"You're afraid the enemy might set up ahead of us?" Patrick said.

"Yes, especially during the last few. We need to be closer to belts four and five. I suggest that we set up outposts, then move as we claim each fulcrum. We can have our ships and troops moved much quicker."

"That's not a bad idea," Solan said. "We can have Stell and her team move supplies to the fourth belt's fulcrum while we're defending the upcoming third belt."

Dane grunted. "That's right. Eventually, the front line will become the air space between those two belts, assuming we can successfully defend our remaining fulcrums."

"I agree with Dane," Patrick said. "An outpost base will provide some defense, at least until the bulk of our forces can arrive."

"Let's make it happen," Solan said.

"One more thing," Dane said. "With your permission, I'd like to run a few ambushes on Lybra while she's moving her forces around. It's a perfect opportunity to cause some disruption and take her focus off our new outposts as we set up. It may not seem like much but could make a difference later."

Solan grinned at Dane, once again glad to have his expertise. "I like it. Gather your team and brief us later."

K

Back in the control room, Solan gathered the council. DiJinn, Ti-Leer, Cord, Vail, and Kamber sat at their respective seats around the table with Stell, Dane, Patrick and their generals seated around the perimeter.

"Dane, do we have the final numbers?" Solan asked.

"As I feared. Twenty-one percent of our forces were lost." Dane handed her a holopad with all the names of the soldiers killed in action.

The group let out a collective gasp and crossed their arms or leaned back in stunned silence.

Solan held Dane's gaze for a brief second as the shock settled in. Then she cleared her throat and stuffed the holopad into her cloak. "It was a tough loss for us. This one's on me. I made the call, and I take full responsibility for it. It was a risk. But now we have a clear path in front of us. We cannot stop Lybra from igniting her fulcrums on the outer belts. What we can do is focus on the remaining fulcrums in our territory on belts three, four and one." Solan motioned to Dane.

"As Solan mentioned, we'll now focus our efforts on defense, which gives us a tactical advantage," Dane said. "We'll also be setting up outpost bases at our fulcrums, then moving from there after each battle."

"Lybra will control the outer belts—we can't prevent that now," Solan said. "We can't afford any more mistakes. You may want to prepare yourselves and your troops. The way forward won't be easy."

"We're planning to run ambushes on Lybra's forces," Dane continued. "I've used this tactic before with great success. Hit-and-run attacks can create disruption, and Lybra won't be expecting it. This may give us an advantage later on."

"Now that we're only defending, we can set up earlier," Solan said. "Dane will start mobilizing forces to the third belt this evening. Stell, I need you to help move supplies ahead of the fourth belt. Any questions?"

The room remained silent as Solan waited. She sensed they were already weary, the sixth belt loss weighed heavy, especially on Patrick and his troops. Solan stood and clapped her hands. "Keep your heads up, everyone. Our forces need us now more than ever. Stay strong and confident, and we'll make it through this together." But she heard the flat tone in her voice and knew the others did as well.

Ƙ

Solan worked with Patrick and Dane to ready the troops for deployment that evening. After that, she found a quiet spot in the Clipton Forest and pulled out the holopad Dane had given her. She scrolled through the long list. It showed the fallen soldiers' names, age, occupation, gender and where they had been from. The longer she scrolled, the more emotional she became.

These were mothers, fathers and siblings. Some were too young to have faced such horrors. She saw teachers, peace officers and factory workers. They came from every walk of life and had volunteered to defend the Skylight System. Knowing they had died under her watch brought tears to her eyes, and she was glad that no one could see her.

Later, Solan found Cord in the hangar bay and pulled him aside.

"Cord, I need a moment."

Cord held her gaze in the dimly lit corridor as troops hurried past. "Shall I assume this is in regard to the first and the eighth belts' fulcrums?"

"I'd like to know more about them. Things will move fast once we get to the end of this. I don't want to be caught off guard again."

Cord rubbed his chin. "It's what lies *beneath* their surface that truly sets them apart, Solan."

Solan tilted her head for a second, then her eyes went wide. She brought a hand to her forehead. "Of course. The particle colliders. Why didn't I think of that?"

"Everyone knows about the Lyrinthum Particle Collider, though it's been defunct for decades. Not many know about Goliath's Gate, though. Both require a great deal of energy to operate. I wonder if that might have something to do with these fulcrums?"

"I think you're on to something, Cord. See what you can find out and let me know."

"Something else on your mind?" Cord asked with a wry smile.

Solan chuckled at Cord's attempted humor. "Yes, more than I care to discuss. But I also wanted to follow up on the ninth belt. Earlier, you said there was no record of a fulcrum there."

"This is true, and I find that intriguing. But remember, it's not really a belt anymore. It's a collection of parts and pieces, and perhaps Albright has another purpose for that memoir, something in a future event perhaps."

"Can you keep researching that too?"

Cord gave her a terse nod. "I sense that you have something planned for it."

"Maybe," Solan said thoughtfully. "I'm trying to decide how important it might be."

"I would wager that it is very important," Cord said. "If you have something in mind, I wouldn't wait much longer.

PART THREE

A LOOPHOLE IN TIME

CHAPTER 44

Return to C9

JET FINALLY WOKE. The bridge of the Armada was dark. Soft beeps from the equipment chirped in the background, and he could feel the deep, soothing rumble of the ship's propulsion system.

He sat up and looked around. Sember lay curled up in a chair, asleep with a blanket pulled up to her neck. Out the front window, Jet could see the electrical storm. From this vantage, he could clearly see it actually was a sphere covering the system from the eighth belt to the first belt. The sphere arched up in an elliptical fashion that spanned perhaps hundreds of kilometers and nearly disappeared from sight. Below him was the eighth belt, and beyond were the broken remnants of the ninth belt. The Armada held its position, hovering just above the electrical storm.

Jet sat back for a moment and stretched, wondering how long he'd been asleep. He felt better now. His strength had returned, the fever was gone, and his stomach grumbled. As he looked down at the electric storm, he had no doubt now that it had been designed for one purpose. To eliminate the human race.

Now what? he wondered.

The reason the Lucem army had failed was because he hadn't been there to ignite the first fulcrum, thus setting the Lyrinthum Particle Accelerator into motion, a.k.a. *Project David.* That had been humanity's downfall—all because he had been in the wrong timeline. Albright had sent him to this cursed apocalyptic world, and he'd seen what he needed to see, at least he thought he had. Yet, here he was, still stranded in time.

Was he missing something?

Then again, what had he assumed would happen? That he'd be magically transported back to his own timeline when he awoke?

Of course not. Because there was something else. Something more that Albright had in store for him. And he had a feeling it was lurking somewhere on the ninth belt.

Sember stirred and stretched. She quickly sat up and looked around the bridge before seeing Jet, then relaxed.

Jet walked over, knelt, and gave her a hug. "Thank you, Sember. You saved my life, again."

"When you didn't return, I knew you needed help. I got the ship as close as I could—"

"And you risked your life by coming out there. I won't forget that."

"You'd have done the same thing." Sember gave him an odd look as he held her. Jet quickly let her go and stepped back.

"You must be starving," she said. "Come on. There's probably some food in the mess hall."

"Hold on, Sember. There's something I have left to do, and I don't have much time—"

She held up a hand. "You can spare thirty minutes. Let's go." She led the way from the bridge and down through the main hull. After several wrong turns, and a few vector accelerators, they finally located the chow hall.

The interior had been abandoned in a hurry, it seemed. Chairs, plates and forks littered the floor. At the far end were several deep freezers and kitchen appliances. They found some rations and bottled water and slid into a booth.

Jet sat across from her and devoured the ration. Sember ate very little as they chatted.

"You want to talk about it?" she said.

He chuckled. "Not really. It wasn't pleasant."

Sember sat back. "I want to hear it. You don't have to give me all the details."

Jet took a few more bites, trying to remember everything that had happened. His memory was hazy and most of it felt like a distant dream. "Well…I guess it was kinda like the seventh belt, only worse," he said. "Those banshees were everywhere, mostly concentrated around the large pyramid. It was a lot hotter, too. I went down the stairs and found the fulcrum. If I hadn't had my staff, I don't think I would have made it as far as I did."

"And…did you find what you needed?"

"I did, though I'm not sure what to do with the information."

"Just seems odd that you had to go through all of that."

"It was a test…at least, I think it was."

"But why?"

Jet looked up from his food and held her gaze. "Preparation. For what's to come. Albright told me several times that I needed to do this, alone. I don't know if I fully appreciated that. But now I understand."

"And yet, you found me," she said, propping her chin in her hand and batting her eyelashes.

Jet chuckled. "I don't know if Albright planned that. But maybe he did. Either way, I couldn't have done it without you." Jet pushed his plate to the side and leaned back, draping an arm over the back of the booth. "Sember. I think I'm beginning to understand why all of this happened. The first and the eighth belts are transmitters, we've established that. But the particle accelerators beneath those two belts are what's powering this dome. The other fulcrums are just receivers."

"Accelerators?" she said. "You mean that old atom smasher in the first belt's hull?"

"Yeah. Decommissioned a long time ago. But what if it was created by Albright for a different reason?"

"I don't follow," Sember said. "I vaguely know some about the one in the eighth belt. The Agency developed that one, but it was kept a secret."

"Not many knew that it existed. It was code-named Goliath's Gate because of its size, and it was developed in secret. At first, I thought it was kept quiet because of the cost to the system. But it had a more sinister purpose. I see that now. And Albright knew it, even a century ago. That's why he commissioned the one inside the first belt. He called it Project David."

Sember tilted her head. "David and Goliath. That's interesting. It's an old legend."

"I'm no expert on any of this, and certainly not about history and legends. But the prophesies are falling into place, just like Albright predicted. I wouldn't have known any of this in my old world. But Sybold knew it and used that knowledge to deceive everyone. I always thought President Harok had pushed the development of Goliath's Gate for political reasons. Now I know that wasn't the case."

"Sorry, I'm not much help. I didn't get involved in politics. I stayed under the radar and out of public view as much as possible."

Jet took a deep breath and let it out. "All I know is there are just two war staffs that can ignite the first and eighth fulcrums to start the colliders. I missed the deadline. You can see the result."

"So, you think all of this is your fault?"

Jet held out his hands. "I wasn't there. That's all that matters." Jet poked at his food. "I just need to find my way back, Sember. If I don't, then millions will die again. All of this can be prevented, but I'm running out of time."

Sember gave him another grim look. "I'll do whatever I can to help prevent this. Did you find any other clues?"

"At the eighth fulcrum, I saw the letter 'S'."

"So, an 'R' on the fifth belt. Then a 'C' an 'A' and an 'S'. Make any sense?"

Jet shook his head. "Maybe. But I don't know what I missed on the other belts. And we don't have the time to go back."

Sember gave him a long look. "Why do I get the sense that you want to go to the ninth belt now?"

"Because I think that's where I'm being led."

"Wonder why?"

"That's a great question."

"Am I coming, too?"

"I hope so."

Sember reached across the table and took his hand. "You asked if I'd be interested in joining the Lucem."

"Yes. I think you'd enjoy that."

"Then come find me if you make it back. Promise me. I'm on the third belt, Vent District."

"Well, well," Jet said and gave her a playful smile. "That's a pretty posh area."

"What can I say? Being a 'genie' has its perks."

"As promised, I will find you." Jet gave her hand a squeeze.

M

They finished their meals and found their way back to the bridge.

"Where to?" Sember asked, settling into the co-pilot seat.

Jet plugged in some coordinates. "C9. We'll start there."

"I'm sorry. C9?"

"It's the ninth largest chunk of belt, deep in the debris field."

"Why have I never heard of it?"

"Because it doesn't exist," Jet said. "At least, according to the maps."

"Who lives there?" Sember asked.

"Lybra Howling. I think you know her."

Sember wrinkled her nose. "And what if this 'C9' doesn't exist anymore? Any other places in mind?"

"There's the old Lucem headquarters, which is inside Memorial Park. Might find something there."

"What happens if we run into this Sybold person?" Sember asked.

"Let's hope that doesn't happen." Jet pressed the thrusters forward, and the Armada hit cruising speed.

Fifteen minutes later, Jet maneuvered the massive battle cruiser into the ninth belt's debris field. All around them were thousands of chunks of metal floating in a hazy cloud of steam. Sunlight shone from behind them, creating a bronze-colored fog. It was impossible to avoid all the random chunks, but they did very little to the Armada's thick armor. In the distance, he finally saw it. The ninth largest free-floating chunk of belt, which resembled a grinning skull. Two large craters mimicked a pair of eye sockets, and a jagged ruptured bulkhead appeared as the maw. It was perhaps two kilometers in diameter.

"Ew," Sember said, her face scrunched up and brows knitted together. "That looks like a bad place to be."

Jet leaned in closer, peering at the surface. "Looks like it's been abandoned. That doesn't make any sense. Lybra's forces won the Fulcrum Wars. This place should be crawling with mercenaries."

"Maybe she moved to a nicer place?" Sember joked.

"No. That's not it. She had everything she needed right here. All that technology, hidden among the debris field. It was a perfect place for her operations. There's something more going on."

"And…I'm guessing we're going down to find out?"

"I'm just following the breadcrumbs. So, yeah. We're going down there."

"At least we don't have to deal with the banshees."

"Let's hope there isn't something worse," Jet said and moved toward the maw of C9. It was permanently wedged open and dark inside.

"Are you sure you want to go in there? What if it's an ambush or something?"

"At least we're in the baddest ship in the system," Jet said. "Hold on."

Jet maneuvered the massive battle cruiser inside the opening. C9 was so vast that it wasn't difficult, though. He turned on the floodlights, and the inside of the hull lit up. The entire base was indeed abandoned. Dust caked the inside and there were no ships to be seen. He carefully docked the Armada, and it latched into place.

Jet grabbed Port-Shear, donned his cloak, and tucked his respirator inside.

Together, they lowered the gangplank and walked cautiously into one of the large hangar bays. Jet held his war staff forward and lit the space. It was drafty inside, and the hull creaked and groaned. It was dark, and there seemed to be no power. The vast bay was in disarray. Littering the floor were hundreds of dead troops. Jet knelt to look at one of them. The soldier's eyes had been burned out, his mouth in a permanent scream of terror.

"What could have done that?" Sember said, her eyes narrowed.

Jet shook his head and stood. "Look. Most of Lybra's troops…the same thing. This was no normal battle. I see the Dreadnaught insignia too. Just doesn't make sense. Lybra won the Fulcrum Wars. Why would this happen?"

"Maybe they fought each other?" Sember said. "Greed conquers all, right?"

"Maybe. Come on," Jet said and led the way forward.

"What are we looking for exactly?" Sember asked, walking close behind him.

"Something tells me we'll know when we see it."

Jet vaguely remembered the internal layout of C9. The night he'd been captured had been the ninth memoir's reveal. But things were foggy. Cord, Vail, Kamber and Bo had rescued him, and together, they'd infiltrated the main control center. He thought it might be a good place to start and moved in that direction. Of course, there were ruptured bulkheads and collapsed thoroughfares to contend with. Their progress was slow.

Half an hour later, Jet paused. "I recognize this area. I think we're close."

They finally turned a corner to see a large control room. It was the brain center for the facility, responsible for running C9. But it was dark and silent.

Sember wrapped her arms around herself, fighting off a brief spasm. "I don't like this place."

"Neither do I," Jet replied. He found one of the displays and switched it on. Surprisingly, it powered up. He worked through the menus and found a map. After searching around, he found an area that caught his attention.

"There," Jet said and pointed at the large chamber.

"What is it?"

"Knowing Lybra and her huge ego, I bet that's her study. Let's go have a look."

Soon, they were standing inside Lybra's personal suite. Not surprisingly, it was a lavish space. Ornate wood paneling, marble floors and exquisite furniture. The walls were lined with bookshelves and filled with thousands of old tombs, along with a few pieces of artwork by Shiloe Van Saint.

They searched the area and found a partially hidden antechamber off to one side. Jet nudged the door open and then covered his nose.

Inside, strung up among the rafters, was Lybra Howling.

Carved in the wood floor below her dead body was a Greek symbol of the Omega.

Jet moved closer, still holding his nose with Sember right behind.

Up close, Lybra had been hung on a crucifix. Her head lulled forward, her gray hair covering her face. Like the troops in the hangar bay, her eyes seemed to have been burned out. She was backlit by a lightwell that shone is a dull, reddish hue. Jet guessed that her body had been there for several months and was already starting to decay. Sember squinted her eyes and turned away from the macabre spectacle.

"Why would Sybold do this?" Jet muttered, pointing at the Greek symbol gouged into the floor. "I always assumed that Lybra would be a loyal follower. Then again, maybe Sybold viewed her as a threat?"

"I think the latter," Sember said and pointed to a nearby desk. "Wonder if that might offer any background?"

Jet walked over and brushed a layer of dust from the holopad's screen. Then he stood it up and pressed play.

The holographic form of Lybra appeared. She sat behind her ornate desk, her appearance haggard and frayed. Jet almost didn't recognize her. Lybra was old, but in the hologram, she looked ancient. Dark circles clung below her eyes, and she was practically skin and bone. She spoke into the hologram.

"Ah, there we go," she whispered distractedly, then paused and scanned the dark corners of her study before continuing in a low voice. She scooted closer to the screen. "Let this be a warning! There is no place to hide, nowhere to go. No amount of guards can stop her. I've seen what she does to her enemies…she takes their soul." She paused again, her eyes darting around the room. "*President Harok!* That snake tricked me! I'll get him for this and Chief Fritt, too. It seems everyone was in on this coup." Lybra slammed her scrawny fist onto her desk and glowered into the hologram, a bit of spittle glistening from the corner of her lip. "I tell you…the prophesies were true. All of them! I knew it all along. Ah, Mister Stroud. Clandestine indeed."

Lybra stood and straightened her shimmering blouse. "I wanted to kill them all, those dirty Heliographi. But the paintings spoke to me again. They told me to seek out the 'one.' Oh, she thinks she's so clever, using those paintings to get through to me…and what choice did I have? Harok fell in line immediately, of course. He couldn't disobey the whispers. And Mister Stroud, who just magically disappeared at the 'perfect' time? Who was left to face her after that? But…I know where the key is." Lybra gave a sneaky smile and a sly wink into the hologram. Jet could see the twitch in her eyes—she'd completely lost her mind.

"I've *seen* the ninth memoir," Lybra continued. "Oh, it is glorious…*clandestine*, in fact. She'll hold that one until the very end."

Lybra went silent, as if lost in a sudden trance. Then she started to hum to herself. She closed her eyes and waltzed around her study, holding out her hand as if dancing with a ghost. "One last dance, my darling Dantier," she whispered. "One more before I join you…because she's coming…coming for me!" she sang and repeated it over and over.

Jet glanced at Sember, who was riveted to the hologram.

Lybra danced for several minutes, and Jet wondered if that was all to see.

Sember reached forward to end the transmission, but Jet stopped her. "Hold on."

They watched for several more minutes when the hologram shook violently, followed by a loud bang. When the hologram settled, Lybra had stopped dancing and glided back to her desk and waited calmly, her hands folded neatly on the lavish desk. There was another loud bang as the door to her study flew from its hinges.

Lybra's expression hardened, but then the color slowly left her skin. Her eyes grew wide in terror, and her lips trembled. She held one hand over her chest and the other in front of her face. She was trying to look away, but something held her gaze as if she was under a spell. Then Lybra began to scream, her eyes turned black, and smoke entrails rose from beneath her hand. A black shadow swept in so quickly that it was nothing more than a blur. When the hologram cleared, Lybra was gone. Her shrill screams echoed through the study, then ended with a sickening crack.

CHAPTER 45
The Third Fulcrum

SOLAN SAT IN her quarters and watched the clock as the noon hour came and went.

Lybra had just collected another fulcrum. And there was nothing Solan could do about it. She gritted her teeth in frustration. She hated to give up on a fulcrum; her competitive nature could barely take it. But it had been the entire group's decision. This was a democracy now, not a dictatorship—Solan would not take that route and become like Lybra, though it pained her to sit idly by. As much as she hated it, they just didn't have the troops to mount another attack. That would certainly be the end of their army. She valued the life of her troops over her own competitive desires. Her greatest hope now was to prevent Lybra's forces from taking one of their fulcrums. Defense was their only option. She just hoped that Jet would return in time to ignite the final fulcrum. If he didn't, it left a window for Sybold, and eventually, she'd make it past their defenses. They could only hold out for so long. If Sybold was to make her 'glorious' return, she was betting it would be then.

Solan left her dreary quarters and strolled through the Lyrinthum hangar bay. It was almost vacant now that most of the troops had been relocated to the third belt. They had taken Dane's advice and set up as early as possible for the next war. Solan had stayed behind to make sure Stell had everything she needed, since she was secretly moving supplies to the fourth belt's fulcrum. They had reviewed the blueprints for that belt and found a large chamber not far away. It would allow them to stash everything there and save precious time after the third fulcrum battle.

A skeleton crew was all that remained behind to assist the young and elderly in Lyrinthum. They were well hidden in the lower passages, and Solan was gambling they'd be safe until everyone could return. And now that operations were winding down on the first belt, Solan could make her way to the third belt and help set up defenses. She made one last round, then boarded her jammer and left.

K

Ten minutes later, Solan uncloaked her jammer and settled into a private hangar bay on the third belt. Skylight City was unusually quiet. She donned her alias and strolled through the streets, aware of the diminished activity in the normally vibrant city.

Solan found access into the belt's hull through a subway tunnel. The air was hot and steamy as she followed several hidden passages Cord had pinpointed on her map. She finally emerged through a side tunnel that spilled out onto the vast field surrounding the pyramid. Beyond, she could hear shouts as Dane's crews were busy finalizing their defenses. Solan found Dane, Jinn and Patrick atop the pyramid.

"How are we progressing?" she asked.

"We're on track," Dane said in his gruff voice. He held out his hand in a sweeping motion. "We have every quadrant covered. Did Stell get her early alert system set up?"

"Yes, along with supplies. I still want our scouts to verify that Lybra sets up her full defenses, though. If she tries to split her forces between the last two fulcrums, we might still have a shot."

They toured the site while Dane went over the details. He had organized a similar defense to the second belt's fulcrum. Trenches had been gouged into the metal hull, and howitzers were anchored to the side of the pyramid. Large vehicles ringed the base with scores of quick response tanks stashed in the hidden recesses beyond. *I've still got a few surprises up my sleeve*, he'd told Solan.

Dane also had sentries patrolling the perimeter of the vast chamber. Skiffs and jammers created a net around the airspace between the third and fourth belts, just in case Lybra decided to arrive early. A tent city had been erected in the field around the pyramid's base. The majority of the Lucem army camped out that night with the troops. There was plenty of nervous chatter among the campfires.

Solan, DiJinn and Dane took time to stroll around the camps and talk with the troops. Having General Dane along helped boost morale, though most of the soldiers no longer looked at the Lucem fearfully. As they walked from camp to camp, Dane greeted most of the men and women by name, which amazed Solan.

With things under control and their early warning systems in place, Solan located the other Lucem for a quick chat. Then, she found a vacant tent and sat on a rug, falling instantly into deep meditation. While her Heliographi raced off through space, she thought about the upcoming battle. Everything seemed to be in place—

she had full faith in Dane. But her thoughts kept turning to Jet and where he might be. There was a growing anxiety in her soul that he might not return. Though she didn't necessarily believe in fate, she prayed that the universe would align in time to get him back before their time ran out.

K

Solan was up early and found one of the dozens of chow tents around the base. Stell had thought of everything, food included. Inside the tents, most of the troops ate quietly. There was some soft murmuring, but she could sense their anxious moods. She took some time out of her schedule to walk among the soldiers and talk with them. She did what she could to help calm their nerves. From one chow hall to the next, Solan soon gathered a crowd as she sat and talked with them. It also helped ease her nerves too, though the tension persisted throughout their camp as the day turned to night. The next morning, they went through the same drill. Sleep. Eat. Prepare.

By the following morning, Solan sensed that everyone was eager to get on with it. She marched along the parapets of the pyramid and scanned the horizons of the vast chamber. It was dark and foreboding that day, very little sunlight filtered into the space as the noon

hour drew near. Solan paused when she saw a flash along the far perimeter wall, but it was hard to make out. Then more flashes joined, and the chamber was suddenly alive with movement.

An alarm sounded, and troops readied themselves for the onslaught.

But it didn't come like last time. During the second fulcrum war, there had been a swarm of enemy troops, vehicles, and ships. Lybra's forces were purposely holding back. Solan checked the time, and it was growing close to the noon hour. Thirty minutes perhaps. *What was happening?*

Then she heard the distinctive sound of incoming fire.

"Take cover!" someone above her yelled.

The troops in her area scattered as explosions hammered the side of the pyramid. Solan dove over the railing to the next plateau, some fifteen meters below. She landed on her feet and rolled to absorb the fall. When she looked up, the troops near her had been vaporized, though the pyramid's wall hadn't even been chipped.

The sound of more incoming fire whistled through the air. Soon, the chamber lit up in colorful explosions. It appeared Lybra was trying to 'soften' their defenses before making her charge this time. She'd learned her lesson from the last head-on assault it seemed.

Solan and the other platoon leaders directed their troops to take cover in the trenches or inside the pyramid. Everyone scrambled toward one of the pyramid's side entrances at ground level, which could only be unlocked from the inside. The doors swung open, and troops flooded in as the fire continued to rain down. Before long, the entire battlefield was vacant except for some smoking vehicles.

They waited as enemy fire continued to hammer the pyramid. It sounded like some angry storm to Solan. Low concussive booms shook the ground for several minutes. Solan smiled, though. The longer Lybra bombarded them, the closer they were to igniting the fulcrum.

When the bombardment finally ended, Solan quickly rallied her troops back onto the battlefield and waited. She heard a roar erupt from the enemy line as Lybra's forces mounted their charge.

"Hold your position!" she yelled to her troops.

The Recon and Freedom Army dropped into position, locked and loaded. Dane's howitzer cannons boomed from overhead, pulverizing the charging enemy line. The Lucem forces opened fire as the enemy line crashed into them. The battle that ensued was brutal. To Solan, it seemed that the enemy troops attacked in a frenzy. They snarled and tore at her, throwing caution to the wind. Up close, there was a crazed look in their eyes.

Like bloodlust, she thought.

Was it driven by some unknown force or sphere of influence? Their last battle hadn't been like this. She immediately thought of Sybold.

But she had little time to consider as she hurled herself into battle. All along the front line, the fighting grew even worse. Down in the front trenches, Solan came face to face with the enemy troops. She saw the sigils, both the Tetrahedron and the Dreadnaughts. Mixed in were several other sigils she didn't recognize. She witnessed their expressions and knew that something unnatural was affecting them. Their eyes were a shade darker, almost like charcoal covering their iris. Below their eye sockets were dark circles. They screamed and moved with an energy she'd not seen before. She even saw one bite into the neck of a recon troop. Behind the enemy soldiers were the M-Class mechs and some heavy vehicles. This time, the Mechs didn't lead the charge. Lybra held them back and let the foot soldiers take the brunt of the incoming fire.

With the bloodlust driving the enemy soldiers, along with the backing of the mechs, the Lucem army continued to lose ground. Solan watched as their forces gradually retreated from trench to trench. Solan eventually found herself isolated with perhaps a few dozen recon troops surrounding her. Her staff blazed as it deflected incoming rounds. She could feel her staff, *Mal-Frear*, begin to whisper. It sounded like a warning to her ears.

She turned just in time to block Joshia's blow aimed at her head.

The grin on her half-sister's face was twisted, almost a leer. Her glowing eyes seemed a bit dimmer, and Solan could see that she was under the same spell as the other troops. Joshia dropped and rolled, her own staff a glowing blade of destruction. She, too, had received a vessel. Solan recalled the name, *Mal-Voln*, from the Book of Vishmu. *The ancient Serpent of Obfuscation.*

Joshia slammed her war staff into the ground, which caused a massive concussive blast that instantly killed half the recon troops around her. Solan immediately leapt and engaged Joshia, taking her focus. She yelled over her shoulder for the troops to retreat. Joshia grinned, then shoved back at Solan. They circled each other, staffs at the ready. Around them, the battle continued, but soldiers on both sides avoided the two Heliographi. Energy pulsed from their staffs. Solan waited for Joshia to make her move.

"Why, Joshia?" Solan yelled over the explosions.

Joshia narrowed her eyes, then a confused look or moment of clarity, Solan thought. But it was quickly gone. "Just following orders, *sister*. Nothing personal."

"What is happening to you?" Solan said. "What has Sybold done?"

"That's not for me to say. You'll understand soon enough." Joshia grinned, then laughed as she rushed toward her. Solan noticed that her forces had fully

retreated. There was a flood of enemy troops building around her and Joshia. Hundreds paused their fighting and watched now, though they still held their distance.

Joshia gripped her staff in both hands and slammed the shaft against Solan's. The two leaders pressed against each other, sparks flying from the contact as if the two staffs detested each other. Solan could hear the entities roaring, a spectral scream that rang out through the chamber.

Solan backflipped and reset. Joshia lunged and barely missed Solan. Her Atrum half-sister was quicker than most others. Solan was facing her equal. She was in a dangerous situation—facing a powerful Atrum and surrounded by a growing crowd of enemy troops. Her forces had all retreated, and the battlefield was nearly empty of Lucem troops.

Joshia was relentless. She pressed in, swinging her staff with enough force to crater the ground. Powered by some unearthly rage, Joshia didn't give any breaks. Soon, Solan was being forced back, unable to return any blows. She was in full defense. One slip, and she was doomed. The enemy troops held their ground, though, knowing that interference meant death. Joshia wanted this for herself, Solan sensed.

Solan finally made a mistake. She wasn't quick enough to block a sweeping roundhouse kick. It landed in her stomach, knocking the wind from her and she flew backwards. Joshia was on her immediately, bringing her staff down toward Solan's forehead. Solan reached for her staff but was too late.

At the last instant, a blurry figure rolled in. Its staff appeared from thin air and wedged between the ground and Joshia's staff. The blow from Joshia's staff hit so hard that the impact knocked all the troops off their feet. Joshia's face contorted in rage as she stepped back in confusion.

Solan lay on her back, trying to figure out what had just happened. Then, Vail uncloaked and unnotched her staff from the ground. Joshia backpedaled as Solan flipped to her feet.

"What do you think you're doing, Vail?" Joshia hissed.

"It's none of your concern anymore," Vail shot back.

Joshia's look of confusion turned to anger.

Solan stood next to Vail, their staffs at the ready. The enemy troops around them looked on, uncertain what to do. Beyond, Solan saw several pairs of glowing eyes begin to emerge and approach them. Bofisto and Sojahn stepped into the circle followed by Brit, Bo, Tetra, Myranda and Mosstrom last.

Several things happened in that instant.

The opening above the pyramid began to grow wider and the ground shook violently. Solan looked up just as a squadron of jammers swept in and scattered the enemy troops.

Solan gripped Vail's arm and pulled her. "Let's move."

The larger oculus drenched the pyramid in daylight as the noon hour finally hit. A blinding white lightning bolt arced from the pyramid and shot through the oculus above. Lybra's army sounded the retreat, and everyone turned and rushed toward the perimeter walls. The Lucem army cheered and launched fire into the retreating army.

Solan paused long enough to look back at her half-sister, Joshia. She stood like a statue among the fleeing troops, her staff gripped in one hand. The look on Joshia's face was one she'd never witnessed before. Solan felt as if she was staring at a zombie. Her inner color had always been on the darker side, being an Atrum. But now, it felt black. She wasn't even sure if Joshia was a Heliographi anymore, but rather some immortal abomination.

Amidst the enemy retreat, Solan and Vail cloaked and waited. Ten minutes later, the battlefield was cleared and the war for the third fulcrum was over.

Solan hurried through the battlefield searching for wounded troops. Stell's medics filed in, and stretchers carried the injured to a makeshift triage tent. Eventually, she made her way to the top of the pyramid and found Dane and Patrick, along with the other Lucem.

DiJinn leaned on her staff and favored one leg. "What the hell was that?" she yelled. "Did you see those soldiers?"

"Kinda hard to miss," Cord said. "Sybold's doing, no doubt. She's found a way to transmit some of her influence, and it will only get worse, I'm afraid."

"They were practically throwin' themselves at us," Ti-Leer said and wiped sweat from his forehead. "Not seen anything like it. Complete disregard for their own safety."

"Some call it a *bloodlust*," Solan said. "I think Cord's right. It may get worse as her power grows."

"I thought for sure we'd see Sybold today," DiJinn said.

"She's still not ready," Cord said.

Solan could only shake her head. "For the moment, let's go down and congratulate our troops, then start moving our operations to the fourth belt. No rest for the weary."

CHAPTER 46
A Deceit of Dreadnaughts

JET AND SEMBER stared at the hologram as it slowly faded to static, then shut down.

Neither said a word.

Jet turned to look back at Lybra's body as Sember stood beside him.

"That was Sybold, wasn't it?" she said.

"Yeah. I just thought they would be fighting together, but—" Jet paused and powered up the hologram again. "It's odd, the timestamp. See?"

Sember bent low. "Huh. Is that the right date?"

Jet nodded. "That would mean this hologram was recorded just after the fulcrum wars began, probably close to the third or fourth battle, I'd guess. It seems that Sybold had been influencing Lybra and Harok long ago, maybe even during the memoir reveals."

"Right…the part about Lybra talking to the paintings," Sember said. "That's how Sybold got to them."

"Our leader, Solan, had a feeling something was happening all along, at least the part about Harok acting strangely."

"I was buried in my daily life. I had no idea this was happening in our politics. Now I wish I'd paid closer attention."

"It was Sybold pushing Harok to finish Goliath's Gate the entire time," Jet said. "That must have been why he was so adamant about completing it on schedule. Sybold was trying to time it right. The project was completed right as the fulcrum wars began. Everything fell into place perfectly."

"I guess President Harok and Lybra served their purpose," Sember said, glancing at the crucifix. "Can we leave now? I think we've seen enough."

Jet and Sember left the study. He talked over his shoulder as they walked.

"In the past Skylight, I'd worked out an agreement with the Dreadnaughts."

"The mercenary group?" she asked. "Thought they always maintained a neutral status?"

"Normally, they do. But they seemed to worship this war staff and I used it to persuade them. What confuses me is that I saw several dead Dreadnaughts in Lybra's hangar bay. Looked like they'd been killed in the same way as Lybra, which tells me they were defending her. I want to check the Dreadnaught base and find out if they honored their agreement with the Lucem."

Sember pulled at his arm and stopped him. "You want to go to the Dreadnaught's base?" She shook her head. "I don't know if that's a good idea. Remember, we're in Sybold's territory now. We need to be careful."

"I understand. But maybe there I can find some answers. I'm running out of time."

M

After searching the rest of C9's hangar bays, they found little information except for more dead troops. The base had been ransacked and there were no weapons, gear or food left anywhere. Jet set a course for the Dreadnaught's base, Hurang-R. He hoped that Fritt was there and willing to chat. There was a risk involved, but Jet needed answers, and he sensed his window was closing. He had no desire to remain trapped in this future world any longer.

The Armada made its way into the airspace of the Dreadnaught's base. To say things had changed was an understatement. Their base had grown in size, and construction was taking place with crews working on new buildings. The air was filled with ships, trade frigates, and transports full of minerals and goods. It looked like a major hub now, which he hadn't seen the likes since Skylight City.

Of course, it was hard to miss the SLS Armada. The massive battle cruiser commanded attention, and hundreds of smaller skiffs floated beside it, trying to get a closer look. When they approached the main base, the gate opened and allowed them access without confirmation. Jet could only assume they didn't want any trouble.

Jet turned to Sember and held her hands. "I want you to stay behind. You'll be safer onboard the ship."

"I'd like to stay close to you, in case you need my help."

But Jet knew that if things went sour, he couldn't look after her and fend for himself. Plus, Sember might be used as leverage against him, if caught. "If things take a turn, and I'm not back here in one hour, light this place up, okay?"

Sember looked down at his hands, then nodded.

Once they reached the main port, Jet let the autopilot maneuver the ship into a hangar bay.

"I'll be back soon," he said, changing into his alias. "Keep the doors locked."

Jet was greeted by several officials when he stepped off. He remembered how the base had been a collection of floating chunks of hull, held together by massive steel cables. It reminded him of a gigantic spiderweb. But that web had grown rapidly, it seemed, and there were hundreds of additional chunks of belt now. Things had flourished for the Dreadnaughts, it appeared, and that made Jet even more suspicious.

"Welcome," one of the port officials said, and gave a low bow.

Jet thought it a bit forced but bowed back. "Thank you for receiving me."

"This is quite the ship. The legendary SLS Armada, if I'm not mistaken," the man said. "How did you manage to steel it, mister…"

"It's Clint Kregg," Jet answered, not bothering to shake his hand or explain how he'd acquired the Armada. "I didn't catch your name," Jet said.

"Oh, of course. Forgive me. I'm known as Proast around here. I'm the Port Master in this section."

"Proast. I'm in a bit of a hurry. I need to speak with Fritt and his council."

"Certainly, Mister Kregg. Please, follow me."

Proast turned and led the small group up the winding dirt trails of the central district. The city had definitely grown since Jet had last visited. The hubbub of the markets and trading filled the air, as if things were normal in the system. Jet thought it odd and wondered if these people were even aware of what had just happened. If he didn't know better, it almost felt like everyone had been brainwashed.

With the huge stasis dome surrounding the main district, the port city was protected from the brief period when it crossed into outer space. Other areas of the ninth belt weren't so lucky. The Dreadnaughts had constructed the dome to allow nature to thrive.

They followed a dusty switchback trail that led them up higher until he saw the castle-like stronghold rising through the mist. To Jet, it felt more like a monastery, with its high turrets towering like needles behind a massive entry gate. Once inside, the sounds of the city died down. The wide corridors were drenched in a sunlit haze, giving a mystic feel. Jet followed Proast deeper into the stronghold until they entered the main court.

As Jet recalled, the court felt more like a gladiator's arena and for good reason. Fritt and his council had asked him to fight to gain their allegiance. Jet guessed the amount of blood spilled here from others asking for that same assistance was considerable. Circling the rotunda were hundreds of bleacher seats and the council members perched there, waiting. Sitting front and center was Fritt and his chief advisors. A tapestry of the Dreadnaught's sigil hung from the rafters overhead, backlit by sunlight. A few birds chirped from the darkness above.

They stopped in the center and waited.

"May I ask who you are and why you're here?" Fritt said, and his voice echoed around the room. Like before, he kept his hood drawn and his features masked in shadow. His lavish robes covered his entire body.

"I think you know me, Fritt. I'm here to check on our little agreement. It seems that you might have broken that truce."

Fritt leaned forward, his hands gripped the arms of his throne. "Do we know each other?"

"You swore your alliance to me. Ring a bell? How many have you done that for? Not many, I imagine."

Fritt stood and moved closer to the railing, his eyes riveted on Jet. "Reveal yourself!" His voice rang out, a bit unsteady.

Jet stepped closer and stopped a few meters from the dais. Then he removed his ring and slid Port-Shear from his cloak. Fritt finally lowered his hood. The man's dark hair and beard were braided with white beads. His skin was tanned, his eyes a piercing blue. As he looked at Jet, his eyes grew wide.

"Do you remember me now, Fritt?"

"I see you found your way, Jet Stroud. They claimed you were lost, never to return."

Jet felt his skin flush as he thought about his friends and the rest of the Skylight System. "Your deceit may have cost millions of lives."

Fritt held up his hands and motioned to his surroundings. "Look around you, Jet Stroud. My kingdom has prospered tenfold. What do I care for others who live beyond my realm?"

"At the cost of our system?" Jet asked, stunned. "What about your promise?"

"The Dreadnaughts have always remained neutral. You knew that. And once you disappeared, why then should we be held to that agreement?"

"And still, it seems that you've joined forces with our enemy."

Fritt waved his hand in a dismissive gesture. "Tell me, Mister Stroud, where did you go? If we are to discuss broken oaths, then you abandoned the Skylight System at its most desperate hour. I watched as your enemy swept down upon the Lucem. It seems I made the correct decision after all."

That hit home, and Jet felt suddenly ashamed as he stood there before Fritt and his council. Fritt had a point—had Jet remained, this wouldn't have happened. Yet, he still wondered if Fritt might have backed out anyway.

"Fritt. You'll eventually regret your decision."

"Will I?" Fritt said, and it almost sounded like a laugh. "Do you even know who it is you face?"

"Yes, I've faced her before. She'll tire of you and will destroy your people. She will eradicate the human race."

Fritt turned and sat heavily on his throne. "You may be right, Mister Stroud. But if I were you, I'd be more concerned about my own wellbeing. You've risked a lot by revealing yourself here today."

"I need answers, Fritt, and you're going to give them to me."

"I suppose you're looking for a way back, am I correct?"

"You could say that."

"I have some bad news for you then," Fritt said. He stood and removed his robes, revealing his bare chest. Fritt walked to the railing again, and a few guards opened the gate for him. Fritt approached Jet and stopped short. A swarm of guards moved in from the doors around the arena. Soon, Jet was surrounded by hundreds of Dreadnaught mercenaries.

Jet felt a moment of concern but smiled back at Fritt. "Are you going to tell me the bad news, or just stand there?"

"The only way back is through 'her,' and there, doom awaits. There is no place to hide. Now…if you hand over that war staff, then I might be able to set you up with a parcel of land here, a stronghold and a title perhaps. What do you say to that?"

Jet remained silent as he stared into Fritt's eyes. The man's bare chest was tattooed and scarred from battles. Jet hadn't known that Fritt had once been a warrior, but now it made sense.

"Think about it, Mister Stroud. If you remain here, I can at least make your life comfortable."

"You want this staff? You crave power, do you?" Jet stepped in close, his nose nearly touching Fritt's now. "A word of warning. It would drive you mad, Fritt. Now tell me, where can I find Sybold?"

Fritt continued to smile and stare at Jet. "Hand over the staff and I will let you live."

Jet felt Port-Shear start to wake. It began to whisper loud enough that the nearest guards took a step back. Jet lifted the staff and faced the skull toward Fritt. The man looked at it and his smile faded. Jet watched fear creep into his eyes, and his dark skin blanched. A few of the guards grew nauseous and dropped to the ground.

Jet held the staff in place, letting Fritt get a good dose of Port-Shear. He sensed the staff was enjoying itself. Then, Jet lifted the war staff over his head and slammed it to the ground.

The entire arena quivered from the concussive impact. The banners above fluttered and whipped about as if a storm had suddenly blown in. The sunlight faded and the air grew dark. Then Port-Shear began to roar. The place lit up with a pure white light, and everyone dropped or hid their face. A massive split in the floor ran quickly toward the throne and up the side of the wall. The stone shook and dust clouds filtered down. At first, there was small debris, but then larger chunks of stone fell, and everyone fled. Jet exited as Port-Shear's laughs echoed around the chamber.

As Jet fled, he could hear the voice of Port-Shear reverberating inside his head. Jet could read the Titan's emotions and knew the ancient being wanted to rend these unholy people limb from limb. Stunned men knelt or bowed before the staff as Jet raced out of the stronghold.

He sprinted down the cobbled thoroughfares and back toward the Armada. When he held the staff before him, the crowd parted. He could hear Port-Shear commanding him to turn around.

But Jet ignored it and sprinted along as people looked on in confusion. Eventually, Jet made the port where the Armada had been docked.

But it was gone.

He heard an explosion at the next bay over. Bright flashes of cannon fire drew his attention, and he saw dozens of jammers zip past.

He leapt across the port and followed the skiffs. He continued to hurdle over docking bays, keeping pace with the jammers until he saw the cause. The Armada was being attacked by dozens of frigates and jammers. But the massive battlecruiser appeared unfazed. Railguns and rockets skipped harmlessly off its armor. The

Armada let loose hundreds of cannons and leveled the surrounding ships. Fire and smoke filled the air.

Jet ran to the port directly in front of the Armada and waved his arms, trying to get Sember's attention. The few remaining ships facing off against the Armada were soon plummeting to the ground. Then, the battle cruiser lowered. Jet heard a commotion over his shoulder and looked to see thousands of troops flooding his way.

Just as the Armada's gangway lowered, Jet hopped on, and the cruiser lifted. The troops opened fire on him, but he managed to block most of the rounds with his staff and cloak as the gangway closed. The heavy cannons lit up the surrounding bays and scattered the foot soldiers. Then, the Armada turned and rocketed off.

CHAPTER 47
A Long Overdue Conversation

ΑΒ Δ ΖΗΘΙ<u>Κ</u>Λ
ΝΞΟΠΡΣ ΥΦ ΨΩ

SOLAN SPENT SOME time at the triage unit, trying her best to comfort the wounded. She strolled from tent to tent, talking with the injured troops, reading with them or playing card games. She saw several faces she recognized from the battles. Also missing were many that she'd befriended. It was difficult, seeing their empty beds with charts at the foot of them and the names crossed through. Even after all the wars, she still couldn't overcome her feeling of responsibility to these brave citizens who had sacrificed everything in the name of Skylight. It was something that would haunt her to the end of her days.

Down at the main camp, Dane gave a rousing victory speech that brought plenty of cheer. Immediately after that, he had everyone moving on to the next fulcrum on the fourth belt. The troops were weary, but the recent victory bolstered their mood.

As their forces began mobilizing, Stell's crews pitched in, and the tent city was packed and loaded in record time. Morale was high at the moment, but Solan worried that too much enthusiasm could lead to distractions. She mentioned it to Dane. *I know, Solan. Give 'em a moment, they've earned it. Then it'll be business as usual tomorrow*, Dane had said.

Solan was one of the last to leave the third belt. She spent some time analyzing the glowing fulcrum. The inner sanctum, or glass orb, was filled with strange glyphs. She'd translated some of the Greek text from the fulcrum's base. **o** *nostos*, which meant *zero return*, or perhaps *no return*, at least as best she could interpret. Each fulcrum, as far as they all knew, could not switch its polarity once ignited. Perhaps that's what the glyphs meant.

Solan flew to the fourth belt and immediately helped arrange battle plans and strategies. Later in the evening, amidst the roaring, cheering and partying, she found DiJinn among the soiree and spoke with her.

"I've been considering something, and I'd like your opinion."

DiJinn gave her a knowing grin. "Does this involve another dangerous mission?"

"I'm getting a strange vibe about the ninth memoir, and I'm not sure why. Cord seems to think it has something to do with a future event. The final memoir doesn't fit anywhere on the ninth belt, that we know of."

"So, it has a special meaning?"

Solan could only shrug. "Call it intuition. Something tells me we need to grab it."

DiJinn chuckled. "I don't see how. I imagine Lybra'll have it under lock and key."

"Lybra may not be around anymore, and secondly…lock and key *is* your specialty."

DiJinn watched Solan with narrowed eyes before she finally spoke. "If you believe it's that important, then who am I to argue. When should I leave?"

"Let me talk to Cord. He may have an idea of its general location. As far as when, I think during the final fulcrum. Everyone will be here on the first belt, that gives us the maximum time to acquire it. It'll push your abilities, Jinn. I hate to lean on you again."

Jinn slapped Solan's shoulder playfully. "Don't worry about it. Now, come over here and have a drink. Relax for a moment. You need a break. They need you more than you realize."

"I don't think so. Dane is the one they need."

"Well, a little birdie told me these troops are warmin' up to you, girl. They've seen you in action. Nothing gets more respect from these hardened soldiers than seein' their leaders in battle. That's why they love Dane. You're the same, and they see it. Come on, celebrate with them."

Solan finally agreed, and they found Ti-leer at the heart of the party. Of course, he had his favorite music playing, an Irish folk song that had him dancing on the tables and kicking over mugs. Jinn was right—it was something they all needed, including Solan. Though she felt anxious about the upcoming battles, she allowed herself to kick back and enjoy the soldiers' company. The night of festivities went on late into the evening with plenty of laughter and games.

In the morning, things moved slowly. Everyone slept in and took their time until just before noon. Dane finally marshaled his generals and got the troops moving.

The next day, Solan stood at one of the taller hills in the nearby forest and watched as the fifth belt fulcrum was ignited. Like those before, the black lightning bolt shot skyward and exited the system's protective atmosphere. Though it was far in the distance, the energy pulse moved with purpose, and that foreboding anxiety returned to the pit of her stomach. Their enemy was now just one fulcrum away from collecting all four of theirs. The Lucem forces still had two of their own left.

I

That night, Cord had no desire to partake in the festivities. Instead, he spent his time at the inner sanctum of the fourth fulcrum. It was similar to all the others, wrapped in Greek glyphs and odd math. Most of it was, of course, a decoy. He had known that for a while now——*Albright was so tricky.* But woven in between were secrets, meaningful prophesies for the discerning eye. And he had discovered a few of them, though he'd kept most of it a secret. However, the portion about the ninth memoir he'd brought to Solan's attention. It had reinforced what they both already knew. *There wasn't, and never had been, a ninth belt fulcrum.* The cryptic message also seemed to hint at some future event, which Cord had also guessed. Solan had immediately talked to DiJinn afterwards and Cord suspected she was planning to steal it. If anyone could pull that off, it was Jinn.

Later, Cord moved up top and sat at the apex of the pyramid. He gazed at the stars through the oculus and found himself reminiscing about everything that had happened over the last few months. It seemed so long ago since the day of the Century Eclipse, which was the event that had kicked everything off.

But he found himself longing for the quiet days down in the stacks, researching the old tombs there. He longed for more free time to crack Albright's code, which seemed to be never-ending. That challenge fueled his interests, though, since he honestly disliked all the fighting. While he enjoyed using the war staff and witnessing its power, he found little amusement in ending another person's life. But that was war, and he did what he felt he must. He understood the same thing that Solan did—they were all cogs in the greater scheme. He, too, had a part to play, and he couldn't forget that he *was* the other Skylight Fallout. That had been preordained by Albright himself. Cord was meant to crack his code, which, in turn, might save lives. The breadcrumbs had slowly revealed themselves, a sequential series of events that Albright had masterfully laid out. Cord planned to solve it, even if the cost was his life. And it very well might.

A movement drew his attention, and he turned to see Vail uncloak and sit near him. She pulled her knees up and gazed at the stars, not saying anything. Cord waited for her to spout something off, an insult perhaps or maybe a complex question he had no answer for. But she simply sat there looking up at the stars. Cord felt that strange sensation settle into his stomach again.

"I assume you're here for a reason?" he asked.

"Thought you could use some company. Something wrong with that?"

"That's very thoughtful of you. But I don't require any company. Besides, I don't think that's why you're really here."

Vail shrugged, though she didn't leave or even snap back at him.

Cord rubbed his neck thoughtfully…or was he nervous? The Vail he'd known over the years had been standoffish and a loner. Back then, she would have never sought out his company. But he could sense she was carefully and slowly letting her walls down over their last few conversations. The fact that she was here now spoke volumes.

Cord narrowed his eyes at her. "You mentioned something about similarities between us, do you remember that?"

She nodded.

"I've always done things that border on the edge of the Lucem's principles," Cord continued. "I do what makes sense, and I don't apologize for it. Even though our personalities are different, we view the world through the same lens. Would you agree with that?"

Vail shook her head. "I can't believe I'm even havin' this conversation with you. But yeah, I imagine you're probably right."

"If your beliefs are a little gray, so what? Don't feel bad about the things you've done. I wouldn't."

"Have you ever killed anyone in cold blood?"

"Not yet."

That made Vail pause, a bit shocked. She grinned at him with her head tilted. Cord didn't smile back.

"Vail. I think what we're talking about here is this: can you and I ever be friends."

She crossed her arms. "Well…can we?"

"I think we can both agree things are better between us."

Vail turned a thoughtful gaze to the stars and leaned back on her elbows. "I used to hate you, Ledbetter. You know that, right? So, am I changing, or are you?"

"Bit of both, obviously. We've learned a thing or two over the years. I dare say we've both grown up since university. Would that be a fair assessment?"

Vail nodded. "That would seem to make sense. But frankly, I don't like who I've become. I've killed people for no reason, even when I could have let them live. And every time, I feel a sense of satisfaction. That's the Atrum in me." Vail paused to gather her thoughts, and Cord sensed the mood change. "I want to be around better people, like Stroud, Ti-Leer…you."

There was a moment of silence, Cord not sure how to respond. He knew he wasn't very good at dealing with emotions, especially others' feelings. He was completely out of his element. Empathy felt foreign and extremely uncomfortable, and he hated the weakness it brought. But if Vail was willing to change, maybe he could too, or at least he could try.

Cord did something that shocked him, and apparently, Vail too. He didn't think; otherwise, he would have stood and walked off.

He reached out and gave Vail a hug.

It was the strangest thing he'd ever felt before. It seemed as if he was floating, his head spinning. At first, he was repulsed by the sensation in his gut. But then, it wasn't so bad, now that he was experiencing it. He sensed Vail's shock. She stiffened, and he thought she might push him away or even hit him. But he held onto her and didn't let go. When Vail hugged him back, something within Cord finally let go. It was like a giant chain—one that had always held him back because of E.M., because of his own insecurities—finally snapped and fell away. He sensed the same thing for Vail. She gripped him tighter and exhaled. Then, Vail was crying. He felt tears sting his own eyes. It was a moment that he would never forget.

After what seemed like hours, Vail pushed back and wiped her eyes with the sleeve of her cloak.

"I don't hate you, Vail. I never did," Cord said, hearing the strain in his own voice. "I pushed you away because I was afraid of dealing with my emotions. Jet talks about humility, something I've always viewed as a weakness. Most of my life, I thought winning was the only option and my father beat that into me. I know how difficult it is for you because it's the same for me. What I've always known is this—you have to face your weaknesses. That's how you win. For me, it's been learning how to fail and accepting humility. For you, it's learning to trust others and having patience."

Vail could only stare at Cord. She started to say something several times but paused. If he was confused by his own emotions, then Vail was even more so.

She finally cleared her throat, as if she didn't trust her voice at the moment. "I…I don't really know what to say. I guess…thank you for not giving up on me."

Cord cracked a crooked smile; it felt genuine this time. Like Vail, he'd never had any close friends until joining the Lucem. Whether he admitted it or not, he enjoyed being around them. Apparently for Vail, being around the Atrum hadn't been the same experience. Now, she had a chance to enjoy a whole new group of friends, though it would take some trust on everyone's part.

"If you're planning on sticking around the Lucem, you need to build some trust, starting with Solan," Cord said. "I imagine the others will eventually come around."

Vail gave him another awkward smile, something she was still trying to get used to, Cord imagined. She let out a long breath, as if expelling some tension, then leaned back on her elbows, and Cord joined her. They gazed up at the twinkling stars.

"Cord. How will things end…for us? I mean all of us?" It was simply a question with no spitefulness in it now.

"I assume you know what the second phase of the Prism Effect set into motion?"

"Yes. I know. Hanely Hurse was the first to die, never to return."

"That's right. The second phase put an end to the regeneration of the Heliographi. It would seem our ancient race is coming to an end. Honestly, I still haven't considered specifically how my ending might come. It's best not to dwell on such things, even though I find it a fascinating question."

"Yeah, well, I do think about it. We're all gonna die sooner rather than later. All of us and that's Albright's doing. I still wonder why he did that."

"Perhaps Albright's power was constrained when he set things in motion? Maybe it was a bargain between him and the universe or some higher being? Maybe he *is* the guardian of balance? Who can say?"

"It's beyond me," Vail said. "Still, I can't stop thinking about how all of this will end. I'm worried, which is something I'm not used to. I guess I really have changed."

Cord looked at Vail and waited until she faced him. "Even though I have mixed feelings about destiny, there are forces at work. Each phase of the Prism Effect has come to pass, just as prophesied. I'm slowly becoming a believer in fate."

K

The morning of the fourth fulcrum dawned. Once again, the makeshift camp was alive with preparations and training exercises.

Dane pulled Solan aside and motioned to the area above the pyramid. "See, there?" he pointed.

Solan nodded. "Yes. Another oculus."

"No, beside it."

Solan looked closer and noticed how the holes around the main opening were spaced closely together. "Are you thinking what I'm thinking?"

Dane gave her a slight grin. "If we demolish that portion, it'll provide enough room for our entire air force. Whatever surprise Lybra might have in store, I think we can top her. The Armada is itching for a fight."

"Do it," Solan said and clapped her hands.

There was less than five hours till 'show time,' as Ti-Lerer liked to say. Dane went to work with his team. But Solan found herself feeling anxious once again. This time, they would anticipate the early cannon fire. Lybra had to know she was dealing with a master tactician in Dane. Solan would once again place her trust in the wily general.

At three hours till ignition time, the enemy showed their hand.

Massive numbers of soldiers begin entering the chamber, forcing Dane to sound the alarm earlier than anticipated. The Lucem army hurried into position. Solan spread the remaining Lucem around the base. Then she leapt down multiple levels from the top of the pyramid. Their forces remained under cover from enemy fire. But this time, Lybra's forces continued to push forward.

Solan noticed the same crazed look in the enemy soldier's eyes. Their attack was relentless and the mech units joined in this time. Solan quickly engaged the enemy, focusing on the mechs. But it wasn't long until she heard thoughts from the other Lucem. DiJinn was calling for backup on her side. Solan hated to leave her post, but knew that if Jinn was asking for help, it must be serious.

When she arrived, she understood the distress call. All of the remaining Atrum were trying to overload one side. The push was backed by hundreds of mechs, Tetrahedron and Dreadnaught troops. Leaping down the pyramid was Cord and Vail. Ti-Leer, and DiJinn stood shoulder to shoulder as Solan barreled into a group of mechs to clear the way. In the distance, she could see the Atrum cutting through troops like a fiery wedge, led by Joshia. They would soon be face to face with the Atrum, though Solan noticed there was thankfully still no sign of Sybold.

Solan and the other Lucem held their ground along with the troops. In the back of Solan's mind, she wondered how the other quadrants were holding up. With all the Lucem on just one side of the pyramid, it left the other three sides vulnerable. But what choice did she have? They had to focus on stopping the greatest threat, which at the moment was the approaching Atrum.

They continued to fight off enemy forces as the two groups of Heliographi neared each other. Like a flaming cudgel, the Atrum laid waste to the soldiers in their way. Solan braced herself, knowing they'd be outnumbered, though there was still hope without Sybold present.

Solan could now see Joshia just a few dozen meters away. They made eye contact across the battlefield. Solan witnessed the unnatural aura about her half-sister and knew her condition had worsened. The other Atrum looked much the same—their glow had darkened slightly, their expressions full of rage. It seemed the light surrounding their Heliographi had changed, mutated. Solan barely recognized some of them. If they were related to some ancient Titan's essence, then it had become an abomination. The Atrums' ancient serpent— or *wyrm*—was morphing right before her eyes into something completely different, all because of Sybold's influence.

But at just five meters away, and a platoon of soldiers separating their two groups, there was a huge explosion and a sudden burst of daylight. Everyone paused and looked up.

Dane's crews had finally managed to cut through the upper hull. Several large pieces dropped from above, bringing trees and vegetation with it. The debris hit the side of the pyramid and tumbled down with a loud crash that echoed around the chamber. As if on cue, Dane's air force flooded through the larger oculus. At first, hundreds of smaller jammers raced in, followed by larger war frigates and destroyers. But it was the heavy battle cruisers that drew everyone's attention, led by the massive SLS Armada.

A wave of panic rippled through the enemy line as fire rained down. A cheer erupted from the allies while the enemy line faltered and then crumbled. The tide of battle changed in an instant as their enemy began to flee the battlefield.

Joshia and the other Atrum stood their ground, though, and faced Solan and the Lucem. Neither side moved until a thunderclap shook the ground. A white bolt of lightning leapt from the top of the pyramid. It illuminated the chamber and shot skyward right as the clock hit noon. Ranks of recon troops surrounded the Atrum but held their ground as Joshia stared at Solan. When she spoke, it sounded like multiple voices intertwined together, like tortured souls from some dark well. It made Solan's skin crawl because she knew that it wasn't her half-sister's voice.

It was Sybold speaking through her.

"I'm coming, Solan. Your souls belong to me."

Then the Atrum cloaked and disappeared in a cloud of smoke.

CHAPTER 48

Into the Belly of the Beast

JET AND SEMBER manned the cannons, while the Armada's artificial intelligence did the rest. Jet was suddenly thankful for the battle cruiser's superior armaments. Even without a crew, they were pulverizing hundreds of enemy ships. The Armada's armor was simply too robust for the railguns and missiles. Before they made the airspace between the eighth and ninth belt, half of the Dreadnaught's air force was decimated and the other half fleeing.

Sember sat back and drew in a deep breath.

Jet took a moment and checked their radar. "Thanks, by the way," he said and finally eased back in his seat.

"I figured you were in trouble when those enemy ships moved in. I let the Armada do most of the work and tried to stay nearby. What did you find out?"

"Something you probably don't want to hear."

Sember waited patiently for a few seconds, then raised her hands. "Well, you going to leave me hanging? What is it?"

"I know where Sybold is. We're going to pay her a visit."

Sember's face blanched, and a quick spasm shook her. "Why would we do that?"

"Because that's my ticket home."

"By facing Sybold?" Sember narrowed her eyes. "That makes no sense."

"It's complicated."

"Who told you this?"

"Fritt."

"The leader of the Dreadnaughts?" Sember asked. "And you believe him?"

"Yes."

"Jet. He's a mercenary. The mercenary of mercenaries, in fact. I wouldn't believe him as far as I could throw him. What makes you think he's telling the truth?"

Jet held up Port-Shear. "Because of this. You might say he was under some influence to speak the truth."

Sember gave him a concerned look. "Okay. Let's say he was. How is facing Sybold—on her own turf, I might add—going to get you home?"

"That…I haven't figured out yet. I only know that I have to go through her to get home. And if that's what it takes, then I'm going to do it. My friends need me."

"I don't know. Sounds risky, right? She could be luring you in."

"She is undoubtedly luring me in," Jet said.

"And you think you can defeat her? Jet. Let's be honest. That's a no-win scenario, no offense, of course."

"Look around you, Sember. If there's a chance to avoid all of this, I have to try. It's a small sacrifice, in my opinion. If I can somehow make it past her, millions can be saved, I think."

Jet stood and looked out the front window. Beyond were the remnants of the ninth belt, the muddled sunlight filtered in through the dense haze in an ominous way. "I understand if you don't want to go. If you want me to drop you off somewhere, I will. But I know now this is my path."

Sember thought for a split second. "No. I've come this far. We go together."

"You are right. This is going to be dangerous, Sember."

"If you're set on doing this then I'm coming along. But the Agency headquarters is large. I've been there before. Where would you start?"

"When I was searching for answers in my past world, there was a place in the old Lucem wing called The Hall of Vital Records. It was a conduit between planes created by Christian Albright. I think that's a good starting point."

But Sember still had a concerned look on her face. "Are we announcing our arrival? It's going to be difficult to sneak in. The Armada isn't what I'd call stealthy."

"I'm running out of time, Sember. If I don't get back soon, this future world becomes a reality. If that means busting down the front door with this battle cruiser, so be it."

Sember chuckled. "I always thought Brindall was bold, but he's nothing compared to you. Okay, let's do this."

Jet settled into the pilot seat and set a course for Memorial Park and their old headquarters, Flotsam.

M

Jet found Memorial Park among the debris field. It wasn't hard, thanks to its size. The largest floating chunk of the ninth belt glittered on the horizon as mist and dust bathed it in a reddish light. He maneuvered closer to look inside the large, clear dome and noticed there was no longer a museum inside. Instead, its interior glowed like some fiery forge. He could only imagine what diabolical purpose Sybold was using the once public space for. Most of the hangars were vacant, though, and setting the cruiser down took little effort.

"Sember," Jet said as he unbuckled from his harness. "Are you sure you want to do this—"

"I'm not waiting back this time." Sember stood directly in front of him, arms crossed. "You forget that I'm a soldier with more experience than anyone you know. I've fought in many wars. Plus, you can't stop me."

They stepped off the Armada's gangway, maybe for the last time. Jet looked back at the battle cruiser like he was saying goodbye to an old friend. The Armada had been a lifesaver.

Jet and Sember walked cautiously through the hangar bay. Jet cloaked and scouted ahead, searching for traps or sensors. He led the way to the lower levels, having to shoulder through some of the locked doors. Before long, Jet felt the intuitive voice in his head, which he hadn't heard in a long while. It began to whisper to him, and he knew then he must follow it. One thing became very clear—he wasn't heading toward The Hall of Vital Records after all. They were heading down into the belly of the beast.

К

Solan and crew had successfully countered their enemy's late charge and claimed their third fulcrum. But the first three didn't matter if they couldn't ignite their final fulcrum on the first belt. That one was special. She sensed it was the cornerstone of everything they'd fought and bled for. If they couldn't manage to set its polarity, everything would crumble. Somehow, Solan knew this, and she felt the others did, too. The first belt's fulcrum would decide the balance of power in the Skylight System, and if they failed, Sybold would rule.

Solan also suspected something else.

Lybra hadn't been leading the enemy forces for a while now. She guessed that Sybold had murdered her.

Of course, this didn't come as a surprise. Sybold would have dispatched her as soon as she'd regained her strength. Lybra had served her purpose by building her an army. Harok had done the same by overseeing the completion of Goliath's Gate. They'd both simply been used as pawns.

And now, there was no doubt Sybold would make her appearance at the final fulcrum. They had nothing to counter Sybold, with Jet missing. Furthermore, the eighth belt fulcrum would be ignited tomorrow, and they could not prevent Sybold from setting its polarity. If the eighth fulcrum was similar to the first fulcrum, then

Cord believed it to be a transmitter. Unlike belts two through seven, which were believed to be receivers, the first and eighth fulcrums would transmit something. Solan had an idea what that might be, at least for Sybold.

Bloodlust.

The Serpent Effect,

And with all the fulcrums powering it, that sphere of influence would spread rapidly throughout the system. Millions would be affected, and depending on the first fulcrum's polarity, they would be safe only until it was ignited. The final battle for the first fulcrum meant more than Solan cared to think about. The very survival of the human race hinged on that battle. And yet, the Lucem army was at the end of their endurance. She needed to find a way to rally everyone for their final push. It was all or nothing. Everything they had fought and bled for over the last few months might go down the drain if she couldn't find a way to rally her army. But in the back of her mind, there was nothing she could do to prevent Sybold from taking the first belt's fulcrum unless Jet magically appeared in the next three days.

M

Jet led the way down into the bowels of Memorial Park as Sember followed close behind. He was trusting the 'intuitive voice' now, just like he had throughout his life. The air inside was musty and unused. Dust blanketed the floors as they tip-toed along. This had once been the public jewel of the Skylight System, but based on the smell, it had probably been abandoned long ago.

They took stairwells instead of vector accelerators to avoid attention. As they descended deeper, the air grew heavy and humid. Soon, Jet began to feel the 'sickness' again. Even though they were no longer inside the electrical storm, the air gave him a nauseous feeling the deeper they ventured. He was coming closer to the source.

In his mind, he could hear Port-Shear begin to whisper. The ancient war staff was waking. But its vibe was different now. In fact, it seemed uncertain, perhaps. Jet had not felt that before. Port-Shear's ambiance had ranged from confident to angry to ominous or even childlike at times. But never uncertain. That gave him pause.

Was he doing the right thing?

But it was the only plan he had. Not that he liked it or even agreed with it. He just had no other direction, and he wasn't going to turn tail and run now. He wished Solan was here, or Cord, just to give some advice. But the clock was ticking, and he *had* to do something.

Before long, Jet could no longer hear the intuitive voice. It seemed to have disappeared, or perhaps it had fled. It seemed strange that as soon as Port-Shear had awakened, the intuitive voice went away. Regardless, Jet knew where he was heading now.

Sember pulled at his cloak. "Do you feel that?" she asked. "The air isn't right. It feels like it did back on the belts."

"Yeah, I feel it." Jet held her gaze in the dim light of the stairwell. "She's near."

"You still sure this is a good idea? Maybe we should come back later. You're already tired and I wonder—"

"No, Sember. This is it. I have to do this now. There's no time left. It's okay if you want to go back. You can take the ship and leave. I can do this alone. I *should* do this alone."

Sember paused and took a deep breath.

"I know this is scary," Jet continued and gripped her shoulder. "I'm afraid too. It's nothing to be ashamed of. You don't have to come, Sember."

But she shook her head. "No. I think I was meant to do this."

Jet gave her a quick smile. "Let's move on."

They traveled downward and the air continued to thicken and grow stale. It was like descending into hell, Jet thought. His mood darkened and there seemed to be a weight on him he couldn't shake. It wasn't long until Port-Shear began to whisper again.

After ten minutes of listening to the war staff's babbling, Jet stopped on a stair landing.

"What's wrong?" Sember said, a worried tone in her voice.

"This…thing." Jet held up the staff and almost threw it. "I don't know what's wrong, but…"

Sember scrunched her eyes at him. "But what?"

Jet lowered the staff and took a deep breath. "I just…I need to understand what it's trying to tell me before we go any farther."

Sember looked at him uncertainly. "Sure. What should I do?"

"Just keep an eye out while I'm meditating. Call my name if you need me." Jet settled down on the landing and laid the war staff across his lap. He placed his palms facing down on the surface and closed his eyes and fell into Vishmu.

Jet was immediately transported across the cosmos. His being elongated across light years as he moved into one of the highest planes of existence, calling out for Port-Shear. He let his voice echo across the multidimensions and soon he could sense the being was near him. The presence of Port-Shear was disturbing, almost unbearable. Though Jet's gift permitted contact, it still unnerved him.

Jet slowed, and his elongated form slowly contracted. He looked at Port-Shear, the Titan's jeweled form reflecting time and space. The millions of facets made it hard to look directly at him. Jet did his best to form thoughts, trying to communicate with the being.

…I don't understand… Jet said.

…no time…you mustn't…

…mustn't what… Jet asked.

…no…Rend-Shear…

Jet floated in space, not sure what to make of it. Who was Rend-Shear? But then he knew. It had to be the name of Sybold's war staff—the being, or Titan, who enchanted the black vessel.

…why… Jet asked.

…no time…

…it has to be…

…NO TIME… Port-Shear roared so loud that the fabric of space vibrated.

Jet felt his own temper start to flare. This was his decision, not some being from a distant dimension or plane or whatever.

…it's not up to you… Jet replied.

…NO…YOUNGLING… Port-Shear roared again.

Jet waited to see if there was anything else, but the Titan remained, as if waiting for his response. Jet was afraid to say more, not wanting to anger Port-Shear again. But at the same time, he didn't want his own anger to get out of control. Jet snapped the connection closed.

When he woke from his meditation, Sember was asleep, her head slumped against his shoulder. Jet felt panic set in and checked the time.

He'd been in meditation for nearly five hours.

CHAPTER 49

Ignition Day

THE DAY OF the final fulcrum was upon them. As Solan had predicted, the Atrum army successfully ignited the eighth belt fulcrum two days prior. Solan had felt it, like a cosmic supernova. Those waves had pulsed across the Skylight System immediately after the clock struck noon that day. According to Stell's scouts, the larger pyramid had risen through the belt's hull. Once ignited, the fifth, sixth and seventh fulcrums had joined polarities to combine with the larger eighth fulcrum. An electric storm now covered all four of the outer belts. Whether it was a dome or some sphere of influence, Solan wasn't certain. What she did know was that this 'unnatural storm' would spread if they didn't win the battle for the first belt's fulcrum. The polarity of the second, third and fourth belts currently belonged to them, but Solan felt that would all change if they lost today.

They had taken the last few days to prepare. Tension was at an all-time high around the Lyrinthum hangar bay. Dane had gone over everything with his team and Patrick. Solan and the other Lucem had studied the first belt's fulcrum. Based on what they knew about the eighth belt's pyramid, the first belt seemed much the same.

Oddly enough, that day's war would take place under the Clipton River. In fact, the pyramid was located near Firefly Falls, where Jet had buried his friend, Cutter Jade. Coincidence? Was there something special about that area after all?

Solan spent that morning helping Dane set up defenses while coordinating with Stell and her team to make sure the citizens would be safe. This final battle would be an all-out effort on both sides. Neither would hold anything back.

But in the back of her mind, questions still lingered.

Would Jet return? Would Sybold make her appearance?

Solan knew the answer to the second question. Yes. Sybold would make her appearance today. The first question, she tried not to think about because it was out of her control.

The majority of the first belt had been evacuated. Skylight University was a ghost town, something Solan thought she would never see. The university had never shut its doors. It was a sign of the times, and it broke her heart to witness it. She feared things in the system would never be the same again.

Just after sunrise, Kamber found Solan. "Come, you have to see this!"

Kamber led her down through Lyrinthum and deep into the bowels of the first belt. They neared the site of the fulcrum and the pyramid. The oculus high above had mysteriously caved in. The opening was now large enough for any air fleet to enter.

Solan smiled. "A ray of hope for once, literally. Dane's going to be happy to see this. Time to rework our plans. Find him, hurry!"

As Kamber hurried off, Solan made her way over to explore the area above. Daylight flooded in, and around the edges, she could see tree roots, rock and dirt hanging on. The collapse had rerouted a small portion of the Clipton River, and rivulets of it spilled down several hundred meters through the opening.

While Solan waited for Dane, she studied the large pyramid. It was definitely unique, compared to the others. Though the shape of it was similar, with its stepped plateaus and Aztec influence, the field around it was an actual maze. Deep channels had been cut into the metallic floor, each passaged perhaps ten meters wide. The field was like some intricate motherboard, a network of corridors radiating outward from the base. The channels were tall enough to prevent most troops from climbing over. It would be trench warfare in many areas. *This should be interesting,* Solan mused.

When Dane arrived, he looked up at the opening and smiled broadly. He turned to Patrick. "Ready the air force. We have just enough time to revamp our plans."

Solan walked alongside Dane as they hurried back to the control room. Thankfully, most of their ground defenses were already in place, and last-minute preparations were wrapping up. When they entered the control room, Dane immediately started strategizing with his team. Solan sat in the meeting for a few minutes but didn't stay long. She was of little use—her time would be better spent helping prepare on the battlefield. She hurried back and searched for DiJinn. She found her working with a group of recon soldiers and Ti-Leer.

"Jinn," Solan said and pulled her aside. "Are you about ready?"

"Of course," she said. "Studied the floorplans last night. I have an idea where the memoir might be."

"Good. When the enemy arrives, make your move. Our old base should be fairly empty."

"You realize that Lybra's no longer leadin' their forces."

Solan gave her a tense look. "Yes. Lybra hasn't been around for a while now."

"Sybold will be here today. Are you sure you want me to go?"

Hearing Sybold's name made Solan reconsider for just a split second. "We need the ninth memoir. You're the only one who can get it."

"And how will we deal with Sybold?" DiJinn said and lowered her gaze. "Especially if she's at full strength?"

"I'll find a way to handle it, Jinn. Just focus on your mission."

"Don't take this the wrong way, Sol. But you know taking on Sybold is a suicide mission."

"If Jet doesn't show up, I'll have no other option."

K

At one hour till noon, enemy forces began to arrive. Solan hurried through the ranks of troops, barking orders and encouragement. She held her war staff high, letting its light shine like a beacon of hope. The other Heliographi rallied their troops as well, while Kamber remained within the inner sanctum. Jinn had already departed, and Solan said a silent prayer for her safety.

She was beginning to worry about Dane's fleet, though. She thought he'd have everything ready by now, but there was no sign of him. But she knew they'd had little time to scramble the fleet and ready the crews. It was going to be a close call, no doubt. They would be shorthanded without Dane on the battlefield. But as Solan watched the enemy pour in, so did their air fleet. Apparently, the enemy had been notified about the mysterious opening. She should have known they'd have their spies in place.

Solan readied herself, her eyes trained along the metallic maze in the field beyond. The ground began to vibrate as thousands of troops began pushing across the field and toward them. Solan held her position behind the ramparts of the pyramid. With Dane gone, she was directing the show now.

She gave the signal, and the mounted howitzers erupted. Rounds pummeled the troops as they advanced. Some of the heavier vehicles moved up and absorbed the fire. At the same time, the smaller jammers and skiffs attacked from above. Enemy frigates rained fire down on the pyramid. When Solan looked up, she saw the cargo bays open, and hundreds of troops surged down zip lines.

"To the interior!" she yelled and immediately leapt up the side of the pyramid and toward the top opening.

She made it there just as the first troops hit the apex level. Solan swung her staff, and the vibration it sent forth pushed the enemy troops over the parapet. She was joined by a platoon of recon soldiers, who took aim and started picking off the enemy.

Solan dropped through the top of the pyramid opening and down twenty meters. She landed on her feet next to Kamber, who gripped her war staff and looked up at the troops flooding in.

"Come on!" Kamber yelled, her stance squared and ready.

As the enemy made it past the recon above, Solan and Kamber easily dispatched them. But soon, there were more flooding in and before long, the inner sanctum was filled with Dreadnaught's, Tetrahedron and a few mechs. Solan and Kamber stood back-to-back and dispatched troops. Minutes later, Solan felt Vail's presence as she dropped to the ground behind the enemy soldiers. She slammed her staff on the ground and the remaining troops dropped dead instantly.

Solan looked up to see that the recon troops had set up a heavy cannon and had taken down the drop ships. For the moment, they had secured the inner sanctum.

"Kamber, you got this?" Solan said.

"Of course. Go!"

Vail and Solan rushed up the stairs to the apex level. When Solan reached the top, she had a clear view of the entire battlefield. What she saw made her heart drop. It was full of enemy forces in all directions as far as she could see.

"Where did all this come from?" Vail hissed in disbelief.

Solan had no answer. Apparently, they had held back their reserves for the final battle. It was something they hadn't planned for. "Get back to Cord. He's going to need you."

Solan moved to her own position, which was lower on the pyramid's side but behind the ramparts. She sent orders down to the field commanders when a sector was about to collapse. If it grew worse, she would rush to that spot, clear the enemy—until her troops could shore up the line—then return to her perch. But she could already see that the rhythm of war was moving too quickly. They simply weren't keeping up and would not survive at this pace. In the back of her mind, she wondered where Dane was. *And...where was Sybold?*

CHAPTER 50

Hell's Forge

J ET REACHED OVER and shook Sember awake. Her eyes fluttered open, and she convulsed for a few seconds.

"Jet," she said. "Where did you go? It's been hours."

Jet felt his shoulders slump, and his head rolled back against the stair railing. "I'm sorry. I should've known that would happen. We have to go." Jet stood and pulled Sember with him.

"Can't we wait a bit longer?" she asked with a yawn and arched her back.

Jet shook his head. "We gotta move."

But Sember pulled at his arm. "Hold on. You were gone a while. Did you find any answers?"

They both stood motionless on the landing in the dim light. "I think I finally figured it out. The message in the pyramids—" Jet stopped midsentence and held up his hand. "Now's not the time. We have to go."

Sember took a few seconds, then slowly nodded. "Alright." She held out her hand for him to lead the way.

They made their way down to the bottom of the stairs, where the heat was becoming unbearable. The air was heavier and almost suffocating. It felt like they had just descended into the ninth circle of Dante's Inferno. They continued into a large, metallic antechamber filled with steam, the rusty bulkheads warm to the touch. Jet had never been this deep into a hull before. It was new territory for him. He guessed they were near the stabilization levels, which were at the very bottom of each belt's hull. The gravity even felt stronger down here.

"Stay close," Jet whispered, though Sember was practically on his back.

Jet held Port-Shear in front of him, but the white light was dimmer now. Jet wondered if the Titan was really away or simply pouting from their last argument.

The antechamber had a low ceiling that stretched outward for hundreds of meters. The walls were blackened and sooty. Jet guessed this area had once been used for smelting or some similar function. When they reached the halfway point, he noticed an opening off to each side about every ten meters. The main thoroughfare had branched into dozens of passages. Jet paused.

"What is it?" Sember asked.

"I'm not sure which way to go."

As they stood there, the ground began to quiver. At the far end of the antechamber, a massive iron door opened. Just behind it, Jet could see a glowing red glob that looked like molten lava. It began to flow in their direction. Jet pulled Sember and raced directly toward the flowing molten steel.

"What are you doing!" she yelled.

Jet didn't answer as they sprinted. At the last second, he sprang to his right and down one of the side chambers, where they hunched and waited. They watched the molten steel ooze past until the flow finally stopped. Jet heard the doors slam shut with a resounding thud.

Sember moved forward, but Jet held her back. "Wait a second," he said.

The area beyond was still smoking, too hot to walk on. But as they waited, the steel walls cooled surprisingly fast.

They moved out of the side chamber and closer to the main doors and paused.

"I bet this is on a timer," Jet said and held a hand to the steel. "We just need to wait for it to open again."

"That would explain the heat," Sember replied. "Wonder what it's for, though? Doesn't seem like anyone's home. A bit odd, don't you think? Anyway, it feels like hell down here."

And it might be, Jet thought to himself.

When the ground started to quiver again, Jet pulled Sember close. "Get ready."

As soon as the steel-plated doors slid open, Jet and Sember jumped through, just seconds before the molten flow slid past. They waited off to the side with their backs turned from the heat. Minutes later, the doors slammed shut again.

They stood in a large, multilevel forge, surrounded by massive iron cauldrons. Embers sparked and hissed into the air as red glowing blobs bubbled from the cauldrons. Some thirty meters above were conveyor belts moving parts along. Jet recognized the shape of the torsos, heads and other parts for the M-Class unit. *So, this was where Lybra had been constructing her army.* It was so far beneath the Agency that no one had even noticed. If he had to guess, this had once been a secret Agency operation used for building warships, based on the size of the bay. By the look of things, it had been shuttered ages ago. But Lybra had repurposed it, right beneath everyone's nose. And apparently, things were still running on autopilot, now that she was dead…or was that really the case?

"Come on," Jet whispered and moved up and along one of the higher conveyors. They traveled through the forge and into another large bay. Beyond, he could hear shouting and clamoring. It was a sound he was familiar with. An orchestra of clicking metallic parts, all moving in unison. M-Class mechs. He peered below to see thousands of the units marching around.

Things were beginning to fall into place now.

Sybold must have planned this out long ago and used Lybra to facilitate the operation. Yet, this army had never truly been Lybra's. This was Sybold's doomsday army, one that would enforce her rule of the ninth belt. And it could travel anywhere in the system, since it wasn't affected by the sphere of bloodlust. With millions of surviving citizens now crowded around the broken remnants of the debris field, these obedient machines would carry out her command without question or emotion.

Once again, Jet could see how costly his decision had been. He should have stayed with his friends back in his own world and ignored Albright's quest. *Surely, Albright hadn't meant for things to happen this way.* But in order to find out, he needed to locate Sybold.

К

Solan's feet were suddenly upended. She flew head-over-heels as the mortar blast exploded near her. Mangled steel flew past, the shrapnel just missing several nearby troops. She landed on her side and rolled, using her cloak to shield her from incoming railgun fire. She pulled as many troops as she could with her and moved back, yelling for a retreat up to the pyramid's second plateau.

When she looked up, the recon troops were still holding their ground from the frigates above. But in the distance, she could see more enemy cruisers moving in. It wouldn't be long until the recon troops were sitting ducks from their howitzers overhead.

But she had to focus on her own sector now. She only hoped that the other Heliographi were holding their own side. There was a total of five plateaus on the giant pyramid. They had three more lines of defense left, then the inner sanctum. If Dane didn't get to them soon, all would be lost.

But the enemy's intensity seemed to be growing stronger with each minute that passed. Once again, she had seen the bloodlust in their glazed eyes. It was a reddish film now, slightly different than before. There was also a rancid odor along with inhuman strength. They moved fast and didn't seem to show fear or fatigue. The zombielike troops threw their bodies into the fray with little regard for their own life.

Solan felt Cord bump into her.

"What is it?" she yelled.

"Need backup on the other side," Cord panted. "The Atrum have finally arrived."

Solan groaned. The remaining Atrum easily outnumbered them. That was something they couldn't afford.

"Alright, let's go!" She hated to leave her side, knowing it would collapse as soon as she did. But if the Atrum made the inner sanctum, they were all dead.

As soon as Solan and Cord arrived, she could see the Atrum's war staffs arcing in the distance. It appeared they were trying the same tactic as last time by overloading one side again. This time, they had held back, though, letting their own foot soldiers wear down the Lucem forces. Now, the way was mostly clear with little resistance. Solan counted four Atrum but couldn't tell which ones. She felt her staff begin to vibrate, her vessel sensing the proximity of the opposing vessels. Thankfully, both her staff and Cord's had received upgrades. Perhaps between them, they stood a chance.

As the Atrum approached, they saw Solan and Cord. It was Bofisto, Sojahn, Tetra, and Brit. They moved in slowly, surrounding them.

"My, *my!* If it isn't the great Solan Alexander and Cord Ledbetter," Bofisto mocked. He dragged his staff on the metallic floor, and it shot sparks from where it made contact, leaving a glowing gouge in the steel. "Where is your girlfriend, Solan? Oh, I do wish 'Tiny

Jinn' was here." The huge man flashed a mocking grin at her. The tiny metal daggers attached to his teeth glinted in the dull sunlight.

"I think you need to focus on me instead, or it might be the last thing you do," Solan said through clenched teeth. But she sensed what Bofisto was hinting at—*they'd somehow known that DiJinn had gone after the ninth memoir.*

Sojahn and Brit moved to the left of Solan while Tetra and Bofisto circled to face Cord.

"You sure you want to do this?" Cord asked, lifting his war staff. The modified vessel pulsed with a yellow light that matched his glowing eyes.

"It's not too late," Solan said. "You can resist Sybold's influence."

"It was always too late for us, Solan," Brit said. "And now, it's too late for you. She is near…"

Brit lunged at Solan as Bofisto tried to sweep Cord's legs out and the fight was on.

But Cord hammered his staff down and blocked Bofisto's war staff. Sparks flew as they connected. Cord flipped over his head and landed between Tetra and Bofisto. Their staffs jabbed and parried so quickly it was a blur of light. Meanwhile, Solan had managed to take Brit down and engaged Sojahn. She screamed as she swung her war staff. But Solan was quicker and sidestepped. Sojahn's slower, powerful strikes had little effect. Brit was back on his feet and tried to wrap his staff around her neck and choke her. Solan ducked and brought the butt of her staff into his midsection. She could have used the pointed end and finished Brit off. Yet, she held back, hoping to simply knock him unconscious rather than kill him. But she could see that Cord had no intention of that. He was striking blows that *would* kill. He wasn't holding back.

But Bofisto was an elder Atrum and well-trained. Tetra took a backseat as Cord and Bofisto faced off. With each blow from their staffs, embers lit the air, and the sound of thunderclaps followed.

Solan tried to watch Cord from the corner of her eye, but still had to focus on the two Atrum in front of her. She moved quickly, preventing Brit from circling behind her again. She wanted them in front of her. They continued to spar as the battle raged around them. The troops—both ally and enemy—gave way, creating an island around the Heliographi as they fought. Eventually, Brit made another error, and Solan slashed across his forehead. The end of her staff erupted as she landed the blow. It was enough to knock him unconscious this time, and he dropped to the floor and lay still.

Sojahn jumped over Brit's body and brought her staff down. Solan lifted her staff with both hands and blocked the strike, sending sparks outward in a massive eruption that lit the surroundings. Then she glanced over at Cord just in time to see him block Bofisto. With a quick flick of his wrist, he knocked Bofisto's staff away.

Cord moved in toward the unarmed Atrum, but Tetra stepped between them. Bofisto stood there, not sure what to do as Tetra engaged Cord. Solan could already see that Tetra was completely overmatched. The vessel on the end of Cord's war staff glowed and seemed to whisper. Cord let loose a series of jabs and sweeps, Tetra unable to keep up. Cord saw an opening and lunged. The vessel end of his staff impacted Tetra in the midsection. The blow rang out, and she was blown backwards several meters. Tetra landed on her feet, teetered, then fell forward, dead.

A massive thunderclap echoed around the chamber, and the sunlight dimmed noticeably. Bofisto and Sojahn looked at Cord in disbelief for just a split second. Then Sojahn screamed and rushed at Cord while Bofisto leapt to retrieve his staff.

Solan stepped to Cord's side, still a bit stunned at what she'd just witnessed. She'd known Cord was dangerous and that he was capable of killing. But he could have easily pulled the deadly strike. Instead, he'd stepped into it, knowing it would end Tetra's life.

Bofisto and Sojahn were about to reengage when the ground started to quiver violently. Solan planted her staff into the floor to steady herself. She glanced at Cord, wondering what was happening. Then, the floor began to rise rapidly. Solan looked above to see the entire pyramid was heaving upward, yet it wasn't noon. There was still plenty of time till the ignition.

The pyramid rose steadily as the surface below was ground into dust. To Solan, it felt like they were riding a volcano as it erupted. Solan, Cord, Bofisto and Sojahn were too stunned to continue fighting. She grabbed Cord and pulled him closer to the interior wall as Bofisto and Sojahn slid off the edge and disappeared.

Soon, they neared the top of the large oculus in the belt's surface. Now, she understood that the roof section had fallen away to make room for the pyramid. When the pyramid finally stopped, Cord and Solan stood roughly fifty meters above the surface of the first belt. She could see the Clipton Forest below, and the Clipton River had been diverted around the massive pyramid. Solan checked the time, and there was just thirty minutes left.

Where the hell was Jet!

CHAPTER 51
The End of the Line

JET AND SEMBER sat silently, looking down from their perch. Below were thousands of M-Class mechs marching around the bay floor. He knew there was no way in Skylight he could take on that many mechs, Port-Shear or not. "Come on," he whispered.

They crept along the high conveyor belt, stopping occasionally to listen. But the mechs below had stopped marching and stood at attention now, as if waiting for orders. Jet and Sember moved through to the next bay only to see thousands more of the M-Class mechs. So far, they hadn't seen a single living person. Jet was beginning to wonder if they were the only living things left on Memorial Park.

In the next bay were thousands of jammers, hovering just above the floor. Jet pulled Sember to a stop. "I think we need to make our way down lower."

"Are you crazy?" she asked.

Jet looked over the edge again. "Something tells me those mechs are immobilized for a reason. She's offering me a fair fight."

Sember's eyes went wide, her skin lost its color. "You're frightening me, Jet. You shouldn't go down there. What if it's a trap?" She took his hand.

"I don't think that's how Sybold works."

"You saw what she did to Lybra. How can you trust anything she might offer?"

"Somehow, I just know. Besides…what I was trying to tell you earlier is that I figured out the message in the fulcrums."

Sember arched her eyebrows and lowered her gaze. "What message?"

"Remember those Greek symbols? The ones I almost died to see?"

"But we never saw the ones on the inner belts. We don't know the—"

"Yes, I do."

Sember waited and Jet sensed her concern turn to fear.

"S, A, C, R," he said. "There are nine letters. It spells 'sacrifice,' Sember. I think that's what I'm supposed to do."

"That makes no sense. It could mean any number of things. Are you willing to risk your life on a guess?"

Jet held her hands. "I've lived my entire life listening to my intuition. I've always followed it. I'm following it now. This is what I have to do."

"Jet. Please…don't go down there."

"I have to."

Sember stared into Jet's glowing eyes. He could tell she was close to tears, and in that instant, he felt a sudden pity for her. Sember was all alone in this apocalyptic world. She had no family, no friends. Like him, and all the other Heliographi, she was different and had lived a life of solitude.

"I don't want to be in this world anymore, Jet. Not alone, not without you. I've faced death in so many battles. But living like this is the worst thing I've ever faced."

Jet didn't know what to say to her. He was only doing what he believed was right and that facing Sybold would lead him home. He would either die or make it back. Either way, Sember would be left behind, and he couldn't take her along.

A few minutes passed, both silent. Sember finally released his hands and straightened her shoulders. "It's okay. You need to go, I understand. It's selfish of me to even talk about this right now when you're about to…" Sember couldn't finish her sentence.

"I'm sorry, Sember. I don't know what to say except that I have to do this."

"Go," she said, her voice steady now. "Please, just go and leave me."

Jet gave her one last downcast look, then cloaked and hopped over the edge of the conveyor belt.

N

Vail felt the ground begin to shake, and she tumbled. When she regained her footing, she was surrounded by thousands of troops, both enemy and ally. She'd been helping a group of recon soldiers to hold a portion of the line. But it had collapsed, and everything had gone to hell now. She cloaked and searched for the other Lucem, in particular for Ledbetter. But he'd disappeared among the chaos.

Dammit, Ledbetter! she thought, both in frustration and concern.

But Vail was also fighting an internal battle now. She could feel the presence of Sybold nearby. She was ready to make her appearance known, and that frightened Vail.

This time, she'll kill me if she finds me. There was little doubt of that.

Regardless, Vail wasn't running away. Maybe her new attitude was partially from Stroud's annoying persona already rubbing off on her?

She continued to move toward the pyramid as it rose up through the belt's hull. The steel deck around the base continued to shear in half, and the piercing sound of rending metal filled the vast chamber. The fighting in her area was fierce, and the enemy troops finally overwhelmed the recon army. The crazed Tetrahedron and Dreadnaughts were climbing the steps of the pyramid, chasing the Lucem army inwards. Still cloaked, Vail used her staff to knock troops off and help clear the way as she hurtled up the levels.

Then she heard a familiar voice speak from behind her.

"Well, if it isn't Vail Hart. The traitor."

She turned to see Brit. He held his war staff out in front of him, pointing it at her chest. There was a darker hue to his eyes, and they held a reddish film glazed across them. He seemed to have difficulty controlling his expression, like he couldn't decide to laugh or scream.

"Don't be an idiot, Brit." Vail circled him as troops moved past the two of them.

"She's coming, Vail," Brit said and seemed to finally break through. "Leave now, if you want to live."

"I know what I'm doin'."

"I'm not so sure about that," Brit replied. "She let you live the first time. She won't do it again."

"She let me go unharmed on purpose!" Vail hissed. "You know it, and so do all the other Atrum. Why, Brit? Tell me!"

"You know I can't do that," he chuckled.

"Brit, please." Vail lowered her staff. "I don't want to fight you or anyone else. I just want to know why she kicked me out."

"Maybe she sensed…" Brit paused.

"What," Vail screamed. "What!"

"…that you're not like us. Not anymore."

"What does that mean?"

"That you're not under her control like the rest of us," Brit said in a lower voice, his eyes darting around. "She can't control you."

"Then why didn't she just kill me!"

"I can't answer that," Brit said and finally lowered his staff. "When she's near, I can't think. All I feel is rage and hate. I want to kill. When she's near, don't try to reason with us, Vail. I will kill you because I'm not myself. Go, please. Go now before I lose control again."

Vail held Brit's gaze for a few more seconds. Her old boyfriend, someone she'd known for nearly a decade now. At that moment, he was so different she barely recognized him.

"Goodbye, Brit," Vail said. She pulled her hood over her head and vanished.

M

Jet finally made it to the ground level of the massive bay, though it felt more like some Titan's forge from the depths of hell. He remained cloaked, even though he knew the M-Class mechs could still see him. Yet, they stood stonelike as if being held in check. There were thousands of them organized into neat rows as far as he could see. It was an army that had been built for one purpose. To eliminate the human race.

He walked silently through the rows, searching between the gaps. In the back of his mind, he began to hear Port-Shear whisper again. The Titan was beginning to awaken.

As Jet moved along, he could feel that sickness seeping into his being. It hit him in the pit of his stomach, making him feel nauseous. That feeling moved through him and into his mind, clouding his thoughts and creating doubt. His heart began to race.

Maybe Sember was right? *Maybe he shouldn't have come down here?*

But he pushed the thought away. He would find out soon enough if he'd made the right decision.

Port-Shear continued to whisper louder. *…you are wrong…to be here…*

Jet shook his head. *…leave me alone…*

…you…die without me…youngling…

…fine…it's why I'm here…sacrifice…

…WRONG… Port-Shear roared. *…no time…*

Port-Shear was in his head now. The ancient Titan seemed to lengthen out around him, as if in preparation. Jet felt the sickness continue to intensify in his body and mind.

He was moving closer to her.

Jet held the war staff in front of him. The pure white light flashed and pulsed, sending out waves that engulfed the mechs around him. Everything seemed to warp in Jet's vision.

Move closer, a voice whispered, and it sounded like a hissing serpent.

Closer…

Then, Jet reached a clearing in the middle of the mechs. He walked to the very center, rammed the butt of his staff into the metal deck and closed his eyes in preparation.

The mech units began to stir. They turned, reoriented on Jet and Port-Shear. Then they began to spread out, creating a circular arena.

K

Solan and Cord stood back-to-back as the pyramid finally stabilized. Thousands of troops and mechs clambered up the steps and toward them. Just beyond Solan was the portal leading into the pyramid and the inner sanctum below. If they didn't keep the enemy out, Kamber would be the final defense.

Cord stood in the opposite doorway as Solan readied herself. She closed her eyes and took a deep breath, then looked into the vessel of her staff, hoping she had enough strength left for what might be her final battle.

Solan braced herself.

It only took a few more seconds before the swarm of units crashed into her and Cord. Their staffs lit up in a blur of lightning, shredding the incoming wave. Pieces of mech units started to pile up around them. The parts spilled off the top plateau and rained down onto the next step below. But the mechs kept coming. Solan backed into the narrow opening and felt Cord lean against her. The first hint of fatigue set in as her arms and legs screamed in pain. She didn't know how much longer she could hold out.

Additional Dreadnaught troops soon arrived. Their combined might was becoming too much, even with her modified staff. Minutes passed when she felt Cord

stumble to one knee. It was all the enemy needed, and Cord's body was suddenly thrust into her back. He was literally being crushed against her from the rush of troops pressing in.

This is it, she thought. *This is my final breath.*

As if on cue, the surrounding air lit up with fire and explosions that rocked the ground.

Solan felt the heat of a massive blast, and the troops in front of her seemed to melt away. Suddenly, she could breathe again. She turned and found Cord, then pulled him to his feet. They used their staffs to force the troops back. Another explosion rocked the top of the pyramid.

"What was that?" Cord said through labored breath. "It's not time for the ignition yet."

Solan poked her head through the opposite opening and saw the shadow of a massive battle cruiser descending through the oculus above, followed by dozens of other war frigates. It was the SLS Armada.

Dane had finally arrived.

CHAPTER 52
The Rubicon

VAIL BOLTED IN the opposite direction of Brit. She had suddenly lost control of her emotions and hated herself for it. The memories of her youth came rushing back. The abuse from her parents, her classmates—the hatred and anger that had driven her to be who she was. It had made her strong, independent…lonely and spiteful.

She didn't want to be alone anymore. She wanted to be with people who cared for her, who wanted her around. *People like Stroud. People like Solan and Ledbetter.*

And yet, she didn't belong with the Lucem. They might not run her off like the Atrum had, but they sure as hell would never *truly* accept her. But where else did she have to go?

Vail continued to run, and it felt like her world was falling apart, right in the middle of this damned war. She didn't have time for a meltdown; she could save that for later.

She finally stopped on the third plateau of the pyramid, still cloaked, and sat down with her back against its large step. As the battle continued around her, with troops dying and screaming, she took a deep breath and closed her eyes.

What would Stroud do?

He would fight on. He wouldn't give up on himself or his friends.

And suddenly, it was so clear to her. She would stand with the Lucem. Stand against Sybold. They needed her help. She had vowed to help Stroud anyway, and she wasn't going to abandon him like the Atrum had done to her.

Vail stood and gripped her war staff. As she scanned the battlefield, everyone seemed to be racing toward the apex of the pyramid.

But that's also where Sybold would be.

Vail somehow knew Sybold was on her way there. She would make her appearance at the very top. She wanted that grand announcement to all of Skylight. And that thought still frightened Vail.

So be it! she thought. Vail would cross that line, and there would be no return.

Vail raised her war staff, and the vessel began to glow. It whispered to her, sending chills through her body. She slammed it on the ground. The concussive impact vaulted her up the plateaued steps and over thousands of enemy troops. When she made it to the top, Cord and Solan were nearly overwhelmed by enemy troops.

Vail immediately fell in behind them and began sweeping them off the plateau.

M

Jet stood in the middle of the arena that had formed around him. He could still hear Port-Shear in his head, the Titan clearly upset with his decision.

In the center of the floor, and permanently embedded in the steel deck, were eleven of the Atrum's war staffs in a circular pattern. Only one was missing. Jet looked closer and saw Vail's staff, then Bofisto's, Sojahn's, even Mosstrom's staff, all displayed like trophies.

Jet sensed that he had crossed a line, and there was no turning back.

He had a sudden revelation. *He knew why he'd struggled to fend off the serpent's effect.*

While Sybold had collected the souls of the fallen Atrum, he hadn't collected any of the Lucem souls because…

…because he'd been missing in this world as they'd perished.

It was a morbid, selfish thing to consider. Where Sybold had probably taken steps to usher in her fellow Atrums' demise so she could become more powerful. Like a black widow, using and then collecting her victims, regardless of who they were. Jet began to wonder if the other Atrum had even known Sybold's true intention. That had been her plan all along, and she was much stronger, while he was still just one Lucem.

The thousands of M-class mechs suddenly locked arms, creating an impenetrable barrier. In the bay's fiery light, Port-Shear shone bright, reflecting off the gleaming mechs. The eerie sound of his war staff's moans could be heard around the arena.

In preparation, Jet thought. Port-Shear was readying itself for battle with its equal.

…*prepare*… a voice said, reminding him of the last four and a half years. His journey through Skylight, then the induction into the Heliographi, a path that had led him to this point in time. Had it all been preordained? His life—and perhaps the future of the human race—came down to this.

...sacrifice...

Was that really the answer? Was he making a colossal mistake by facing Sybold right now instead of waiting until he was stronger? But he'd missed his chance to collect the other Lucems' souls—they were all dead now.

A noise in the distance drew his attention.

Beyond was a large cauldron. Its black iron shone dully in the reddish light, the lip of it glowed with molten slag and sent sparks and embers into the rafters high above. A ripple like a wave pulsed through the field of mechs, and they shifted like the parting of a sea to let something through. Then they immediately closed right behind it. Though Jet couldn't see what was causing the ripple, he knew what it was.

Sybold had finally come. The sick feeling in his soul was undeniable.

But it seemed to take an eternity. The entire time, Port-Shear hummed in his sweaty hands. The war staff grew hotter, the skull grinned and morphed in the firelight of the forge.

Finally, the two mechs at the edge of the arena stepped aside. There seemed to be darkness behind them, a fog of evil—a cloud of malice. Jet could see two glowing pinpoints of dark light staring at him beyond.

Those eyes bored through him, threatening to drive him mad. He had faced Sybold once before, during his freshman year at Skylight University. She had tried to murder him the night of the Triclipse. But her eyes back then had been a bright red. Now, they were a black beyond description. The light from her eyes was an abyss, or some ominous black hole perhaps. They devoured all hope and joy and peace. Whatever Sybold had become, it was nothing like her former self.

Finally, Sybold stepped into the arena, and the two mechs closed behind her.

For several minutes, they faced each other. Sybold was short, having possessed the body of a twenty-something-year-old lady. Her black hair was long and straight. She had fair skin, pale and cold, even in the fiery light of the forge, with strange tattoos on her face. Her Atrum cloak clung tightly to her body as she moved. Her features were sharp and pointed, almost too harsh for a human's face. But when he tried to look directly at her, his gaze seemed to be redirected to another part of the arena. It was like using his peripheral vision. He couldn't get a good look at her. A dark aura surrounded Sybold, like thunderheads on the horizon, waiting to erupt.

Sybold held her war staff loosely. It was the same ancient wood, wrought from the first tree, just like all the other war staffs. But there seemed to be a black tarlike substance coating it with snakelike tendrils circling the haft. The dark vessel atop it pulsed in time with Port-Shear. Its black light was the exact opposite of his staff. Inside the faceted jewel, Jet could see the black serpent. Its sinewy body writhed and twisted with hate as it clawed at the walls to get at Port-Shear. This was Rend-Shear, the ancient Titan. Port-Shear's nemesis.

As Jet faced Sybold, their war staffs roared at each other. He dared not make the first move and wondered what Sybold was waiting for. Then she spoke. He heard it within his thoughts, multiple voices speaking at once, all in different octaves.

"Why have you come?" she mocked.

Jet took a step back, yet the tone of her voice compelled him to speak. A rush of adrenaline coursed through him, along with a hint of nausea. He didn't answer, unable to find his voice, but held Port-Shear in front of him.

"You're from a great distance. You do not belong. Port-Shear has been known to do that."

"I'm here by my own decision...to fix a mistake."

"And what do you hope to accomplish by facing me now? You are weak. It's a shame you're so new to this world. At a slight disadvantage, I might add."

"Of course. But that's not really the point."

"I see that you've been in the company of my dear friend Christian. He must know the time is near. I want to thank you, by the way," she hissed. "I could have never achieved this power without your help, the third phase, that is. You were the one fated to initiate it, to allow me to collect my brothers and sisters. Their light has made me strong. So, I ask again. Why are you here? You are not ready. The color of your eyes says so."

Jet maintained his distance from Sybold as his mind raced. "I've already told you why I'm here. To fix a mistake, and I won't leave until that happens."

"As it stands now, your death brings no additional colors to me," Sybold said. "Your Heliographi will be lost, along with all the other Lucem. Oh, Solan was a tough one. She battled the hardest. I admire her. It was delectable, ending her life. Of course, Tyberius was just as tough—like father, like daughter. Albright, well, he didn't even seem to care."

Hearing Sybold speak so casually about his friends' deaths made his blood boil. She was goading him to play her game now, and he almost fell for it.

"And…poor Kamber," Sybold said. Her black lips twisted in a smile of satisfaction. He even noticed how her eyelids fluttered with pleasure. "She was so…innocent. That poor lost soul, all alone, waiting for her lover's return. How very unfortunate that you were in the wrong timeline. It *is* your fault, Jet Stroud. Do you realize it now? All of your friends died because of you! Such a pity when they called your name…and you failed them."

Jet faltered at that. He felt his eyes sting as he held her gaze. The pure malice staring back made his anger grow cold. Fear and doubt threatened to seep in. Her words were affecting him, and his guard dipped. He felt Sybold press her advantage. A few seconds perhaps, and his defense collapsed.

Sybold slithered into his thoughts.

Suddenly, his mind was expanding, being stretched by a pair of vices. His head swam and he couldn't see straight. The sheet-demons were back, swarming around him. Swirling in their masses were his friends—Solan, Cord, Tyberius, and Kamber. They were covered in the white sheets, floating aimlessly, lost in another dimension, unaware—oblivious. Lost forever in Sybold's menagerie.

Jet swung his staff blindly at the demons as they floated near him. He felt himself gradually slipping down a dark well. His grip on reality faltered. Jet knew if he didn't fight through this, he would never return, and all hope for the human race would disappear. But strangely, the visions began to fade, and the swirling sheets diminished and disappeared. When Jet opened his eyes, he saw Sember barreling toward Sybold. It was enough to distract her and break Jet's trance.

Sybold dodged Sember with ease and brought her war staff around in one smooth motion. She held Sember in a headlock, her staff pulled tight across Sember's throat, and she began to quiver and shake with spasms.

Jet froze, holding out his hands in a plea. "Please…let her go."

Sybold's black lips curled into an evil grin. "Ah, I see you actually *do* have a friend left. And who might this

lovely one be? Someone important, it seems. But you must know by now that this one belongs to me."

Jet stared at Sybold in confusion.

"Are you really so blind?" Sybold whispered. "Did you think that stumbling upon anyone in this hell was that easy?"

Jet's eyes grew wide as he looked from Sybold to Sember, who was convulsing so badly now that she could barely stand.

"Yes…" Sybold hissed. "I've manipulated this one to guide you. Her sole purpose was to make sure you made it safely to me. This one has blindly led you to your doom."

"Just…let her go," Jet continued. His voice trembled as he looked into Sember's wide eyes.

"I'm so sorry, Jet," Sember said. She had finally managed to overcome the spasms, but her voice was uneven and fearful. "You said sacrifice, but it was meant for me. It's alright. You can let me go now. It's what you need to get back, and I have nothing left." Sember gave him a weak smile, then she rammed her head backward and into Sybold's nose. Blood gushed when she made contact, and Sybold screeched. Without another word, Sybold pulled on her staff and snapped Sember's neck. Jet watched in horror as Sember's eyes went blank, and she slumped forward, dead.

Sybold lifted her staff and kicked Sember in the back. Her body flew across the arena and landed on the cold steel deck.

Jet dropped to his knees and crawled to Sember's lifeless body.

He felt defeated already, and his battle hadn't even begun. Yet another friend he couldn't protect. He thought of Professor Sylvant, Cutter, and all the other Lucem who'd died. Yet Albright had chosen him for this quest. Even with the powerful war staff, he couldn't protect those around him. Jet struggled with his emotions as he collapsed to the floor, Sember's body next to him.

"You have made me a demigod, Jet Stroud!" Sybold bellowed. She slammed Rend-Shear onto the metal deck, and sparks shot upward like an erupting volcano.

Jet stood and glared at Sybold. At that moment, his fear faded. Sember's sacrifice had given him a second chance, and he wasn't about to waste it. He held Port-Shear aloft and the war staff quivered with the anticipation of battle. Its pure white aura pressed against the darkness of Rend-Shear in the forge's fiery light.

"So be it," Jet said and stepped forward.

CHAPTER 53
A Final Stand

SOLAN AND CORD managed to fight back the flood of troops, thanks to Dane's intervention. But now, enemy warships swarmed in and forced Dane's air fleet to engage them instead of the ground troops. The fulcrum's ignition was just minutes away and if they didn't set the polarity, they would miss their chance to claim it. That might mean the other fulcrums would convert, which would spell doom.

In her mind, it seemed like everything was beginning to align. Even the morning sun cast a long shadow across the apex of the pyramid from the system's outer loops, like some approaching prophesy—either impending doom or angelic salvation, she knew not. Everything she held dear was balanced on the tip of some great cosmic fulcrum, and the heavens seemed to hold its breath, waiting to see which way fate would tip. Their long war between good and evil stood in the balance, and a momentous decision was to be made shortly. Everyone around her played a part now. They were like tiny cogs in a great clock. Every piece mattered, and if one of those gears slipped, the whole assembly would malfunction. For better or worse, Solan would play her part until the very end.

Regardless of what fate may have in store, Solan would fight until her last breath. Her path was clear—she had to hold the enemy at bay and wait for whatever destiny lay ahead for the Skylight System and perhaps the human race.

The little reprieve they'd experienced from Dane's interference had faded, and the enemy forces were surging again. Dreadnaught's, Tetrahedron, and M-Class mechs pressed forward in a relentless onslaught. Cord and Solan both—even with their powerful war staffs—were down to their last stand. Several minutes passed, and Solan's entire body screamed in anguish. She'd pushed past her physical limit, fighting off hundreds and perhaps thousands of troops. Just as her energy waned and slipped, she noticed a flashing light pulse between the bodies of the troops before her. A bluish-green explosion sent soldiers flying in all directions. About ten rows back, Solan saw Vail leaping between the troops and hammering down on them. Behind her was a full platoon of recon troops she had gathered with her. Solan almost wept at seeing them. She'd never been so thankful to see an Atrum before, and it gave her a sudden surge of energy.

Minutes later, Vail broke through with the recon soldiers. Solan nearly collapsed as she gripped Vail's shoulder.

"Thank you, Vail. I thought we were alone."

"Not today, Solan," Vail said. "I'm here till the end this time."

Cord slipped around and gave Vail a hug. Solan noticed the surprised look on Vail's face. "Clever Atrum," he said with his crooked smile.

"This isn't over yet," Vail said and directed the recon to take up positions around the entryways.

Above, Dane was managing to hold the enemy war frigates at bay. But several of his ships were badly damaged and smoke filled the air. They'd probably get no more air support from him, at the moment.

Solan risked a glance over the edge of the pyramid. Bounding up the large steps were several blue and purple colored lights.

"Looks like we've got company," Cord said. "Vail, are you ready to face a few of your old friends?"

"I wouldn't call them friends," Vail said and gripped her war staff.

"You're not alone, lass."

Solan turned to see Ti-Leer materialize behind them with his war staff held at the ready. He had several cuts and bruises across his face; his wiry beard was caked with dirt and blood. "Oi, it's been a rough go, but I made it to the top. Where's all the action?"

"It's on the way." Solan smiled at Ti-Leer and grasped his shoulder. Then she turned to face the Atrum heading their way. "This is it. If the Atrum gain entry, they'll block us from getting inside to ignite the final fulcrum. We must keep the path clear. The four of us have to hold this entry point—"

"The five of us," Kamber said and stepped from the opening. "There's no point in keeping me down there anymore, Solan. I can't ignite this fulcrum, and you know that."

Solan looked at Kamber and felt a moment of guilt. But Kamber was a full-fledged Lucem. She was formidable and deadly. She gave Kamber a wink. "The five of us then."

Solan moved to the edge of the pyramid's first plateau, flanked by Kamber and Cord on her right and Ti-Leer and Vail on her left. The dozen or so recon troops readied their railguns and took aim. Flooding up the steps was the second wave of enemy troops. Solan saw Joshia leading the charge, followed by Mosstrom,

Bofisto, Sojahn, Myranda, Bo, and Brit. They were outnumbered again, but they still held more of the upgraded war staffs.

The leading edge of the enemy crashed into the Lucem and the recon troops. The fighting was intense at the apex of the pyramid. Each time it seemed like they were about to collapse, one of the Lucem would step up and push the line back. But she could see a gathering horde of enemy troops beyond, swarming the steps. It was as if the floodgates of hell had been ripped open. She wondered where their own troops were. Surely, they hadn't all been decimated.

Above, Dane's fleet was still holding the enemy air force at bay. At the center of the fray was the SLS Armada. It launched an assortment of rockets and cannon rounds into the enemy foot soldiers, but it didn't seem to matter. Solan and the remaining Lucem were being forced deeper inside the entry portal, and they were soon back-to-back.

On the horizon, something flashed like lightning. Solan immediately recognized the color, though. It was the same one she'd seen during the first memoir's reveal.

The black light of the first vessel.

She felt her heart sink. She knew who had finally arrived, and so did everyone else.

With one eye on the Atrum in front of her and the other on the disturbance beyond, Solan yelled for her troops to stay focused.

But the enemy forces stopped and backed away, almost in fear or reverence. Soon, there was a ten-meter gap between the front lines of both sides. The sound of war diminished and went silent.

The Dreadnaughts, Tetrahedron and mech units parted to let Sybold through.

Solan hadn't seen the Atrum leader since that night at Skylight University over four years ago. Then, she had controlled a different body. The young lady she now possessed was medium height, with pale skin and a face that looked distorted in the reddish light. But Solan also noticed her eyes. That once bright red glow had changed. Now it seemed darker, a deep maroon perhaps.

Sybold hopped up the five-meter-tall steps of the pyramid with ease and stopped in front of Solan. The other Atrum gathered around behind her and waited for her command. Solan looked down at Sybold and held her gaze while leaning on her staff. She tried not to show any signs of fatigue, but she was out of breath.

"The great Solan Alexander," Sybold mocked. Her voice intertwined in multiple pitches. Solan knew that tone. It was the sound of someone who was beyond hope or salvation. Utter blackness—devoid of light.

"You won't get past us, Sybold," Solan said with as much conviction as she could muster. She had to, for the sake of those near her. Solan's resolve was the only thing preventing the others from fleeing the pyramid. Some of the nearby recon troops couldn't even look at Sybold's face. Others were on their knees or looking in the opposite direction.

"Why do you lie? For the sake of these lost souls you call friends?" Sybold replied. She held Solan's gaze, as if searching her mind for a weakness—a chink in her defense that might allow her in and ruin her mind. But Solan kept her thoughts closed, hoping her training over the years would pay off. She was trying to keep Sybold focused on her, so the others didn't have to face that test. "I owe you, Solan," Sybold said. "Or should I say, I owe your father and Albright for what they did to me. I suppose you'll do."

"You shouldn't be here, Sybold. You're an abomination. This breaks the laws of our—"

Sybold's laughter sent a chill through Solan. It reverberated around the pyramid top. "I do not bow to any rules, Solan, especially Albright's. Soon, I will be beyond the laws of any universe."

"That's what you think, Sybold. But there are always rules or nothing would exist. There will be a price to pay for what you've done."

"Says who?" Sybold hissed. "Are you an expert on such matters? I think not. But why don't we send you to a place where you can find out?"

Sybold lifted her staff and struck it to the ground. Power surged through the blackened wood of the war staff. The dark vessel pulsed, and the other, lesser war staffs seemed to falter in its presence.

Solan hefted her staff and readied herself for her final battle.

CHAPTER 54
Ethereal Battlegrounds

JET FELT AS if his heart had been ripped out. Meters away lay the dead body of Sember. She'd made the ultimate sacrifice by giving Jet an opportunity to stand against the demon that circled him. It was yet another friend who'd died because of him. His anger flared, and adrenaline surged through him now. His resolve was as high as it had ever been. But he knew that didn't mean much against what he was facing.

Jet understood why Sybold's appearance looked different now. Her eyes had grown darker, black, in fact.

She had been collecting other Atrums' inner light as they were extinguished in battle, never to return. It was the combination of all those darker colors. Since Jet had gone missing in this world—and his past world—it had prevented him from collecting the other Lucems' light as they'd been snuffed out.

Once again, it was such a morbid thought, one that almost made him nauseous. He now had the ability to collect his friend's lifeforce to strengthen himself. All of this had been conceived by Albright but set in motion by Jet. Certainly, Albright had known it would allow Sybold to do the same.

He couldn't beat Sybold right now because she had the strength of every Atrum. She had indeed become a demigod as Jet remained a single Lucem. It made sense why Port-Shear had warned him so fervently to avoid this conflict. The odds were beyond uneven.

But in his heart, he knew Albright had wanted him here, at this moment. Albright wanted him to see this apocalyptic future world and Jet had done that. He had seen things that would help guide him back in his own world now. Only, he couldn't get back there.

Sybold moved in, and Jet cleared his thoughts to focus.

She struck with Rend-Shear, and sparks flew as he brought Port-Shear up defensively. He could hear the two Titans' war scream as they made contact. There was no turning back now—he had crossed the rubicon. Someone wasn't walking out of here alive.

Sybold held Rend-Shear in contact with Port-Shear for several seconds, as if priming her staff for battle. She stared into Jet's glowing gaze, her face just inches from his. The aura from her skin made him feel frightened and queasy. He'd never been so unnerved before. But he forced his thoughts on all his training over the years. He let the memory of all the positive people in his life reinforce his mind. They were counting on him, perhaps waiting for him back home, and he hoped it wasn't too late. He was in the fight of his life, and he sensed that all of humanity hung in the balance.

Jet felt as if he were in a trance, watching the event from above like some ghostly spectator. His body seemed to float as his war staff moved on its own. Sybold lashed out, strike after strike, hammering down on Port-Shear. Sparks flew, and the air grew thick with embers.

The thousands of M-Class mechs looked on, stonelike and unmoving as the battle unfolded. Sybold also attacked him mentally as she flew around the arena. It was a deadly dance of steel and lightning. Whether by some greater power, or perhaps strength granted by his war staff, Jet wasn't sure. But somehow, he managed to defend against Sybold's unrelenting onslaught.

Sybold cloaked and disappeared, only to reappear behind him in a cloud of smoke and dust. Each time, she seemed to whirl faster until the air around them was a blur of white and black lightning. The flashes erupted in greater arcs as the staffs did battle, each one roaring at its counterpart. It was an ancient war between mythical beings. Sybold of the Omega class, and Jet of the Mu class. Two Primes, representing the light and the dark. Their weapons, beings from a higher plane of existence…the equal and opposite of all things.

Jet continued to look down over himself as the battle raged on. He thought he could see galaxies now. Stars lit the cosmic background as the arena and mech units fell away. Soon, it was just him and Sybold floating among the inky blackness of space. Gradually, other beings began to appear. Jet could see the Titans from the court of stars. They gathered around the peripheral of the spatial arena, both above and below. Eternal beings, there to stand witness to the epic battle that was taking place between the Serpent and the Prism. A war that had been prophesied, thousands of years in the making. An eternity seemed to pass as Sybold continued to attack while he defended. Jet began to wonder if it might go on forever.

…*no time*… Port-Shear whispered, which broke Jet's concentration.

And then it happened.

Sybold landed a blow on his head.

Suddenly, Jet was back within his physical being, his head spinning and his heart thudding. The blow rang like the concussive wave from a supernova. He stumbled backward, trying to regain his bearings. Sybold immediately pressed in, and Jet was barely able to lift his staff and parry the blow.

…no time… Port-Shear whispered again.

Jet tried to focus while listening to Port-Shear. What did it mean? No time? Maybe *not* time?

Not the right time!

He finally realized what the Titan had been trying to tell him.

Then a stray thought came to him. Something from a distant conversation, perhaps? Or had it been something Sybold had said?

You're from a great distance. Port-Shear has been known to do that.

Port-Shear had the ability to transport him, and not just from place to place, but through time! That's why Jet's gift was so important. He could withstand the rigors of time travel. He could withstand the presence of these higher beings.

Jet was beginning to understand Albright's ploy.

All he had to do was get Port-Shear to transport him back. He didn't need to be in some mystic pool or special conduit. He had already *unlocked* his gift. Albright had asked him to 'perfect it now.' And Port-Shear had been the key all along. Albright had wanted Jet to *cheat the system*, in a sense.

Somehow, he had to *provoke* Port-Shear into transporting him. And the way to do that was by…

…sacrificing himself.

Jet understood what he had to do now. But would Port-Shear follow through?

He lowered his war staff and stood defenseless in the middle of the cosmic arena.

Port-Shear roared in disapproval. He sensed the Titan willing him to move his arms and defend himself. But Jet remained motionless as Sybold advanced.

She raised her staff high.

The Titans around them spoke in cosmic winds and shocked wonder. The court stood in disagreement…in objection to his method.

Then Sybold swung Rend-Shear down at Jet's head.

But the descending staff slowed, then gradually stopped just above his forehead. He looked up to see everything around him frozen as if time stood still. Jet looked down at Port-Shear. The end of the vessel was glowing white hot, like a dying star. It pulsed with massive waves of light, the frequency growing rapidly until it was a solid white light that rippled across time and space.

Jet felt his body begin to phase in and out of existence. His mind felt riddled with missing information, recent memories that were no longer available. The staff grew so hot that he nearly dropped it. Then, the white light enveloped him and everything else. Jet's entire world fell into a swirling mass of light and stars.

CHAPTER 55
Final Ignition

SOLAN FACED SYBOLD, her staff at the ready. As she looked into her deep red glowing eyes, she already knew what the outcome would be. But she had vowed to 'play her part', regardless. They began to circle each other as the battle around them suddenly commenced. The Lucem and Atrum flew at each other as the troops did the same.

Just as Sybold moved in, a roar filled the chamber. Solan turned to see a large Agency skiff barreling down on their position. It was moving in too fast, and everyone leapt out of the way as it crashed down. It leveled the stone portal, sending chunks of stone and steel outward. As the dust settled, three blurry figures emerged from the cockpit and materialized.

A smile stretched across Solan's weary face.

Her father had finally returned. With him was the young Shiloe Van Saint and the teenage Christian Albright.

Sybold backed away uncertainly, and the other Atrum gathered near her.

"I'd say the odds are a bit more even now, wouldn't you?" the young Albright trilled. The seventeen-year-old boy was tall, his blonde hair long about his shoulders. He had a knowing smile on his face and didn't show any sign of fear as he held Sybold's gaze. Next to him, Tyberius Alexander and Shiloe Van Saint stepped from the wrecked skiff. All three held up their war staffs and hammered the ground. The three staffs unfurled to full length. They had apparently taken the conversion ritual and were ready for battle.

"You were never alone, Solan," Tyberius said and stood next to her. His silver hair and white beard, full and flowing in the morning light, his tall frame commanding. "I see we're in a bit of a predicament."

"Isn't that usually the case?" Solan muttered.

The Atrum gathered around Sybold as the Lucem stood near Christian Albright.

The young Albright faced off against Sybold. "I see that you've figured out my code. But do you know the extent of it, I wonder?" Albright spoke without hesitation, and his confidence strengthened the others.

"You're a fool for handing me this power," Sybold said. Her tone was filled with contempt and veiled anger. "It will be your undoing, and this world will burn under my rein. I have seen the future. Your gamble will not pay off."

"Fate will decide which way the fulcrum swings. Not you. Not me." Albright lifted his staff and held it at the ready. The red vessel lit the wreckage atop the final pyramid. The powerful Titan, Kal-Wist, Solan recalled from the memoirs.

"Once a fool, always a fool. So be it." Sybold lifted Rend-Shear above her head and swung it at Albright, and the fight was on. The other Heliographi rushed at each other, and the clash lit up the top of the pyramid as fighting continued below them. The colorful array strobed in flashes of blue, green and red lightning. Solan felt her fatigue fall away, being near her father and Albright now. She let loose a battle cry and fell in next to her fellow Lucem.

Several minutes of intense hand to hand fighting took place. Cord tangled with Mosstrom, while Sojahn, Bo and Brit met Shiloe, Ti-Leer and Tyberius. Kamber rolled on the ground with Myranda. Solan faced her half-

sister, Joshia, as Bofisto clashed with Vail. And at the center of it all was Sybold and Albright.

Precious minutes passed as the Heliographi fought atop the pyramid. At the apex of the strange fulcrum, the fate of the human race would be decided. It seemed to be a standoff, though. Neither the Atrum nor the Lucem could make any progress. But Solan felt a pressure building, like waking from a dream, and a moment of clarity was upon them.

Suddenly, a huge blast sent everyone flying through the air. When Solan gained her senses, she saw Sybold on one knee and her war staff planted to the ground. She had channeled a massive pulse, strong enough to clear the entire top of the pyramid. Every troop and Heliographi had been thrown off the top tier and tumbled down the steps of the pyramid.

Solan rolled to her elbow, still groggy, and looked to see Sybold's cloak flutter as she moved inside the entry portal and disappeared.

M

Jet remained in a state of limbo.

He didn't seem to have a body or a physical presence. He was simply floating without a form. It was a thought—or memory perhaps—that had once been Jet Stroud. It felt different than Vishmu. This was a feeling of omnipotence, if he had to guess. He knew things that the human mind couldn't comprehend. He knew that he could travel to other places, that he could shift or *phase* through dimensions or higher planes of existence. He could see time and how it flowed through the fabric of space.

But it was all because of Port-Shear. Only with the Titan present could he bear witness to all the strange and glorious things before him. Otherwise, he was nonexistent. This was part of his 'gift', and it only worked in conjunction with Port-Shear. Had Albright outwitted the cosmic rules? Had that been why the Titans at the court of stars objected to Jet's action? Had his actions potentially upset the balance of things? He'd forced Port-Shear to use its powers, allowing him a way out of his predicament. Jet had found a loophole in time by tricking the Titan. *"Albright was so sneaky!"* he could almost hear Cord whisper.

But he didn't care, he only desired to get home to his friends.

But time still seemed to be frozen, as though it didn't matter in this realm, whatever realm he was in. Jet was simply along for the ride as the Titan guided him across time and space. He could sense Port-Shear simmering with anger, though. It had done the only thing it could to save him and transported him away from certain death, all because the time hadn't been right.

Jet wondered why. What difference did it make to a higher being like Port-Shear if he lived or died? Jet imagined his life was insignificant to a Titan. According to Albright, there was to be a final, prophesied battle between the Serpent and the Prism. Either the timing had been wrong, or the odds hadn't been even. So, what if Port-Shear had been tasked with seeing Jet safely to the finish line? That made some sense. Port-Shear might have used up some of its own essence in order to save Jet, which would cause the Titan harm. Only time would tell, and Jet's ability to communicate with Port-Shear was feeble, at best.

Jet felt his essence begin to slow, and his thoughts begin to compress back to reality. Time seemed to flow again, like it was struggling to catch up. Lights flooded his mind, a jumble of colors that joined to create that same white light he'd seen while facing Sybold. Then, a thunderclap sounded, and Jet felt his body solidify. He held on to Port-Shear with all his strength, afraid to let go. His shoulder slammed into a hard surface, and suddenly, he could breathe again. His head spun as he looked up and took in his surroundings.

Jet stood to his feet and his legs threatened to buckle. He was inside a space he recognized. It was a fulcrum's inner sanctum, though he didn't know which one. Near him was a clear encasement with a memoir inside of it. Above, he could see daylight pouring in through the narrow throat of an oculus. There were explosions beyond, and the ground shuddered with the vibrations of war. He could see a great battle raging above, and his mind began to fill in the gaps. Port-Shear had brought him back to the present day. Jet wanted to drop and kiss the ground. He felt a sudden rush of gratitude and relief at being home again. Now he had work to do, and he needed to make up for lost time.

K

Solan tried to come to her senses after Sybold's massive EMP blast, but she felt groggy and disoriented. The Atrum leader had already entered the pyramid and would make the inner sanctum quickly. If she did, there was no hope of any of them breaking through, not even Albright.

A loud thunderclap rocked the pyramid with so much intensity that Solan's ears popped. It was followed by a pure white light that flooded from the inner sanctum below before quickly fading.

What in Skylight was that? Solan thought.

She leapt to her feet and scrambled up the steps of the pyramid. She had to get to the inner sanctum before the timer hit zero. Without Jet, her best hope was to prevent Sybold from setting the polarity of the last fulcrum.

Solan called out to the other Lucem, willing them to meet her below. She found Tyberius standing at the entry portal.

"We must hurry," he said, readying himself for the leap downward. "The time is near."

"What was that noise?" Solan said as she followed him inside.

"A Titan has returned."

Tyberius and Solan nearly ran into Albright, who was standing at the top, waiting for them.

"What do you mean?" Solan asked. "A Titan?"

"That was a tear in the space-time fabric," Albright said. "Only a Titan can achieve that. Jet Stroud has returned, and he must face Sybold. We can only bear witness but not interfere."

"That doesn't mean we can't have a better view," Solan said.

The three of them hopped down the stairs and toward the inner sanctum below. Soon, Solan could sense the other Heliographi filing in behind them, both Atrum and Lucem. It was a mad dash to the bottom to see what was happening, though she could already see flashes of light as Jet and Sybold engaged in battle.

M

Jet finally understood where he was now. The timing had been impeccable, the placement perfect. It was the final fulcrum, and the holographic timer above the fulcrum was nearing zero.

He looked up to see sunlight spilling through the oculus and barely noticed the narrow staircase leading down. Rushing his way was the blurry figure of a Heliographi. He knew immediately who it was, based on the sick feeling in his stomach, though the effect wasn't as strong as before.

The figure hopped over the stairs with twenty meters left and landed with a thud. Sybold used her staff to absorb the landing and uncloaked.

She looked much the same as the future Sybold, though her eyes were not as black but more of a dark maroon color. When she faced him, he saw the look of surprise in her expression, and he immediately understood why.

His own eyes had changed, too.

His return must have allowed him to gather the deceased Lucems' Heliographi: Booker, Annaka and Harriet. If he listened closely, he could almost hear them speaking encouragement to him. He felt different now. Stronger and more aware. It was a power he'd not felt before.

Sybold tried to probe his mind, but he was able to deflect her with ease. Unlike the future Sybold, this version wasn't a full demigod yet. Then again, neither was he. There was confusion in her expression, as if she knew something was out of place.

"I see that you have gathered souls," she mocked. "Your color has shifted. Now you know this is a race."

"I know what your goal is. But this fulcrum is not yours to take."

"Impressive," she hissed. "Your confidence grows in the face of death. But I will take what I want."

"This isn't the last time we'll meet," Jet replied. "We both know that."

"Let us see what fate has to say about that!" Sybold leapt at him, her staff hammering down.

Jet raised his war staff and blocked the strike. But he sensed that Port-Shear was weary and drained. Regardless, Jet felt energized, renewed almost. He would need all of it.

However, Sybold was buoyed by her knowledge and skill, where his background was limited. She was drawing on millennia of expertise.

They moved around the base of the fulcrum, trading jabs. Jet could see the large holographic clock ticking away at the top of the fulcrum. There were just minutes left now, but time seemed to slow as the epic battle ensued.

From the corner of his eye, he saw the other Heliographi starting to fill the space around them. He was surprised to see Tyberius, Shiloe, and even Albright. The entire remaining entourage of Heliographi surrounded Jet and Sybold, spectating but not interfering. He could hear them cheering him on. Solan clapped and yelled. Ti-Leer dropped to his knees and pounded the ground in excitement. Kamber hid her face behind her hands, barely able to watch. Vail had a concerned look on her face as she followed their movements.

Jet felt encouraged by his friends while the Atrum screamed back. The clock continued to count down to zero, though, and Jet had to find a way to stay near the fulcrum. But each time he drew closer, Sybold drove him back. As they continued to struggle, Jet had a flashback of the future Skylight and how that battle had ended. But this time, he felt less afraid and more confident.

The fulcrum began to glow with just seconds left. Sybold had managed to work her way in between. Her staff's black vessel glowed with dark light while his did the same. Both Rend-Shear and Port-Shear were primed and ready as the moment neared. Sybold backed toward the fulcrum, continuing to block him out. Time was almost out when Jet heard Port-Shear speak to him.

...strike...

Jet hammered the ground with the end of the staff. The metal collars sizzled with electricity, and a large EMP erupted, sending Sybold and everyone else flying. He sensed that EMP had drained all of Port-Shear's remaining energy, and the staff felt suddenly cold in his hands.

But now the way was clear.

The holographic clock struck zero, and the end of the vessel shone a pure white light.

Jet placed the war staff into the keyhole.

The air around the inner sanctum swirled, and a massive lightning bolt erupted from the top of the fulcrum. It shot up through the oculus, followed by a thunderclap that sent him flying backward. The bolt seemed to suck the oxygen from the air as it arced upward and along the horizon. Jet heard a groaning, like gigantic steel gears were moving beneath the ground. The Lyrinthum Particle Accelerator, which hadn't functioned in decades, suddenly whirred to life.

Through the opening above, Jet could see the color of the sky change to a golden hue. It was like a soft filter had descended around the sun, drenching everything in an angelic light.

Jet heard the unmistakable sound of a stasis dome form in the atmosphere above them. It hummed like windchimes in the air, a soft white noise that sounded like music.

All the Atrum inside the inner sanctum held their hands to their ears. Their faces twisted in anguish. Jet could almost feel their pain from the soft, barely perceptible music. Sybold immediately cloaked and vanished while the other Atrum followed her up the stairs and out of sight.

Jet reached for Vail, hoping to protect her. But she, too, was in some sort of pain and fled the inner sanctum and disappeared from sight.

J. Wint

CHAPTER 56
A Price to Pay

THE ENTIRE GROUP of Lucem stood around, blinking in shock and wonder. No one spoke for several minutes at what had just happened. Solan lay on the ground, her eyes closed. Ti-Leer looked to be hyperventilating. Tyberius stood, eyes closed and mumbling something while Albright simply stared at Jet with a knowing smirk on his youthful face.

Jet had so many questions. But he continued to lay on his backside, staring up at the lightning bolt above.

He closed his eyes and felt a calmness sink into his bones.

Someone fell on top of him and wrapped their arms around his neck. He felt kisses on his cheek and brow. When he finally came to his senses, Kamber's face was just inches from his, tears on her cheeks. The other Lucem piled on top of him or knelt beside him. There was so much chattering and hugging that he could barely make sense of what was happening. Ti-Leer shook him by the arm, a stout grin beneath his beard. Cord shook his hand, a crooked smile on his face. Solan ruffled his hair while Tyberius looked on, arms crossed and smiling in amusement. But behind all of them, Jet's eyes didn't leave the tall, teenage boy. Christian Albright had finally rejoined the Lucem.

"There's still a war raging above, people," Solan said. "Let's move up top and do what we can."

The line of Lucem raced up the stairs and stood at the apex of the pyramid. What Jet saw shocked him.

The battlefield was mostly vacant of enemy troops now. Perhaps seeing the large white lightning bolt had caused them to flee. All Jet could see were their own troops, sifting through the carnage that lay around them. The fighting had even spilled over into the nearby Clipton Forest. Trees had been leveled and charred where the most intense fighting had taken place.

Jet moved to the edge of the pyramid's first plateau and sat down, letting his legs dangle from the ledge. It was mostly silent, except for the soft musical hum of the golden dome above.

"Heaven's Shield," Tyberius said. "It is said to be one of the most beautiful things to behold…I'd have to agree, now that I see it."

"What does it mean?" Jet asked as the other Lucem gathered around.

Tyberius looked to Albright and held out a hand, as if giving him the stage.

Albright moved to sit next to Jet and laid his war staff down, then leaned back on his elbows as he gazed up. He playfully kicked his feet as he sat with a smile on his boyish face, like decades of worry had finally gone away. "It means that we are protected…for the moment, at least. A safe haven for all those who seek peace. Now, the battle will move back to the front line."

"Which is where, exactly?" Jet asked.

"The air space between the fourth and fifth belts," Albright said, "as I had anticipated. Soon, our enemy will regroup and create a net around that airspace. They will try to prevent any further passage in or out."

"It would appear the Skylight System is now split into two portions," Solan said. "Have we simply extended our civil war?"

"This battle is long from over," Tyberius agreed.

"Those enemy troops were under Sybold's spell," Jet said. "Bloodlust, isn't that what it's called?"

"Yes," Albright said. "The source is from Sybold's Titan." He stood and began pacing, his hands behind his back. Once again, it was odd to see the tall teenage boy speaking with such authority and knowledge. "It's time I share some secrets with the entire group. It's been a long while coming. But with the recent events, I see no reason to hold on to many of them. The fourth and final phase of the Prism Effect has been initiated."

"Which is?" Solan asked.

Albright raised his hands at the golden dome high above. "Heaven's Shield."

"And, the Serpent's Effect," Tyberius added with Albright nodding approval. "The four outer belts also have their own protective shield, too. It holds influence over all who reside within it."

"And we've seen what that looks like," Ti-Leer said. "Zombies, the lot o' them…everyone who didn't make it out at least."

"The first and eighth fulcrums were designed as transmitters, as you've probably guessed. Their particle accelerators are the power source, both Goliath's Gate and Project David," Albright said. "The rest of the fulcrums are receivers. Their polarity is locked in now, and fortunately for us, we control the first four belts. But that doesn't mean a fulcrum can't be destroyed or reversed."

"What about the ninth belt?" Jet asked. "Why did you not provide a fulcrum there?"

"It was destroyed in the meteor storm," Albright said with a wink, and Jet could tell there was more to it. But apparently, it was one of the secrets Christian wasn't willing to give up just yet.

Ti-Leer looked at Jet and crossed his arms. Then he nodded his head. "What's wrong with your eyes, lad?"

Jet looked around the group, then shrugged. "How should I know? I haven't looked at myself in a week or so, Ti."

"Cut the crap," Ti-Leer said. "You *know* what's happenin', don't you."

Jet sighed, not sure he wanted to get into such a discussion at that moment. The guilt he felt about what was happening to him already had him on edge. "I'm not sure I'm the one to explain it, even if I cared to."

Albright glanced at Tyberius, who stepped into the center of the group. "I can answer that, Ti-Leer. The second phase of the Prism Effect triggered what we refer to as an 'extinction event.' But it was the third phase that allowed two Heliographi to gather souls. More specifically, another Heliographi's inner light, once it has passed. Of course, you already knew this, I believe."

Jet looked around the group and gave a weak smile. "Yeah. Sybold may have mentioned it."

"Why are you not the prime?" Kamber asked Albright.

"I was never meant to be, at least not in this universe. It's always been the order of the 'M' symbol. I devised and created the phases only. It has always been my duty to ensure that certain 'rules' were in place and followed."

"Certain rules?" Kamber asked. "Is that why you didn't get so involved?"

"Part of my purpose here is to create and observe. I am bound to follow the rules. Everything requires balance. Whatever actions I take must apply equally to both the Atrum and Lucem. I know that doesn't seem right, considering the nature of who I am and what Sybold has done, but it is the way of our race."

"Who sets those rules?" Jet asked. "Is it the Titans?"

Albright looked at Jet. "I see that you've met our friends."

"I don't know that I'd call them friends," Jet replied. "I just followed the path you sent me on, which led me to their court with Brindall and my friend Cutter. I was trying to plead our case to them, hoping they'd send help. I guess that didn't work out so well."

Albright only smiled and gave him a wink, as if he knew something more. "Worth a shot, wasn't it?"

"All this talk about Titans and rules," Kamber said. "What happened to you, Jet? Where'd you go?"

Jet gave a tired sigh. "You wouldn't believe me if I told you."

"You owe us an explanation, lad," Ti-Leer said. "After all we've been through, we deserve that much. Let's get to it."

Jet paused for another brief second, then held up his hands. "Alright…fine. If you must know, I was trapped in the future. My war staff, Port-Shear, apparently has the ability to teleport me. I guess we took it one step too far and I ended up months in a future Skylight System. Only, I guess it wasn't in this timeline…" Jet rubbed his forehead. "I'm still confused about that. I don't know."

"A future timeline?" Cord asked. "Fascinating. What can you tell us?"

"Just that—" Jet paused as he looked around at his friends. He recalled those disturbing images of them. Solan, Ti-Leer…knowing that they were all dead, lying in the ash and dust of the ruined belts.

"What is it?" Kamber asked. She placed a hand on his arm.

"It's…nothing. I really don't want to talk about it. At least, not right now."

"I'm still waitin' to hear 'bout your eyes," Ti-Leer prodded, poking his war staff at Jet. "It ain't natural and I miss your lovely turquoise color."

Jet gave them all a serious look, then held Albright's gaze. He waited to see if Albright might speak, but he remained silent, as if wanting Jet to confirm what they all knew.

"I…I uh. Apparently, gathering souls makes me stronger. When you all pass away, your light joins with mine. That's why my color is changing."

"Jet," Solan said and laid a hand on his shoulder. "It's okay. None of this is your fault."

"We gonna die sooner or later, lad," Ti-Leer said. "If we do, might as well be for a good cause. Am I right?" he said and clapped Cord and Kamber on the back and chuckled, though no one else laughed.

To Jet, it was still a morbid thought, and he tried not to dwell on it. "I feel so bad about this, guys. I hate the whole idea of it." Jet turned to Albright. "Why did you make this the third phase?"

The young Albright gave him a knowing look, then spoke without hesitation. "You already know why. Sybold is too powerful. Only I could face her. But in this universe, you are the prime. The Prism Effect, and all four of its phases, was the only way we could give you the power to face her. It gave the human race a fighting chance. But I had to allow Sybold the same power so that balance was maintained, as was decreed by the Titans. By allowing you both to collect other Heliographi, in theory, it puts you on equal ground. Otherwise, you could never defeat her and our world, our universe, would not survive."

"You're creating demigods, Albright," Jet replied. "It just doesn't feel right."

"We are like living vessels, infused with the essence of celestial beings. In that regard, we were already like minor gods, I suppose."

"But what you're doing is making Sybold and me much more powerful."

"I've struggled with that very thought for centuries, Jet. No matter what decision I contemplated, I knew the final war would come, regardless."

"You're talking about the battle between the Serpent and the Prism again?" Jet asked.

"Yes. And it will be upon us soon."

"Well, for what it's worth," Ti-Leer said and clapped Jet on the shoulder. "I'm okay knowing you get my goods, lad."

Jet looked away, gazing out across the smoking battlefield. It broke his heart knowing that the only way to possibly win this war was that his friends had to die. *He didn't want to live in a world without Cord, and Solan…and Kamber.*

Everyone waited. "I'm sorry," Jet said and turned away. He felt tears sting his eyes as he gazed off in silence.

"Albright," Cord said, breaking the silence. "Why doesn't Sybold just kill off all the remaining Atrum right now, if this is true?"

"A Heliographi's inner light cannot be collected in that manner, I made sure of that," Albright explained. "Sybold knows this. When an Atrum dies in battle, only then will it work. No other way."

"Strange rules," Cord said. "It makes no sense in my view. Seems like there's always a little room to 'bend' things a bit, no?"

Albright gave Cord a boyish grin. "Maybe. And you can bet Sybold is searching for loopholes right now. I guess we shall see what can *bend* and what will *break*."

"There's one other thing I don't understand," Jet said. "Why didn't Sybold or I gather Heliographi as soon as the third phase was set into motion? It only worked when I returned from the future Skylight."

"Because Sybold already knew what an unbalanced world would look like, she had an unfair advantage. It was just one reason you were sent to the future Skylight. You needed to see that unbalance first to understand the consequences. Upon your return, the third phase was allowed to move forward."

"Just one reason?" Jet asked.

"There are others," Albright said.

"Like what?" Jet continued.

"What else did you find in the future Skylight?"

Jet thought for a moment. "There were some clues I found around the fulcrum's bases."

"What else?" Albright said.

"Well. I also met a friend—"

Albright snapped his fingers at Jet. "Yes, you did, didn't you."

"Her name was Sember. Sybold took control of her to guide me."

"While Sybold regained her strength, she has been acting as a puppet master," Albright agreed. "She excels at manipulation. Her endgame in this is the same as the essence of the Titan that imbues her. She delights in chaos, death and destruction."

Jet gave Albright a side glance and arched his eyebrows. "Wait. Is there something else about Sember? Did you know her?"

Albright only continued to smile at Jet, his arms crossed. But he said nothing. Jet knew then that there was more to Sember's story.

"So, what should we do now?" Kamber asked, changing the subject with a suspicious glare in Jet's direction.

Albright looked to Tyberius, who in turn faced Solan and waited for her to speak.

She glanced at them both. Then shook her head. "Oh no. *No.* I've had enough. The lead passes back to Tyberius."

"It will not," Tyberius said. "It remains as is."

"Father. We are in a mess right now and people are dead and—"

Tyberius held up a hand. "Are we in a mess? Everything is in place as it was meant to be. The fourth phase has been set in motion. Heaven's Shield is providing safe haven for millions of citizens, thanks to your leadership. I'd say you've done quite well, my daughter."

"And many are dead as well." Solan frowned and shook her head. "I don't want this anymore. Please."

Tyberius placed a gentle hand on her shoulder. "This was meant for you and you alone, Solan."

She took a deep breath and let her head lean back, her frustration evident. Everyone stood around with arms crossed, not sure what to say. So much information had passed in just a short time that everyone seemed to be processing it all.

"Fine," Solan finally said. "We need to tend to the wounded first. I take it we are safe for the moment, but I want scouts surrounding the fourth belt's airspace. Find Stell and the other generals. We need to take inventory and gather what resources we have left—"

The silence was broken when a jammer suddenly materialized from above. One of its wings was missing, and it was smoking. It veered low and a bit too fast. It hovered, then thudded onto the stone plateau.

Everyone raced over to the wrecked jammer. Solan hopped to the front of the nose and ripped the windshield free. Inside was DiJinn, her face bruised and bloodied. Solan freed her from the harness and set her gently on the ground.

The other Lucem knelt close.

Solan pulled DiJinn's robe back and saw the gash in her stomach and looked away. "She needs help," Solan said in a raised voice. "Hurry, get a medic!" Solan looked to be on the verge of panic as she glanced around desperately.

Solan stood to move, but DiJinn reached up and pulled at her cloak, bringing her close enough to whisper in her ear. Solan leaned in as tears streamed down her face and pressed her forehead to DiJinn's. She gripped DiJinn's hand and spoke softly. "No, Jinn. Please don't go like this. I still need you."

DiJinn managed a weak smile and brushed Solan's black hair back from her ear. Then she handed her a metallic scroll, which was smeared with her blood, leaned in and whispered something to her.

Then, she was gone.

CHAPTER 57

A Time for Peace.
A Time for Grief.

ΑΒΓΔΕΖΗΘΙΚΛΜ
ΝΞΟΠΡΣΤΥΦΧΨΩ

LATER THAT DAY, all of the Lucem met in the Clipton Forest at the familiar clearing.

In the center, surrounded by tall pines, was a wood pyre. Solan laid DiJinn's body on it, wrapped in her Lucem cloak. The sun was setting behind Heaven's Shield, and the strange golden hue shone down in otherworldly god rays. Everything was bathed in the amber light as a few fireflies gathered around them. The barely perceptible music fell from high, calming their nerves.

Jet had never seen Solan in such a state before. She seemed to go through a cycle of emotions: anger and rage—sorrow and regret. As they stood silently in a circle, heads bowed, Jet imagined everyone was considering their own mortality. There had been so much death and destruction over the last few months, and for it to end like this made him feel that much worse. Jinn had been there with him since his induction into the Lucem. She had saved his life on many occasions. And now, she was gone. Worse, no one knew how it had happened. There was a hole in the pit of his stomach that made him feel sick. But mostly, he felt sorrow for Solan and wondered how she'd come through this.

Next to Solan stood Shiloe. Her expression was one of confusion, her wide eyes darted around the darkened clearing at the shadows beneath the tall pines. Jet knew the teenage Shiloe had been through a lot over the last century, and he wondered if losing Jinn would make things worse for her.

Next to Shiloe stood Albright. The tall, blond-haired teenager looked at her confidently, squeezing her hand, which seemed to settle her nerves.

Ti-Leer stood next to Albright. His nose was red, his matted hair even more tangled than normal. He constantly shook his head and muttered under his breath, as if chiding himself perhaps, or maybe second guessing why he hadn't been there to protect Jinn.

Tyberius stood on Solan's other side. His weathered face looked haggard, the lines around his eyes a bit deeper than normal. He clasped his hands behind him, waiting silently.

Jet stood across the clearing and next to Kamber. He felt her interlock her fingers with his and she laid her head on his shoulder. She sniffled as everyone waited for Solan to speak.

"I wanted to say a few things," Solan said, after clearing her throat a few times. She looked around the circle of Heliographi. "I decided not to tell anyone about Jinn's death, at least not yet. I wanted just the Lucem here today. I…my friend held a special place in my heart, in all our hearts. I can't tell you how many times she saved my life or bailed me out of a tough situation. I relied on her so much over the years. We had something not many had—she seemed to know me better than anyone. Jinn was the first one to befriend me when I joined the Lucem. She showed me the ropes around the Agency, along with Ti-Leer." Solan gave Ti-Leer a long look. "Well…I know that she'd want us to go on. Her sacrifice to gain the ninth memoir may decide the fate of our race and this war. Only she could have brought it back to us. Let's do her a favor and make the most of it. She would expect nothing less from any of you. She'll be missed sorely."

Solan bowed her head and stood silently, letting the sounds of nature take over. Then she lit the pyre.

Everyone stood around, lost in their own thoughts as the wood burned, hissed and popped.

Jet raised his head and looked up at the sky and the embers floating upward, his eyes glowing a bit whiter than before. The guilt he felt at that moment made his heart ache.

M

Jet didn't sleep that night. He stayed out in the Clipton Woods until dawn. He needed time alone and wasn't ready to see anyone yet, including Kamber. He wanted to sort out his feelings and prepare himself for all the questions and attention first. The other Lucem seemed to sense this and gave him the time and space he needed to decompress.

At dawn, he made his way back to Lyrinthum. Jet noticed Solan talking with Dane in the hangar bay. He stopped and watched from a distance but didn't approach them. He could tell that Solan was sharing the news about DiJinn. The look on Dane's face didn't change as he listened. He remained stoic, unflinching. But Jet could sense that he was breaking inside.

Albright held on to the ninth memoir, which DiJinn had sacrificed her life to bring home. He knew that Albright would keep it well-hidden and well-guarded. When Albright was ready, Jet assumed he'd share more about what the ninth memoir was designed for. Jet only knew that Sybold would be furious when she found out it was missing. What DiJinn had done for them all might be the deciding factor in this conflict. Only time would tell.

Solan remained in the hangar bay. If she was second-guessing her decision to send DiJinn for the ninth memoir, she didn't show it. Instead, she chose to be around the troops and citizens, directing them and taking on the leadership role. Jet found encouragement in her decision. She wasn't giving up, and Jet knew she wouldn't. It would be a slap in the face of her beloved friend if she did.

After talking with Stell, it was decided to spread out her informants along the front line. Every spy and scout in her organization was on the move to the air space between the fourth and fifth belts. Outposts would need to be established along the fourth belt. Early detection and defense were now the most important missions for them all. They would also need to recruit more soldiers. The final fulcrum had been costly to their troops and resources, though their enemy was likely in the same situation.

Dane moved the Armada and the rest of the fleet into position between the fourth and fifth belts in hopes of deterring any future attacks until they had regrouped and replenished. Meetings were held to discuss tactics. For the moment, Solan had decided to dig in and defend

until they could understand what they were up against. Though Tyberius and Albright were in the meetings, they remained silent and stayed in the background.

Jet found out later that Linon had fallen in battle. Now, his son Patrick was leading their army. Patrick volunteered to relocate the majority of his forces to the fourth belt as well, just in case Sybold tried to make any moves.

Jet had a ton of questions for Albright, but he had conveniently slipped away unannounced with Shiloe. Now that Heaven's Shield was in place, Jet wasn't in a hurry to track him down. He assumed that his questions would be answered in due time. Besides, Shiloe and Albright had earned a break, and everyone gave them space during this period of peace, however brief that might be.

M

On the following day, Jet felt better. He hadn't realized how much energy he'd expended in the lead-up to the battle with Sybold. After a full day of meditation, he finally met Kamber at Firefly Falls.

The hidden glen had been geographically relocated, at least somewhat. After the first fulcrum's pyramid had risen through the topography, things had shifted. Though it hadn't destroyed the landscape or anything like that, it was certainly a new landmark on the horizon, which could be seen through the tree canopy. The waterfall had partially been rerouted as well but still looked and sounded majestic. As usual, the air was filled with fireflies buzzing around. In addition to the fairytale setting was Heaven's Shield. Its melodic sound and golden hue blended in with the green and yellow luminance of Firefly Falls. The crashing sound of the falls, mixed with the soft chiming of Heaven's Shield, felt like something out of a daydream. If Jet sat and listened long enough, he thought he could hear voices singing.

Jet and Kamber sat at the foot of Cutter's grave, leaning against each other. Jet felt almost shy again, being near her. They had had so little contact over the last several weeks that he wasn't sure what to say at first.

"What was it like?" Kamber asked and wrapped her arms around his shoulder. "You said you didn't want to talk about it. If you still don't, I understand."

Jet felt a momentary flutter in his stomach as she leaned in. "No…it's okay. I probably need to talk about it." He paused for a moment, trying to recall all the events. "It…well. Everything was gone."

He felt Kamber stiffen next to him. "Gone? What does that mean?"

"The trees, the buildings…everything was burned to the ground. Smoke filled the sky, there was only ash and dust."

"Who did you see?"

Jet held her gaze, not wanting to say it. But Kamber waited, apparently intent on hearing the full tale.

"Well, yeah. I saw some people."

"Who?"

"There was a girl by the name of Sember. She was what they call a genie."

"A what?"

"Someone with genetically modified genes, the last of her kind. She saved my life and got me to the end. I wouldn't be here without her sacrifice."

"She…died then?" Kamber asked.

Jet took in a sharp breath, thinking about that moment again, and had to look away. "Sybold killed her. Sember knew she would die, but still…she chose to help me."

Kamber considered, an uncertain expression on her face. "So, you faced Sybold in both worlds? How did you survive her in the future?"

"Facing Sybold was my ticket home. I knew I couldn't beat her, though. I tricked my war staff, or the entity within, by trying to sacrifice myself in battle. Albright had known the timing wasn't right and that the Titan would be forced to use its power. In the end, it worked. But at a cost, I think." Jet pulled the compressed war staff from his cloak. The wood and metallic contraption remained cold and dormant and had been so since the fight with Sybold, in fact. Jet wondered if he'd permanently broken the war staff.

"Did you see what you were supposed to?"

He'd seen *more* than he wanted, actually. He gave Kamber a weak smile. "According to Albright, yeah. I understand now what the third phase set off, though Albright could've warned me. But I guess he wasn't allowed to do that, and I had to witness it myself. I saw what would have happened had we failed to claim the last fulcrum. I saw the destruction of the human race."

"Albright mentioned something about Titans. What was that all about?"

Jet chuckled and leaned back against the boulder. "Imagine the strangest dream you've ever had, then multiply it by a thousand. How's that?"

"That strange, huh?"

"It's something I can't even explain. I was just floating amidst the stars as these 'Titans' stood judgment over me. I was pleading for their help, but it never came. I still don't understand that part, though I feel like I was meant to be there. At first, I thought that was Albright's true quest for me, not seeing the future Skylight. Cutter was also there." Jet paused, leaning back and looking at his friend's grave. "I've been wondering. After what happened to Jinn, it made me think about my gift more—" He stopped again, trying to find the right words.

"What is it, Jet?" Kamber asked, sensing his hesitation.

"What if I could use my gift to change fate…rewrite it? I can travel through time, if Port-Shear allows it. I could bring Cutter back, and Jinn—"

Kamber gripped his arm and sat up. "Jet. No. Don't talk about such things."

"But I could save him and Jinn and the others."

"We've talked about this. What happened to them was meant to be. You shouldn't venture into such thoughts."

"But why not? I mean, if this gift was meant for me—"

"Listen to me, Jet," Kamber said and pulled him around by the shoulders. "We live in the present. Not the past, not the future. Please. Stray from those thoughts. Trust me, it's not the right way. Neither would Cutter or anyone else want for such a thing. Let it go. Okay?"

Jet held her gaze, then took a deep breath. "Yeah, alright. I guess we have other things to think about anyway."

Kamber stood. "Yes, of course we do." She pulled him to his feet, guided him to the edge of the rocky shore, then shoved him into the lake. She giggled, undressed, and dove in after him.

CHAPTER 58
Somber Greetings

AFTER A LONG and eventful night at Firefly Falls with Kamber, Jet slept in the next morning. At the mess hall, every Lucem was there, chatting softly and eating or drinking coffee. On the table in front of them was a board game with a few twenty-sided dice, mostly ignored, though. They all sat huddled around each other, and he could read the room. The mood was somber, with DiJinn still on everyone's mind. As he looked on, he felt a sudden rush of love for them all. This was his true family now, and they would need each other now more than ever in the upcoming days.

Ti-Leer was red-nosed and puffy-eyed. Jet could see he'd spent his night with his magic flask, mourning the loss of DiJinn. Other than Solan, Jinn had been closest to Ti-Leer. They had been like siblings, attending Skylight University together about fifty years ago. Both had been inducted into the Lucem at the same time, similar to Jet, Cord, Vail and Bo. Making that connection, Jet felt Ti-Leer's grief.

Next to him was Cord, who sat quietly with a bowl of untouched gruel in front of him. Cord had his eyes closed and seemed to be asleep, though Jet guessed he was lost in thought about the events of the previous weeks or some secret he'd unearthed, perhaps.

Kamber sat across from them, yawning and scratching at her disheveled hair. She wrapped herself in her cloak and fought off a shiver. A steaming mug of tea sat in front of her as she blinked and rubbed at her bleary eyes. It brought a smile to his face as he stared at her, unnoticed in the doorway.

Shiloe and Albright had also returned from their brief sabbatical. They were always near each other now. Jet assumed that Albright would never let her out of his sight again. They'd spent a century apart, finally being reunited just recently. The two teens sat, elbows on the table, looking around at the others and smiling on occasion, but mostly listening.

Solan and Tyberius sat next to each other, talking quietly. Solan had dark circles under her eyes, and Jet knew where she'd spent the night. The clearing in the Clipton Forest had become her home-away-from-home. Unfortunately, Solan had spent too much time there of late. The clearing had become more of a burial ground these days. For Solan, Jet felt a deep empathy, knowing how much it hurt to lose a close friend, and Jinn had been more than just a friend. Though Solan upheld her stoic façade, he knew she was struggling. The loss of Jinn had affected them all. She had been the glue that connected many Lucem to each other. Jet felt that familiar pang in his heart again with Jinn as he had with Cutter. It was a feeling that seemed to be *on repeat* lately, and it would continue, if Albright's prophesy were true. The extinction of the Heliographi would continue to count down to either one or zero—a mystery that still remained. Either Jet or Sybold, and only the final war between the *Serpent and the Prism* would determine that. Even Albright didn't know the true outcome.

Of the four phases of the Prism Effect, the third one had been the most difficult for Jet. The 'first phase' had been set in motion by Shiloe, Albright and Sybold nearly a century ago. It had separated each Heliographi's true color through a physical condition that caused their eyes to glow, misleadingly known as *ephebus mortem*.

It wasn't until the Century Eclipse just a few months back when the 'second phase' had been revealed. Albright had prophesied that a special Heliographi would set it into motion. Secretly, he had devised two Skylight Fallouts, though. Hanley Hurse, the Atrum, had died to set it into motion, while Cord was the other one who had cracked the splinter code. It was the *extinction event*, which prevented Heliographi from respawning.

But the third phase had been set into motion by Jet himself, just after the Heliographi Memoirs had been unearthed. At the time, he hadn't known the full extent. Only recently had he discovered the true purpose: a prime's ability to harvest other fallen Heliographi. Jet and Sybold were becoming demigods, all of which had been Albright's doing—his claim that it would even the playing field between the two. The problem was that the others had to die for Jet to realize his full potential. He was too weak to face Sybold on his own, and now the others were being 'sacrificed' because of that. It made him sick to his stomach.

And now, the 'fourth and final phase,' *Heaven's Shield* and *The Serpent Effect*. Each phenomenon a protective dome, as best Jet could understand. For the Lucem and the citizens who had made it out, the inner four belts now possessed a protective sphere that provided safe haven. The outer belts—the fifth through the eighth belt—had a much more sinister sphere of influence, one that he had already witnessed in the future Skylight. That 'bloodlust' spell of madness had nearly driven him insane. Life there, as he knew it, would not be pleasant for anyone who'd been left behind.

So far, there had been very little conversation about the 'gathering of souls.' As Jet stood quietly at the threshold, looking at his dear friends, he wondered what they thought about that part. Of course, they would support him, he had no doubt. Still, there had to be some internal conflict, he assumed. He wondered how he would feel, if he knew his prophesied death would come soon, only to strengthen another Heliographi. It didn't seem fair, but there was nothing he could do about it now.

Jet finally entered the chow hall, and the others greeted him. It was a half-hearted cheer that Jet waved off with an awkward grin. He sat down next to Cord as everyone went back to their conversations.

As he sat there, he felt slightly disconnected from reality. Surrounding him were his friends, alive and well, unlike the future Skylight world where everyone had been dead. *Maybe he was still suffering from the trauma? Maybe he would never get over that?*

"You don't seem yourself lately," Cord said.

Jet glanced at him, then shrugged. "It's been a rough few weeks, I'll admit."

"I understand," Cord said and lowered his voice. He partially turned his shoulder to shield himself from the others. "We have a lot to discuss."

"What's on your mind?"

Cord did something then that caught Jet by surprise. He began to blush.

Jet furrowed his brow, then cracked a smile. "Something you want to tell me?"

"Well…I have a favor to ask."

"Okay. I'm guessing it's an *important* favor."

"I need your help, if it's not too much to ask."

"With what?" Jet said, shoveling a spoonful of lukewarm gruel into his mouth.

"I'd like to locate Vail." Cord was no longer blushing and stared directly into Jet's eyes.

"What?" Jet said and nearly spit out his food. "Is this a joke?" he whispered. "I mean, you two can't stand each other."

"She saved my life, Jet," Cord said.

"Yeah, and you saved hers. We've all saved each other's lives on more than one occasion. So what?"

Cord maintained his blank expression.

Jet sensed he wasn't sure what to say, or maybe he was processing his feelings. "There's more going on, Cord. What is it?"

"I don't have a lot of close friends."

"Sure you do. Ti-Leer, Solan, Kamber…*me*."

"Well, that's correct, to some degree. But this is different, I suppose."

"Are you talking about your feelings for Vail?"

"Can you help me or not?"

Jet set his spoon down and crossed his arms. "Yes, of course. Vail is a friend of mine, too. But I want to know why, Cord."

"I…" Cord blushed again. "I guess I kind of like her, if you must know."

Jet gave Cord a quick nod, then patted his narrow shoulder. "There you go. Wasn't that easy?"

Cord smirked and lifted Jet's hand off his shoulder.

"Alright Cord. But I need another day or so. And Solan's not going to like it."

"She can't stop you. You know that, right? I don't think any of us can now. Besides, Heaven's Shield should give us a long break."

"Yeah, I guess so. But we have a lot to consider now, with setting up patrols and outposts along the fourth belt."

"I understand. But I think Vail's gonna need us. She's been expelled by the Atrum, and she can't survive under Heaven's Shield. I assume she'll be somewhere on the ninth belt, hiding from the Atrum."

"Or down on earth," Jet said. "Alright Cord. Here's the deal. I'll help you, but I need a favor too."

"Anything," Cord said.

"When I was in the future Skylight, I met a girl, a genie—"

"You met a genie?" Cord interrupted and his attention perked up. "Now that's fascinating. I didn't know there were any left. That program was abandoned long ago."

"Well, I did. And she saved my life by sacrificing her own, in fact. I made a promise to find her and bring her in. She last told me she was somewhere on Skylight City in the Vent Quarter, I think."

"Very well," Cord said. He stood and straightened his cloak. "Find me when you're ready. Don't wait too long."

M

Later, Jet found Solan in the hangar bay. She was rushing around and directing traffic with Stell. Jet knew he'd find her there, buried in her work. It was her way of keeping her mind off Jinn, he assumed.

As predicted, she wasn't happy about his little mission. But she grudgingly gave her permission and asked that both he and Cord hurry back.

"There's a lot of preparation ahead, and our enemy will be on the move soon," Solan said.

"Solan," Jet said and stopped her. He grasped her by the shoulders until he had her full attention. "You need to take a break. Spend some time away or with your father or something. Pretending that nothing happened isn't going to fix anything."

She faced him, hands on her hips. "No, Jet. I hear what you're saying, but I can't right now."

"You've got to get past it—"

Solan raised a hand. "This is my way of doing that. Please, let's not talk about it, at least not right now."

Jet nodded, though a bit uncertain. He worried about her. Solan had been so wound up with the memoirs, then the fulcrum wars, and now Jinn. Of course, the return of her father, who refused to take over the Lucem again, didn't help either. It was a lot of pressure for anyone. He knew from experience that Solan would eventually reach a breaking point. "Alright, Solan. Just get some rest then."

Jet turned to leave, and Solan placed a hand on his shoulder and stopped him. "Before you leave, I wanted to thank you, Jet. I know you went through a lot for us all. That hasn't gone unnoticed."

He held her gaze and felt his skin flush. "I thought about you and all of these people. I knew Albright meant for it to happen like that. It's what pulled me through the dark times."

"I think that's why you were chosen," Solan said. "When you get back, we can talk more about it, when you're ready, of course."

Jet gave her a weak smile. "Let's make a deal. You get some rest, get away from all of this. Then I promise you I'll share everything I experienced on my quest as soon as I get back." Jet held out his hand.

"Deal," Solan said and shook his hand. "See you soon, Jet."

M

When Jet told Kamber he was leaving, he thought she was going to punch him in the face.

"We're finally back together and have some free time and you're leaving again?" she said, her voice raised and hands on her hips.

Eventually, Jet managed to calm her. He reassured her he'd be back soon enough.

She gave him a hug and a kiss. "I suppose…I should be grateful to this girl. What was her name? Sember?"

"Yeah. I promised to find her and bring her into our group. I think you'll like her a lot."

"And you're also going to find Vail?" Kamber continued. "I don't know if I like that very much."

"Cord's idea," Jet said and held up his hands. "That was the deal."

M

Jet took one last stroll around the first belt that afternoon. He sat out in the woods alone, listening to nature, enjoying it more than ever. After his nightmare trip to the future Skylight, he realized how important it was to him. Just like Albright had once proclaimed, *nature is at the center of Skylight, as it should be.* He walked through the Skylight University campus, which had resumed classes. That made him smile and brought back some fond memories of his freshman days. At least some things were returning to normal. He only hoped that Heaven's Shield would hold up in the days and months ahead.

M

The following morning, Jet and Cord loaded up their jammers.

"Well," Cord said, leaning against the nose of his jammer. "Vail or Sember first?"

"Dunno," Jet replied. "He took out his Lucem badge and held it to the light. "Face up, Sember. Face down, Vail. Sound fair?"

Cord shrugged his narrow shoulders and gave Jet a crooked smile. "Your call."

Jet flipped the badge in the air and caught it on the back of his hand, covering it with his other. He lifted his hand after a brief pause, and they both looked down.

ΑΒΓΔΕΖΗΘΙΚΛΜ
ΝΞΟΠΡΣΤϒΦΧΨΩ

DIJINN KNEW THIS would be a dangerous mission.

It was a gut feeling. Though she'd been on so many of them over the last fifty or so years, this one felt different. She'd be lying if she didn't admit to herself that she wasn't afraid. Most missions, she felt an excitement, an exhilarating rush of adrenaline. It was something she loved—that challenge of breaking in and stealing secrets, or hearing a private conversation, or seeing information not meant for her eyes. But right now, there was a sinking feeling in the pit of her stomach.

This might be her final mission.

And Solan knew it, too.

Was gaining the ninth memoir really that important? Apparently, to Solan, it was. She'd always had good instincts in such things, and DiJinn was trusting in her now. The only way to get the memoirs was by using DiJinn's gift.

She pushed the fear down. Damned be her emotions. The challenge had been laid before her, and she would attain the memoir no matter the cost. After all, Solan was right: this was the perfect time to go after it. While the battle for the final fulcrum was raging, she would infiltrate Lybra's stronghold and find it. Though she hated the thought of her friends battling without her, DiJinn had to focus on this important mission.

She pushed the thrusters into overdrive, then engaged the impeller system. Her jammer cloaked, and the vapor trails disappeared.

Making it to the ninth belt didn't take long, and soon, she was cruising through the debris field. She eased back on the controls and searched for the hidden pathway to Lybra's secret headquarters, C9.

Moments later, she saw the spherical-shaped chunk. Its resemblance to a human skull was unmistakable: hollowed-out eye sockets and a grinning maw, ominous in the dusty sunlight.

DiJinn settled her jammer among the ruined field of rock and dust, which was crispy and charred from exposure to outer space. She hopped out and cloaked, finding a ruined vent to make her way below.

Part of her gift was her intuition, which she assumed was the same for all Heliographi. It was something she didn't quite understand, just that it involved subtle nudges, like a whisper or inner voice. For her, that meant directions: *go this way, hurry, or wait…* Each time, it got her to the place she needed to be. Right now, that voice was loud and clear, and she had a vision of where she needed to go. The ninth memoir was hidden in the lower bowels of C9. Her intuition was also warning her that she wasn't alone.

DiJinn traversed through the old, vacant corridors. She could see that most of the stronghold's security precautions had been moved. It seemed that the final fulcrum battle today took precedence. Lybra—or perhaps it was really Sybold calling the shots now—had relocated almost all her resources to the first belt. All eyes were trained on that location, and of course no one would be crazy enough to attempt infiltrating Lybra's inner lair. DiJinn had all the advantages she needed, and she would need every bit of it to pull this off.

The temperature climbed the lower she went. The humidity also increased, along with her pounding pulse. Jinn focused on her gift, leaning into it, and soon, she found the right passages amongst the rusty bulkheads.

The lower she went, the more unstable her footing felt. It shifted beneath her feet, like something moved within the bottom levels.

Among the sheared bulkheads, an orange light glowed and pulsed from ahead. It strobed as a fan with giant blades passed steadily in front of it. When she neared, she paused, trying to time the intervals. The whooshing caused a strong breeze to gush through the passage. She waited, closed her eyes and tried to time the oscillations. One more deep breath, and then she leapt forward, rolling through and just beyond the giant ventilation blades.

Once inside the dark chamber, she let her eyes adjust. The walls spanned up and out of sight. Surrounding her was some sort of strange mechanism. Pistons, valves and other odd equipment snaked up the side walls and into the darkness beyond. Directly in the center of the space was a dais with a spotlight shining down on it. Sitting in the middle was a small metallic encasement. The ninth memoir.

And almost certainly a trap.

DiJinn smiled inwardly, though. The game was on, one she intended to win. Her anxiety lessened now as the thrill of the challenge took hold of her. She studied the area, her cloaked figure hidden in the shadows as she considered.

But she could see nothing alarming.

Still, she knew that, as soon as she took the memoir, the trap would spring. There was something else here, a guardian in hiding, and it would give chase the moment she touched the memoir. She knew this because her gift was whispering it to her, warning her.

She prepared herself. She would have to be quick. The escape passage beyond would likely close the moment she touched the memoir. Seconds mattered now.

DiJinn channeled her inner Heliographi. One last breath, then she made her move.

In a blur of speed, she grasped the memoir. As soon as her fingers closed around the tube, the sound of grinding metal filled the chamber, and the fan stopped spinning. The grate over the tunnel was quickly closing. She leapt into the tunnel and rolled just as it slammed down behind her. DiJinn was instantly to her feet and running.

Then the guardian awoke.

The entire chamber behind her shifted and seemed to morph.

It began to reassemble and align in a way that revealed four legs, then a long torso and a pair of clawed arms. The head of a massive mech unit phased from thin air, and it stood inside the chamber. Its shiny surface was faceted, almost like silver armor or scales. Its head was connected with rods and pistons, forming a long, sinewy neck. The thing's mouth looked like a dark cave, and it had dozens of sharp dagger-like teeth—some sort of mechanical dragon from hell. But it was the red glow of its eyes that gave her pause. The dragon-mech launched itself directly toward her and the memoir.

DiJinn sprinted down the passage as it began to collapse around her. A loud thud echoed down the tunnel. When she exited, everything caved in behind her. Through the dust, she could see a silhouette. Like some futuristic dinosaur, the giant dragon-mech stepped toward her.

DiJinn felt her heart leap to her throat. She turned and searched for the tiny air duct she'd entered through, found it, and dove into the vent just as the mech swiped at her. Its claws gouged several channels into the steel bulkhead, just missing her feet. She clambered up through the cramped vent while the unit continued to scrape through the bulkheads just behind her.

Through the maze of ducts, she followed her intuition's lead. When she exited the ductwork, she found the long stair and leapt up the flights two at a time. Halfway up, the robot finally made it through the last steel bulkhead. It immediately homed in on the memoir and launched itself at her. She barely managed to stay in front of it, all the while wondering why they had not seen any of these giant mechs before. It was evidently some new prototype, one that was obviously the next in line to replace the current M-Class unit. If there were more of these giant mechs coming, the Lucem would be in trouble.

But she had to focus on surviving this one right now.

She finally made it to the surface of C9 and scrambled up through the left eye socket. She found her jammer. Just as she was about to hop in, the ground near her softened, and a sink hole developed. Then the surface erupted in a shower of dirt and steel. She nearly lost her balance and fell into the void that had formed just meters away. One massive foot poked through and slammed down. The mech's claw grazed her side, pressing into her cloak and nearly pulling her down into the sinkhole. The blow was enough to thrust her against the side of her jammer. Her head spun, and stars formed in her vision when she hit the hull of her skiff. She nearly passed out.

But somehow, she managed to roll and avoid the rest of the dragon's strike. Then, the thing was rising through the cratered sinkhole. She watched in horror as its shoulders appeared and dirt began to pile up around it. The sound of rending steel filled the air as the giant continued to squeeze through the void.

She regained her balance and hopped into the cockpit, fired up the engines and slammed the thrusters. Just as she lifted off, the mech brought its other foot down on the tail fin of her skiff. The jammer yawed and spun, sending her into a tailspin. She pulled on the controls, managing to steady it. The dragon mech was almost completely through the opening now. Due to the damage, her skiff had lost some of its maneuverability. Smoke poured from the ruined tail as she cloaked the ship, which thankfully still worked. But its speed had been compromised, and she wasn't ascending as quickly.

The mech unit closed on her ship quickly and leapt. It brought both of its front arms together in a clapping motion that just missed her skiff. The concussive impact rocked her into another tailspin.

DiJinn realized she was doomed. Even though she'd managed to bring her skiff under control again, she'd never be able to outrun the dragon mech, once it took flight.

But to her surprise, the thing remained planted on C9's surface. It appeared the new prototype had no propulsion system, unlike the smaller M-Class units. Or maybe it hadn't been developed yet. Either way, she was beyond its reach now, and she finally settled back and breathed a sigh of relief.

That's when she felt the blood running down her leg.

With all the adrenaline and excitement, she hadn't noticed the large wound in her lower abdomen from the mech's claw.

A shooting pain rocked her left side, and she doubled over in her seat. She was losing a lot of blood and knew she had to hurry back. Now that she had the ninth memoir, her priority was to deliver it safely to Solan. Passing out from loss of blood would leave her floating in no-man's land. Her jammer would eventually be found, and probably not by the right people.

She gritted her teeth and pressed the thrusters forward, hoping her skiff wouldn't fall apart. The jammer shuddered as the rockets flared into overdrive.

If her judgment was correct, the Lucem army was in the midst of the fulcrum war. Soon, the fulcrum should ignite. If the polarity was a black lightning bolt, it meant that Jet hadn't returned, and her sacrifice to attain the ninth memoir was pointless. She kept her gaze trained on the horizon of the first belt and held her breath as the time neared.

As if on cue, a bolt of lightning shot skyward.

She gripped her console so tight that her knuckles turned white. Seconds seemed to turn to minutes until she finally saw the color of the large bolt of lightning.

It was a pure, white light.

DiJinn felt tears sting her eyes.

Jet Stroud had returned.

In her heart, she felt pride settle in. The Lucem had done it. Perhaps there was hope for the human race after all. Through all their recent misfortune, loss and sacrifice, they'd succeeded. And now, all their hope, and perhaps the fate of the human race, depended on Jet Stroud.

Then, a strange golden hue descended around her jammer. She felt a sudden peace settle into her soul, one that she couldn't explain. The pain in her side seemed to lessen, though it still remained. It was just enough to keep her from passing out. She could make it home now, and she set a course right for the first belt and the lightning bolt that danced on the horizon.

But she was weak, and her vision continued to grow dim. The floor of her jammer was soaked with blood. Her only goal now was to place the ninth memoir in the hands of her friend and love, Solan Alexander. She had one last thing to tell her before the end.

She nosed her jammer downward, the white bolt of lightning growing larger in her vision. She could see a pyramid, which was the source of the bolt. This one was larger than the others and had pushed up through the ground in a way that had caused the Clipton River and forest to divert around it.

Atop the pyramid she saw a group of people—all the remaining Lucem. A smile eased across her face as her eyes slid closed. She used her last bit of strength to nudge the skiff into a horizontal position, but she was too weak to slow its speed. In her drowsy state, she felt the skiff hit the ground, and the sound of rending steel filled the cabin. Her skiff cartwheeled a few times and came to a rest.

DiJinn heard the windshield being ripped off, and strong hands lifted her out. She heard screaming and frantic talking. Her pain was mostly gone now. In the background, she could hear music. It was a soft melody, like the pitter-patter of rain on a spring day. She could also hear singing, and birds and a chiming in the breeze. Beneath it all was a soothing whisper. Whether it was a voice or the wind, she didn't know. But her pain continued to subside as her vision turned white. DiJinn finally opened her eyes and looked into the face of Solan Alexander. She held back her tears and handed Solan the memoir. She closed her fingers around it and gripped her hand, then pulled Solan close.

Solan leaned down, and brushed DiJinn's her hair back with a smile.

DiJinn managed one last sentence.

"Don't cry for me. I will be with you forever. I love you, Sol. Make this sacrifice worthy."

[illegible]

EPILOGUE 2

A Divine Parody

OCTOBER 31, 2136, A.D.

ΑΒΓΔΕΖΗΘΙΚΛΜ
ΝΞΟΠΡΣΤΥΦΧΨΩ

CHRISTIAN ALBRIGHT FINALLY had it within his possession.

His hands shook as he looked at the Titan's essence. Something unheard of on this plane. Star-light from another dimension was dangerous, and he had to contain it soon before it became antimatter. The special vessels he'd designed would hold for millennia before diminishing, and he had all twenty-four ready to go now. These vessels would form the headpiece for the future staffs, a tool that would be crucial to the survival of the human race.

His lab equipment had been pieced together from spare parts and equipment. It was a monstrosity, not something for the faint of heart. But what he was attempting had never been tried before, nor should it. "It wasn't meant to be," Tyberius had told him. "You should rethink this." But Albright had always followed his own beliefs. His foresight was his gift, and he felt this was the right thing to do.

Everything had been prepared decades ago, and he had waited for this moment in time. The amount of labor and thought had been painstaking. But finally, the night was here. The conditions were perfect; his lab was ready. The unnatural electricity from the storm blowing in was something straight out of a horror story. An unearthly creation was at hand.

Above his rotunda shaped lab, lightning crashed in the windows high above. He had placed all the vessels on the large metal basket. Each of the twenty-four headpieces glowed a unique color of a Titan's essence. Once the vessels were ready, he would separate them from each other, and ensure they were reunited at the opportune time. He couldn't afford to have them brought together too soon, or things wouldn't progress as planned. No. The timing had to be perfect, and he would rely on the ghosts of past Lucem to protect the remnants until the proper time.

With everything in place, and the storm of biblical proportions peaking, Albright watched as the large iron basket was hoisted up. The cylindrical stone shaft reflected the lightning flashes with greater intensity. When the twenty-four vessels finally made it to the top, he opened the clear dome. The iron basket emerged into the approaching storm. Christian Albright waited anxiously. His timing had to be perfect. If he reacted just a split second too late, the conditions would falter and there was no telling how long he'd have to wait for the next opportunity.

Lightning coursed through the air, and still, he waited. Atop the stone turret, tall lightning rods quivered in the wind, waiting for the right lightning strike. Minutes passed, and his hand hovered just over the controls.

Finally, he sensed it was time and slammed his hand onto the button.

The vessels opened just as a bolt of lightning coursed through the cables. It supercharged the basket, bathing everything in energy. The fury of the storm had been captured. Soon, the basket was practically glowing with an eerie light. It cycled through all the colors of the spectrum, pulsing like a heartbeat. Albright let it stay there for an hour, watched as the storm disintegrated and dispersed. He dared not touch the basket or vessels until then.

Finally, he lowered the iron basket.

He hurried over to inspect the vessels. They lit up the inside of his lab. He heard them speaking to him. "Voices of the Titans," he whispered. Their haunting language made his skin prickle. His smile grew to a maniacal grin as he gathered the twenty-four vessels.

"They're alive," he whispered. "They're alive…"

EPILOGUE 3
A Hostile Takeover

ΑΒΓΔΕΖΗΘΙΚΛΜ
ΝΞΟΠΡΣΤΥΦΧΨΩ

RIVEN SYBOLD DIDN'T HAVE A BODY. There was no form or physical traits to her. She was a shade. It was the only way she could break the laws that the Titans had bestowed upon the Heliographi. To leap over the respawning process was something strictly forbidden. Regardless, it was her only route, and she cared nothing about the consequences. If she was to be ready on time, this had to be done. Doing so had weakened her inner light, though. It would take years to recoup her strength.

What she had done was a 'one-time-only' opportunity, at least until she had the war staff and vessel. She'd never be able to achieve this again until she had those relics. Once the Titans discovered the loophole, she felt sure they would take safeguards to prevent future occurrences. But thanks to Rend-Shear, the Titan had secretly helped her do this. The power of that Titan was aligned with her gift. Known as the *Disruptor*, breaking rules was his blessing to her, and once she had the vessel, she could forgo the respawning process. Forever.

She wondered if Albright was even aware of Rend-Shear's true abilities. *Perhaps he hadn't considered what the 'disruption' of laws entailed?*

After all, this had been Christian's doing. He and Tyberius had set her back decades by assassinating her physical form. Not out of retribution, of course. That was not Christian's way and never had been. The two Lucem knew she'd guessed their plan: she was moving too quickly. Sybold had been determined to disrupt the timeline early and ensure the Lucem *prime* didn't receive the Titan's vessel. But now her plan was ruined. The backup plan would have to do.

But for her backup plan to work, she needed the ideal host, and there were only so many available for her. And after a few years living in stasis—a form of limbo— Sybold had finally found the one. The twenty-four-year-old girl had been on her radar for some time. A rebellious Skylight University student named Bellisa. She'd been a problem child most of her life. Breaking rules, causing fights, getting kicked out of her home…murder.

Yes, Sybold hissed. *She was perfect. Just the right type.*

Overtaking her soul would be easy, given her background and nature. But this was the *forbidden* part, in the eyes of the Titans. Those self-righteous, pompous beings who couldn't find the time for humans. Why should she care if they didn't care? If Sybold worked quickly, they'd be too late to act. Besides, they wouldn't interfere. That duty had been appointed to the Heliographi, or rather, the Lucem. And Christian was too absorbed in his own projects to intervene anyway.

It was Christmas Eve. Other students were at home with their families. Bellisa had stayed at school, having no family to return to. She sat in her dorm room like she did every night and hacked through company firewalls. The girl broke down corporate entities, transferring large amounts of credits and leaving their mainframes in shambles.

Sybold moved into the cramped dorm room, a two-dimensional shade that clung to the back walls and worked its way closer.

Bellisa's long black hair shone in the glow of the hologram. Her tattooed arms with clan symbols ran up to her shoulders and even extended onto her face. Pierced ears and nose…permanent black lips.

Sybold's shadow remained just feet away, the girl unaware. She listened in to her thoughts, which were dark and tinged with evil and malice. It gave Sybold the shivers.

As minutes passed, Belissa rubbed her arms and looked behind her, searching the corners of her dark room. Belissa finished her meal and bent back to her work on the stolen holopad.

Sybold had given her this one last free moment. It would be the last time Belissa would think on her own—the last time she'd remember her own name. The rebellious girl with black hair and lips would now be known as Sybold, leader of the Atrum. Sybold felt she was doing this girl a favor. She was freeing her from the miserable life she'd chosen for herself. She had only herself to blame.

Sybold detached from the wall and floated in behind the girl.

Belissa stiffened, and her eyes grew wide with terror. The glow of the red eyes in her holopad made her want to scream. But the eyes held her captive as Sybold entered her being and disrupted her soul. Belissa's screams went unheard in the dorm room tower. As the clock struck midnight on Christmas Day, Sybold stood and smiled into the hologram. She had work to do, and the citizens of Skylight needed a new ruler.

Thank you for reading The Serpent Effect. I truly hope you enjoyed it. If you don't mind doing me a small favor, please consider leaving a review on Amazon or your favorite website. Reviews are critically important to a writer's work and help get the word out. Additionally, please consider heading over to the website www.theskylightseries.com and sign up for updates, information and special offers. I'd love to connect with you and talk about this series and hear your thoughts and ideas. Once again, thank you. This would not be possible without your support.

J. Wint

J. Wint